The Table Of Stories

University Assaut

University Assault By: Nelson Amador

Chapter 1 University of Washington 1980

It was a new school year then Alex drove to park his car by Husky stadium then as Alex was parking then Alex backed out and parked his car then Alex got out his car then Alex got his 3 suitcases out of his trunk he then pressed a button on his remote on his chain that looked the car so no one would steel then Alex started running to the campus then as Alex got into the dorms he then checked himself in and got his classes and went to find a dorm then as Alex was walking to find a dorm then Alex found a sign that said "dorm for sale" then Alex got out his wallet and went to a pay phone to call the person who was sailing the dorm "hello?" the operator said "oh yes hello the names Aussmen, Alex Aussmen I'm just interested on buying that dorm of yours is it still for sale?" Alex asked "yes it is Mr. Aussmen it's for 45$ to buy" he said "okay I'll mail the money to you if I ever see you" Alex said then Alex hanged up the phone then Alex gave the money to clerk then Alex set up his stuff and his clothes in the closet then he set up his bed then as Alex was done, Alex then looked on his schedule and he had English to go to then Alex ran where the English class was then as Alex got there he then took out a book and waited for the bell ring then as Alex was reading then he saw a strange person with black hair then he had a camera then as Alex was reading then he kept looking at his backpack and it was filled with maps and also other stuff then as class started Alex then had to write an easy for the English class then as Alex got out of class he then bumped into a girl with brown curly hair "oh I'm so sorry" Alex said "that's okay" the girl said "I'm Alex" Alex said "I'm Jeanne" Jeanne said "so what class are you heading to" Jeanne asked "oh PE you?" Alex asked "same here" Jeanne said then Alex walked with Jeanne to class then as Alex was walking then Alex saw something on Jeanne's wrist it was a bracelet it had purple and black "what's that?" Alex asked then Jeanne looked at the bracelet "it's new bracelet I got" Jeanne said "Jeanne what is your last name?" Alex asked "Kaymen what is yours disco boy" Jeanne said "Aussmen" Alex said "Aussmen that's pretty intersecting name" Jeanne said then as Alex and Jeanne got to PE then somebody attacked Alex then Alex got forced against the wall "I want your money freshmen" the thug said then as Alex was struggling to get free then Alex felt one of his taser guns that Michael gave to him for a gadget he could use just in case to defend himself then the thug was about shove him into the wall again then Alex did a back flip and kicked the thug in the face and got out his tacer gun and shot him then the thug was knocked out then Alex took the thugs wallet and got and kicked then kicked the thug in the face and headed to PE then as Alex was changing into his Jog shirt and jog shorts then headed to the track "runners take your marks and go!!!!" the coach said then Alex started running and Alex was really fast and Alex did 4 laps then Alex saw thing rise up that where platforms then Alex jumped through the platforms then he got to the finish line "your time 7:51" the PE teacher said then as class was over then Jeanne thought Alex was fast "wow that was good Aussmen" Jeanne said then Alex went to change then as he got out Jeanne was in front of the boy's lock room "so

Alex what do you want to do" Jeanne said "I don't know I was thinking there a fancy restaurant in University village" Alex said "okay well try to take a cab" Jeanne said "it's okay Jeanne well take my car" Alex said "really but aren't freshmen not supposed to have cars" Jeanne said "um yeah but I never fallow those stupid rules" Alex said "yum bad boy" Jeanne said "I know" Alex said

Chapter 2 Alex's new girlfriend of a life time

Then Alex pressed the button on his keys on his controller on his key chain then the car opened the doors then Jeanne did a girl laugh then Alex and Jeanne got into Alex's 1980 Ford Panther but it was red it looked like a Lamberguni that Alex drove in 1978 when he went to Los Vegas to save Dona from Bolden then Alex started the car and drove to University village then Alex put on music in the car then Alex took a right turn to by Eddie Bauer store and then Alex parked his car by the Eddie Bauer then Alex got out of the car "where do you want eat? Jeanne" Alex asked "the treasure club that's a good fancy restaurant" Jeanne said "okay" Alex said then Alex and Jeanne and went inside the treasure club restaurant and got seated "welcome to treasure club what will it be for you guys" the waiter said "I'l have the New York steak" Alex said "and for you young lady" the waiter said "oh chicken enselata" Jeanne said then the waiter took the menus "tell me about your self Mr. Aussmen" Jeanne said "oh well last year I graduated from Tahoma high school last year and I choose to come to University of Washington and so far I love it here you?" Alex asked "I went to high school in Los Angles but enough about me what about you what kind women are you intersected in Alex?" Jeanne said with a sexy smile on her face staring at Alex "well. Nothing really it's really boring" Alex said "really?" Jeanne said "yes" Alex, said, "so what are studying to be Alex?" Jeanne asked "I don't know yet" Alex said "so your just studding anything that's there that's very interacting Alex" Jeanne said "yeah" Alex said then as they finished up dinner Alex then drove Jeanne back to University of Washington then Alex parked his car in front of Jeanne's apartment "thanks for dinner Alex" Jeanne said "your welcome Jeanne" Alex said then Jeanne smooched Alex for 13 minutes then Jeanne got out of the car "bye sweetie" Jeanne said then Alex waved at Jeanne then Alex then as Alex was driving then a group wearing purple jumpsuits where spying on Alex "the freshmen is driving back to campus over" one of the guys said that person was strong and intimating "I have him too Jack send two Seniors to beat him up" his boss said then as his boss was sitting his chair in his office his office was huge and there was a pool table, a royal chair like one of those king chairs, then there was animal heads, a flat screen TV, and bar table with a lot of beers tabs the man in the chair was skinny his face looked very boyish looking, he was tall, had black hair, and his hands where big for a skinny guy "keep spying on him and send in enforcements" he said "yes Mawloy" the thug said then Mawloy hanged up the phone then as Alex got out of his car then he got the keys of the car and started walking back to his dorm room then as Alex was walking then a thug pointed a gun at Alex "hello Mr.Aussmen now walk" the thug said then the thug in the purple suit pointed the gun at Alex then Alex jumped in the air and punched him in the face and then another thug showed up pulled out a PP7 and tried to shoot Alex then Alex

jumped on a bench and kicked the thug in the face and grabbed the thug's gun and shot both of them and stole his gun and wallet and ran to his dorm room then another thug in a purple jump suit saw the 2 thugs that got shot and contacted Mawloy "Mr.Mawloy we got bad news the thugs you sent they got killed by the freshmen" the thug said "what find out who this freshmen is EMEDAITLY!!! IS THAT CLEAR" Mawloy screamed and then he hanged up "yes sir" the thug said

Chapter 3 exploring University of Washington with the seniors

Then the next morning Alex got up and turned off his alream and got dressed then as Alex was getting dressed he then looked in his backpack for some extra gadgets that Michael gave to him just in chase he was in trouble then as Alex was in the tour then one of the security camrea then as Alex was looking around then one of the seniors "hey Auss you listing" one of the seniors said "oh I am" Alex said then seniors turned their back and Alex and rest of the group kept walking then the camera kept zooming in "it's the guy that killed one of out guys" one the thugs "research about it him" Mawloy said then as the camrea kept zooming in it then researched Alex "Secret agent Alex Aussmen went to Tahoma high in 1976,77,78, and 1979" one of the thugs said "smart boy he is" Mawloy said "send in the security guards to arrest him and kill him" Mawloy said "yes sir" his thug said then he pressed a button that the guards came out then Alex saw the guards come out and then kept on walking "keep on going Freshmen" the professors said then Alex got tackled by one of the security guards then Alex kicked one of security guards in the face then another guard tried to catch Alex but then Alex ducked punched him in the stomach and whacked him in the face and ran off then Alex started running University of Washington and guards where coming after him then guards were shooting at Alex then Alex jumped off walls then he went to the 2nd floor then Alex hid inside a girl's lockeroom "sorry about this girls I'm hiding from someone" Alex said then the naked girls in the lockeroom just chuckled and kept looking at Alex and thought Alex was really sexy then Alex got out of the locker room and looked around and kept running then Alex jumped out a window and did a summer salt then Alex jumped into a tree and then stole a motorcycle and road off in the motorcycle and road around University village and went off a jump around the Unversity park then Alex's landed on the ground and kept going then the cops where riding in nice 1980 motorcycles chasing Alex in the park then Alex road into the hills of University village and then road by the flower stores and then he kept riding into the neighborhoods by University village then Alex took a right turn and started headed into downtown Seattle then more guards chasing him then Alex started shooting a dart gun at the guards then Alex fell off the motorcycle then Alex got out his PP7 gun and started shooting the guards then Alex shot the last guard then Alex got back on the motorcycle and lifted the motorcycle and hoped back on the motorcycle and headed back to University of Washington then as Alex went back then as Alex went back then there was a dance in the gym in University of Washington then as Alex went back to his dorm he then dark blue jeans and got on a blue shirt and bought a leather jacket and got sliver bandana and tied it around his neck and got a new sliver watch and got black disco pants even the 70's tennis

shoes where over but Alex knew that he can still make some sort of fashion and then he got a moon ring at the store to go with his watch then Alex took a shower and then headed to the dance then as Alex was in line he then saw the gym just going crazy then Alex started warming up jumping then as Alex got in then started dancing to electric slide and started snapping his finger then he clapped and started doing new dance moves and then Alex Jumped in the air and then moved his arms and moved left and right then started disco moves and then Alex pointed at a random hot girl as he was dancing then Alex did a cartwheel then did a backflip in the air and landed on one foot and kept on dancing then moving his hips and then Alex jumped in the air and then put his right floor in and started moving shoulders then he clapped his hands and went down low and then raised up again and then Alex kicked his right leg out and spine and moved his arms back in forth and twisted his head to the left then Alex moved his head left and right then Alex spined around in circles then without actually realizing it but Jeanne was watching him dance "hey Alex what's up" Jeanne said "oh not much just dancing what about you?" Alex said "oh good when did you get here" Jeanne said as the music kept on going Alex really couldn't hear her "you want to dance?" Alex asked then another song came on called lucky star then Alex and Jeanne danced then Alex grabbed her hand and spine her then Jeanne lowed her self and put her hand on hand and Alex's legs and then Jeanne raised up and started kissing Alex on the face and on the neck then she kissed Alex on the lips then Jeanne put her hands around Alex then Alex lifted up her then Alex spined her in the blue disco light then Alex lowered Jeanne and then Alex raised her up then Jeanne smooched Alex for the rest of the song then everybody in the gym clapped and thought Alex was really good when he was slow dancing with Jeanne "wow that was really good Alex" Jeanne said "thanks Jeanne you didn't have a date?" Alex asked, "no I was going to go with him but he is always busy" Jeanne said "what does he work for" Alex said "well I don't know he works University as the like the president or something I can never know" Jeanne said "do you want to come back to myself?" Alex asked then without knowing Jeanne passed out "Jeanne?" Alex said then Alex found out that she was poisoned by one of Mawloy's thugs then Alex lifted Jeanne in his arms then Alex ran to his Loutus Esprit that he parked by the dorm and took Jeanne to the hospital then Alex drove as fast he can then he took right turn into the hospital and picked up Jeanne and Alex ran into the hospital "hi sir can I help you" the nurse said "yeah my friend here has been poisoned and is there a doctor that can help her and fast" Alex said "yes sir we will get a doctor for her right away" the nurse said then Alex was waiting in the hospital waiting on what Jeanne's heath was if it was bad or good then Alex kept on waiting for 30 minutes then a nurse ran to Alex "is she okay" Alex said "she is okay and the good news is she can go home" the nurse said "thanks doc" Alex said Then as Alex got in the hospital room he then kissed Jeanne "are you okay Jeanne?" Alex said "yeah I'm okay Alex" Jeanne said "I'm going to find the person who did this to you" Alex said then Jeanne got out of the hospital bed then the next morning Alex went to his classes and talked to Jeanne in the halls on the campus "hey Jeanne what's up" Alex said "nothing much" Jeanne said "how are you feeling? "Alex asked "I'm feeling okay I'm just really engeryced by the median that the doctor gave me" Jeanne said then as Alex was about to leave he then turned back "hey Jeanne do you want go out to dinner and go to a movie on Friday? "Alex asked "oh my god yes I would love to baby boy "Jeanne said then Jeanne ran up to Alex and just smooched Alex for 30 minutes and unbutton his button up shirt he wearied with tie then Alex knew he was late for class then Alex ran to class then Alex made it to class and Alex was just thinking about what fun things he would do Jeanne and she was the only thing Alex was thinking about and he fantasized about her and Alex loved her curly hair when he was kissing her she was just the most classy girl ever she wearied high heels and she would wear these really sexy outfits she would go from dark blue jeans and wearing a strap shirt with a really sexy dark blue jacket and she would wear red lipstick and had these big volume high lashes too on her eyes then as classes where over Alex then through out the week Alex spined a lot of time with Jeanne and Alex was with her a lot and Alex even speed time with her in her dorm and they loved talking and walking to class together then on Thursday Alex helped her with her homework and they enjoyed each others company and she just loved Alex and they loved listing to music together then as Friday rolled around Alex just couldn't wait to go to the movie with Jeanne and Alex just knew it was going to be fun

Chapter 4 Mawloy's plan to destroy the principal of University of Washington

Then after his last class Alex then got his backpack on and headed to find Jeanne then Alex started running to find Jeanne then Alex went to Jeanne's dormroom "hey you ready to go" Alex asked "yeah I just got to get my purse" Jeanne said then Jeanne ran back into her dorm and got her purse and Alex drove his Loutus to a fancy resteraunt in downtown Seattle and the food was great and so was the resteraunt then Alex took Jeanne to see a movie in downtown Seattle then as they got out the movie Jeanne just loved the movie "wow that was such a great movie thanks for taking me Alex" Jeanne said "your welcome Jeanne" Alex said "you want to go swimming" Jeanne said "sure yeah" Alex said then as Alex and Jeanne got back to UW Alex and Jeanne then sneaked into a swimming pool then Jeanne changed into her bathing suit and jumped into the pool "come on Alex jump it" Jeanne said then Alex stole a bathing suit from the lockeroom and jumped into the pool then Jeanne splashed Alex did a girl chuckle then just paused and just smoched Jeanne then Jeanne picked up Alex and threw him in the deep water then Jeanne laughed then Alex laughed then as Alex was getting to the surface Jeanne then swam to Alex put her hands around him and just smooched him then Alex put her hands on Jeanne's hips Then as Jeanne was kissing Alex then something was wrong and the lights where shut off "oh god it's dark" Jeanne said then Alex knew that someone turned off the lights in the swimming pool then Alex got out of the pool and got out his PP7 gun and went into the lockeroom then a thug punched him in the face then Alex got up and shot him then as Alex was getting out he went to go find some other thugs then other thugs then grabbed Jeanne then Alex ran to the swimming pool and shot the thugs with his PP7 gun "are you okay Jeanne said "yeah I'm okay Alex" Jeanne said then Alex saw other thugs come in "lets get out of here" Alex said "where?!' Jeanne said "my place trust me" Alex said then Alex and Jeanne and ran to Alex's dorm room and just started running in the halls then as

they got in Alex's dorms Alex got dressed and got on a black spy suit "Jeanne stay here your safe here" Alex said then Alex then loaded up his gun and went to go find the thugs then Alex kept running the whole night then Alex saw the thugs going to secret floor on the campus then Alex shoot the lock and broke into the floor and a lot of people where wearing purple and black jumpsuits "holy shit" Alex thought then Alex hided behind a wall then a Goth dude came by then as the Goth dude was coming by "where the hell is my ring!!!" the Goth dude said then Alex pulled out his PP7 gun and shot Goth dude in the head then he fell to the floor then Alex looked in his pocket and stole his money and found the keycard to get into the bosses room then Alex hid behind and shot another Goth dude coming by and shot him as he was walking then Alex ran to the main room then as Alex got to entrance he then tested the keycard but the card didn't work then Alex put a mine on the door knob and see the bomb "001" was the number of the minutes he set it then he broke into the bosses room "what the hell was that?!" Mawloy said "FREZZE!!"Alex yelled "my, my welcome to University of Washington Alex Aussmen muahahahahahahahahah" Mawloy said then Mawloy got out of his seat and Mawloy was really scary looking and had mo hawk which was a hair do with that had only hair in the center of his head and left and right ends where bald "so finally great to meet you Mr. Aussmen the famous Alex Aussmen from Tahoma high school muhahahahaha" Mawloy said then he had wig to cover his Mohawk and it was brown hair it liked like john F Kennedy hair style "I'll tell you every bit of my little evil plane first I kill the principal at University of Washington so I become the principal of both University of Washington and Washington state university despite your efforts Mr. Aussmen you will never stop me because of that Autistic brain of yours the makes you weak it's true Alex I know everything because I work for RAD muahahahah" Mawloy said "wait a minute RAD?,RAD?" Alex was thinking "now why the hell would you want to do that that's pretty stupid plan Mawloy and you will never win" Alex said "cause then the money goes to me and I got the money that UW always finaces along with WSU's money and I steel them and they go out of business also kill principals of every University in America and then blow all of them even their football stadiums with this button right here Mr. Aussmen" Mawloy said "you will never get away with this Mawloy "Alex said "oh I think I will cause I'm smart Goth gangster Mr. Aussmen and that loves money muahahahahahahahahahahahahahahah eheehhahahahahahahahaha" Mawloy said then Mawloy went up to Alex and tried to whack him with his money Cain then Alex grabbed on to the Caine then Alex punched him in the face and threw a grenade then Alex escaped and took some of cash from Mawloy "KILL HIM!!!"Mawloy said then Alex got out his gun and started shooting thugs with PP7 gun then as Alex was running then jumped out the window and Alex kept on running then he pressed a button on his remote that told his lotus esprit to come then Alex jumped into the car and then got in the driving seat and threw the stolen money in the back seat and drove to downtown Seattle to find the principal of University of Washington then as Alex parked his car by hotel by the Seattle aqruim and saw some thugs pulling a gun then Alex took out a A33 riffle sniper and shot the thugs "hello Mr. Aussmen I'm Owen Olson CIA" Owen said "Aussmen. Alex Aussmen" Alex said then as Alex and Owen where with each other they went into a hideout with gadgets "Nice Owen meet me in UW in like 6 minutes and try to find more thugs okay" Alex said "okay dude" Owens said Then as Alex drove back to University of Washington and saw Jeanne walking to class and Alex just spied on her then somebody grabbed her then Alex started running "Jeanne?!" Alex said then a thug put a knife to her neck "you fallow me she dies" the thug said then Alex started running and got in the car and started up the car then he speeded up the car and chased the car that had Jeanne in it then Alex took a right turn into downtown Seattle and then found the car going into the garage at an IREI store then Alex got his A33 riffle and then he pulled out one of his hookers and shot his hooker gun and the hooker and zoomed up there and got into the boss room and then Alex started running then he found the thugs taking her to elevator then Alex got into the elevator and found a button then Alex put a glove on his hand to read the finger print on the button to get up to that room then Alex got up there and found Mawloy pointing a gun at Jeanne then Alex pointed the riffle at mawloy "games over Mawloy now let her go!! Alex yelled "you have been messing with me for the last time Aussmen now you will get a big gangster beating" Mawloy said then Mawloy was going to punch Alex then Alex ducked and punched Mawloy in the stomach then Alex whacked Mawloy in the face then Mawloy punched Alex and pushed Alex against the wall then Mawloy punched Alex and gave Alex a big black eye then Mawloy got out a knife and cut Alex's arms then Alex smacked Mawloy's hand then Alex tackled Mawloy then Mawloy tried to punch Alex then Alex grabbed his riest and punched Mawloy in the face then Alex pushed Mawloy into a wooden wall and then Mawloy got a cut by his right eye then Mawloy tried to grab Alex then grabbed on to rail and spined around the rail and kicked Mawloy in the face then as Mawloy was going to get up then Alex picked up a metal stick and whacked Mawloy in the face with a metal stick then Mawloy jumped in the back then Mawloy whacked Alex in the back then punched Alex in head from behind then Mawloy got up and grabbed pistol and pointed the gun at Jeanne and they went to the last floor then Alex got up and got his PP7 gun out of his pocket then Mawloy tied up Jeanne then Mawloy set up traps

Chapter 5 stopping Mawloy and stopping the assault

Then as Alex was climbing then Alex got to the elevator Alex then found out that the elevator was broken then Alex got out of the elevator and climbed up the rope then Mawloy with an evil smile pushed the intercom button "take this elevator coming up" Mawloy said then as the elevator came down then Alex got in the elevator then "your too late Mr. Aussmen in 31 minutes I will destroy every University in America and your little sweet Jeanne" Mawloy said then as Mawloy was going to press the button he was going to open the trap door "so long Mr. Aussmen" Mawloy said then Mawloy saw that no one was going down then Mawloy saw Alex "you did want me to fall didn't you Mawloy" Alex said then Alex pulled out his PP7 gun "where Jeanne?!" Alex said "my, my the autistic freshmen in love with the college girl how romantic muahahahahahah" Mawloy said "your times running out MAWLOY!!!" Alex yelled "so is yours Mr. Aussmen, so is yours" Mawloy said then Mawloy pressed button on a rocket launcher and blew up the wall then Alex hid behind a wall and loaded up his gun "you shot your last bullet Mawloy now it's my turn" Alex said then Alex shot Mawloy and threw grenade at him and blew up Mawloy and Mawloy then Alex shot the remote the controls the bombs the blows up University then Alex ran to Jeanne "Alex!" Jeanne said "Mawloy?" Jeanne asked "dead and we will be dead if we don't get here" Alex said then Alex hooked a hook on his backpack "grab on to me and don't let go what ever you do Jeanne" Alex said then Alex jumped off the building then Jeannie started screaming then Alex pressed a button that disabled the controls that controls the schools getting blown up then Alex pressed a button on his watch that blew up the Mawloy's headquarters in University of Washington then Alex and Jeanne landed safely "I love you Alex you're my hero" Jeanne said "it was nothing Jeanne" Alex said then Jeanne smooched Alex as they where in the air as Alex lowered down

Chapter 6 the finish to a great year

Then as Alex came back to University of Washington and it was summer and then Alex took Jeanne to Los Angles and they took a plane to Los Angles and stayed in a hotel in San Diego "beautiful sunset" Jeanne said, "I know it is you know what else is beautiful. You "Alex said then Jeanne jumped in Alex's arms "you want to go the beach?" Alex asked "yes yes" Jeanne said then Alex carried her to the beach then Alex layed down on the beach with Jeanne in her hands then Jeanne smooched Alex then Alex lifted Jeanne up and Alex and Jeanne went into the ocean and splashed each other then Alex smooched Jeanne while lifting her "oh Alex" Jeanne said

D.I.S.C.O.

001

D.I.S.C.O

By: Nelson Amador

Chapter 1 Downtown Seattle 1981

As Summer came Alex completed another year at University of Washington then as Alex ran to his dorm he then thought about some plans you might have then as Alex made up those plans then Alex as was thinking Alex then herd a knock on his door then Alex went to open the door "hey cutey" the girl said then it was a girl with brown hair wearing robe on and she looked like she just got out of the shower "hey what's up?" Alex said as he was smiling "I'm so sorry to bother you but my friends told me about you and your really hot" the girl said "no,no it's great that you came" Alex said then the girl just smiled and just jumped on Alex and started kissing Alex then as Alex was kissing her then Alex untied the girl's robe and then her pink robe fell of her and then slowly the robe slipped off her and she was butt naked then the girl unbutton Alex's shirt and took off his shirt and then took off his jeans "oh Alex your so hot my friends were right" the girl said then as the it grew night time Alex then put some music on in his dorm room and put on "all time high by Rita Coolidge" then Alex kept kissing her "oh Alex" the girl said then Alex just kept on smooching her "you are the most sexist man alive Alex" the girl said "thanks I don't know really know your name miss but thank.." Alex said then the girl just kept on kissing him on the lips then the girl rolled around then Alex gave her message and kissed her back and her arm "oh Alex baby" the girl said then the girl turned back then she raised up her blanket and then the girl dropped the blanket and then Alex saw her nakedness then the girl just hugged Alex and started kissing him "you want to go to a party tonight?" Alex asked "party but I don't have clothes on" the girl said "I will buy you some what happened to your old clothes" Alex asked "my roommate burned them last night and said he would pay me 900$ if I ran around the campus butt naked and I lost he said he would burn all my clothes even my bra and my underwear and I haven't wearied any clothes for 4 weeks and I have had to wear robe everywhere in the campus I went" the girl said "oh" Alex said "alright lets go" Alex said then Alex opened the door then the girl just started smooching him for 20 minutes "I love you you are awesome" the girl said then she just kept on kissing him and she then took off her robe again and this girl was just not afraid to show her nudity "man you just love sex do you" Alex said "I know I'm Ronica Manilo by the way" Ronica said "I'll see you later Alex baby" Ronica said then Ronica without putting on her rob Ronica then started running to her dorm with out putting on a rob to cover her nakedness then she just jumped in the air and blew a kiss at Alex and did a girl chuckle "wow she is awesome" Alex said then as Alex sat on his bed "who's the naked girl in the halls Alex?" a voice said then Alex turned back "Michael? What are you doing here?" Alex said "oh you didn't hear I transferred her Alex so what's up dude" Michael said "oh nothing dude" Alex said "really because?" Michael said "because it doesn't look like nothing you just like a nude girl in your dorm room dude you are a god" Michael said "we first of all Michael she is not swinger like you would see in those 1960's movies dude 2nd she came to me because she lost a bet with her roommate and her roommate burned all her clothes and she has to wear a robe to cover her nudity so she would not get kicked out of here" Alex said "well as the britsh would say she is fit and your lucky to have her" Michael said "I know dude" Alex said then Ronica then ran back to Alex's dorm and kissed him "so when do we leave baby" Ronica asked "right now hope in my car baby girl" Alex said then Ronica ran to Alex's 1980 lotus Esipert he drove last year then Ronica got in the car "wah whooooooo" Ronica yelled "man this girl is just a dare devil she's like afraid to run around the campus naked Alex, you should marry her" Michael said "I could if she wanted to" Alex said Alex then got to his car "so what store are we going to Alex" Ronica said "I think there is a Nordstrom in downtown somewhere but you have to stay in car because you would get arrested in downtown Seattle if you where running naked so just stay in the car" Alex said "okay Alex baby" Ronica said then Alex stopped by Nordstrom in downtown Seattle then as Alex was looking in the store for clothes for Ronica Alex then got tons of fancy clothes and lots of sexy underwear for her then as Alex went to the casher the casher then looked at Alex "who the hell are these for?" the casher said "there for my girlfriend" Alex said "why so much" the casher said "because my girlfriend has no clothes and she doesn't even have any clothes on" Alex said "so she's naked in your car" the casher said "yeah" Alex said with sarcasm "well good for you man" the casher said "I'll tell you I what man since you have a naked girlfriend in your car i will give you a 79% discount" the casher said "thanks man" Alex said then Alex got her shoes, high heels, and tennis shoes and also socks too then as Alex came back with the clothes "oh Ronica I bought some clothes for you" Alex said "oh thank you Alex your my sexy little angel" Ronica said then Ronica smooched Alex and got out of the car "Ronica, Ronica there is security staring at his you do know that" Alex said "yeah I don't care baby I just want to love you up angel boy" Ronica said then Ronica just smooched him "oh baby

girl" Alex said

Chapter 2 Alex's new roommate

 Then that night Alex and Ronica went back to University of Washington then Ronica put

on her clothes for the first time in 4 weeks then as Ronica was lucking for lip gloss then

Ronica jumped into a air vent and stole lip gloss from another girl next dorm down from

Alex and Ronica just grabbed the lip gloss then she was back in like 3 seconds then she

was back in the bathroom then as Alex knocked on the door "Ronica are in there?" Alex

asked then Ronica found out she had dust in her hair then Ronica without thinking she

took her clothes off and went into the air vent that was on the celling and sneaked into

Women's locker room that was locked "Ronica you in there" Alex asked then Alex got

out his x-ray flashlight to see through the walls then Alex found out that Ronica was not

in there then Alex started looking for Ronica "Ronica?!" Alex said then Alex ran and

then Alex layed by the women's locker room then Alex felt a girl's hand tugging him

then Alex got pulled into the girl's locker room "hey baby boy" Ronica said "Ronica are

you crazy I can get in trouble if I'm in girl's locker room and.." Alex said then Ronica

smooched Alex then Ronica just took Alex's clothes and unbutton his shirt "Alex this is

your lucky day baby boy" Ronica said then Ronica took Alex's pants, socks, shoes, and

underwear then Alex and Ronica went into the showers and got wet then Ronica just

smooched Alex then Alex and Ronica fell on the floor of the showers "wow I love

touching your six pack" Ronica said "oh thanks" Alex said then Alex and Ronica slept in the women's locker room the hole night and Alex was just captured by Ronica's sexy

voice, body, and romantic sexuality and Alex was clueless about everything that went on

that night

Chapter 3 new highways in downtown Seattle

 Then as time reached morning Alex then got up "oh my god what happened last night

then as Alex got up he then locked around for his clothes "I'm naked that's just great

Ronica stole my clothes and now I'm naked in the women's locker room great" Alex said

then as the Washington Huskie cheerleaders came in the locker room then Alex saw a girl

with blonde hair taking off her clothes to take a shower then Alex saw a dude in the

locker room with a video camera then as Alex saw him he then cocked him and killed

him then the girl with blonde hair was about to walk over to Alex "hey sexy" the blonde

girl said "oh hi I'm so sorry miss it just my girlfriend and I last night where going to a

nightclub and then she sneaked in here in the middle of the night and we took a shower in

here and then I woke up and she stole my clothes and that's why I'm naked" Alex said

then the blonde girl started laughing at Alex "it's okay what's your name" the blonde girl

said "Aussmen…Alex Aussmen" Alex said "Debra Chambers I'm the head Huskie

cheerleader here" Debra said "so who was the girl you where with last night Alex?"

Debra said "oh I was with Ronica Melino" Alex said "oh the naked girl that runs around

naked all the time around the campus" Debra said "she's not a swinger" Alex said then

Alex was about to undress the thug then as Alex was undressing him he then found out it

was a robot "oh shit" Alex said "great now what I'm I going to do" Alex said "well you

can have my clothes" Debra said "yeah but I don't think you would last very long being naked" Alex said "yeah I would try me" Debra said "fine where are the clothes then"

Alex said then Debra took off her jeans and sweet shirt underwear and her bra and Debra

was naked "that's it sweet shirt and jeans no socks" Alex said "well thanks Debra" Alex

said "oh by the way you can have the rest for your girlfriend Alex" Debra said "what

about you?" Alex asked "don't worry about me I'm be able to mange then Alex kept on

walking back to his dorm room Then as Alex got back to his dorm he then changed out of

the clothes Debra gave him and changed into a suit and neck tie and headed out the

campus and headed to downtown Seattle then as Alex got into his lotus esprit car Alex

then drove to Seattle Center and then he went to the fun forest and then Alex went inside

the food court and got Cheeseburger and then as Alex was done Alex then headed to class

to the library then as Alex was coming out of the food court then a random was fallowing

Alex then he pulled out a walked talke "got him boss" the thug said then as Alex headed

around the EMP theater Alex then saw the thug trying to attack then Alex grabbed him

and threw off the ledge then Alex pulled out his PP7 and pointed the gun at him "who are

you working for? Tell me!!!" Alex said, "I can't tell you dude he would kill me man" the

thug said "what makes I won't!!!" Alex said then Alex was starting load up his gun to

shoot "okay man I work for this guy name Peter Disco and his headquarters is in north

Seattle that's all I know" the thug said "thanks" Alex said then Alex pushed him against

the wall "if I see another one of your guys spy on me I kick their ass" Alex said then Alex

ran to his car and drove back to University of Washington then as Alex was driving Alex

then saw a disco club around North Seattle then as Alex parked his car into the parking

space then without knowing then the street opened up then area holding the car was in

elevator and then the car went into garage and Alex didn't know where he was

Chapter 4 Michael's garage under University of Washington

Then as Alex got out of his car he then walked to the another room and it was like a part office part and there was an elevator and the floor Alex was on was a gadget factory Michael built "oh wat up Alex like me new apartment?" Michael said "yeah this is like our gadget factory you built" Alex said "oh yeah dude it is I will show you some new gadgets dude" Michael said then Michael and Alex walked to a table "new watch a 1981 citizen eco drive watch has diamonds on it and the diamonds are used for burning steel if you ever trapped and it could be used for burning bad guys too" Michael said "awesome dude" Alex said "yes anyway moving on, these are new head phones but are they" Michal said then Michael opened up the top and it was hooker gun that can be used as a hooker to up to buildings if Alex need to sneak into places or hideouts "awesome Michael anything else" Alex asked "well new shoes these are 1981 Nike shoes but what's this" Michael said then Michael pressed a button on the both of the shoes "these are roller shoes just in chase if your getting chased anywhere for any reason you can press the button and wheels will come out of bottom of the shoes" Michael said "but won't I need helmet?" Alex asked "well..if can balance your self pretty you have good balance don't you Alex?" Michael said "I think I do" Alex said "good and that is oh by the way since you have a new girlfriend here is more cash it's 99,000,000$" Michael said "where the hell did get this shit" Alex said "I have ways" Michael said then as Alex was looking around Alex was trying to find a way out of the garage "um Michael?" Alex asked, "yeah dude" Michael said "how the hell do I get out of here?" Alex said "oh just take that elevator up and you should be able to meet Owen up there" Michael said "you where with Owen?!" Alex said then Alex went to the elevator and took the elevator up and ended up in library in University of Washington

Chapter 5 going to the nightclub with Ronica in downtown Seattle

Then as Alex got back to his dorm room Alex took a shower in the boy's locker room because he thought if he took a shower in his dorm Ronica would steel his clothes like she did the previous night then as Alex took his clothes and then as Alex was using shampoo to wash his long hair then Alex used bar of soap then Alex herd a door opened then Alex looked and then Alex saw Debra in the boys' locker room looking through Alex's clothes and she was wearing a leather jacket and really dark blue jeans with shades then Alex saw Debra looking at his driver's license then Debra put an invitation by Alex's clothes then Alex just kept washing hair then as Alex was washing his hair Alex then saw another girl come into the boys' locker room and it was Ronica then as she came into the locker room Ronica then took off her shirt, pants, heels, underwear, and bra and Ronica was butt naked then as Alex was looking at Ronica getting undressed Alex put his head back into the shower then Ronica saw Alex in the shower and then Ronica went into the shower and just smooched Alex "hey baby boy" Ronica said "hey Ronica what's up" Alex said "oh nothing much just in the shower naked with you so how about you" Ronica said "oh same here so Ronica how did you know that I was taking shower in here" Alex asked "oh I'm just guessed that you where in here" Ronica said then Ronica just smooched Alex on the lips and then Ronica jumped on Alex and her legs just raped around Alex's upper body and Alex made out with Ronica then Alex and Ronica just layed on the shower floor then Ronica just layed on Alex then as Alex was laying down then Ronica then just layed on top of Alex and her breasts just pressed against Alex's chest then Ronica just put her arms around Alex and just layed on him then Alex kissed Ronica on the shoulder and on her back and on her neck then Ronica touched Alex on the face and just kissed Alex on the lips and then Alex as Alex got up then Alex saw the invitation that Debra left on Alex's clothes then as Alex looked on the piece of paper and said that Alex and Ronica were invited to a party in North Seattle by the Nordstrom and by the shopping mall Then Alex got on one of his suits the next night Alex's suit was black with blue button up shirt and with a sliver tie it kind of looked like a 70's suit then Alex combed his long hair then Alex as was done then Alex got out of his dorm he then saw Ronica in a purple disco clothes with pink disco pants, silver heels, and a purple strap shirt with sharps on her shoulder and she wearied the shirt without a bra and Ronica just looked gorgeous and she was wearing red lipstick "ready to go Ronica?" Alex asked then Ronica just went into Alex's arms with an exciting feeling "yeah" Ronica said then Alex and Ronica drove in Alex's lotus esprit and drove to North Seattle and Alex found the night club and took a left turn and got into the Seattle highlands shopping mall area and saw the night club and Alex was just amazed that how much people from University of Washington where in live then as Alex found parking Alex then parked in a parking space then as Alex and Ronica got out of Alex's car Alex pressed the button on the key chain that put the door lock that Michael added into the key chain then Alex and Ronica got in line into the night club and the night club was called "D.I.S.C.O" and it was grand opening and the owner of the night club was former Washington graduate name Peter Disco then as Alex was in line then the guard saw Alex and Ronica "you guys can go in have a great night" the guard said then Alex saw the night club and it was awesome

"wow" Alex thought then Ronica was just dancing and then Ronica did a back flip then

Ronica jumped in the air and let her hair fly then Ronica then did hand stand then Ronica

did another backflip then Ronica used one hand to keep her self balance then Ronica

started doing disco dance moves but her dances where very different from Alex's then

Ronica put on finger in the air then started spinning around then Ronica snapped her

fingers then Ronica pulled Alex and Ronica then bended down on her 2 legs and then she

jumped in the air and started spinning in the air and then Ronica used on foot to keep her

self balance and then Alex grabbed her waist and Alex then spine her around for 20

minutes then Ronica jumped off a wall and did a back flip then Ronica did more disco

moves and then she started spinning and then did another cartwheel then Ronica made a

gun sign with her hand used as a dance move and started moving her 2 hands one hand as

the gun sign, one was holding the other hand then Ronica did another backflip and Alex

started dancing disso moves then Ronica grabbed Alex's hand and then Alex lowered

Ronica then Ronica spined Alex around in circus really fast then they ended doing a

kissing sign then crowd just clapped "that is one extremely flexible girl" on the people in

the club said then Alex and Ronica just sat down on the seats then Ronica just layed

down on Alex's shoulder "wow that was amazing Alex" Ronica said "no that was all

you" Ronica said then Ronica just kissed Alex on the lips then Ronica put her arms

around Alex's neck then without knowing Debra then saw Alex and Ronica kissing him

"oh there's the naked girl in love with Alex" Debra said then Disco saw Alex then as

Alex and Ronica where making out on the chairs then Debra saw them "hello Alex"

Debra said "oh Debra hey, Debra this is Ronica, Ronica this is Debra" Alex said "yeah I know you are you're the lead cheerleader for the Washington huskies" Ronica said "so do you guys want to meet Disco" Debra said "sure we would love to meet Disco" Ronica said "good" Debra said

Chapter 6 meeting Peter Disco

Then as Alex and Ronica went up the stairs then they entered a 2 doors then as they got into the room Alex then just stood amazement "wow" Alex though in his mind "hello Mr. Aussmen" a voice said then Alex and Ronica turned their heads to a man with a white tuxedo with a black button up shirt with a black neck tie he was an average height was muscular had black hair and his hands just had muscles on both of his hands "please sit down Aussmen" Disco said then Alex sat down and so did Ronica "so how did you like my new club?" Disco asked "oh it's great Mr. Disco" Alex said "good and who's this young beautiful lady?" Disco asked "this my girlfriend Ronica Manilo" Alex said "pleasure to meet you" Disco said then as they where talking then Debra then came into the room "oh Debra did you met Alex and Ronica?" Disco said "oh yes baby" Debra said then Debra kissed Disco on the lips "you guys board there is pool on the deck" Debra said "oh okay thanks Debra" Alex said "no thank you" Debra said then as Alex and Ronica went outside then they just saw the swimming pool and they just stood amazement "wow because the pool was as long as a football field they was diving board a water slide and it was 8 feet deep on the deep end "come on Alex lets go swimming" Ronica said "oh but I don't have a bathing suit and.." Alex said then as Alex was talking Ronica then took off her heels and then she untied the back of lacing in back of her strap shirt then she threw her shirt off the roof then she took her pants and her underwear and then Ronica was butt naked then Ronica went skinny dipping "come on Alex it's so warm in here" Ronica said then Ronica did a sexy laugh then Alex looked around and then Alex unbutton his shirt and took his socks and shoes and dress pants off and his underwear then Alex jumped in the water then Ronica started swimming and splashing Alex then Alex went under water and touched Ronica's waist then Alex just kissed in her on the check then Ronica just put her arms around Alex's neck and just smooched Alex

Chapter 7 streaking in Seattle

Then as Alex was smooching Ronica then Debra came on to the deck "steel their clothes and then kill them" Disco said then Debrea without Alex and Ronica knowing Debra stole their clothes then as Alex and Ronica where done swimming Alex was just shocked their clothes were gone "oh my god Ronica have you seen are clothes?" Alex said "no..but that's okay well find a way out of here" Ronica said then Ronica then ran saw something from the pool and then Alex saw a jumpsuit then as Alex was putting on the jumpsuit then Ronica just found pipe and climbed down then "wahoooooooooooooo" Ronica yelled as she got down then Alex climbed down "Ronica come back here and put some clothes on" Alex said then Ronica did a cartwheel then she did a backflip then "come on Alex you should try this" Ronica said "I don't know I don't think it's not good idea" Alex said then Ronica ran back to Alex "oh come on Alex please go streaking with me" Ronica said "no thanks we have to go back your dorm" Alex said then Ronica then

Ronica then unzipped Alex's jumpsuit and then Alex lifted his legs but still had no idea what Ronica was doing with his jumpsuit "hey!! That's mine I need that seriously" Alex said "great I'm naked again because of you" Alex said "haha" Ronica said "don't haha me" Alex said "come on Alex have some for a while" Ronica said "fine but if we get arrested I'm telling it was your idea" Alex said then Alex and Ronica just ran around North Seattle and then Alex then ran to University of Washington then Alex was tired, naked, and thruster but Ronica was feeling the exacted opposite Ronica was just always filled with energy but the good news is that they never got arrested and they got back to University of Washington in one peace then as Alex and Ronica came into the dorm Ronica then jumped on to the bed and covered her nakedness then Alex went into bed with her then Alex just slept "Alex thanks for letting me stay here and you're a great guy" Ronica said "you're welcome Ronica" Alex said then Ronica started smooching Alex for the rest of the night

Chapter 8 Disco's plane reveled to Alex

Then over the next 2 weeks Alex started realize that Disco was up to something big but Alex didn't know what it was then as summer hit late July Alex went into his lotus esprit and went to the night club then Alex parked his car and used his hooker gun that Michael gave to him then as the club was closed for the night Alex was in a black jumpsuit then Alex shot the hooker gun to deck Alex then jumped to the deck then Alex saw security guard with a flash light then Alex tripped him and then punched him in the face and stole his wallet and then Alex started running then Alex pulled out a PP7 and hid behind a wall and saw something in container and it was purple and silver "oh yes my new make-up project that will be on the market to every lady in the US and with this make-up this can go girl's clothes and eat all the clothing they have even underwear, bras, and also buildings in the US and with this product every girl in the US will have bathing suit nobody can stop me now muahahahahahahahahahahahahahah" Disco laughed then Alex pressed a button on his head set "Michael I think we have huge problem in Seattle right now" Alex said then a guard saw Alex then a lot of the guards started shooting at Alex then Alex pulled an A33 riffle out of his backpack and started shooting the security guards then Disco saw Alex "it's Aussmen kill him" Disco said then the guards ran then Alex punched them in the face and kicked them in the face then Alex was done then an unknown assign pointed a gun at Alex "hello Alex" a voice said then Alex turned back then it was Debra then Debra whacked Alex in the face "good work put him in the steam room" Disco said then a bunch of the other security guards

Then Alex woke up in another room that was in a spa room and Alex was in his underwear "Alex Aussmen great for you to join us" Disco said "its old news Peter" Alex said "oh lovely of you to say Mr.Aussmen" Disco said "so do you know what my plan is going to be" Disco said "yeah you're going to use silver and purple make-up and use it as Nano bots to destroy women's clothing and underwear and using it to destroy all the great buildings in downtown Seattle" Alex said "very impressive Mr.Aussmen but your only half correct" Disco said " I will also use the make-up and polite the all the lakes in the state of Washington with the makeup and the makeup will be used to eat up all sorts of clothing and buildings especially women's clothing so when girls go swimming they come out of the water with no bathing suit and it will happen to every one Mr.Aussmen and then as that happens then buildings and trees will destroyed and we will have destroyed Washington state" Disco said "that's a very stupid and perverted plan Peter but you will never get away with this" Alex said "muahahah oh really Mr.Aussmen because I think I will win with all these gadgets I have Alex" Disco said "start the spa" Disco said then Debra started the machine that lets the Nano bots get out of the cautioner then Alex used his foot the destroy the Nano bots then Alex started running then Alex got a pair of pants that where dark blue then Alex stole a purple button up shirt and then Alex stole a blue Addis jacket and wear the jacket then Alex used a DD4 gun and started shooting the thugs then Alex escaped from Disco's headquarters and knew that this was the reason Ronica had no clothes on when she met him because Disco used on her and used it on her clothes and the Nano bots ate all of Ronica's clothes and Alex knew that Disco had to be stopped and he had to warn Ronica fast

Chapter 9 Final fight on the Alki beach dock

Then as Alex was running then he then saw a 1981 Delorean then as Alex saw the thug driving the car Alex then grabbed the thug and took out his DD4 and shot him then Alex stole the car and started driving back to University of Washington then Alex saw other thugs driving then Alex put the car on Drive and Alex started driving really fast then as Alex was driving by the freeway then thugs got out RC33 riffles and started shooting at Alex then Alex found buttons in the car then Alex pressed the button that was purple then Alex pressed the button then out of the back of the car machine guns then Alex pressed a button on strearing wheel then machine guns in back of the car started shooting and then the bullets knocked out the tires then other cars feel off the freeway then another thug car speeded up then the driver started shooting at the windows then Alex ducked then Alex speeded up and then Alex's car went on top of the other and then the car flipped in the air then as the car was upside down Alex then got out his PP7 gun and shoot at the thug then Alex found green button and pressed the button and the car flipped back to normal then Alex started speeding up and took an exit turn into downtown Seattle then Alex kept driving all over downtown Seattle then Alex turned left on hill that heads to University of Washington then as Alex got to the campus Alex then parked the car by University library then Alex got out of the car and started running then Alex's watch started ringing then Alex pressed the button on the watch "Aussmen here" Alex said "hey Alex Ronica is by Huskie stadium be careful dude there is a lot of Disco's thugs by the place" Owen said "thanks Owen" Alex said then Alex herd thugs in back of him then one of them pulled out a sniper riffle then Alex pressed a button on tennis shoes then roller wheels came out of the bottom of the shoes then Alex started roller skating around University of Washington then the other had skateboards and then as they where on the skateboards then they pulled out AKS 74U riffles and started shooting at Alex then as Alex then pulled and DD4 out of his backpack and started shooting at the thugs then Alex kept on roller skating to get Huskie stadium then more thugs chased after Alex then Alex reloaded his DD4 and shot more of the thugs that where chasing him then more and more thugs where on Alex's tail then Alex skated by bank of America arena then Alex then jumped of the stairs and did a back flip and landed on his legs and kept on going then Alex fell then Alex realized more thugs where chasing him then Alex got up and kept going then Alex left a grenade where he was and started skating really fast then as thugs where chasing Alex then the grenade exploded and killed the rest of the thugs chasing Alex then as Alex got by bank of America arena Alex then saw Ronica by in the stands then Alex skated to the parking lot of Huskie stadium then as Alex got to the entrance Alex then pressed the button on his tennis shoes and skates went back into his shoes then Alex ran to where Ronica was "Ronica hey what's up" Alex said "oh nothing much Alex I'm just hanging out up here you?" Ronica said "oh nothing much I was just roller skating" Alex said "you roller skate?" Ronica asked "yeah just a little bit" Alex said then Ronica did a girl laugh then Ronica and started kissing in the stands then Alex and Ronica where kissing for 20 minutes in the stands of Huskie stadium "you want to do something today baby?" Alex asked "like what baby?" Ronica said "I don't know like get a bite to eat or go to a movie" Alex said "sure I want go to a movie maybe tonight baby" Ronica said then Ronica kept on kissing Alex more and more

Then as Alex and Ronica where kissing then thugs showed up and then without knowing then a gun was pointed at Alex's head "hello Alex" a thug said then one of the thugs punched Alex in the face and grabbed him by the T-shirt "Alex!" Ronica said then the other thug grabbed Ronica by the arms then the thugs put duck tape on her mouth then Disco came into the stands "oh good Aussmen is knocked out boys take Ronica and Alex to the limo" Disco said then the thugs picked up Alex and Ronica and put Alex in the trunk then Ronica was in the back seat "let me go" Ronica said "shut up" Disco said "hello Ronica it's been a long time since we have dated but now that's all about to change my dear thought you can just run away from me bad idea sweetheart" Disco said then Disco looked at the clothes Ronica was wearing "nice clothes baby I wonder why bought you all of these?" Disco said "Alex did" Ronica said "oh you and Aussmen we that will really change once I kill him in Alki beach in west Seattle muahahahahah" Disco said "you monster please don't baby" Ronica said "oh yes I will baby girl and I will find a great death for you baby girl" Disco said "muahahahahahahahahahahaha" Disco laughed then as they got on a boat and started heading towards a factory deport then as they got there they then got out of the car "Debra take her clothes off and put her in the container" Disco said then Debra grabbed Ronica opened the container then Ronica got out a knife and cut up everything then Debra took off Ronica's jacket and cut up her straps and took her strap shirt and then her shirt then Debra cut Ronica's Bra straps then Debra took her pants and underwear off and Ronica was butt naked in the container "please let me out please baby please don't burn my clothes" Ronica cried then Ronica started crying not because she was not wearing any clothes but she thought Alex was dead in Disco's trunk then Alex found a way to get out of the trunk then Alex started running to find Ronica before it was too late then Alex then started running to find Ronica then Alex took out his A33 riffle and shot a bunch of thugs then one of the thugs then the other thugs started shooting back at Alex then Alex shot them and kept on running then the head thug was looking for Alex then Alex pointed the riffle at him "where's Ronica!!?" Alex yelled "I won't tell you man" the thug said then Alex was about to load up "okay, okay she's in the red container 23" the thug said "thanks" Alex said then Alex grabbed him and threw him off the factory and into the water then Alex started running around the factory looking for Container then Alex found the #23 and used on of Michael's gadgets to open the lock then Alex open the door with all his might then Ronica turned her head as Alex opened the door "Alex!!" Ronica said then Ronica cried "it's okay I'm here Ronica" Alex said then as Alex and Ronica where hugging then other thugs caught them and then they used duck tape on their wrist and took them to main control room "Aussmen what a surprise you survived in my trunk" Disco said "like my new plan in 5 minutes my Nano bots will eat every clothing in every lake in the state and also every ocean" Disco said "it's great news Peter but your crazy mastermind in the end" Alex said "thanks Alex" Disco said then Disco was getting ready to arm the Nano bots then as Alex watched then Alex head butted one of the thugs then Alex kicked another thugs in the stomach and then he stole his PP7 and shot the last 3 thugs then Alex shot the active button "you stupid fool" Disco said then Disco was about to punch Alex then Alex punched Disco in the face then Disco threw Alex against the wall "you have been melting with my plans for the last Mr.Aussmen" Disco said then Disco tried to whack Alex in the face then Alex jumped in the air and kicked Disco in the face then Alex tackled Disco and then Alex punched Disco in the face then Disco pulled a knife and tried to cut Alex then Alex grabbed on a rope then kicked Disco in the face then Disco got hit so hard that he fell off the window and into the Puget sound

"AHHHHHHHHHHHHHHHHHHHHHHHHHHHHHHHHHHHHHHHHHHHHHHHHHHHHHHHHH HHHHHHHHHHHHHHHHHHH!!!!!!!!!!" Disco screamed then Disco got eaten by the sharks then Alex got off the rope "are you okay Ronica" Alex said then Ronica just smiled and hugged Alex "oh thank you for saving me my little angel" Ronica said then Ronica smooched Alex then Alex and Ronica tried to get off the main control center then Alex jumped into a boat and so did Ronica then Alex started the boat and went back to downtown Seattle then the factory exploded

Chapter 10 the flight to Florida

Then the next 3 days Alex and Ronica bought tickets to Florida then as Alex went on the plane with Ronica Alex just enjoyed every minutes he had with Ronica then as Alex was on the plane Ronica then started getting smooching Alex "can I get you lovely couple" the flight attendant said "just soda please" Ronica said then as flight attendant then she got grabbed and then the person who stole her clothes and it was Debra then she threw the original flight attendant out of the plane with no clothes on and Debra put on the flight attendant then as Alex and Ronica where kissing then Ronica instead of getting Ronica soda she got her a beer then she walked to Alex and Ronica's row then Debra pulled out a gun "hers your bed Ronica and Alex" Debra said then she pointed the gun at Alex and Ronica "now get up put your hands behind your head" Debra yelled then Alex and Ronica then without thinking Ronica then kicked Debra in the face then she knocked the gun out of her hand then Ronica then jumped on the celling and stomped on Debra then Alex was about to make sure if she was knocked out then Debra got right back up and slapped and Alex and grabbed him then Ronica knew Alex was in trouble then she used a vacuum in the plane and vacuumed Debra's clothes "hey what you....those are my clothes give them back our I kick you like can of whop ass!!!" Debra said then Ronica then just smiled and kept on vacuuming and vacuumed all of some of Debra's clothes then as Debra looked all beaten up Alex then got out a Nano bolt liquid in his pocket "Debra you left this back in Alki beach in Seattle I believe it's one of yours? Alex said then Alex threw it Debra's clothes then the Nano bots started eating up Debra's clothes bra, shoes, and underwear and then Debra was butt naked then once they where over the gulf of Mexico then "let me go" Debra said "I hope you know how to swim because you will need it Debra" Alex said then "really" Debra said "no!!" Alex said then Alex pushed Debra out of the plane with no Para shot and no clothes on "AHHHHHHHHHHHHHHHHHHHHHHHHHHHHHHHHHHHHHHHH!!!!" Debra yelled then

Alex got back to to his seat "what happened Alex?" Ronica said "she went skinny flying" Alex said "oh Alex you didn't" Ronica said "oh yes I did" Alex said

Then as Debra landed in the gulf of Mexico and she then splashed into the ocean and then she saw some boats "hello can anyone hear me hello?" then boats kept on going passed her then back on the plane the plane landed on and Alex and Ronica drove to Miami beach and then as Alex layed down Ronica then layed down next to Alex "I love you my sweet little angel" Ronica said "Ronica if I ever asked you to marry me would you do it?" Alex asked "yes I would Alex baby I love you a lot" Ronica said "come on lets go swimming baby" Ronica said then Ronica took off her swimsuit then she ran into the ocean then Alex ran in with her and then she started laughing then Alex smooched her "baby you're the best" Ronica said then Alex kept smooching her in the ocean then as Alex and Ronica where kissing then Ronica got out of the ocean with no clothes on then she just saw Alex and just started walking like she didn't even carried about her body then Ronica ran out of the ocean and Alex then lifted up Ronica up in his arms and put her on the towel and then she started laughing and kissing Alex "if might be time to go home soon" Alex said "Alex take on one more trip after Florida please" Ronica said "don't worry baby girl I will" Alex said then Alex kept on kissing Ronica in the Florida sunset "oh Alex" Ronica said

An American Autistic Secret Agent & The American Bankruptcy

An American Autistic Secret Agent & The American Bankruptcy
By: Nelson Amador

Chapter 1 Prologue

It was a really a normal fall day in New York city and a lot of businessmen & women were going back to work and then all of sudden, a women with black hair got off a bus and she went into the wall street and she went into the wall street building and as she went into the building, she went into one of the elevators and she headed up to around the 90th floor in the building and some of the wall street stock brokers were watching President Reagan's voodoo economics speech and a lot of the people were excited because of business people were getting really huge tax cuts from the federal government and people were just celebrating like crazy and then there was one young gentlemen that was waiting for his interview and then the young man turned to the girl "are you waiting for an interview?" he asked her "maybe you tell me" she asked "well it's such a great time because a lot of business are going to be making a lot of money" he said "oh wow that is really cool" she said "wait are you cop?" he asked and all of a sudden she pulled out a ice ring out of her purse and she punched the young man and she put the ring and she started stabbing the guy in the neck and blood started coming out of his neck and the girl grabbed by the neck and all of sudden she threw the guy off the ledge "AHHHHHHHHHHHHHHHHHH!!!!!!!" he yelled and a lot of the people saw him on the floor "oh my god he is okay?!" a women asked "somebody call 911" another person said and then ambulance came and as they came the girl with the black hair stole the young man's wallet and then she walked over to a 1980's computer and she pulled out a microchip and all of a sudden she started steeling every sort of credit card information and she sucked all the money into her credit card and her balance was around 999 billon dollars on the card and a lot of information was just flashing in her eyes and then she turned off the computer and she walked out of the wall street building with a sliver & gold credit card and the ambulance was around the New York exchange

Then all of a sudden a limo picked her up and she got in the car "well I was able to get another 10 billion dollars so that will make my bank account 999 billon dollars and boys that is a lot more fucking money then our US president" she asked "wow that is really incredible Gloria" one of the thugs "guys, you know why I really hate wall street, because this country just really pisses me off because of how wealth is just waved around like candy bars and wall street will be no more" Gloria said as she looked at the window and the limo kept on driving off "well when I get hold of all that cash not only will start going on a shopping party but I my plan is to put this country into a bankruptcy so that every American business in this country will be bankrupt and the US government will have to put restrictions like fuck!! Think about it, no more big buildings, no more wall cards, no more private sectors, and also

no American agencies to help the needy & retarded people in this country!!!!!!!...nothing can stop me now!!!!!!!!!!!! MUAHAHAHAHAHAHAHAHAHAHAHAHAHAHAHAHAHAHAHAHAHAHAHAHAHAH AHAHAHAHAHAHAHAHA HEHEHEHEHEHEHEHEHEHEHEHEHEHEHEHEHEHEHEHEHEHEHEHEHHEHEHE HEHEHEHEEHEHE AHAHAHAHAHAHAHAHAAHAHAHAHAHAHAHAHAHAHHHAHAHAHAHAHAHAHAHAHA HAHAHAHAHAHAHAHAHA!!!!!!!!!!!!!!!!!!" Gloria laughed and the limo kept on driving off into the shadows and some of the banks around them were starting to loose money.

Chapter 2 University of Washington 1982

As the day began, Alex was sleeping in his dorm room and as Alex got up from bed he then went to take a shower and as Alex went into the shower he put on some Old spice shampoo and he started washing his hair and his body and then as Alex got out of the shower and as Alex got back to his dorm room and he started to "what a feeling" and Alex was dancing like a goof ball "wahoooooooo!!!!" Alex yelled with excitement and then Alex put on some really some gold jeans, a Jack Sikma jersey, a purple tennis shoes and Alex started walking to his classes and he took Photography and as he got to class a lot of really hot girls were waiting for him "hey Alex" one of the girls said and Alex winked at one of them and Alex started loading his camera and Alex started taking pictures of the girls he was assigned to take pictures "alright ladies work with me show me some love" Alex said and Alex started taking photos and Alex took around 50 pictures and 10 of each girl and then Alex went into a room to develop the pictures and then after his class, Alex gave the pictures to his professor "thank you Alex" his professor said and Alex started going to his English class and Alex was a really great writer, because of his disability he was really slow but he wrote very beautiful and then as Alex was done with one of his 6 paragraphs paper he passed a note to one of his classmates and it said "if you have the time, can you please correct my paper?" the sticky note said and then the same guy that Alex gave the note to started heading to Alex's dorm room and the boy knocked on Alex's door "password." Alex said "dude I don't know your damn password let me in" the boy said "alright I will give you hint: who is my favorite Angel from Charlie's Angels?" Alex asked "is it...Farrah Fawcett?" the student asked and then all of a sudden Alex let him in "come in my man" Alex said and then the student walked into his room "anyway I'm glad you noted me man" the boy said "your welcome Roger you know I can be a little slow but anyway here is the paper" Alex said and Alex handed his paper to the student and Roger started correcting his paper "I think your missing some periods I believe because there is a lot of run on sentences" Roger said "alright sure I can do that" Alex said and all of a sudden Alex just started making another paper and he wrote more shorter sentences "say Alex why in the hell do you know never tell me about your job you have?" Roger asked "because Roger it is a very secret job" Alex said "do you like work for the government or something because you do know that government jobs are increasing ever since Reagan took became president" Roger said "well Roger I don't plan on working for president Reagan" Alex said "but aren't you a republican though Alex?" Roger asked "yes I am Roger but it doesn't matter who are president is, I will never work for the government I love working for myself" Alex said "but what about hanging out with 50 different women isn't kind of hypocritical?" Roger asked "no because those things I do define my political beliefs such as I believe relationship should be between a man and a woman and hell if you are with more women, more power to you." Alex said, "Okay that does make sense" Roger said, "Anyway how are you coming along with that paper?" Roger asked "I made some corrections on it so it should be a lot more clear" Alex said "alright sounds really awesome" Roger said and then that night as Alex fixed up his paper, Alex started walking to a dorm party and he knocked on the door and one of the people let him into the party and there was dancing and tons of 80's music blasting and Alex started playing beer pong and he ended up throwing 3 balls in the cups and Alex was dancing at the party and was making a lot of really crazy 80's dance moves and Alex got really drunk at the party but all of a sudden and Alex passed out on the coach and at the same time as Alex was passed out on the coach, Gloria arrived at the University of Washington Campus and she started looking at the security cameras at the campus looking for Alex and she was walking in the halls and then she saw the door and she knocked on the door and Alex got up and he was in underwear and Alex open the door "Mr.Aussmen?" Gloria said "yes this is Alex" Alex said "Mr.Aussmen, my name is Gloria Shipmen I hear you are one of the best agents in the Seattle area. I was wondering if you wanted to do a job?" Gloria said "I'm sorry I'm a really busy college student and I have classes" Alex said "actually Alex, we have talked to your professors and they said you can go" Gloria said "are sure this is a really good idea?" Alex asked "come with us Mr.Aussmen" Gloria said and then all of a sudden Alex started walking with Gloria and Alex got on a purple T shirt with red jeans and Gloria and Alex got into a limo and the limo driver started driving to the airport "so Alex have you herd of wall street?" Gloria asked "yeah I have it's in New York and that's were people invest in the stock-market" Alex said "....you are half correct Mr.Aussmen but no...it's more then that, we are talking billons of dollars and people who invest their companies in the stock market and they get points. They also can get money there and you get customer's money and put it into your pocket" Gloria said "so what's in it for me?" Alex asked "....oh what a very hilarious questions. Reason you're brought along is because I believe some people with autism like you are not very bright and very unintelligent and are considered not very favorable and are seemed social unacceptable in society..." Gloria said "you on the other hand are a man with many gifts Mr.Aussmen not only do you have this unexplainable disability but you seem to be a very intelligent and people see you as socially acceptable and not mentally retarded Mr.Aussmen. But I will get to the point, I want you with your incredible autistic brain of yours to steel money from the top money stock companies and once you do that I will

pay 66 million dollars and that way you can be the richest man in Seattle and you don't have to go to college" Gloria said "but I love going to UW" Alex said "oh of course you do Mr.Aussmen but think of it as you are doing me a favor my dear and you will be known as the smartest man in America if you do this Mr.Aussmen" Gloria said "okay what if I get caught?" Alex asked "you will not get caught Alex "Gloria said and as the limo got closer and closer to the airport the limo door opened "and remember Alex, I will be watching you" Gloria said and Alex got out of the limo and the limo left "so did you really mean all those things that you said to him?" the limo driver asked him "oh hell no. he is retarded, stupid, and very intelligent. It's time to crank this up a notch..." Gloria said and then all of a sudden Gloria picked up the phone "yeah I would like to a report a bank robbery" Gloria said and without being aware of this, Alex started walking to the gate that was heading to a flight to New York city and as Alex was on the plane, he slept on the plane and the plane landed in New York City and Alex got on a taxi and he started heading to the 1st cooperate building in the city and Alex got into the car and he started looking at the city of New York and Alex got out by the World Trade Center and he started walking to a company called "Simon & Carl's Technology" Alex started walking inside the company and as he walked into the building he went into one of the buildings and Alex went into the elevator as Alex got into the elevator, he got off around the 78th floor in the building and Alex sneaked into a room where the safe and then a security guard saw Alex "hey your not part of the staff!!!!..." the guard yelled and all of a sudden, Alex punched the security guard in the face and kicked him in the balls and Alex threw the security guard out the window
"AHHHHHHHHHHHHHHHHHHHHHHHHHHHHHHHH!!!!!!!!!!!!" the guard yelled and Gloria saw the footage of the guard falling and Gloria started laughing "wow that stupid mentally retarded son of a bitch actually beat the guy up he is smarter then I thought" Gloria asked and then Alex grabbed around 400,000$ of money from the safe "HIT THE ALREAM!!!!!!" another security guard yelled and Alex took out a PP7 gun and he started shooting at the security guards and shot them in the head and Alex started running to the elevator and as Alex got out the elevator several police cars showed and Alex went to a pay phone and dialed Gloria's number "hey I got the money" Alex said "brilliant Mr.Aussmen we will pick you up real soon" Gloria asked and all of a sudden, Gloria's limo picked up Alex "great you were able to get 4,00,000$" Gloria asked "what is this money going to be for anyway?" Alex asked "that is for me to know and you to find out Mr.Aussmen" Gloria asked "now your next task will be to rob the JP Morgan company and as for you I don't see it being very impossible" Gloria said "for this task, you will need go undercover as a stock-broker and you will meet a man name Joseph Wilson and your plan is to get the key card for around 999 billon dollars and you want to put all that money into..." Gloria said and then Gloria pulled a microchip "this microchip into one of their computers and download the money and get out of their without no distractions. I will also get you some stock broker clothes as well" Gloria said "and remember this day will take a couple of days so I will expect you to get

the key card around 4 weeks" Gloria said and as the day got started, Alex started in a hotel that was in Brooklyn and he laid on his bed and he looked at the view of the city

Then later on in her office, Gloria sat in front of camera and then a man dressed in a gold suit with a silver tie, a silver button up shirt "so how are the plans coming along?" the man asked "oh they are going very well" Gloria said "oh that is really good to hear" the man asked "Alex Aussmen is working for me and doesn't even know where the money is going into. The man must be more stupid then I thought. I think I will be able to get 999 billon dollars in no time with this retarded piece of shit working for me" Gloria said "sounds really good now I do expect that he will get that money and we will cause the biggest bankruptcy that not even president Reagan will not even be able fix it" the man said "oh yes I agree" the man said "where is the boy now?" the man asked "I got him a hotel in Brooklyn but if I wanted to right now, I could send some guards to beat his mentally retarded ass up and throw him into a dumpster and frame him" Gloria said "alright well I must be off I will see you around" the man asked and for the rest of the night, Gloria sat in her office and she looked at the window

Chapter 3 Exploring JP Morgan & Meeting Helga Bynes

As Alex walked into the JP Morgan building, he went into an elevator and he went to the JP Morgan floor and sat down and as he was sitting down a beautiful girl with black hair showed up "hello welcome JP Morgan I'm Helga Bynes are you new working at this job?" Helga asked "oh yes I am my name Aussmen…Alex Aussmen" Alex said "it's a pleasure to meet you. Our last stock broker died yesterday from some sort of killing a couple of days ago" Helga said "oh no yikes I'm sorry that's awful" Alex said "yeah I know it was really sad" Helga said and Helga & Alex walked over to a private office and Alex was really shocked "wow this is a really cool office" Alex said "well anyway since you are new, I don't expect to get a lot of stock points. But try to get as many as you can" Helga said and Helga left and Alex was all alone with computer and Alex turned the computer "alright Alex, I want you to click on the money memory button" Gloria said and Alex clicked on the button "alright now you are going export some of the money to another application. Now do you have a key card that I gave you?" Gloria asked "yes I have it" Alex said and Alex got out of the key card and plugged the card into the computer "now start getting that cash Seattle boy" Gloria said and as Alex was steeling money, he started seeing all the stock percentages and Alex was just amazed at how wall street worked "oh my god!!!..." Alex said and all of a sudden, the money amount got around $55,000,000 in the key card and then all of a sudden the alarm went off and a lot of workers "WARNING!!!!, WARNING!!!! SOMEONE MUST HAVE HACKED INTO YOUR BANK ACCOUNT!!!!!!!!" the speaker said all of a sudden, Alex unplugged the key card from the computer and he started running and a lot of security guards with PP7 guns came up and then back at the hotel Gloria started pressing a button on the 1980's mac computer "NOW LETS SEE HOW YOU DO WITHOUT YOUR GOOD HEART YOU MENTALLY RETARDED PIECE OF SHIT!!!!!!!!" Gloria said and Gloria pressed the button and all of a sudden a microchip started planting into Alex's autistic brain and the microchip started controlling Alex's personality and his autistic brain "now your under my control FUCK HEAD!!!!!!!!!" Gloria said with a bitter and evil voice and as the guards came, they pointed their guns at Alex "HANDS UP!!!!!!" the guards yelled and Alex smiled his vision was red and his vision was revised to target the guards and Alex kicked the security guard in the face and shot him in the head, another security guard tried to grab Alex, Alex just cringed his teeth with anger and punched the security guard in the office and slammed his head against the wall and blood started coming out of his head, all of a sudden more police and SWAT came into the building and Alex used his autistic brain to beat up the SWAT team, as the SWAT team came after Alex, Alex grunted his teeth with anger and took out an A33 riffle and shot 88 bullets at the SWAT policemen and killed around 30 policemen and Gloria was watching this through the security guard and she started laughing at the dead policemen and laughing hysterically "oh this is too easy!!!" Gloria said and she kept on laughing and Alex started running to the elevator "Stop that young man!!!" another cop yelled "red team shut down the elevators!!!!!" another SWAT team and Alex used his red Autistic vision and all of a sudden Alex threw 5 grenades at the SWAT team and the floor exploded in flames and Alex got to the 1st floor and as he was looking around with Gloria's autistic controlled red vision in his brain, Alex saw a motorcycle in a leather jacket and Alex with a pissed off look on his face walked up to him "HEY THIS MY BIKE SHIT-HEAD!!!!" the motorcycle said and all of a sudden, Alex punched the biker in the face "alright now your in big trouble you little shit!!!!" the biker said "OH REALLY?! LIKE FUCK I AM!!!!" Alex yelled and then Alex dodged all the biker's punches, Alex grabbed the biker's wrist and shot him in the neck and threw on to the street and the biker ended up getting run over by a car and then Alex took off the dead biker's clothes and he put the clothes on him and Alex took off flying on road going at 88 miles per hour in New York city and all of a sudden 5 SWAT cars started coming after him "pull over to the curve this is the New York police department you are under arrest!!!!" the SWAT team yelled back at the hotel, Gloria laughed and pressed another button that controlled Alex's brain that made Alex pull out a rocket launcher and Alex got out a rocket launcher Alex pointed the rocket launchers at the SWAT team and Gloria started laughing "DIE NEW YORKERS DIE YOU PATHIC MOTHER FUCKERS!!!!!!!!!!!" Gloria yelled and Alex shot the rocket launcher blowing up 4 SWAT cars in flames "blue team don't let that guy get to Manhattan" another SWAT car said and Alex kept on running and Gloria pressed another button that made Alex increase the speed on the bike "now lets go on this ramp shall we" Gloria asked and all of a sudden Alex went off a ramp and Alex was able to get Manhattan with no problem "now Alex get to Brooklyn and deliver the money" Gloria said and as they were a lot of chaos by the JP Morgan, Helga got out of the building and she started noticing some clues and picked up Alex's ID card and Helga took the subway to Long Island to her apartment and as she got home, she put Alex's ID card under a microscope "sounds like this is someone that is from here but how was he able to get through the police" Helga asked herself out-loud and Helga walked over to her phone in her house and Helga's caller was someone was a very beautiful girl that was tall, she had brown & blonde hair, she had a really fit body with big breathes and she answered the phone "hello?" she said "hey Renee I'm on this really huge case. What do you know about Alex Aussmen?" Helga asked "nothing why?" Renee said "well anyway he came into my work and I think he stole money from my business. Bring Jay along with you and meet me at the library in Brooklyn" Helga said "alright okay Helga" Renee said

Later that night, Helga, Jay, & Renee were at the library in Brooklyn and they started looking at different books "so what else happened?" Jay asked, "He then stole the company's money using some sort of keycard. But I don't get it though what is somebody from Seattle doing in New York City?" Helga asked "that is a really good point maybe he has family." Renee said "well we gotta to find out who this guy is" Helga said "we have to investigate this guy because no ordinary person would have been able to get by NYPD" Helga said and so the 3 people started looking at books around crime and Jay found a section about Alex "I found something Helga and here is what is it says" Jay said "Alexander Aussmen born in April 8th 1959 in Seattle, Washington" Jay reads "also Mr.Aussmen has high functioning Autism" Jay continued to read "but that is impossible nobody with autism can do all those things that he did" Helga said "I'm assuming he has like bad ADD or something to the point where it makes him really smart or he got chemically tested as a baby" Jay said "but there is no sign he has ADD because I met him he didn't seem like he did" Helga said "well something or someone must have been telling him what to do" Jay said "I think we just need to keep an eye on him" Renee said "well I don't know where he is now but I will look for him" Helga said

Later that night, Alex came back to the plaza hotel and as Alex got into Gloria's hotel room, he started touching his head and his vision went back to normal "oh man up it's not that bad" Gloria said "what the hell did you do to me?!" Alex said "oh I controlled you Mr.Aussmen so that way your disability wouldn't hold you back and so you would get past those guards more faster. It seems we took a great chance on you. Now where is the damn card?" Gloria asked and Alex handed Gloria the key card full of money and Gloria started looking at the card "sounds like you got a lot of money Mr. Aussmen...I was very happy that I was able to steel from JP Morgan one of the biggest companies in this stupid country" Gloria said "what are you going to need all that money for?" Alex asked "oh that is such a funny question Mr. Aussmen and that is something your going to have to find out" Gloria said

Chapter 4 Shipmen's jewelry warehouse

The next morning, Alex woke up and as Alex woke up he was received a piece of paper that said "meet by my warehouse in Queens, NY DO NOT BE LATE!!!!!..." The note said and Alex got dressed really quickly and he ran out of the hotel and he took the subway to Queens and as Alex got there he looked around Queens and he saw a strange gold warehouse and saw Gloria's henchmen guarding the door and as Alex walked in "like my new warehouse Mr.Aussmen?" Gloria asked "why in the warehouse?" Alex asked "remember when you asked what I was going to do with the money, well this is what I am going to do with the money" Gloria said and all of a sudden the henchmen reveled a lot of gold gems getting turned into gold liquid and in the machines, the gold liquid was making fake gold and sliver and all of sudden Alex turned back and he saw a lot of dollar bills getting burned in flames

Then all of a sudden, Alex saw some henchmen grabbing a stock broker and they started beating him up and they stole his credit card and his debit card and then Gloria just laughed at him and she pressed a button and a lot of hot liquid gold feel on the beat up stock broker and the stock broker was dead and he was covered in liquid gold and the gold dried out "you see Mr. Aussmen I'm going to make all sorts of fake money that nobody will notice and pretty soon the American economy will break down and pretty soon a lot of stupid people will be begging for money and every business will run out of huge money because I will steel it all" Gloria said "you see it Alex I will build my own fortress in Iceland were nobody will be able to find me and my fortress and soon with my wealth I will become the most powerful criminal that nobody will ever stop me and don't worry you will still be paid 56 billon dollars" Gloria said and then a henchmen started looking up Alex's personal information and then the henchmen walked up to Gloria and whispered in her ear "or on a second thought Mr. Aussmen, it turns out your services will not longer be needed you stupid mentally retarded piece of shit!!!!!!" Gloria said and then all of a sudden 4 henchmen tried to grab Alex and Alex punched one of them in the face and then Alex kicked another henchmen in the face and then Alex jumped up in the air and whacked the 3rd henchmen and then Alex took out a huge staff and electrocuted Alex "AHHHHHHHHHHHHHHHHHHHHH!!!!!!!..." Alex screamed and then Gloria punched Alex in the face and then punched him in the jaw and blood started coming out of his mouth "MUAHAHAHAHAHAHAHA I always knew you were so stupid Alex I knew I could use you for personal cover because nobody in this country takes people with disabilities seriously and now that I have all the money that you stole for me, your services will just no longer be needed and you stole all that money for nothing. Lock him in the gold liquid room!!!!" Gloria said and then the henchmen came and Alex was put in the same room were the stock broker died and then henchmen dumped 45 million dollars on Alex and Gloria walked up and she lit a match "Have a nice death Mr.Aussmen because I'm pretty sure your life was not really significant because of your disability and because of that I hope you burn in hell you mentally retarded non intelligent SHIT-HEAD!!!!!!!!!!" Gloria yelled and then she dropped the match and money

started burning all around Alex and Alex was tied up in ropes "power up the gold liquid" Gloria said and then one of the henchmen powered the machine the gold machine started pouring gold liquid that makes making the flames more stronger and Alex just struggled to get free and then Alex started reaching his pocket and Alex noticed that he had some bubble gum and then Alex started chewing the bubble gum and all of a sudden, Alex spit the gum out and gun landed on the gold liquid hose and all of a sudden, the hose exploded and Alex lit one of his lighters and he burned the ropes and Alex got free and Alex jumped through glass window and broke through window and Alex picked up a PP7 and then a bunch of Gloria's henchmen started shooting at Alex and Alex dodged some of the bullets and Alex shot some of the henchmen in the head and then more henchmen came and Alex loaded up the PP7 gun he shot more bullets and shot 6 henchmen in neck and Alex started running to escape out of the warehouse "STOP HIM HE'S GETTING AWAY DON'T LET STUPID SON OF A BITCH GET AWAY!!!!!!!!!!!!!!" Gloria yelled and then more henchmen came and Alex got into a huge fist fight and Alex dodged most of their attacks and Alex slammed one of them against the wall and punched them in the back, another henchmen tried to whack Alex in the head with a metal bar and Alex did a backflip and another henchmen tried to punch Alex in the head, Alex dodged the punch Alex punched the henchmen in the face and kick him in the stomach, the 3rd henchmen tried to kick Alex in the face, Alex grabbed the henchmen's leg threw him against the wall and Alex grabbed his Magnum Cap Pistol and then Alex broke through another glass window and he punched the henchmen that was controlling the buttons for the gold liquid machine and shot him with the Magnum cap Pistol and then Gloria kicked Alex in the face and then Alex avoided most of her attacks and then Alex kicked Gloria in the stomach and she was forced into the gold liquid machine and then Alex shot at a gold container and then a lot of gold liquid came down on Gloria
"AHHHHHHHHHHHHHHHHHHHHHHHHHHHHHHHHHHHHHHHH!!!!!!!!" Gloria screamed and then Gloria was covered in gold liquid and Alex ran out of the warehouse as fast as he could and Alex started running to the nearest subway he could find and Alex went down into the subway stop and he went on a subway that headed back to New York City but as he went on the subway, Jay & Helga saw him go on the subway and so they started fallowing him

Chapter 5 The Rise of a Bankrupt America

As Alex was on the subway, he was super tried from all the running and from all the fighting and shooting Alex then looked at his watch and it was around 1:00PM and he kept looking around to see if any of Gloria's henchmen came out of the warehouse but nobody was on the subway accept him and Alex was looking, Jay & Helga saw him "there he is" Helga said and then as Alex got to Manhattan, Jay all of a sudden shot a tranquilizer bullet at Alex and Alex got electrocuted and then Alex passed out "that worked out just fine" Jay said "we have to take him to my house and ask him a few questions" Helga said and a couple hours later, Alex was sitting down in a kitchen and then Renee & Jay walked in "where am I?" Alex asked "your in Brooklyn" Jay said "we saw you work with Shipmen's group steeling money from all the wall street companies and we can play this the easy way or the hard way" Renee said "look overall I have nothing to do with it. But I will talk, Shipmen's plan is steel billons and billons of dollars from every wall street company to build a gold liquid machine that would kill people with liquid gold" Alex said "the reason she came to me was because I had a disability and she said that nobody would take seriously so that's why she came to me" Alex said "alright those are some good answers" Renee said "we also read about your record as a secret agent in Seattle, Washington I think you could really help you us" Renee said "I would love to help you guys" Alex said and then Helga came into the kitchen and she sat down "so Alex, were do you think Shipmen is going to strike next?" Helga asked "none of us don't know but I think she has most of the money to build the machine and she is going to strike New York City first" Alex said "well we have to act fast. Where do you think she is controlling the machine from?"" Helga asked "it has to be in time square because of Wall Street is in that area" Alex said

Then meanwhile around Wall Street Gloria and her henchmen were able to get into a secret elevator and they went to the top of the building and then all of a sudden a huge computer screen showed up and then the man dressed in the gold suit and sliver tie appeared on the screen again "hello Gloria, it seems that are massive plan is really working out." The man in the gold suit said "it is working just fine we have around 1 trillion dollars to build the gold liquid machine and then we can destroy this city" Gloria said "excellent what about that Alex Aussmen boy from Seattle" the man in the gold suit said "Unfortunately Mr.Aussmen escaped from my warehouse but my henchmen will be able to track him down and also kill him" Gloria said "I'm sure they will Dr. Dollar" Gloria said "also with this amount of money we will be able bankrupt this whole country and not even President Reagan will have an answer for this type of destruction and then all of the Untied States' money will all ours!!!!" Dr. Dollar said "also Alex does come..." Gloria said all of a sudden Gloria reveled herself and she had massive and brutal gold cuts on her face, some parts of her body, and her right arm and right hand were painted gold "very evil look Gloria" Dr. Dollar said "you want to see what else I can do?" Gloria said and all of a sudden, one of the henchmen put a gold beam around her hand and she blasted a golden laser at the wall and blew up the wall "that is very powerful with that weapon, Alex Aussmen will be defenseless and the money will in your pockets Nobody can stop us now BRAHAHAHAHAHAHAHAHAHAHAHAHAHAHAHAHAHAHAHAHAHAHAHAHAHAH AHAHAHAHAHAHAHAHAHAHAHAHAH MUAHAHAHAHAHAHAHAHAHAHAHAHAHAHAHAHAHAHAHAHAHAHAHAHAHAH AHAHAHAHAHAHAHAHAHAHAHAHAHAHAHAHAHAHAHAHAHAHAHAHAHAH AHHHHHHHHHHH MUAHAHAHAHAHAHAHAHAHAHAHAHAHAHAHAHAHAHAHAHAHAHAHAHAHAHAH

**AHAHAHAHAHAHAHAHAHAHAHAAHAHAHA
BRAAHAHAHAHAHAHAHAHAHAHAHAHAHAHAHAHAHAHAHAHAHAHAHAHAHAHAHA
HAHAHAHAHAHAAHAAHAHAHAHA!!!!!!! Dr. Dollar laughed and then as Dr.
Dollar was laughing, a lot of golden bombs started to be planted over Wall
Street and all over time square**

**Then later that day, Alex & Helga started looking around some of the buildings
in New York City and they started looking around the Empire State building.
Jay & Helga went into the elevator and Alex pressed the 90th floor button and
then as they got out of the elevator, they saw that the floor was a factory "oh
my god" Helga said "this has to be one of the factories that Shipmen was
working on but I don't think she did this alone" Alex said "do you have any
idea were one of the credit cards that she stole?" Helga asked "no but we are
going to find out soon" Alex said then Alex & Helga started looking around
more and more and then they went into a cart and as Alex was driving the cart,
Alex started noticing a lot of money being transmitted into a lot of computers
through printers and then Alex took out his camera and then as he was done,
Alex & Helga ducked under covered money and then one of the workers
double checked the cart and it passed through and then Alex & Helga got out of
the cart "is there a way you can send my photos to Jay & Renee?" Alex asked
"yes I can" Helga said "Alright I want you to get out of here and end those
photos to them and I will meet you in Brooklyn in 3 hours" Alex said "and what
are you going to do?" Helga asked "I'm going to find out who really is behind
all this mess" Alex said and then Helga started running out of the factory and
then Alex took out a Edison Giacatolli cap gun and he started spying around
the factory and then Dr. Dollar started walking around and he look tall,
skinny, he had facial hair that made him look a pharaoh from ancient Egypt
and he had a gold and sliver cane and he wore bronze dress shoes and he
looked like Michael Jackson "what in the hell?!" Alex said "so it appears
everything is going right as planed I will call Shipmen in a little bit to tell her
to get started on the machine" Dr. Dollar said and then a factory worker came
and then he spotted Alex and all of a sudden Alex whacked him in the head
with his gun and shot him in the neck and blood came out of his neck and Alex
went closer and closer to Dr.Dollar's office and then Alex sneaked into the
office and he went under the desk and as Dr.Dollar came into the office Alex
showed out of nowhere and he punched Dr. Dollar in the face and Dr. Dollar
took out his golden staff and he tried to whack Alex in the face 8 times, Alex
dodged all of Dr. Dollar's attacks and all of a sudden, Alex kicked Dr. Dollar in
the stomach and Alex grabbed him by the shirt and shoved him against a glass
window and gave Dr. Dollar a cut on his forehead and Alex punched him in the
face again and gave him a black eye and Alex punched him in the jaw "where
are the records?!" Alex yelled and Alex took out a PP7 gun and pointed the gun
at his head "I will never tell you Mr. Aussmen, but I know that soon I will have
every money recorded in every single computer in the world and not even
somebody as smart as you will be able to stop me" Dr. Dollar said and all of a
sudden Dr. Dollar took out a kitchen knife and he suddenly stabbed Alex in the**

arm and blood started coming out of the upper part of his arm and all of a sudden the beatings that Alex gave on Dr. Dollar were starting to go away "you see Mr. Aussmen the money that I'm using will be used to heal all my beatings and soon my laser beam will over-heat every human being in this country and that is final phase in my plan" Dr. Dollar said and all of a sudden, Dr. Dollar grabbed a remote and the remote started making noises and noises started driving Alex crazy and Alex was just covering his ears "AHHHHHHHHHH!!!!!..." Alex yelled and Dr. Dollar whacked Alex in the face and grabbed him by the neck "and now it's time to destroy the world and it's also to die of a very deadly and bloody beating Mr.Aussmen" Dr. Dollar said and Dr. Dollar started stabbing Alex in the neck harder and harder and blood started coming out of Alex's neck and a couple of guards came and grabbed Alex by the arms and they started punching Alex in the face and giving him all sorts of beatings and all of a sudden, Dr. Dollar walked over and he pressed a green button and then all sorts gold laser beams started to fire at Alex "this deadly gold laser beam will burn all of your skin and soon this laser will plant a nuclear laser bomb and will blow up New York City and will work it's away throughout the country and with this plan we owe it all to you kid!!!" Dr. Dollar said and then Alex was able to get free from the guards and he kicked both of the guards in the faces, another guard tried to attack Alex but Alex dodged the guard's attack, and Alex kicked the guard in the stomach and knocked him out and the other guard grabbed Alex and Alex threw the guard to the wall and took out his PP7 gun and shot him in the head, all of a sudden Dr. Dollar grabbed from behind "can you feel the pain Mr.Aussmen because this is the pain New York city is going to feel!!!!..." Dr. Dollar said and all of a sudden Alex got into rage and grinded his teeth and back punched Dr. Dollar in the face and Alex grabbed Dr. Dollar and punched him in the face 6 times, Dr. Dollar then kicked Alex in the stomach and forced against the floor, Dr. Dollar tried to stomp on Alex's face, Alex summersaulted and avoided the attack, Alex got out and Dr. Dollar tried to punch Alex 9 times, Alex dodged all of the attacks, Alex tackled Dr. Dollar and forced him against the wall and Dr. Dollar head-butted Alex and gave Alex a bloody lip, Alex grabbed Dr. Dollar and saw one of the golden knives on the floor and Alex grabbed the knives and Alex all of a sudden stabbed Dr. Dollar in the top of the head, Alex stabbed him again in the both of the shoulders, Alex took the last knife that was bigger and Alex stabbed Dr. Dollar in eye and all of a sudden, as Dr. Dollar was dead, Dr. Dollar pressed the green button and a bomb count down "the floor will self destruct in 40 minutes and Alex started running and he jumped through a glass window and he landed on the floor of the factory and the floor was catching fire and a lot of guards had a lot ZMG gun firing at Alex, Ale took out reloaded his A33 riffle and Alex started firing the A33 riffle gun and firing more then 200 bullets at the guards killing 50 evil factory workers as Alex took the ammo of the guards and Alex noticed the countdown of the bomb reached 10 minutes and Alex started running as fast as he can to the nearest window he can find and as the factory floor on the empire state building exploded Alex jumped through glass window and Alex started sky-diving and Alex was in free fall and Alex pressed a button on his spy-watch and a helicopter came out of the head of the watch and became a handle and another handle extended to the other hand and it Alex used both of his hands to grab on the helicopter handles and all of a sudden a rocket launcher & a machine gun showed up in the other arm and all of a sudden Dr. Dollar's helicopters showed up and the helicopters started firing bullets at Alex and Alex started firing his rocket launcher and Alex ended up blowing up one of the helicopters and Alex started flying towards Brooklyn and more helicopters showed up chasing Alex "this is your last warning Mr. Aussmen we have the orders of Gloria Shipman to capture you!!!!!!" the helicopter pilots said and Alex started firing his machine gun at 5 helicopters coming at him and Alex blew up 3 helicopters in flames and Alex started flying faster and faster and 2 remaining helicopters started chasing him and more bullets started firing at Alex and Alex dodged the bullets and Alex reloaded his rocket launcher and he fired 4 rockets out of his rocket launcher and the helicopters exploded in flames "AHHHHHHHHHHHHHHHH!!!!!" the pilots yelled and Alex fell into Brooklyn and he started finding Helga's house in Brooklyn and as Alex was flying faster and faster, Alex ejected himself from the helicopter and Alex was sky-diving into Brooklyn and as Alex was in free fall, Alex pulled one of the Para-shoots and Alex free fall really softly into Helga's roof and Alex jumped off the roof "Alex are alright?" Helga asked, "Yeah I'm fine" Alex said, "Oh my god you are hurt come on lets get inside" Helga said

Alex & Helga went inside of Helga's house to get away from more helicopters coming and as they got into the house, Helga went to go look for some Band-Aids "I was able to find these will these help?" Helga asked, "Yeah they will help" Alex said Alex started putting on the Band-Aids using Neosporin to heal the cuts that Dr. Dollar gave to him "oh my god it hurts so bad" Alex said then Renee & Jay showed up "what the hell happened to you?" Jay asked, "I was in a really bad fist fight" Alex said "did you find out anything new?" Renee asked "yeah I did I found out that not only are they are killing stock-brokers and steeling their money, they are using the money to build a gold laser bomb that would start in New York City and move along to the west coast" Alex said and "the laser is going to over-heart the whole world and burn people" Alex continued "but then what happens to the money?" Renee asked "with that plan I do not think there is going to be currency" Jay said "he's right" Alex said "that means we are really running out of time and we would need to stop them really fast" Renee said

Back in New York city around Manhattan in a different building, Gloria and her thugs walked in and Gloria activated one of the biggest computers and she took out 4 different credit cards that were stolen from different stock brokers around wall street "my plan is 100% complete and now it's time to blow up New York City as well know it" Gloria said "and the world is...GOLD!!!!!" Gloria said and all of a sudden Gloria pressed the gold button and then a lot of stock numbers were coming into her head and a lot of money was getting sucked out of the wall street and a lot of people were getting shocked and very confused "what my savings is gone!!!..." a random person said and Gloria just laughed and she pressed another button a lot of laser gold laser bombs were starting to explode all over Manhattan and people were dying of over-heating and also people's bank account in their computers started exploding in flames and people were dying in flames and the heat was killing and laser beam explosions started reaching Brooklyn "the explosions!!!" Jay yelled and all around a lot of things around them were exploding in flames and Renee, Jay, Helga, & Alex ran out of Helga's house and Helga's house exploded "you guys get to the subway and find a safe place that is only place the bombs will not hit" Alex said "and what are you going to do?" Jay asked "I have to stop them" Alex said "are you crazy you are going to get killed" Renee said "yeah I know I might be a lot different most of you guys but I have to save the world weather I die or not" Alex said and all of a sudden Alex started running towards the bomb and then Alex pressed a button on his spy-watch and Alex jumped in the air and the helicopter came out of his spy watch so did the handles and Alex grabbed on to the handles and Alex started flying really faster towards Manhattan

All of a sudden, Gloria saw Alex flying "Shipman its Aussmen!!!" one of the guards said and Gloria looked through the window "oh I know the best thing option how are we going to care of Mr.Aussmen" Gloria said and then all of a sudden, Gloria pressed a button and a lot of helicopters showed up and they started flying towards Alex and they also had rocket launchers and all of a sudden they started firing bullets and rockets at Alex then Alex started dodging all the bullets and the rockets and Alex fired back and he fired 600 bullets at the helicopters and the helicopters exploded in flames and Alex flew faster and Alex found Gloria's headquarters and Alex started running inside the building and Alex knew he had to stop Gloria and her evil awful planning before the world blew up in laser beams

Chapter 6 An American Autistic Secret Agent

As Alex got into the building, he knew what he had to do. Alex then took out a DD4 pistol and suddenly 6 guards "you will never get of here alive!!!!!!!!" the guards yelled and then Alex had a pissed off and angry look on his face and Alex shot all of the guards in the face and Alex started running really fast and more guards came and he had ZMG guns and they started shooting at Alex, Alex went to go find cover and he reloaded his gun and Alex started shooting at more guards that were shooting at him and Alex started running to the elevator and he noticed that the last floor was beeping gold "Shipman!!!" Alex said with anger and Alex pressed the button and the elevator opened and 5 guards showed up and Alex took out a ZMG gun and shot guards in the head and Alex got into the elevator and he pressed the button to the 500th floor in the building and then as Alex was in the elevator, Gloria then powered up the building that controlled the whole building and all the city of New York City

"TIME TO TAKE CONTROL OF THIS BITCH!!!!!!!!" Gloria yelled and Alex got out of the elevator and he was on the top "good luck with the floor that you are on Alex because you are going to need the level that you are on because I don't know if this went through your head, but I can control New York City and this building with 900% of my brain. Isn't that wonderful that I can do that. NOW DIE RETARD DIE!!!!!!!" Gloria yelled and then Gloria pulled an orange lever on the computer and the elevator above Alex started coming down and it was coming towards really fast and Alex jumped off the elevator and Alex grabbed on to the sliver rope and Alex started climbing on to the rope really slowly "YOU CAN'T WIN ALEX!!!! MY PLAN TO TAKE CONTROL OF NEW YORK CITY MY IQ WILL DESTROY THE CITY AND THERE IS NOTHING YOU CAN DO ABOUT IT!!!!!!!!!!!" Gloria yelled, "yes there is!!!!..." Alex said and then Alex started climbing really fast and Gloria pressed on another button to drop down another elevator and Alex swing to the next rope and Alex kept on climbing and Alex got to the floor and she saw a pen-house as he climbed up and then all of sudden a giant claw hit Alex in the face and the pen house disappeared "MUAHAHAHAHAHAHAHAHAHAHAHAHAHAHAHAHAHAHAHAHAHAHAHAHAHAHA HAHAHAHAHAHAHAHAHAHAHAAHAHAH HEHEHEHEHEEHE HAAHAHAAHAHAHAHAHAHAHAHAHAHAHAHAHAHAHAHAHAHA YOU FAILED ALEX YOU ARRIVED REALLY TOO LATE AND NOW MY PLAN IS GOING TO PUT NEW YORK CITY IN SHAMBELS AND ALSO PUT AMERICAN ECONMEY INTO FLAMES AND THANKS TO YOU, I AM THE ONLY PERSON THAT HAS AROUND 999,000,000,000,000$ AND WALL STREET & THE AMERICAN ECONMEY IS DEAD MUAHAHAHAHAHAHAHAHAHAHAHAHAHAHAHAHAHAHAHAHAHAHAHAHAHAHAH AHAHAHAHAHAHAHAHAHAHAHAHAHAHAHAHAH HAAAAAAA AHAHAHAHAHAHAHAHAHAHAHAHAHAHAHAHAHAHAHAHAAHAHAHAHAHAHAHA HEHEHEHEHEHEHEHEHEHEHEHEEE MUAHAHAHAHAHAHAHAHAHAHAHAHAHAHAHAHAHAHAHAHAHAHAHAHA!!!!" Gloria laughed and Alex had a really pissed and angry look on his face "and now...I'M GOING TO KILL YOU AND FINSH YOU OFF!!!!..." Gloria yelled and all of a sudden the claws came out of walls and they tried to scratch and attack Alex and Alex dodged most of the attacks but then one of Gloria's robot claws grabbed Alex and Alex struggled to get free and the claws started chocking him "and it's now time to kill stupid people like you!!!" Gloria yelled and all of a sudden, Alex planted a bomb on one of Gloria's robot claws and the bomb exploded in flames "AHHHHHHHHHHHH!!!.." Gloria yelled and Alex jumped off one of the claws and Alex pressed a button on his spy watch and his spy helicopter and Alex started flying and suddenly a really giant robot showed up and it was a golden robot and the robot started trying to shot at Alex. Alex dodged some of the robots attacks and Alex started 8,000 bullets at Gloria's golden robot "AHHHHHHHHHHHHHHHHHHHH!!!!!..." Alex yelled as he was firing the bullets at the robot and inside the robot, Gloria pressed another button that fired a missile at Alex and Alex tried to fly really fast but the missile hit Alex from behind and the helicopter on Alex's spy watch broke and Alex started flying and Alex pressed another button on his watch, and rockets came out of Alex's shoes and a grenade launcher came out of Alex's backpack and Alex started firing grenade at Gloria's robot and Alex hit the head of the robot and the robot's head exploded and the robot started falling a part "MY ROBOT MY BEAUITFUL ROBOT!!!!!...THIS BATTLE IS NOT OVER YET!!!!! ALEX AUSSMEN CURSE YOU!!!!!!!!!!!!' Gloria yelled and Gloria started falling down and then Alex landed inside the computer room and Alex started running inside the credit computer lab "oh my god how am I going to work this?" Alex said and then Alex looked at the computer and Alex noticed that the accounts were getting connected into the large computer screen and then as Alex was working on the computer, all of a sudden somebody from behind hit him in the head with a golden cane and the person grabbed Alex by the neck and threw against the wall, Alex tried to punch him in the face, but the person kicked Alex in the balls and punched him in the face and gave him a huge black eye "MUAHAHAHAHAHAHAHAHAHA you thought you killed me think again Mr. Aussmen" Dr. Dollar said and Alex felt very week and all of a sudden Gloria showed up "you thought you could take both of us on think again Mr. Aussmen, I'm much more smarter then the average human being with all this technology I can control with my brain!!!!" Gloria said and then a robot claw grabbed Alex and Gloria punched Alex in the jaw and blood started coming out of Alex's mouth and Alex's teeth were red "I finally captured the autistic secret agent Alex Aussmen and you thought could escape from people that are much smarter then you and my wealthy then you. I believe Gloria and I are going to give you a good and nice jail beating" Dr. Dollar said "you know something, you are right you guys are much smarter then me. But aren't you guys forgetting something?!" Alex said and then Alex pulled Gloria's keycard out of his pocket "I was able to get every bank account you stole back to their companies before you attacked me" Alex said and then Alex slowly pressed a button on his spy watch and then a missile came out of Alex's spy watch and the missile fired at Dr. Dollar and Alex was able to get free and Alex kicked Dr. Dollar in the face and shot him in the stomach and Dr. Dollar was dead for good.

Gloria then tried to punch Alex in the face, Alex dodged all of Gloria's attacks. Gloria then took out an electric knife to stab Alex, Alex dodged all of the attacks, Alex jumped up in the air and Gloria grabbed Alex from one of his legs and slammed to the ground and Gloria grabbed Alex's head from behind and shaved him against the wall, Gloria then kicked Alex in the face "I owe you a very bloody death Mr.Aussmen!!!" Gloria said and then without noticing Alex grabbed one of Gloria's bombs "Now time to kill you once and for all!!!!" Gloria yelled and then Alex grabbed a metal bar in the building and Alex whacked Gloria in the head with a metal bar and Alex kicked Gloria in the head and Gloria then grabbed Alex by the right foot and then grabbed Alex's bomb button "ahahahahahah I will and now I'm on the edge of seven-teen!!!!!!" Gloria yelled "you mean on the edge of getting blown up!?" Alex said "what?!" Gloria said and then Gloria started trying to find the bomb and Alex kicked Gloria in the stomach and Gloria started getting electrocuted really badly "uh oh!!!...AHHHHHHHHHHHHHHHHHHHHHHHHHHHHHHHHHHHHH!!!!!!!!!" Gloria yelled violently and as Gloria was getting electrocuted, the huge computer screen in the credit card computer lab was starting to get destroyed and the money was going back to the cooperate companies and the floor exploded into flames and Alex grabbed the Gloria's keycard and as Alex was falling down, Alex through a bomb at Gloria's building and Gloria's building started explode and so did the helicopters on top of the building and the golden laser exploded in space and Alex pulled on the Para shoot and Alex free fallen really nice as things behind Alex exploded into flames and as Alex landed on the ground most of wall street was really destroyed from all the damage and Alex started looking around and he felt big sense of shame and sadness and Alex walked into the New York Stock Exchange building and all of a sudden Renee, Jay, & Helga showed up "ALEX!!!!!!!" Helga said and they started running to Alex "Alex you did it you saved the world and the American economy from going into bankruptcy thank you so much Alex" Helga said "we owe you one man" Jay said and then all of a sudden Helga smooched Alex on the lips and all of a sudden Alex used a hock shot and zipped his way to the 3rd floor and Alex pulled Gloria's keycard out and all of a sudden the wall street building started turning on again and the numbers on the screen were turning into positive numbers with a lot of pluses and back in hidden areas, the New York police department started telling people that the area is safe and the bomb has been disabled and a lot of people were cheering "my savings are back!!!" another citizen said and other people's bank accounts were back in running again

Chapter 7 rebuilding New York City, Coming Home and meeting President Reagan

As Alex came back to Seattle, he took the bus back to University of Washington and as he got back Alex was just exhausted from the mission and what he had to do and so he just laid on his bed and the next morning Alex walked to University village and he went to the hospital to get the injuries checked out and the doctor said he was going to be alright but he had to take some medicine every night so that the cuts would heal themselves and after that, Alex headed to a Mexican restaurant and he ate a taco and then after lunch, Alex then headed home and he played the old NES and Alex started 6 Pepsi and then as Alex was playing video games, Roger came into Alex's dorm-room "dude what the fuck happened to you man you look like shit" Roger said "I had to do another secret mission" Alex said "damn dude" Roger said "did you meet any hot girls?" Roger asked "well there was this one girl that worked in New York city around wall street" Alex said "do you have her number?" Roger asked "no I don't Roger I wish I did though" Alex said "but anyway we are going to a house party in Bellevue it's in Redmond you want to come a lot of people are going to be there" Roger said "alright sounds really fun I would love to go" Alex said

And as Roger & Alex came the house was 4 floors big and there was a deck and there was a 99 feet deep pole and there was a lot of people going really crazy "dude Roger this place is hopping" Alex said with excitement "I told you would like it" Roger said and as Roger & Alex got into the party a lot of people were doing all sorts of activates such as dancing to Madonna, playing cards, playing pool, people swimming in the pool, playing darts, some crazy college students jumping on a tramplon, some people roller blading and Alex went swimming and he started dancing to 80's music and as Alex was dancing he saw a girl that looked like Helga and Alex's vision started going really slow and Alex started having massive fantasies of Helga "oh yeah Helga is a sexy lady" Alex said as he was wasted and the girl ran up to Alex "hey Alex I didn't know you were going to this party" Helga said "I don't know the owner of this party" Alex said "well I just want to say thank you I was wondering if you wanted to go on a date sometime" Helga said "that would be really nice and really wonderful" Alex said and Alex started spinning Helga in circles "WAHOOOOOOOOOOOOO!!!" Helga said in excitement and Helga put her arms around Alex's neck "you are super sexy when you are in normal clothes. Are you usually this fun?" Helga asked "when I'm not doing any secret agent work oh yes" Alex said and then Alex put his hands on Helga's waste as they were under the 1980's disco ball and Helga smooched Alex on the lips and throughout the night Alex & Helga did a lot of things at the party and had a lot of drinks at the party in Redmond and as Roger dropped them off, Alex & Helga started making out massively and they started heading towards Alex's dorm room and they started taking each other's clothes and the next day Alex & Helga went to Seattle and had their 1st date and went on a couple of dates because of this mission, Alex had around 300,000,000$ and Alex bought Helga a lot of 1980's clothes did a lot of fun things around the state of Washington and they went swimming in green lake in Seattle and then strangely enough around Saturday the presidential helicopter arrived around University of Washington and the President's helicopter showed up "hello Alex. I am very proud of you not only saving New York city but you saved America's economy from going into bankrupt and for killing those bastards" President Reagan said "oh it was nothing Mr. President" Alex said and then President Reagan put his arm around Alex and Alex got ride in the presidential Helicopter and Helga came along as well and as they were flying, Alex saw New York City was back in full gear again and Alex got to tour the white house again President Reagan threw a huge ball party for both Alex & Helga and people wanted to handshake Alex and greet him

"My fellow Americans tonight we are here to honor Alexander Aussmen because 5 days New York City was attacked by 2 terriosts that wanted to destroy America's economy and put people on the streets and bankrupt our wonderful country. But I think because of how strong we are we were able to pull through out and also 99 million people now have jobs and our economy is stronger then ever and also our authority is stronger with someone like you in the world Alex. Also even though you have Autism, your coverage and your bravery saved our country and I would proudly give you the Medal of Honor" President Reagan said in his speech and all of a sudden President Reagan put the medal over Alex's neck and Alex & Helga got a picture with President Reagan and later that night Alex got meet Nancy Reagan "we can't thank you enough for what you did in New York City. I hope every American can learn from you" Nancy Reagan said "oh thank you Mrs. Reagan" Alex said, "So what is Seattle like?" Nancy Reagan asked "well it is really different" Alex said "yeah I thought you would say that I remember back in 1980 when my husband was campaigning Washington is a very democratic state but I can't deny you live in a very beautiful city" Nancy Reagan said "oh thank you Mrs. Reagan" Alex said "also Alex you are always welcome to come here we need more secret agents like you that fight for our country" Nancy Reagan said and she walked off

After that night Alex & Helga headed back to Seattle. Alex headed back to school and he did most of his classes as usual and Alex hung up his medal of honor in his dorm-room and he also hung up his picture of Ronald Reagan in his room and the next day as Alex got done with his homework done Helga threw Alex a really huge party and a lot of loud playing 80's music and people were barbequing on the roof and people were mostly celebrating his welcome home party and people were drinking, and going crazy and also Jay was at the party "do you know where Alex is?" jay asked "I don't know" Helga said and then Alex showed up "where were you?" Helga asked "I was hanging out with Roger" Alex said "hey thanks for this party by the way" Alex said "your welcome you earned it Alex" Helga asked and then Helga & Alex started dancing and then Alex picked up Helga "wahooooooooo!!!!!!!" Helga excited and then she started laughed and Alex pressed a button on his spy watch and a hock-shot wire came out and Alex & Helga started making out on the roof of his dorm room "dude way to go Alex. You da man" Roger said and Alex & Helga were making out on top of the roof top of UW dorm-room Alex was staying in "oh Alex" Helga said

She Woofie
pool
U
F

Chapter 1 Miami Florida 1982

As he was laying in the sun Alex just looked at the sun and Alex knew that he was a Junior at University of Washington and knew time was going by really fast then as Alex was eating breakfast Alex was looking at the beach and knew that Alex has been in Miami for a couple weeks but for some reason Alex was going to marry Ronica but Alex never knew why he could never keep girls for a long period of time because he never cheats on the girls he is with then after breakfast Alex then got dressed into jean shorts and sandals and a Hawaiian shirt then as Alex was walking a girl with blonde hair wearing a huge hat with a rose on it then she started fallowing Alex then Alex got his new car and it was a 1982 Chevrolet Corvette Coupe and after Alex paid for the car Alex then got into the car and drove up to Tampa Florida and then Alex saw a mall in Tampa and it was huge and there was a beach then Alex looked in the stores Alex looked for some new clothes then the girl kept spying on Alex then she pulled a camera and took a picture of Alex as he was getting new clothes Alex got new black shoes, new ties, and new dress shirts then as Alex went back to his car then a person caught up to Alex "Mr.Aussmen, Mr.Aussmen there is a person that wants to see you" the random person said "okay sir" Alex said then as Alex kept on walking then the man got knocked out with a jar then Alex pulled out his PP7 and was about to shoot then from behind Alex then got hit by a baseball bat then Alex was knocked out then as Alex got up then Alex found out that he was tied up and it turned out nobody wanted to see Alex it was a plot by Alex's old enemy Sergio Finland "good evening Mr.Aussmen" Sergio said "I thought you died in 1976" Alex said with rage "oh no Mr.Aussmen I survived the

explosion that night in 1976 I didn't know you lived in Florida now Mr.Aussmen how Ironic for a former special Ed Kid that went to Tahoma high school HAHAHAHAHAHAHAHAHA" Sergio said "what the hell do you want with me?!" Alex said "I want you to spend your junior year at Transition Aussmen and then this whole thing of looking for you will be over" Sergio said "and what if I don't accept I can't leave University of Washington I love it there better than being a Special Ed kid back in Maple Valley" Alex said "well too bad Alex my boy because where on a boat taking us back to Seattle and prisoning you back in Tahoma transition and you spending your cool life there with no people like you Alex nobody as cool just mental retard idiots BRA

HAHAHAHAHAHAHAHAHAHAHAHAHAHAHAHA HAHAHAHAHA" Sergio laughed then as Sergio was laughing Alex then had a really pissed off face and had angry look on his face then as Sergio was about to tie up Alex then Alex head butted Sergio then Alex untied himself and started running away "STOP HIM THAT AUTISTIC STUDENT FROM UNIVERSITY OF WASHINGTON IS GETTING AWAY!!!" Sergio yelled then a thug was about to punch Alex then Alex dodged the punch and kicked the thug in the balls then Alex found an A33 riffle and started shooting the thugs and then as the thugs where dead then there was 2 thugs left "KILL HIM!!!" Sergio yelled then Alex kept on shooting the thugs then as the gun was out of bullets then Sergio tried to stab Alex then Alex grabbed Sergio's hand really tight and kicked Sergio in the stomach then Sergio tried to punch Alex in the face then Alex kicked Sergio in the face and then Alex punched Sergio in the stomach then Alex grabbed his button up shirt and slapped him really hard and then Alex took out his PP7 and shot Sergio Finland in the head then Sergio pressed the bomb button and that set the bomb then Alex started a motor boat and then Alex started driving the motor boat back to Miami Florida then the RAD Headquarters boat exploded then Alex was driving he was wondering where he was and he was in the gulf of Mexico by the state of Texas then Alex kept on driving then Alex head South more and then he found boat launch pad and dropped the boat there and walked off the boat then everybody stopped and stared at the boat then as a random person was looking at the boat Alex then found a "for sale" sign and put the sign on the boat "it's for sale if you want it" Alex said "oh thanks man" the person said "how much you want for it?" Alex asked "like 39, 000, 00$" he said "deal here the insurance and the keys" Alex said "okay thanks man" the person said "you're welcome dude" Alex said then Alex pressed a button his remote that made 1982 Chevrolet Corvette Coupe come to him then Alex got back in his car and drove back to his hotel in Miami Florida then as Alex parked his car Alex then got his key and then went into an elevator and went into his hotel room then as Alex was in the hotel room then Alex pulled out his PP7 and thought it was another RAD thug that was working for Sergio and Alex started loading up his gun and began to point and shot

Then out of the shower it wasn't a thug or a person working for Sergio instead it was beautiful naked teenage women that got out of Alex's shower "oh hello Mr.Aussmen do you like what you see" she said "you're a beautiful girl" Alex said "what's your name?" Alex said "She Woofe yours?" She Woofe said "Aussmen, Alex Aussmen my dear" Alex said

Chapter 2 the girl who loves dogs

Then as She Woofe was going into the bathroom she then got dressed and then Alex just staried at her with a smile on his face "are you watching me change?" She Woofe asked then Alex just kept on smileling with no reply "I will take that back as a yes" She Woofe said then as Alex kept stairing at She woofe Alex then saw her putting her bra on then as She woofe then with hesiastion then she desized not to wear a bra and unhooked her bra and took the bra off and even took off her bottoms and she then put a blue, and green dress on and she was naked underneath the dress then as She Woofe zipped up her dress she then put red lipstick then she put on heels "you ready to go?" She Woofe asked "sure" Alex said then Alex and She Woofe went into Alex's car and Alex drove to a resteraunt by Miami Beach "you want some music?" Alex asked "sure baby" She Woofe said then Alex turned on the radio and the radio was playing "Love hangover" by Diana Ross then She Woofe started shaking her head and she started dancing to the song in Alex's car then she shaked her long blondie hair back and fourth then She Woofe started snapping her fingers and she started singing the words to the songs then as She Woofe was dancing then Alex found a parking spot by Emeril's Miami resteraunt then as Alex found parking Alex then got out of the car and went to the other side of the car to open the door for She Woofe "thanks baby" She Woofe then as She Woofe kept on walking Alex then walked with her and started checking her out and she had the most sexiest walk Alex has ever seen "wow now I know her name is She

Woofe cause she is like a sexy female dog" Alex thought in his head then as Alex kept on walking "hello welcome to Emeril's Miami beach I will seat you lovely couple right over here by the beach and I will bring you guys your menus" the waiter said then as Alex and She Woofe where seated "so how long have you been in Miami for?" She Woofe asked "for about 2 weeks now" Alex said "so where are you from Alex?" She Woofe asked "I'm from Seattle" Alex said then She Woofe started laughing "bull shit!!!" She Woofe said "hows that bull shit I really am from Seattle" Alex said "because you look like your from Cailforna not Seattle because I hear in Seattle in rains there a lot" She Woofe said "I know" Alex said with sarcasem then as Alex and She Woofe where talking then after they ate Alex then drank a beer and She Woofe drank 2 beers "wow are you okay babe?" Alex said "I'm fine sexy boy!!!" She Woofe said with a silly yell "wow do you want to rest on in the back of the car?" Alex said "sure baby" She Woofe said then Alex went into his car and put She Woofe in the back seat then as Alex was getting tired then he drove his car on the beach by Miami beach then Alex put the car lever on parking and just sat in the driver's seat with a tired look on his face then as Alex was sleeping then as She Woofe was drunk she then started making dog sounds and started barking like a dog "wow that dog is so cute I just want to go swimming with it" She Woofe said "mype you can do it tomorrow baby girl" Alex said then without thinking She Woofe took off her heels "can you unzip my dress" She Woofe said then as Alex got up then She Woofe unziped her dress and then She Woofe threw her dress in Alex's car and started running around Miami Beach butt naked "wahooooooo hahahahahahahha" She Woofe laughed then She Woofe then ran on the dock and everybody on the dock just staried at her nudity "She Woofe get back here" Alex said then She Woofe then jumped off the dock and into the beach water "come on Alex jump in" She Woofe said " I can't I don't have a swimsuit" Alex said "I don't have one either just get in sexy boy" She Woofe said then Alex took off his clothes and jumped into the beach with her then She Woofe kept on splashing Alex "hahahaha" She Woofe laughed then Alex tried to swim to She Woofe then She Woofe just swimed back to shore then as She Woofe got back to Shore then she went to the back seat and she was tired "tired?" Alex asked "yes I'm hella tried Alex I want to go to sleep" She Woofe said "well you can stay in my hotel room" Alex said "okay" She Woofe said then Alex got his clothes back from dock and put his clothes back on and then went back to the beach and then Alex drove back to his hotel room in Miami then Alex drove back to the hotel Alex then parked by his entrance then Alex turned the car off and then put his keys in his pocket and then opened the other door and lifted She Woofe's naked body in his arms and then went into the hotel then Alex went into the elvator and pressed 31th floor then hopefully there was no stops and there was then as the elvator got to the 31th Alex then lifted She Woofe up and opened the his hotel room "are we there it daddy" She Woofe said as she was tried and drunk "yes we are baby girl were there" Alex said then Alex set She Woofe on his bed then as Alex set She Woofe on her bed then Alex took a shower because he wanted to get the salt water off him so it wasn't on his bed then as Alex got a towel on Alex then went to sleep but then out of no where She Woofe then woke up "sorry I can try to see blankets on the..." Alex said then as Alex was stumbling over words She Woofe then got into the covers with him and then she started kissing Alex then She Woofe then took Alex's towel off

Chapter 3 finding clues in Miami airport

Then the next day Alex then looked out the window and the sun was bright and it always bright in Florida then as Alex got out of bed She Woofe then started touching Alex everywhere "you have such a nice ass" She Woofe said "it's so firm and rounded" She Woofe said "you want to feel mine" She Woofe said then She Woofe then got out of bed and she was butt naked under the covers then She Woofe then standed up and Alex stopped and staried at She Woofe's nudity and her body was like a body of a beautiful goddess and her hands where soft and she had blue painted nails on her nails, and had long brown and blonde hair, and also her hand where really beautiful too then Alex then started kissing her

Then later day around that 3:00PM Alex then went to go to Miami airport to pick up Michael then as Alex was waiting then he saw a guy with Blondie hair "Michael" Alex said with excitingly "hey Alex what's up dude" Michael said then Michael saw scares on Alex forearm "dude what happened on your arm?" Michael asked "oh nothing it's just that Sergio was after me back in Tampa yesterday" Alex said "oh-no Alex that guy is an asshole he's been looking for special Ed kids everywhere back in the Washington and looking them up in Tahoma Transition he's been doing it for 2 years" Michael said "is he still doing it and please don't say that he is doing it here" Michael said "it's okay Michael Sergio is dead I shot him" Alex said then as Alex getting his bags in the back of Alex's car then a bunch of gangsters where spying on them "hey boss we know where the guys are heading to we can take them" the gangsters said then the gangsters then got into their cars and started chasing Alex then Alex turned his head and noticed that the gangsters where fallowing "Alex we got bad guys on are tails" Michael said then Alex pressed a button by shifting lever in the car and then a missile fired from in back of the car and fired at the gangsters then more gangster cars started chasing them then Alex got an AKS-74U and started shooting at the gangsters "don't worry man will take a left turn into Jacksonville hang on Michael" Alex said then Alex turned a left turn into Jacksonville Florida then Alex drove around the town of Jacksonville for a little bit then more of the gangsters kept on shooting at Alex's car then Alex opened up his window and took out his AKS-74U and kept on shooting and then all of the gangsters where dead "that's the last of them" Alex said "who in the hell were those guys?" Michael said "I don't know but I probley think those are RAD gangsters working for the evil Special evil ED organsasion RAD come on lets get of here" Alex said then Alex drove out of Jacksonville and back to downtown Miami and then Alex parked by the hotel "where's your hotel Alex?" Michael said "it's in there" Alex said then Alex got Michael's bags out of the trunk then as they got to Alex's hotel room "nice suite man" Michael said "thanks bro" Alex said "okay Michael you stay here I'm going to look for the guy trying to kill us" Alex said then Alex put on a headset and a suit and tie and went out to go find more RAD gangsters then Alex got into his car and headed into downtown Miami looking for gangsters then Alex looked around the crazy sits that where around the Miami area then Alex saw a RAD agent going into a strip club then Alex went into the strip club trying to find the RAD agent then as Alex was in the strip club he then saw a Special Ed kid he looked around 18 years old but he had the same type of body Alex had but a different face and different disability "hey buddy what's up" Alex said "who the hell are you man" he said "look man they got RAD agents everywhere looking for guys like us and they want to kill us" Alex said "I don't believe you man" he said "you won't beileve me now but here's the thing..dude I had to go through it when I was in high school in the 70's you would have to go through in this decade if you don't get out of here I'm serious" Alex said then a gun got pointed at Alex and the person's head "don't move Special Ed students where taking you back to Tahoma transition now get the HELL UP" the RAD gangster said then as they where walking Alex then turned back into the RAD agent and punched him in the face and took out his PP7 and shot him "lets get out of here" Alex said then Alex and the person started running through the strip club and Alex kept on shooting "what's your name sucker?" the person said "Aussmen…Alex Aussmen" Alex said then Alex started shooting at more RAD agents "I'm Perry Brid" Perry said then more agents kept on shooting and shooting "my car is outside lets go" Alex said then they both ran to Alex's car and got out of the strip club then Alex started the car and got out of the Miami area "I'll take somewhere safe kid" Alex said then more RAD agents where shooting at Alex's car then Alex got out an A33 riffle and started shooting at the RAD agents then as the gangsters died then Alex took Perry to his hotel room "who where those guys?" Perry said "RAD agents" Alex said "I know there is some in Washington state but what the hell are they doing in Florida?!" Perry said "that's what I'm trying to find out dude" Alex said then Alex kept on driving back to his hotel room and Alex went to sleep and wondered if She Woofe was safe and Alex knew that RAD was still out there after all these years but he didn't know who they where working for since Sergio got shot by Alex but Alex had find out who the new leader of RAD was and fast.

Chapter 4 the RAD boss

Then as Alex got in the hotel Alex and Perry went into the hotel "so where's our room" Perry asked "it's in that suite over there" Alex said "look stay here Perry and I'm going to find out who this new RAD boss is" Alex said "okay Alex" Perry said then Alex ran out of the hotel and started to look for She Woofe then Alex got into his car and started driving looking for She Woofe then as Alex drived around downtown Miami Alex then saw her by an office then Alex parked by meter "She Woofe are you alright" Alex said "yeah I'm okay Alex" She Woofe said "oh thank god I thought you got kidnapped" Alex said "oh I didn't get kidnapped Alex I'm okay" She Woofe said "so do you want to come inside my apartment" She Woofe said "sure" Alex said then Alex and She Woofe went into She Woofe's apartment and then as they went inside She Woofe's apartment Alex was just amazed of how the apartment looked like it was the beautiful apartment Alex has ever scene it had a waterfall a swimming pool her bed room and shower was on the 2nd floor then her kitchen was on the left then there where trees and grass with flowers and everything looked beautiful "wow" Alex said "She Woofe it's beautiful" Alex said "I know you might like it Alex baby" She Woofe said "you want to know the best part" She Woofe said "what?" Alex said "the best part of this apartment is that I can run around naked when I ever want to I bet that must turn you on" She Woofe said "that's hot" Alex said then without thinking She Woofe then started taking her clothes off and then she took her strap shirt off, her jeans, her heels, her bottoms, and her bra then She Woofe then undid her and ran into the swimming pool then Alex watched She Woofe go into the swimming "come on Alex baby jump in" She Woofe then Alex took his clothes and went into the pool with nothing but his boxers on then She Woofe then Alex started smooching She Woofe then She Woofe dived underwater and started taking off Alex's boxers then She Woofe then started swimming with her back to the surface and then her breasts started to show then She Woofe then started smooching Alex more and more "you want to go upstairs" She Woofe said "yeah" Alex said then She Woofe got out of the pool and ran upstairs to her bedroom with out putting on a rob then Alex went upstairs then She Woofe started making out with Alex then Alex and She Woofe then fell on She Woofe then Alex and She Woofe then got under the covers and started kissing "oh Alex baby don't stop" She Woofe said

Then as Perry and Michael where in Alex's hotel room then they herd a knock on the door then the RAD the agents broke the door down "you two are under arrest" a RAD agent then Michael and Perry started running outside to the hotel "where do we go?" Perry said "I know where" Michael said then Michael and Perry ran to the sidewalk "taxi!!" Michael yelled "yeah sucker" the taxi driver said "yeah take us to Orlando Florida please" Michael said "sure brotha" the taxi driver said "dude do you know anybody in Orlando?" Perry said "yeah dude Owen Olson he's a CIA agent that has worked with Alex he'll help us" Michael said

Then back at She Woofe's apartment Alex then was getting his clothes on "where are you going baby" She Woofe asked "I gotta make a phone call to Michael" Alex said then as Alex dialed Michael's number the phone then rang but still no answer "oh-no RAD agents got him" Alex said "do you know where they could be" She Woofe asked "well I know Owen Olson is in Orlando mype they went there" Alex said "lets go" Alex said then as She Woofe put her clothes on and then got out of She Woofe's apartment then Alex and She Woofe then ran to Alex's car and then Alex turned on his car and then he put the car on revers and got out of parking and then on drive then Alex started speeding to Orlando,Florida then as Alex was driving then RAD agents where in blue cars and they started chasing Alex and started shooting then Alex pressed a button by his radio then the car dropped grenades then the RAD cars got blown up then Alex took out a PP7 and started shooting at the other RAD cars that went infront of him then Alex then took out DD4 pistol and started shooting at the tires of RAD cars then Alex kept on driving he then saw Mileage sign that said "Orlando 14 miles ahead" the sign said then as Alex kept on driving he then took an exit to enter Orlando then Alex tried to remember what house Owen lived in then Alex remembered that Owen lived by downtown Orlando then Alex drove into the city and started looking for the apartment Owen was staying in then Alex drove into the garage Alex then parked into a parking spot "lets go" Alex said then Alex and She Woofe then got out of the car and took an elevator to get the 39th floor in the apartment in the building then as the elevator stopped at the 39th floor Alex and She Woofe got out of the elevator and Alex and She Woofe started looking for Owen's apartment then Alex found Owen's apartment #3947 then Alex knocked on his door then Alex herd the door open "Owen what's up" Alex said "hey Aussmen what brings you to Florida and who's the lucky girl" Owen said "oh this is She Woofe" Alex said "pleasure to meet you baby" Owen said "hey have you seen Michael and Perry here? "Alex asked "yeah I have I saw Michael and then saw a short guy with a buzz cut" Owen said "that's Perry" Alex said "so are they here?" Alex asked "oh yeah they are here there just on the couch asleep" Owen said "awesome" Alex said "Owen we might need your help.." Alex said "oh I already know Alex about your problem RAD is at it again trying to kill Special Ed Kids the CIA is been after RAD too" Owen said "do you know where their fortress is at or what area around Florida it might be in?" Alex asked "it's around the University of Florida area yes and it's a tall office building that is blue trying to disguise itself as a University of Florida medical building" Owen said "do you know where in that area because there are like two Florida gator colleges one in Tampa, one in Tallahassee" Alex said "Tallahassee dude" Owen said

Chapter 5 sneaking into the RAD head quarters in Tallahassee, Florida

Then that night Alex then put on a black jump and drove to Tallahassee, Florida and started looking for the headquarters then Alex saw the University of Florida and then Alex saw the building "there it is" Alex said then Alex used a hooker gun to hook himself up to the building then Alex started climbing up the building then Alex so far just saw doctors running from room to room then Alex kept on climbing up then as Alex got really up Alex then saw a special Window that was steel gold then Alex used his mine to try to blow up the window then Alex set the time for 14 seconds then the mine then blew up and then Alex swinged himself up and broke into the building then Alex took out his A33 riffle then Alex saw RAD agents walking in the hallway then Alex then shot at them and then stole the keys to get into 74th floor in the building then Alex stole their wallets then Alex found an elevator in the room and Alex then took the elevator to the 74th floor then as the elevator stopped on the 74th floor Alex then used the keys to get into the 74th floor then as Alex got into the floor then RAD agents spotted "IT'S AUSSMEN KILL HIM!!!" the RAD agents then Alex used his A33 riffle and shot at them then Alex started running then more RAD agents then started shooting at Alex then Alex started shooting more and more then Alex then saw a Landry shoot then Alex jumped into the shoot then Alex started sliding down then Alex got to the final floor then Alex started looking around the room and the room looked like a factory then Alex saw a more RAD agents lining up a line of people in line they looked like people that where Alex's age then Alex knew who they where they where Recourse kids then Alex watched the line progress then Alex saw a container of water if it even was water it was deep and bubble then as Alex started watching the recourse kids then they had to take their clothes off and go in the container water butt naked then Alex kept on watching then one of the RAD agents then turned on the machine that powers the container then they started electrocuting the recourse kid that was in container and then Alex kept on watching with scared look on his face as he was holding the A33 riffle "Michael, Owen I think you guys might need to see this" Alex said then Alex started recording it on video then the naked recourse girl got out of the container and then Alex saw the girl walking into another line of naked people getting into a stolen UPS truck then Alex saw the their clothes getting burned as they where getting in line to get on truck "oh my god!!" Alex said silently " I wonder where they are taking them?" Alex said then Alex thought for 9 seconds "oh-no Alex there getting shipped to Tahoma transition I have to warn Michael" Alex said then Alex stopped recording and then started running out of the factory the same way he got in then RAD agents saw Alex running and started chasing him then Alex started shooting at the RAD agents then Alex was out of bullets then with knowing someone then body slammed Alex into a wall and knocked him out "boss we got Aussmen" the RAD agent said then on 90th floor a small person replied "good work boys bring him up here" the man said then the thugs handcuffed Alex and bring him to the 90th floor in the University of Florida medical building then as the elevator stopped then Alex was brought into the room "good evening Mr. Aussmen" the man said "who the hell are you?!" Alex said "oh yes I'm Lucas Stonemen welcome to Tallahassee, Florida Aussmen so glad to finally to meet you bra hahahaha or should I saw memory loss you hehehehegeh hahaha" Stonemen said "is that what the hell your doing to those resource kids by making them go skinny dipping into a container of electric water and erasing their memory and putting their naked bodies into a stolen UPS truck and sending them back to Tahoma transition in Maple Valley Washington" Alex said "oh no Mr.Aussmen not only do I erase their memory but I lower their IQ to 0 that way I send them back to Seattle and then they go back to Tahoma transition and let them die with no knowledge and let them run around the city with knowledge what so ever not even put any clothing on them too bra hahahahaha" Stonemen laughed "you are the biggest piece of SHIT!!! I HAVE

EVER FACED!!" Alex said "bra hahahahahahahahahahahahah heheheheh why thank you Alex" Stonemen said "now I know why RAD has been after Michael and I you wanted the do the same thing to us now I know why Sergio passed the torch to you because you are as stupid!!, insane!!, brick like you" Alex said "wow Alex you are most smartest Special Ed kid I have scene too bad once I get your sweet She Woofe she will be brain less just like all those naked IQ less resource kids getting shipped to Tahoma transition in the stolen UPS truck bra hahahahahahahah hehe hahahahahahahahahahahahahah" Stonemen laughed then Alex then broke out of his handcuffs and punched Stonemen in the face then Alex got video tape he recorded earlier and got it back "STOP HIM HE'S GETTING AWAY!!!" Stonemen said then Alex got out an ZMG gun and started shooting at more the RAD agents chasing then Alex then got on to the roof and then Alex remembered that he had a para shoot in his back pack then Alex jumped off the building then Alex started sky dive then Alex looked at his watch then pressed a button on his citizen eco drive watch that made the Alex's car turn into a plane then Alex's car took up into the air then Alex grabbed on the handle of the car and got into the car then more RAD agents then got into a helicopter and started chasing Alex then they started shooting missiles then Alex turned the flying car around and shot back at them then Stonemen then survived as he launched his para shoot then Alex started flying back to Owen's apartment to tell Owen and Michael what Stonemen was planning and had to stop all this before it's too late.

Chapter 6 revealing the truth about Stonemen's plan

Then as Alex came back "hey guys" Alex said "hey Alex what's up bro" Owen said "nothing much dude I got footage of what RAD is planning and I got it on tape" Alex said then Alex put the tape in the VCR and then Michael, Alex and Owen watched "oh my god that's what they are doing and that was the reason they where after us" Michael said "yes Michael they are putting naked resource kids and putting them into container of electric water and erasing their memory and their IQ percentage that's what they have been doing Michael" Alex said "I believe you Alex where's She Woofe?" Owen asked "I don't know I have to find her fast" Alex said then later that day Alex went to go look for She Woofe then Alex drove to Miami to look for She Woofe then Alex saw her walking into a fancy hotel in Miami then Alex went into a bathroom and changed into a suit and neck tie then Alex started fallowing She Woofe then Alex saw her go by the swimming pool then She Woofe started petting a dog and the dog started licking She Woofe "hey She Woofe" Alex said "hey Alex" She Woofe said "She Woofe do you want to do anything tonight" Alex asked "sure Alex" She Woofe said then through out that day Alex spined a lot of time together and really loved each other then as night time came around Alex and She Woofe then went to go eat at a nightclub in southern Florida then Alex ate dinner then they went dancing in the nightclub then Alex started doing really cool dance moves then Alex started spinning and also did the moon walk then Alex did a cartwheel then Alex spined She Woofe then Alex lowered She Woofe just had a smile on her face then Alex did disco moves then Alex then did a cartwheel with one hand to end the dance then everybody in the nightclub clapped "that was pretty

young thing by Michael Jackson" the DJ said then as Alex and She Woofe were done dancing then unforantlety RAD agents showed up "hello Alex it's pity that I caught you too you must be Alex's new girlfriend" Stonemen said then a RAD agent picked up a beer bottle and whacked Alex in the head with it then Alex fell flat on his face "take him to the car" Stonemen said then Alex and She Woofe then where in the car

Then as the drivers where driving the RAD car Alex and She Woofe then got tied up "so stupid of you Mr. Aussmen despite your good knowledge you have not out smarted me with me my brain of mind heheheheh hahahahahah" Stonemen said "okay Lucas this stops now" Alex said "no can do Aussmen now that I have girlfriend I will use her and erase her knowledge and memory of you hahahahahahah" Stonemen said then She Woofe had scared look and then had a tear come out of her left eye "guards kill Mr.Aussmen and send the girl in line with the Recourse kids Immedelty" Stonemen said then the guards arrested Alex and then as they where walking Alex then remembered that Michael gave him liquid laser gun that would melt any metal when needed then Alex used it "hey" the guards said then Alex kicked the guards in the face and knocked them out then Alex started running and then Alex then went to go find She Woofe then Alex went to 74th floor and started looking for She Woofe then as She Woofe was in line they already put She Woofe in the container of electric water then as the worker turned back then Alex pulled out a PP7 "drop it give me She Woofe's serum" Alex said then Alex punched him in the face then She Woofe was put in the She Woofe in the UPS truck then Alex then got into the truck then She Woofe started barking and she was butt naked and then She Woofe then jumped Alex "okay girl heel girl I got something for you" Alex said "drink this" Alex said then She Woofe started barking and barking then Alex opened the serum and She Woofe started drinking the sirem then She Woofe's brain started gaining everything her IQ and memory where all coming back to her "ALEX!!!" She Woofe said as she hugged Alex "I thought I lost you thank god" She Woofe said "we got to find you some clothes" then Alex stole a dress for She Woofe to wear and heels "I gotta to stop this plan before they get to Miami airport" Alex said then Alex picked up a phone and started talking "hey stop the UPS truck immedtly!!" Alex said then back on the 90th floor Stonemen then answered the phone "WHAT!!?" Stonemen yelled "AUUUUUUUUUSMEN!!!!!!!" Stonemen yelled then Alex loaded up his PP7 and broke the door down into his office "you called..games over Stonemen!!" Alex said then Stoneman then pulled out a machine gun and tried to shot Alex then Alex hid behind a table "bye,bye Mr.Aussmen hahahahahahahahaha" Stonemen said then Stonemen then tried to stab Alex with a knife then Alex then punched Stonemen in the face then Stonement then kick Alex in the face then Alex tackled Stonemen then Stonemen then picked up ZMG gun "it's the end of road Aussmen" Stonemen said then Alex saw a KF-7 riffle then Alex then ducked on the ground "no it's the end of the road for you" Alex said then Alex started shooting Stonemen then Alex shot Stonemen 21 times then Stonemen then feel out of the building then Stonemen was dead then Alex started to find She Woofe "Alex what happened Stonemen?" She Woofe "he's dead lets get out of here" Alex said then Alex and She Woofe started running then Alex pressed a button on his watch that made his car turn into a plane then Alex's car then got the helicopter pad "come on" Alex said then as She Woofe and Alex then as the car took off Alex then threw a mine for 1 minute and Alex then typed on the mine "001" on the mine then Alex threw it at the helicopter pad then the RAD headquarters exploded then Alex flew the plane back to Owen's apartment and the day was saved.

Chapter 7 She Woofe and Alex's weeding

Then through out a few weeks Alex and She Woofe really loved each other and did a lot of things together in Florida and then Alex then just realized that She Woofe was the one that Alex just really loved then one night as they where in Miami they where laying down by the sand "She Woofe will you marry me" Alex said then Alex pulled out a ring "oh wow Alex it's beautiful yes" She Woofe said "by the way is She Woofe your real name" Alex asked "no it's Sarah Alison" She Woofe said then Alex and She Woofe started smooching on the beach

Then the next morning Alex and She Woofe then planed the hole weeding and it was on Miami beach then Alex got a tuxes and Owen and Michael wearied suits then as Alex saw her Alex was really amazed of how great she looked then as the pastor was talking Alex and She Woofe just looked at each other romantic "Alexander Allan Aussmen do you take Sarah Alison to be your lovely wife" the pastor said "I do" Alex said then Alex putted the weeding ring on She Woofe " I now pronounce this couple Mr. and Mrs. Aussmen you may kiss the bride" the pastor said then Alex smooching She Woofe then everybody in the weeding started clapping then Alex kissed for 30 minutes then Alex fanished that Alex and She Woofe under a disco ball in a disco club then as the disco ball shinned in then Alex and She Woofe fell into the ocean then started splashing each other and laughing then She Woofe's weeding dress came off then she took off her heels then She took off her bra then She Woofe was butt naked then Alex started kissing her in the ocean "Alex, She Woofe you guys will be late for the reception" Michael said "just leave those love birds" Owen said then She Woofe took Alex's button up shirt then Alex kept on kissing She Woofe and touching her and She Woofe started laughing more and more "oh Alex baby"She Woofe said

The Native New Yorker that loved the University of Washington College student Runaway

Chapter 1 New York City 1983

As Alex was walking on the streets Alex started to think about his days as a high school student in the 1970's not to say the 80's weren't good but Alex just thought things in those in days where better and less changing because Alex hasn't went to University of Washington in 2 years then as Alex kept on walking he then stopped at McDonald's and got some lunch and ate a burger there then as Alex was done with lunch he then kept on walking around Manhattan then he walked around the World trade center and then took a picture and Alex was married to She Woofe but what happened in Florida after the weeding some RAD agents found her and killed her and Alex kept on flashbacks of She Woofe then Alex called a taxi and then the taxi "where to Brotha" the driver said "time square" Alex said then as the driver drove Alex to time square then as Alex was walking around time square in New York then Alex saw the Casablanca Hotel and then Alex went in there for reservation then as Alex went up to his room then Alex was just amazed of how much he got it was suite then as Alex set his stuff down by the bed then Alex then got on a button up shirt and neck tie and suit jacket and suite pants and started walking around New York city then Alex went to restraint in time Square and went upstairs and then waited for menu and then saw a girl very beautiful blonde hair and it was really blond hair and went up to her waist then Alex started staring at her then Alex just looked at her with a smile on his face with his right hand under his chin then as she was waiting for her drink then without thinking Alex then went up to her and without thinking "hello sexy lady" Alex said "hey baby boy" the girl said then Alex kissed her hand "oh baby you are soo sexy" she said "what's your name sexy boy?" the girl

said "Aussmen..Alex Aussmen" Alex said "Stella Robertson pleasure to me you Aussmen" Stella said "so what brings you to the big apple handsome" Stella asked "oh just staying here for a couple weeks then I have to head back to Seattle" Alex said "you live in Seattle I want to go there some time getting me wet just turns me on I like you Aussmen" Stella said "so are you here with your boyfriend or anything like that?" Alex asked "no I don't have a boyfriend" Stella said "wow I thought you would" Alex said "oh your so funny Alex" Stella then as Stella was touching Alex's face then she started feeling a lot of stuffiness on Alex's face then Stella started making out with Alex then Stella then jumped into Alex's arms and started moaning "hey no making out in public restraint" the waiter said then Alex raised his number one finger then Stella and Alex got out of the bar and Stella was kissing Alex "you want to go back to my suite" Alex said "yeah baby boy where is your suite" Stella asked "uh..in Time Square around Manahan" Alex said "what hotel?" Stella said "the Casablanca Hotel" Alex said then later that night Alex and Stella went into Alex's suite and Stella just kept on kissing Alex "I feel like getting wet can we take a shower I love showers" Stella said "sure anything for you baby girl" Alex said then Alex and Stella took their clothes off and went into the shower and started making out and touching each other then as they got tired Alex then laid on the Shower floor and Stella then put her hole body on Alex "oh baby that was beautiful" Stella said "oh thanks baby" Alex said then Stella started getting turned on again and started making out with Alex then as they where kissing then Alex's hotel phone rang "I'll get that baby" Alex said then without putting on a robe to cover his privets Alex then answered the phone "hello?" Alex said "hey Alex what's up bro" and it was Michael on the phone "Michael hey what up bro how did you get my hotel number in New York" Alex asked "Owen found out and told me dude" Michael said "oh right so where are you dude?" Alex asked "I'm heading to New York city and what hotel are you staying in dude?" Michael asked "I'm Michael this might not be a great time bro because I'm in the middle of something" Alex said then as Alex was on the phone the without knowing Stella then got out of the shower with out covering her nudity and went on the same line as Alex and Michael's conversation "hello?" Stella said "who's this Alex are you there bro" Alex said "this is Stella Alex's new girlfriend" Stella said "you sound like Farah Fawcett Alex what the hell is going on up there?" Michael said "nothing Michael call me when your in Time Square" Alex said then Alex hanged up the phone then Stella ran and hugged Alex's from behind and started feeling Alex's abs "so what do you want to do tonight?" Alex asked "well I want to go out to eat and then go dancing what do you say disco boy" Stella said "yeah I'm done for that Stella then Stella then put her arms around Alex's neck then Stella took her towel off the then she jumped into Alex's arms and Alex was excited for tonight and knew that tonight was going to awesome

Chapter 2 the date with Stella in Brooklyn and night dancing in a night club in New York city

Then as the day got to night time in New York city Alex then got a new car from Michael that was from the best car dealer in New York city then Alex got the car and it was a 1983 Bentley Musslann and it looked awesome for his date with Stella it had a GPS map in the car by the radio and Benknockelers is you need them for zooming into anything suspesish and also a red button that can be used as a laser if you press it to beam anything that could melt steel and it can also be verstila which mean that it can be in subways and be in the water and be in the air too then as Alex was driving Alex then was looking the GPS map and then the GPS told Alex to take a left turn into Queens and then Alex found that Stella was staying an apartment in Queens, New York then as Alex was waiting for Stella Alex then herd a door close and then Alex looked back and Stella just looked like a model and then she had nothing on under her leather jacket accept for a Bra under the coat and her Blond hair just sparkled as Alex looked at her hair and she was wearing a sliver bracelet on her wrist and a sliver necklace with a tiny silver heart on it then as She saw Alex's car "wow I love your car Alex it looks hott just like you" Stella "thanks Stella" Alex then as Stella got in Alex's car she then took off her leather jacket and showered her black and white Bra to Alex "wow" Alex said in amazement and Alex tried not focus on Stella's breath "aren't you cold?" Alex asked "no baby boy I'm not cold at all I like the cold ness if fells like sexy boy like you is touching me everywhere and it just turns me on right now" Stella said "wow" Alex said then Stella started making out with Alex in his new car then she unhooked her bra and

just started kissing Alex "I love you Alex" Stella said "I love you too Stella" Alex said then as Alex was starting up her car then Alex started driving the car to a restaurant called "Acappella restaurant" in New York city then Alex was driving to find a parking place then Alex parked by the restaurant then as Alex parked his car Stella then put her leather jacket on without putting on her white bra then as Alex and Stella went in the restaurant the place was hopping there was a dance floor on the 2nd floor then Alex and Stella were seated and then as Alex was seating he was thinking at the time Alex went out to dinner with Michelle Millard in 1979 and that was in his senior year in high school then Alex and Stella got their floor they talked about everything "so what high school did you go to Alex?" Stella asked "I went to Tahoma high school from 1976 to 1979 what about you baby?" Alex asked "I went to school Albany and then I go to Rutgers and now have a job working a news paper company" Stella said "awesome" Alex said "yeah I really like it what do you do for a living Alex?" Stella then for the for the first time in his life Alex paused and Alex felt he didn't want to tell Stella that he had Autism and he was secret agent working for himself and about he has to go after RAD "I'm still looking for a job" Alex said "aren't you worried about money" Stella said "I have a lot of money so I'm not worried what matters is that I have you baby" Alex said then Stella was just amazed at Alex's answer "I feel the same way too baby" Stella said then as they where done with eating they then went to the 2nd floor and went dancing they then showed up as everybody in the dance room where dancing then Alex and Stella started slow dancing then Alex started realizing that Stella was everything Alex ever wanted she was very loyal to Alex and just loved him then Alex and Stella then kissed in front of the disco ball as they where slow dancing then Stella then rested on Alex's shoulders then as they got out of the dance room Alex then put Stella on his bed then Alex took his clothes and then laid next to Stella then as Stella opening her eyes then saw Alex naked and started chuckling then Alex started making out with Stella "Alex stop it, Alex" Stella said then Stella just started laughing then Alex put Stella's clothes on the ground "I love you Alex So much" Stella said "I love you too Stella" Alex said then Stella started kissing Alex on the lips and then they kissed for the hole night

Chapter 3 Stella's evil Ex boyfriend

 Then the next morning Alex and Stella was were sleeping next to each other then Stella put her head on Alex's abs and started kissing Alex everywhere abs, chest and lips then Stella's alarm went off "oh my god I'm sooo late I gotta go I'll be back around 4:00 Alex" Stella said "okay Stella I love you Stella" Alex said "I love you too Alex" Stella said then as Stella got up from bed she then got her clothes and ran out of Alex's hotel room naked "Alex can you come with me so I don't get kicked out" Stella said then Alex smiled and went with her in the elevator and Alex then got into the elevator then Stella was butt naked in the elevator then Alex got into the elevator and started making out with her then as the elevator stopped then people getting just where shocked "oh my god there's a naked women in the elevator" one of the people said and got out of elevator "I should get changed" Stella said then Stella then got a bra on and put her underwear and put some jeans and a sexy trap shirt that was purple then as the elevator stopped at the lobby Stella kissed Alex and left to go to work then Alex staring at Stella and just smiled "what a beautiful girl even with clothes on she is very beautiful" Alex thought in his head

Then Alex went back to suite then his phone rang "hello?" Alex said, "hey Alex I'm in New York where are you dude?" Michael said "I'm in my suite are you coming man?" Alex said, "yeah I'll be there in 20 minutes" Michael said "do you want to me anywhere?" Alex asked "yeah meet me by the empire state building" Michael said "okay" Alex said then Alex hanged up the phone and headed to the empire state building and then took an elevator then Alex started looking around and Michael was not there then a random thug attacked Alex from behind then Alex got up and then punched him in the face then kicked him in the stomach then three off the building then another then tried to punch him then Alex dodged the punch and body slammed then Alex jumped on the ledge and then Alex took out his gun and started shooting at the thugs then another thug tried to whack Alex then Alex ducked kicked the thug in shins then Alex got up started running then on of the thugs tried to attack Alex then Alex grabbed his hands to avoid getting tackled then Alex pushed him against the wall then another kick in the Alex then Alex ducked then did a cartwheel kick and kicked him in the stomach then as the thugs where dead Alex then tried to find Michael then Alex found walkie-talkie to use then as Alex was trying to use it a person behind a door was spying on Aussmen then Alex used his hooker then started looking for Michael then Alex started looking for Michael then as Alex was looking around on the building then the person that was spying on Alex was looking at one of his security cameras "I will hunt you down Aussmen and it will be brutal Mr. Aussmen" the man said then as he went out in public and then put on a human glove hand and headed out

Then as Alex was running he then climbed down the apartment stair cases and then as Alex got to sidewalk he then went to a pay phone to call Michael then Alex dialed his hotel number "hey Michael it's me Alex I was going to meet up in the empire state building but some thugs got to me and I had to escape where are you man" Alex said "I'm in Brooklyn just meet me there okay dude" Michael said "okay Michael" Alex said then Alex went back to his hotel and went into garage and got into his car and drove Brooklyn the Alex took a left turn into Queens, New York then as Alex saw Michael walking on the sidewalk "hey Michael what up" Alex said "oh nothing much dude so how are you doing bro" Michael said "good I'm staying in Time Square I can get you hotel in same hotel is that okay" Alex said "that's okay I have something on the roof of the hotel that I can see if there's any thugs shows up at your hotel" Michael said "sweet" Alex said then later that day Michael set up all of his spy gear on top of the hotel Alex was staying in then later that day Alex was waiting for Stella to come back around 4:00PM then as Alex was waiting then he saw someone with blonde and brown hair "hey Alex this is Richard Stomber" Stella said "oh hey nice to meet you" Alex said "Stella tells me everything about you Mr.?" Stomber said "Aussmen. Alex Aussmen" Alex said "oh awesome name Mr. Aussmen" Stomber said, "so how do you and Stella know each other?" Alex said with hesitation "oh I used to date Stella Aussmen" Stomber said "how long did you guys go out for?" Alex asked "for 2 years" Stomber said "nice" Alex said then Alex and Stella and Stomber went into Alex's suite "beautiful suite you have here Alexander" Stomber said "um Richard can you please call me Alex" Alex said then as Alex asked Richard then was giving out information about Alex on an ear phone and Alex spotted it on his ear "who does he work for?" Alex thought then later that night as Richard left Alex was very skeptical about what Richard was doing or who he was working for "do you like Richard Alex baby" Stella said "yeah Richard is awesome" Alex said but Alex didn't mean that and Alex knew that Richard was working for somebody but Alex had to find out and fast before Richard gets more information about Alex and more of Alex's past

Chapter 4 finding the clues in the New York's state capital

Then later that night Alex was on the roof of the hotel thinking about what Richard is and why he is after Aussmen and what for "hey Alex are you okay?" Michael asked "I'm okay Michael so how's Owen doing?" Alex asked, "He's doing well he still lives in Orlando" Michael said, "why did you ask?" Michael asked "just wondering" Alex said then as Alex was sitting on the roof then he found piece of paper that said "RAD industries Albany, New York" the piece of paper said then as Alex was looking on the piece of paper then Alex saw Richard's name on the paper

"Michael we have situation!!" Alex said, "What's wrong Alex?" Michael asked, "Stella's ex boyfriend is a RAD AGENT!!!!" Alex yelled, "Oh could this be possible?" Michael said "I don't know Michael but now I know why he called me Alexander cause he was RAD agent working RAD and looking for more special Ed kids in New York city but for some reason he wants to go after me" Alex said "why in the hell would he want to do a god damn thing like that?!" Michael said "cause that's way it is with RAD a lot of the agents are jerks and they call you by your formal name to make you look weak and try to capture you I have to tell Stella" Alex said "is there an address on the paper?" Michael asked "yeah it's Albany, New York's state capital" Alex said "I'm going there to find out what's going on in that city" Alex said then Alex then got a suit on went drove to Albany, New York to try to find out what was going on in Albany

Then as Alex got into his car he then started driving to Albany, New York then as Alex got there then he got out his camera that he has had since 1979 then Alex took pictures of the guards and the guest and it seemed that there was a party at the RAD office building then as Alex was walking he then saw a guard walking then Alex took out a PP7 and shot him then Alex stole his ID card and used it on himself and made his own and replaced it with an unknown name then Alex got into the party he then sneaked through in through an air vent cause he didn't want to risk people finding out he was then as Alex was in the party he then went into the bathroom and changed into a different suit and it was with a black shirt, black suit jacket, green neck tie, and the rest was black and even Alex had black dress shoes and they looked like disco shoes then as Alex went out of the bathroom Alex then saw a lot of people that were wearing fancy clothes then Alex went downstairs then as Alex went downstairs then a lot of the people just turned back and a lot of the girls just fell flat on their backs when they saw Alex and a lot of the women there was Alex was the most sexiest man at the party then Alex went to bar area "Budweiser with lemon" Alex said "coming up sir" the bartender said then the bartender got his beer ready then as Alex was drinking then from behind Stella saw Alex "Alex?" Stella said then Alex turned back then Alex saw Stella in the most beautiful and sexist dress "wow Stella you look amazing" Alex said "you want to dance with me" Stella said then Alex and danced to native new Yorker by Odyssey then Alex started dancing with Stella "I'm didn't think you would show up baby" Alex said then Alex lowered Stella then Alex raised Stella back up then Alex spinned Stella then Stella chuckled and started laughing then Stella put her arms around Alex then Alex picked up Stella and smooched her for 20 minutes "oh Alex" Stella said "let me increase your vocabulary baby girl" Alex said "oh I love that very much Mr. Aussmen" Stella said then Stella just started smooching Alex more and more then Stella just died with laughter "so what do you do for a living?" Stella asked Alex "you know it has something to do with being a secret agent" Alex said "that turns me on if you're like a secret agent your like James Bond 007" Stella said "oh I'm totally better then 007" Alex said then Alex spinned Stella and kissed her on the lips for 20 minutes "you want to go upstairs have sex upstairs?" Stella asked "sure why not" Alex said then Stella chuckled and then Alex and Stella went upstairs then as Richard was at the party he then was looking for Aussmen "sir we got a problem your ex just ran off with the an known man with a green tie" the guard said then he showed the video of Alex and Stella making out in the hotel taking each other's clothes off "its Aussmen kill him" Stomber said then as Alex was hearing the guards coming "Stella we have to go" Alex said then Stella got her dress "Alex why we have to leave?" Stella asked, "Stomber sent guards to go after us" Alex said "Richard why would he do that" Stella said "I don't know come on lets go" Alex said then Alex got out of the party and "what car?" Stella "well take my car" Alex said then Alex and Stella went into Alex's car and started driving back to Time Square in New York city then as Alex was driving then RAD agents where chasing Alex then Alex pressed a button that launched rockets of Alex's car and blew up their cars then Alex saw more as he was driving then pull the lever in his car then shot a missile and shot at the last car "where's your apartment?" Alex asked "it's in queens" Stella said then as Alex was driving to Manhattan he then took a right turn into Queens then Alex found Stella's apartment with his GPS then Alex parked his car by a meter then as Stella got out of the car she then zipped her dress "thanks for taking me home baby boy I love you Alex" Stella said "I love you too Stella" Alex said then Alex got out of the car and walked her to her apartment then as Alex opened her door then Stella smooched Alex "I love you Alex baby" Stella said then Alex touched the place where Stella kissed him and Alex really thought Stella was the one and even though Alex got married to She Woofe back in Florida after the weeding they never made it official that they were husband and wife and also She Woofe died right after Alex left to New York from Miami then as

Alex was driving he was thinking about Stella and her sexy and beautiful smile she had

Then as Alex was driving then something in front of him hit his car with a grenade then Alex's car was destroyed but Alex survived then a random person punched him in the face then Alex had a black eye then as Alex was knocked out on the road he then saw Richard walking to him then Richard kicked Alex in the face and gave him bloody lip "good evening Mr. Aussmen" Stomber said then Stomber kicked Alex in the stomach "you stay away from Stella you stupid autistic dumbass!!!" Stomber said "oh I yeah that's right I know all about you Alex your school history why you have to runaway so RAD doesn't lock you up in Tahoma transition back in Washington state" Stomber said "and also Aussmen I can tell Stella all about your history of yourself and make her break-up with you and back with me Alex you probley don't know what I'm saying cause of your disability and can't react normally hhahahahaha" Stomber laughed "I'm more smarter then you waste head" Alex said "wrong Aussmen my plan will cause RAD and I to build machines that cause damage to New York city with this button" Stomber said then Stomber pulled out a remote that can power the laser to damage New York city and time square and no one will stop me" Stomber said then Stomber punched Alex again in the face "I DON'T GIVE A SHIT!!! IF YOU HAVE A DISABLLITY I WILL BEAT EVERYBODY WHO HAS BEEN WORKING WITH ME OR AGINST ME AND BEAT THEM UP WHEATHER THEY HAD DISABLLITY OR NOT" Stomber said "throw the Special Ed Student in the Hudson river make sure nobody finds him" Stomber said then the guards put Alex in the car and drove to the Hudson river and threw Alex in the Hudson river and left him

Chapter 5 saving New York City and Stella from Stomber

Then as Alex was in Hudson River Michael then found where Alex was "Alex, Alex" Michael said then Michael pulled Alex in his motorboat "how did you find me?" Alex said "GPS" Michael said then Michael drove Alex back to shore then as Stella was in her apartment then she was captured by RAD agents "hello Stella" Stomber said then Stomber knocked her out with sleeping gas "put her in the car now" Stomber said then the guard put Stella in the trunk in the limo then Alex saw that Michael repaired his car then Alex hopped in his new car and speed up "I will take care of the lasers you save Stella" Michael said then Alex put his foot on the gas and drove to Queens to find Stella then Alex was driving then he took a right turn into Queens then as Alex got there he found a note on Stella's bed "hello Aussmen this is Stomber if you want to save Stella you will come to time square and face me and stop my plan if you can brahahhahahahahahahahahahahahhahahahahahahahahahahahahahahahahahahahah" the note said then Alex got back to his car and drove to time square to go look for Stomber's headquarters in time square

Then as Stella was getting grabbed she was screaming then Stomber pulled his faked hand out of his claw hand that covers the claw "what are you Richard?!" Stella said "oh Stella my sweet Stella you are now going to die for being with that stupid Aussmen when you should have been joining me" Stomber said "never" Stella said "Aussmen is more awesome then you will ever be" Stella said "WRONG!!!"Stomber yelled "that stupid autistic idiot will never find you and if he does he never get by and he will get sentsioned to death I grantee it" Stomber said then Stella had a shock "please don't kill Alex please Richard don't" Stella said "I'm sorry my dear you betrayed me by sleeping with him take into the cold storage and freeze her" Stomber said then the guards took Stella and put her in the cold freezer butt naked "someone help me" Stella cried then Alex got on a different suit on and found the hideout and where they were it was on the roof of the one of Coca-Cola logo lights then Alex went into the hideout and pulled a DD4 pistol then Alex turned back and shot a guard then body slammed another guard against the wall and punched the crap of out of him then Alex started running in hallways "Stella?!" Alex yelled then Alex saw the cold freezer and opened the freezer door then Alex used his laser heater to crack the ice Stella was in then the ice broke and Stella was cold inside and out "Alex" Stella said then Alex hugged Stella "Stella thank god are you okay?" Alex said, "yeah I'm alright" Stella cried then Stella hugged him "I missed you Alex" said then guard caught them and arrested them

"Hello Stella and Alexander Aussmen" Stomber said "no more games Richard!!" Alex said "here's my plan to destroy time square and Broadway forever hehehe hahahahahahahahah" Stomber laughed "not going to happen Claw boy!!" Alex said "lets just see about that Mr. Aussmen" Stomber said as he pointed his claw at Alex then Alex saw that Stomber was going to press the button then Alex head-butted Stomber then Alex pulled out his PP7 and started shooting at the rest of the guards "warning time square will be destroyed in 24 minutes" the intercom said then Stomber got up and pointed the claw Stella's neck "Alex!" Stella cried then Stella screamed as she was getting claw pointed at her neck then Alex pointed his PP7 and Stomber "jigs up claw boy let her go!!" Alex said "not chance Aussmen she's mine and always will be mine will never fall for you Aussmen brhahahahahahhaha hehe hahahaha" Stomber laughed then Alex loaded up his gun "I will shot you I swear to god you son of a bitch!!!" Alex said then Stomber then threw Stella then tried to stab Alex with his claw then Alex jumped in the air then Alex kicked Stomber in the face then Stomber kicked Alex in the face then Stomber did an evil smile and tried to stab Alex again but then Alex grabbed his wriest really hard and punched Stomber in the face then Alex then found gasoline and sprayed gasoline at Stomber and killed him

"Come on Stella we gotta get out of here" Alex said then Alex lifted up Stella in his arms and tried to find in escaping route to get out of the roof then Alex used his watch to disable to electric trying to destroy time square then Alex used his hooker and then Alex and Stella got out of burning down headquarters "Stella are you okay? Alex asked "yeah I'm okay baby boy" Stella said then Alex lifted up Stella and kissed her on the lips "Stella I will never found another girl like you and you're the most beautiful and sexiest girl in the world Stella Robertson will you marry me?" Alex said "yes Alex I love yes I will marry you Alex" Stella said then Stella said then Stella smooched Alex and Alex and Stella's weeding and this time this one was official and for real

Chapter 6 you're a beautiful native New Yorker

 Then later in 3 months went by fast and Stella and Alex were planning their weeding then as Alex was getting married he then saw Stella in the most beautiful weeding dress Alex had ever seen and as she was wearing red lipstick then as ceremony was almost over Alex was getting ready to kiss Stella for the first time as Stella's husband "I now pronce you Mr. and Mrs. Aussmen" the pastor said "you may kiss the bride" the pastor said then Alex smooched Stella then Michael and Owen and Stella's parents where clapping and really happy for them then as Alex went into the limo and they where driving to JFK airport to take them to their honeymoon "I love you Alex" Stella said "I love you too Stella" Alex said then Stella smooched Alex for 20 minutes then Alex was really happy that he finally found the women that loved him a lot and Alex wanted to spinned every minute with her

Then as Alex was kissing her Alex then saw RAD agents on their tail "LOOK OUT!!!" Alex said then as Alex hugged Stella with all the might he had then the limo got hit by something then the limo driver was killed by a gun bullet "Stella are you okay?" Alex said then Stella was shot by the RAD agents and Alex was shocked "Stella wake up we need to go home" Alex cried "Stella wake up" Alex said Alex found out that Stella died by a gun bullet in back of her hand then Alex just kissed her then a cop came saw them "it's alright it's quiet alright she's just sleeping will be in Seattle soon Stella there's no hurry to grow up Stella you're a beautiful native new Yorker" Alex cried and Alex head tears in his eyes then Alex then kissed Stella's hand then Alex looked at Stella again then Alex started crying and had tears in his eyes as he was crying then Alex then lowered his head and hugged Stella and Alex just flashed backed to every moment with her and flashbacked to all the things Alex and her did together and flash backed to when they were in Alex's suite and Alex smooched her "Alex stop it" Stella said jokingly then Alex just kissed her more and more and Stella just laughed "oh Alex" Stella said

Fire Down Below

Chapter 1 Los Angles, California 1984

Then it was a very sunny day in Southern California then Alex got out of a cab and then was exploring downtown Los Angles then Alex started walking then Alex then saw a building that was gray and it looked like an office building and Alex was having as much fun in California as he could because Alex knew that he was still sad after Stella's death back in New York and Alex left New York and headed back to Seattle and University of Washington and finished up college and graduated from University of Washington and then moved to Anthem, California and moved into a house there and his house was really cool it had 3 story house the 3rd floor was his room and his command center when ever he had to do any missions for any reason the 2nd floor was his TV room where he had hug couch that was leather and also had other couches too and a really fancy remote to power the TV and Alex also loved video games and there was also a bar in the TV room too but another thing too that Alex was so smart he found a way to hook his TV on the wall and extend the size of the with to be as wide as the wall in 2nd floor by using all of his gadgets then also in the room was sournd sound to the TV and the room looked very classy then there was 1st floor witch was Alex's Kitchen and on the right was the garage were Alex kept all of his cars dating all the way back to 1976 when he was Sophomore in high school and to 1984 and Alex also had a closet too that had every suit he had and also disco clothes and dark blue jeans and leather jackets and Alex just had a lot of clothes then as Alex was done in Los angles Alex then went back to his house in Beverly Hills and then Alex parked his car into garage then Alex got into his house and went into his house then Alex got into his room then Alex looked his

camera and then saw some thugs steeling from a house and Alex didn't know if they where RAD agents or if they where regular thugs then Alex then went outside to see what was going on then Alex pulled out his PP7 gun then Alex hid behind a wall in his garage then Alex shot one of the thugs in back then the rest of the thugs started shooting and shooting at Alex then Alex summer salted in back of another car then Alex loaded up his gun and kept on shooting at the thugs then all of the thugs were dead then Alex looked at the stolen things the thugs where after then Alex looked in one of the boxes then Alex saw a lot of jewelry in the boxes then Alex then took pictures of the jewelry and then put the boxes back in garage of other person's house then as Alex put the jewelry back into the garage then the other thugs showed up then Alex was shocked then without thinking Alex took out his PP7 and shot all the thugs then Alex did a back flip and shot the last thug in the head then Alex escaped back to his house Alex then opened his door to get into his house Alex and then went to sleep

Chapter 2 trouble in Southern California

 Then in Sacramento, California the governor then was making speech to house of congress in state capital then Governor then was talking about how Crime is becoming a big problem in the state now and then as he was getting to talk about educational future then some RAD agents where hidden behind one of Congress house of respective then without knowing one of RAD agents shot one of the Congressmen from the state of California then the place went nuts then a man with a 1930's suit on was staring at everybody screaming then he walked away went into a RAD van and left Sacramento

 Then in Los Angles then a beautiful girl by the beach in a bikini she had black hair and her bikini was purple then as she was playing with her friends playing volleyball she noticed a car coming by Laguna beach then as she was looking at the car she then smiled and waved at the car like her boyfriend was in the car or something then without knowing then the driver of the car pulled out a sniper riffle and shot her but it didn't kill her it just gave her a medicine shot on her back then she passed out then the people in the car turned out to be RAD agents and then they too her bikini off and put her in the trunk and burned her bathing suit and drove off

Then in San Diego there was a college student that got beaten up by RAD agents and kidnapped him and then took him all the way to the state of Arizona and beat him up in the desert "where's the safe" the RAD agents said "I don't know please don't hurt me man" the college student said then the RAD agents then grabbed him and in the car and then drove him to Colorado to the Grand Canyon "this is what it feels like when you escape us" one of the RAD agents said "no,no,no please don't do this" the college student then the RAD agents pushed the college student into the Grand Canyon then they went back into the car and drove back to Los Angles and it was dreadful how Alex was asleep through all this because something was going up

Chapter 3 meeting Farah Firelin

then it was 5:58 then Alex's alarm went off then Alex took a shower in his house then Alex was listing on his radio "rock the casbah by the clash" then Alex went down stairs and made himself breakfast and a breakfast sandwich with beacon, turkey and Tillamook cheese on the eggs then Alex made an ice coffee drink and then looked at the news paper and then as Alex got to important part that he was interested Alex then got his remote and turned his radio off then looked at one of pages in the Los Angles times that 3 Recourse/Special Ed. College students from USC where killed yesterday one in Sacramento, one in Laguna beach, and one in Denver, Colorado and he was also from USC then Alex was thinking in his head "I do not like the looks of this" Alex thought then Alex went upstairs and got on some dark blue jeans and a purple and red button up shirt and had black shoes on then Alex herd a knock at his front door then Alex went to answer the door and it was Owen "morning Aussmen" Owen said "morning dude" Alex said "did you see the paper?" Owen asked "yeah it does not look awesome it's terrible" Alex said "I know dude does Michael know anything about this?" Owen asked again "no but I will tell him he also said that I might get a new car today or something" Alex said "oh yeah it's outside and you will really like Aussmen" Owen said then Alex and Owen went outside in front of Alex's house in Beverly Hills and Alex was amazed at what the car looked like it was a 1984 Ferria "oh it looks awesome Owen" Alex said "I knew you would like it and it will be great on your missions too" Owen said "thanks Owen you really didn't have to do this" Alex said "you're my friend Alex friends help each other" Owen said "thanks man" Alex said then Owen threw the keys at Alex "here's the keys" Owen said "thanks" Alex said then Alex went back into his house and got his wallet and then Alex went inside his new car and drove to downtown Los Angles "have fun Aussmen" Owen said

then Alex was driving to downtown Los Angles then Alex looked for a parking garage to park his car then Alex then drove to Anthem and then Alex really didn't know where to go then Alex found a parking place to park his car then Alex walked around downtown Los angles then as Alex was walking around the city Alex saw a girl driving to Venice Beach then Alex went back into his car and saw the car and fallowed the car to Venice beach then Alex then took a right turn then saw the driver then the driver was a red headed girl she was skinny, her breaths where huge and she had blood eye lashes and she had sparkles in her eye "okay it might be a college student and if it is she is probley groupie" Alex thought to himself it then Alex saw her then Alex saw her changing into a bathing suit and then her legs sparkled as she was changing then she was butt naked outside then she got on a top and her bottoms then Alex just stared at her beauty then Alex went to a swimming suit and bought his swimsuit then Alex changed and then walked around Venice beach then Alex saw a lot of hot girls at the beach then Alex dove into the ocean and went swimming into the ocean then a lot of the hot girls in bikinis just saw Alex and just eyed him and the girls the girls went "oh lala" the girls said as the saw Alex swimming in the ocean and saw Alex's six pack then Alex found the girl with red hair then Alex went to go fallow her then she was going to a bar then Alex just eyed her and at her sparkly eyes "sir can I get you drink" the bartender said "yeah a bud light please" Alex said then as Alex got a bud light he then just kept staring at her and then Alex turned back and started drinking his beer then the red headed girl then went to bar table "hey" Alex said "oh hello do I know you?" the girl said "no I just moved here from Seattle the names Aussmen,…Alex Aussmen and you are?" Alex said "Farah Firline so are you still in college Mr. Aussmen" Farah asked "not anymore baby girl I just graduated from the university of Washington this year" Alex said "oh that's sexy so your bachelor now awesome sexy boy" Farah said "yeah" Alex said then the girl then sat closer and closer to Alex to the point where she was about to kiss him "this doesn't make you wearied out does it I just love hanging out with sexy guys" Farah said "no that at all baby girl" Alex said then Farah just smiled and then she started smooching Alex then Alex started touching Farah's checks and started kissing her then Alex lifted up Farah and then went out of the bar then went on the sand and then Alex ran to his car and went to his car and got a beach towel from his trunk of his car then Alex went back to the beach and Farah and Alex went on Alex's beach towels "ooooh" Farah said in a romantic voice then Farah took off her strap shirt and then Farah was topless then Farah took off her bottoms then Farah was butt naked on the beach then Farah just hugged Alex to cover her body and her nakedness like Alex was a towel then Farah was touching Alex's face and she kissed him on the lips for 20 minutes "do you want to go back to my place" Alex asked "no will go to my place to have sex" Farah said then Alex and Farah then started driving out of Venice beach and Alex took a freeway to get Farah's place then as Alex was driving Farah then told him to take a right turn into the USC campus "you go to USC?" Alex said "hell yeah I go there wahooooo" Farah yelled then Alex parked his car then Alex and Farah started making out on Alex's car then Farah jumped on Alex then Alex carried Farah to her dorm room then as they got into Farah's dorm room then Alex and Farah kept on making out then Alex fell on Farah's bed and then Farah jumped on Alex like a dog and started making out with Alex then Alex took his shirt off then Farah took off her shirt, bottoms, and her sandals and Farah was butt naked then Farah took Alex's pants then Alex and Farah went under the covers and Farah kept on making out with Alex then as Farah and Alex where kissing in bed then some thugs in suits where spying on Alex and Farah making out and it could only mean that RAD was gunning for Alex and maybe Farah

Chapter 4 the USC campus

 Then as time reached 6:00AM then Alex fell asleep Farah was hugging Alex's naked body and Farah was kissing Alex's chest and his face "oh my god that was best sex ever" Farah said "I know" Alex said "so what are you studying to be at USC?" Alex asked, "I'm studying to be an NFL cheerleader" Farah said "wow that's awesome what team do you want to cheer for?" Alex said "I either want to cheer for the Dallas cowboys or the 49ers because Joe Montana is sooo sexy and if I wasn't a cheerleader I would sleep with them" Farah said "awesome" Alex said "so are you just using me or something because I look like Joe Montana?" Alex said in confusing voice "no cause your really hot too Alex your like my fire down below" Farah said "awesome and very true" Alex said "so what are you doing today don't you have a job or something" Farah said "I do but it's not very known though" Alex said "oh really" Farah said "so what classes do you have today if I may ask" Alex said "oh I just have cheer and a bunch of boring classes" Farah said "oh I'll see you around tonight is that okay" Alex said "okay Alex baby I'll see you tonight" Farah said then as Alex go on some cloths then Alex noticed some of the thugs in suits where checking out the men's bathroom and they found some 1979 tennis shoes in the bathroom that looked muddy or something then Alex just stared with shock and thought "I was never at USC something wired is going on" Alex thought then Alex kept on walking out of the campus then he herd noise in a garage can then Alex opened the lid and it was resource college student in there tied up in duck tape and Alex was shocked "are you okay buddy" Alex said "yeah I'm okay I just got kicked out of USC cause I was former special Ed student in high school and then some thugs in suits then kicked me out and put me in this garbage can" he said "what's your name dude?" he asked "the names Aussmen….Alex Aussmen" Alex said "Zach Dolmen" Zach said then Alex got him out of the can and then Alex looked in his backpack "I think I might know who those thugs might be Zach" Alex said "what are they?" Zach asked, "They are RAD agents" Alex said, "so do you have a place to stay?" Alex asked, "Well I did stay in a dorm but now they probley got all my stuff" Zach said, "you can stay at my place" Alex said "where do you live?" Zach asked "Beverley Hills" Alex said then Alex took Zach into his car and then Alex turned the car on and dropped off Zach off at his house "you stay here I'm going to find out who kicked you out" Alex said "okay Alex" Zach said then Alex drove off and headed back to USC campus and then Alex promised that he was going to see Farah again and Alex might take Farah out to dinner

Chapter 5 taking Farah out to dinner and investigating what happened to the special Ed College students

 Then Alex was driving he then went his nearest clothes store and then got new blue jeans, a purple T-shirt, black dress boats and they looked like Michael Jackson's boats, then he got a new necklace but it wasn't a piece necklace it was a heart necklace with wings, then Alex got sliver aviator sun glasses, and he also got a black leather jacket and it sparkled then as Alex got out of the fitting room the women in the store just eyed Alex and also starred at Alex walking out of the store then as Alex was walking of the store Alex then left 300$ on the clerk for the clothes then Alex got back into his car and then drove to the USC campus to pick up Farah then as Alex got there he then his park his car in the parking lot Farah then eyed at Alex "oh my god you look sooo fine" Farah said then Farah kissed Alex on the lips then Farah jumped on Alex "so where are we going go to" Farah asked "my dear Farah the question isn't what are we going to do the question is what aren't we going to baby girl" Alex said "oh baby" Farah said then Farah kissed Alex and then went into his arms then Alex and Farah went into Alex's car and then drove to downtown Los Angles then Alex turned up his music really loud and then Farah then was flipping her red hair in Alex's car then Alex found a restaurant in a mall in downtown Los Angles then Alex then found a parking spot and then Alex turned the lever on his car to put the brake then Alex and Farah got out of Alex's car and then Alex pressed the remote on his key chain to look his car then Farah put her hands around Alex's arms and then she laid her head on one of Alex's shoulder then Alex and Farah got into the mall then Alex and Farah then found a restaurant that was a

steak house then Alex went into the restaurant and they got seated then Alex ordered steak and then Farah got a burger as Alex was done eating and so was Farah then both Alex and Farah drank 2 bud lights then Alex paid for dinner and then headed out of the restaurant "thanks for taking me to dinner Alex baby" Farah said "your welcome Farah" Alex said then Farah smooched then as Farah was kissing Alex then a special Ed college student was sitting on a chair then a RAD agent then pointed a gun at him "get up" he yelled then the person got up and then he tazered him and put him in a bag then Alex herd the screaming "RAD!!" Alex thought "Farah we got out of here" Alex said "why baby nobody it watching us" Farah said then the RAD agents then pulled out a gun and started shooting at Alex then Alex herd the gun bullets "come on" Alex said then Alex grabbed Farah's hand then they started running then Alex pulled out a PP7 and started shooting at them then Alex fired 15 bullets at the RAD agents then Alex and Farah got into Alex's car "get in" Alex said Farah then got out of the car and she was scared "it's okay I'm here Farah just stay clam" Alex said then Farah had tears in her eyes "are those guys trying to kill me?" Farah cried "I don't know but I'm going to take you to my house in Beverley Hills hang on" Alex said then back in the mall the RAD agents saw Alex's car "its Aussmen get him" the RAD agents then the RAD agents called 2 cars and then they got into the car and they started chasing Alex then Alex took a right turn into the freeway to get to Beverley Hills and then Alex noticed the RAD agents chasing them then Alex pressed a button on in his car then Alex's car then started firing bullets at the RAD cars then the cars where knocked out and the RAD cars below up then Alex turned the machine guns off in his car and then continuing to drive to Alex's house

Then Alex parked his car in his driveway by his house and then Farah and Alex got into his Alex's house "Farah are you okay?" Alex asked, "yeah I'm okay Alex" Farah said then Alex got upstairs and then Michael and Owen where upstairs "hey Alex" Michael said "hey dude what's up" Alex said "who's this girl?" Owen asked "oh Farah this Michael and Owen, Owen and Michael this is Farah" Alex said "pleasure to meet you two" Farah said "so how do you guys know Alex?" Farah asked "I went to high school with him" Michael said "what about you?" Farah asked "since college" Owen said "awesome" Farah said then Zach was on the couch sleeping and then Alex poured a keg of bud light to wake him up "what the hell" Zach said "okay Zach I need you answer some questions" Alex said "okay well when I was kicked out there where some people at the USC campus and another thing you gotta know is that the students that got killed where my friends" Zach said "oh-no that's terrible" Alex said "do you know who is behind all this?" Alex asked "no but I can tell you this I did see the person's face he controls everything at USC and is main popular kid and he hates Special Ed college students and he also hates resource students as well" Zach said "okay, okay slow down Zach do you know what he might look like?" Alex asked, "well this dude wears a suit and he also loves money and he has black hair and a crose crop hair and is the same height as you" Zach said "so this guy is rich?" Alex asked "yes fitly rich so rich that he can control anything he wants on the USC campus even the head master's office if he wants to" Zach said "okay thanks Zach" Alex said then Alex went up stairs in his house to talk to Owen and Michael

 "Hey guys I found out who might be behind all of this" Alex said, "okay who is he?" Michael asked "well I don't know his name but he is the richest kid in the USC campus and he wears suits and he loves to be in control" Alex said "damn so your after a millionaire" Owen said "yeah" Alex said then Michael got on the computer and looked up some people on the USC campus that might be rich then as Michael was on the computer he then found a name "hey we got a name Doug Starrson formal stock exchanger and wall street apprentice age is 20 and his hair is black" Michael said then Alex looked on the computer "yep that's him" Alex said "how are you going to find a way to meet or find him? "Owen asked "well I think can't miss him because he always loves for a challenge so I think he might meet me" Alex said "okay you can investigate his house his house is in Pasadena, California a little bit North of here I want you to go there and find out what Starson wants with any Special Ed kid on the USC campus and find out who killed the 3 college students and Alex be carful and don't die" Michael said "I'm on it" Alex said

 Then Alex then got out a black jumpsuit and then got in his car and drove to Pasadena, California and then Michael then set a GPS system in his car to find the house then as Alex got into the house and then got in through an air vent to get into the house then Alex got out a PP7 gun just in case there were any guards in the house then Alex then found an office in the house and then Alex found a list of students that were Special Ed on a death list and then Alex was looking through and then Alex took pictures of what Starson was going to do with all those people then a girl with blonde hair then herd Alex's camera clicking then Alex felt a gun pointed at his head "hello Mr. Aussmen" the girl with blonde hair said then in back of Alex was the blonde haired naked college girl with a gun her hand pointed straight at Alex then Alex put his hands up "this is just not your night isn't it sexy boy" she said "look miss I don't know if your in a relationship with Mr. Starson but I don't want to hurt you miss" Alex said "it's okay Alex baby I won't…haha you really thought I was going to shot you" she said "wow you really got me did you" Alex said "I'm Eliot" she said "so what are you doing at Starson's house naked" Alex asked "I'm going out with him" Eliot said "oh now I see why" Alex said "so do you have the photos?" Eliot asked "yeah I have them right here" Alex said "awesome Alex and congrats" Eliot said "thanks" Alex, said, "so do you know where Starson usually goes after his classes?" Alex asked "oh you he usually watches me cheer" Eliot said "oh that's cool my girlfriend is cheerleader" Alex said "cool what's her name?" Eliot said "Farah Firline" Alex said "oh I know that girl she is good" Eliot said "yeah" Alex said "well goodnight and don't worry I will turn these in to the CIA so you will have nothing to worry about Alex" Eliot said "thanks" Alex said then Eliot walked back to bed and then Alex ran out of the house and went back into his car and drove back to Beverley Hills and Alex then thought why haven't I seen this Starson dude but Alex knew he was going to meet him very soon and Alex had to be ready.

Chapter 6 meeting Starson and watching Farah cheer and going to a nightclub in Los Angles

Then as Alex got back to his house then he got out of his car and then went upstairs and then Alex took his clothes and his underwear off and then slept in his bed then Farah then got out of the shower and then Farah then took her towel and she was butt naked then she slept with Alex next to him then Alex turned to Farah and started kissing her and touching her then Farah also touched Alex everywhere then Alex lit up some candle in his bed room then Alex kept on kissing Farah in his bed

Then the next morning Alex then got out of bed and took a shower and then as Alex got out of the shower then Farah then put her hands around Alex "morning sexy boy" Farah said "morning baby girl" Alex said then Farah kissed Alex on the lips "so what are your plans for today?" Farah asked we I don't know I think Owen, Michael and I might go to Universal studios and go on a couple rides what about you?" Alex asked "well I have cheer and then I might go to 49ers game" Farah said "awesome who are they playing?" Alex asked "oh you noisy sexy boy you are" Farah said then Farah kept on kissing Alex on the lips for 10 minutes then Farah got dressed and then Alex gave her ride to the campus then Alex dropped Farah "hey are you going to ninners game with me?" Farah asked "yeah I will come with you sure I will" Alex said "awesome anyway I gotta go see you baby boy" Farah said then Farah got her cheer bag and then kissed Alex on the check and then started running to cheer then Alex just smiled and then starred at her and then Alex drove back to Beverley Hills to pick up Michael and Owen and then Alex drove Anthem to go to Universal studios

 Then Alex found a parking spot and also got out his cash to get into the theme park "you got the cash?" Owen asked "yep I do guys" Alex said "good lets go" Michael said then Alex, Michael and Owen got in line and Alex then got out his cash and paid to get in then as Alex, Michael, and Owen got in they then saw a dude with black hair and he was wearing a suite then he turned back "well hello Mr.?" Starson said "Aussmen…Alex Aussmen" Alex said "Doug Starson" Starson said, "so Mr.Aussmen welcome the OC Mr.Aussmen have you been to California before?" Starson said "no this my first year here cause I graduated from the University of Washington and I moved here to the golden state" Alex said "what about you" Alex said "I go to USC which is the best school in the PAC 10 Husky boy and I invest in best people that have a talent and a future" Starson said "oh interesting" Alex said "thank you Alex" Starson said "wait how did you know my first name was Alex?" Alex asked, "Guessed I seem you have talents Mr.Aussmen do you have job Alex?" Starson said "I have one…it just a very secret job" Alex said "oh well it was nice to meet you Mr.Aussmen" Starson said then Starson shock Alex's hand and left "I don't like that dude he seemed like he was trying to find things in you like your identity" Michael said then as Alex was walking with Owen and Michael then Starson then was staring at Alex "boys found out any information about Alex Aussmen and then…kill him" Starson said then as Alex was having fun at the park with his friends he then at the end of their visit to the theme park Alex noticed that something was not right then Alex herd a gun getting loaded

"DUCK!!!" Alex yelled then Alex pulled Owen and Michael down "Alex what the hell is wrong with you" Owen said then they turned back "okay now I why you said duck" Michael said "lets get out of here" Alex said then Alex pulled a ZMG gun and started shooting at Starson's thugs trying to kill them then they ran to Alex's car "Michael, Owen get in the car" Alex said then Alex started his car then started the car and then Alex then tried to drive to safe place where the thugs might not get them then Alex drove to parking area by Disneyland "Disneyland are you crazy" Owen said "well do you another plan?" Alex asked "no" Owen said then they got out of the car and started running and getting chased by the thugs then Alex then jumped over the turn style entrances "out of the way" the thugs said then Alex then tried to find a place to hide then Alex and his friends got into Tomorrow land then Alex then Alex lost Owen and Michael "oh god where do I hide now" Alex thought then Alex noticed that there was parade going on then Alex get one of the parade floats and dressed up as Disney charter and then went on the float then Alex dressed up as Mickey Mouse then they where playing "Disco Inferno" during the parade then Alex was really scared and was really nervous what he should do then Alex started doing disco moves on the Disneyland parade float and snapped his fingers like old times and also did his disco moves "look at Mickey Mouse getting his groove on the float ladies and gentlemen" the announcer said then Alex did more disco moves on the Disneyland floats and then everybody started clapping and Alex jumped on the floats and did a dance move after dance move and snapped his fingers and then did more disco moves and then they where playing "young hearts run free" during the parade then Michael Owen where looking for Alex "where the hell is Alex?" Owen said "ah Owen…." Michael said "oh yeah ladies Gentlemen this might be the best Mickey mouse cause of all the disco moves and getting his 1970's on I like those moves" the announcer said "Alex what the hell are you doing get off of there man" Michael said "Alex get off of there man" Owen said then Alex couldn't see them and just kept dancing away

"Where the hell are they taking him we have to get Alex" Michael said "ah Forinterland go to Frointerland" Owen said then as the parade was over everybody in parade that played the Disney charters just high fived him "ladies and gentlemen this trophy for the best dancer goes to…..Mickey Mouse come on up here" the announcer said then Alex ran up there and gave him a big old hug "what's your name son you look awfully young" then announcer said "Aussmen…Alex Aussmen" Alex said "Aussmen that's a cool name give it up for…Mr. Alex Aussmen" the announcer said then Alex then got out of his costume "Alex" Michael said "Michael, Owen" Alex said "what in the hell were you thinking dude going on the god damn Disneyland parade float" Michael said "I don't know at first it was getting away from the bad guys and then I got into to the groove of it I'm sorry guys" Alex said "dude don't listen to Michael he's stupid we are happy for you dude and by the way you have to pick up Farah in 90 minutes in counting" Owen said "holy shit!!! Farah we gotta go guys" Alex said then Alex and his friends ran back to his car and they drove to the USC campus to pick up Farah but then Starson's thugs then where talking to Starson "boss we lost Alex in Disneyland" the thugs said "report back to the hideout NOW!!" Starson yelled "yes sir" the thugs said

 Then Alex then went back to the USC campus and then without waiting Alex then walked in and he was watching Farah cheer "lets go…Torrents…lets go wahooooo" Farah said then Alex just smiled and watched her perform and she was an awesome cheerleader then as partice was over Farah then picked up her palm plams and then walked and then Alex wised at Farah "Alex oh my god you where watching me perform oh I love you baby" Farah said "your such an awesome cheerleader I want you to have this" Alex said "what is it?" Farah asked "it's Disneyland dance trophy I won earlier today and I wanted you to have it" Alex said "oh that's sooo sweet of you Alex and where not going to the ninners game..Let's go dancing at a night club" Farah said then as Farah was hugging Alex Starson then was looking at Farah and Alex "enjoy that Special Ed girl Alex…because she won't last muahahahahahahahahahahahah hahahahahahahahahahahah" Starson laughed

Then later that night Alex and Farah then went to go dancing at a night club downtown Los Angles and then Alex got on his Seattle suit which was a suit that had a green button up shirt, a diamonded green colored neck tie and black disco pants and jacket and Farah then was wearing a blue dress with sliver heals and then as they got there Alex and Farah where the first ones to get into the night club then as they got in Alex and Farah started dancing to "Fire Down Below by Tina Charles" and then Alex did his best disco moves and then Farah and Alex did the tango then

Alex danced really good then Farah did a cartwheel then Farah then moved her shoulders and her body up in down then Alex shaked his head as he was dancing then Farah ran to Alex then Alex lifted up Farah in the air then everybody in the nightclub cheered then Farah also did disco moves and then her eyes started to sparkle under the disco ball then Farah moved her hands and shaked her body and then Alex twisted Farah 3 times then Farah put her hands around's neck and then the song was over and everybody clapped "that was Fire down Below by Tina Charles" the DJ said "oh my god that was so much fun thank you for taking me baby" Farah said "your welcome Farah" Alex said then Farah smiled and just smooched Alex on the lips and then she took her silver high heels off and then went on Alex's lap and they had a great time and then after dancing Alex then went home Farah then got to Alex's room "I'm going to get naked in your room Alex and I know that turns you on" Farah said "hell yeah that turns me on" Alex said then Farah laughed and then she smiled and went upstairs and got naked in Alex's room and then as Alex went upstairs Farah was in Alex's room butt naked then Farah went up to Alex and started smooching him "oh that feels good baby" Farah said then Alex smooched her more and then they fell on Alex's bed but then as they where making out on Alex's bed some of Starson's thugs where video tapping them and Starson was watching it in his dorm room "muahahahahahah oh yes once I get my hands on Alex's pretty girlfriend nothing can stand in my way and USC and all of the theme parks in California will be no more muahahahahahah hahahhahahahahahahahahah muahahahahah bra hahahahahahahahahahahahahahahhahahahah mauahahahahah hahahahahah"

Starson laughed

Chapter 7 Farah's past and Starson's evil plan

Then Alex got up from bed at around 6:30AM in the morning then Alex took a shower then as Alex was looking the mirror then Alex started shaving then as Alex was done then he herd someone come into the house then a special Ed Kid was walking by Alex's house and the person was one of Amber's friends then one of the RAD agents took out a gun and shot him and then broke into Alex's house then Alex saw 2 RAD agents broke into Alex's house "Alex!!" Farah said "Farah" Alex yelled then the RAD agents where starting to kidnap her and then she started screaming as she was getting into the RAD vans then Alex saw Farah getting kidnapped then Alex got dressed into a purple shirt and then got on his black leather jacket and then his dark blue jeans and black leather boats that looked like motorcycle boats then Alex ran to his car and started chasing the kidnapper by driving his car then all the RAD agents where firing guns at Alex then Alex pressed a button by his radio then his machine gun started firing at RAD agents car and then the car took a Sharpe right turn into Anthem then Alex continued to fallow them into Anthem then Alex saw that they where heading into Universal studios and then Alex parked his car and then started running into the theme park looking for Farah

Then as Alex got into the theme park Alex then looked around the theme park looking for what kind of way the found to get into the CEO building then Alex found a rock center then Alex got in line for the ride then as Alex was on the ride then a person with a suite and he had a taser then Alex looked back and saw the RAD agents trying to kill him then Alex kicked one of them in the face and then he punched the other one in the face then Alex fell through a trap door and then Alex started sliding on a slide then Alex fell flat on his face on the ground then 2 RAD agents grabbed Alex by the arms and just started beating the crap of him and then gave Alex a black eye and a bloody lip "enough boys let me have a whack at the former Special Ed student from Tahoma high school muhahahahahaha" Starson laughed "where is she?!" Alex said "muahahahah oh yes I have her right here Mr. Aussmen" Starson said then Starson pressed a button and then Farah was in ice cold arctic water butt naked "if you don't hand me your college degree in less then 17 minutes your sweet Farah dies Mr. Aussmen" Starson said "wait a minute this explains the killings of the Special Ed students from USC that where killed a few weeks ago you have been taking their college degrees and burning them and also taking their money" Alex said "correct Mr.Aussmen not only do I burn their college degress I also steel their money out of their own bank accounts and I save them up to blow up the USC Campus and blow up all the theme parks in Southern California" Starson said "and by the way Alex did you even know that Farah was just like you a Special Ed student in high school but looked like a regular student more then a Special Ed student muahahahaha" Starson laughed "I'm sorry Alex I didn't want you find out like this" Farah said then Farah had tears in her eyes then

Alex then flipped the table over and then beat the crap out of the RAD agents then Alex loaded up a gun and shot the RAD agents in the head then Starson punched Alex in the face "you little stupid Autistic fool trying to escape and now I beat the crap out of you Mr.Aussmen" Starson said then Alex kicked him in the face and then Alex picked up a chair and slammed the chair and punched him in the face "this is not over Aussmen" Starson said "really cause I think it is" Alex said then Alex picked up a D44 gun and shot him in the head then Alex hacked into Starson's computer and disabled the countdown for bomb to blow up USC then Alex then opened the container to get Farah out of the ice cold water then Alex got Farah out of the water "Farah, Farah wake up" Alex said then Alex started running out of the office and back to his car and then Alex opened the door to the back seat and but Farah's naked body in the back seat with a warm blanket covering her body then Alex started driving to the USC campus

 Then as Alex got there he then went into Farah's dorm and but her in the warm shower then Alex then went to a payphone to call Michael "hello?" Michael said "hey Michael it's me Alex I just wanted you to know that the mission is complete" Alex said "good job Alex thanks to you the bomb to blow up USC and the theme parks in southern California has been disabled and Starson is dead well done Alex" Michael said "thanks dude we have to celebrate somewhere do you have any ideas?" Alex asked "lugene beach or Disneyland our my ideas" Michael said "okay me and Farah will meet you there" Alex said then Alex hanged up the phone and then Alex came back to Farah's dorm room and Farah was better "Alex!" Farah said, "Farah oh thank god are you okay sweaty" Alex said "yeah I'm okay baby thank you for saving me you're are a really good boyfriend Alex" Farah said "oh thanks Farah" Alex said then Farah just hugged Alex and smooched him on the lips

Chapter 8 staying in the Sleeping beauty Castle in Disneyland

 Then night time came and Alex and Farah then went to go to Disneyland and Michael and Owen where in tomorrow land "where the hell is Alex now he told me that he and Farah were going to be here" Michael said "don't worry Alex will be here" Owen said then as Owen and Michael where in line to get on space mountain Alex and Farah where in the sleeping beauty castle above Fantasyland having dinner up there "I always wanted to have dinner in the sleeping beauty castle in Disneyland" Alex said then Farah was in a sliver dress with golden heels then Alex poured Champaign into Farah's glass then Farah started smooching Alex on the lips and the moon was in the background then Alex lifted up Farah and then Farah took off her dress and then Farah was butt naked then she got under covers and then Alex took off his suite and got into the covers with her

Then Michael then went on his walke talkie and called Alex in the castle "Alex you there?" Michael said then Alex was kissing Farah then the phone rang "hello?" Alex said "Alex where the hell are you promised that you would meet me and Owen here" Michael said "dude shut up let him do what he wants Michael he'll show up" Owen said then Alex turned off the phone then Farah and Alex started having sex on the bed "I love you Alex" Farah said "I love you too Farah" Farah said "Alex, can you take me to Disneyland tomorrow please" Farah said "sure darling we will" Alex said then Alex kept on kissing on touching Farah "no, Alex" Farah said joking then Farah started laughing then Alex just smooched her for 20 minutes and she kept laughing "oh Alex" Farah said

The Run Away Nighty way

The Runaway Night way

By: Nelson Amador

Chapter 1 key Arena 1985

As people where going into the Seattle Super Sonics game in Seattle Center then it was a very cold day in downtown Seattle it was January 12th 1985 and people were about to watch the Sonics play then as people where getting in Alex then showed up in line with dark blue jeans and a Seattle super Sonics sweatshirt on with Joe Hasset's number on it and Alex was also wearing a ski coat too over the sweatshirt then Alex handed the person his ticket to get in the game and then Alex looked at his ticket to see what row he was going to be sitting at then before the game Alex bought himself a cheeseburger and an icee and fires with ketchup then Alex got to his row and then started watching the game and then as Alex was watching the game a very tall girl with brown hair she was 6'4 height and she weighted about 117 pounds and her arms had muscles too and her legs were also muscular as well then Alex kept on watching the game and watching the Sonics shoot points and dripple the ball down the court then the girl with brown hair then walked in Alex's row and then she was also wearing pink jeans with a purple shirt that said "I love the Sonics" and it also said " rock concert today around Vancouver Canada" then Alex then put on his sun glasses too close up with the player playing then the girl with brown hair then starred at Alex and then she sat by Alex "excuse me is this number 352" she said "oh yeah it is my dear sit down" Alex said "awesome" she said "what's your name?" she asked "I'm Alex" Alex said "Summer Nightway such a privilege to finale meet you Mr.Aussmen" Summer said "oh thanks why is that?" Alex asked "because I hear a lot of awesome things about Alex" Summer said "wow really?" Alex said "yeah I you have a very sexy face under those glasses" Summer said "very true" Alex said "so where do you live Alex?" Summer asked "I live in Beverley Hills in California I used to live in Washington state and I also graduated from the University of Washington" Alex said "what high school did you go to" Summer asked "ah Tahoma high school" Alex said "class of 1979" Alex said "awesome I went there in the 70's too I think I've seen you before" Summer said "what year did you graduate there? "Same class as you sexy boy that's how I know everything about Mr.Aussmen" Summer said "you don't by any chance know about all my relationships I have had…do you?" Alex asked "no" Summer said "good" Alex said then Alex and Summer watched the Seattle Super Sonics game and then Alex and Summer went outside of the arena together "wow that was so awesome" Alex said "yeah that was pretty awesome hey Alex do you want to go to a concert tonight it's in Vancouver do you want to come?" Summer asked "sure...wait in Vancouver, Washington?" Alex asked "no in Canada" Summer said "oh" Alex said then Alex then out of his wallet he pulled out his passport so he can get into the Canada then Alex and Summer then walked around downtown Seattle "so how are we getting there?" Alex asked "in my groupie van" Summer said then Summer then ran to the van and then jumped right in the back and then so did Alex "welcome Summer and who is this gentlemen" the driver asked "oh this Alex Aussmen" Summer said "hello Alex I'm Troy Tenderloin I will be your driver do the two of you have your passports" Troy said "got mine" Alex said "who are we going to watch perform?" Alex asked "Michael Jackson he's on tour in Canada so we are going to watch him perform then they drove to Vancouver and Alex was excited to go to rock concert then as they got there they then saw an area where they can stand "ladies and gentlemen here is Michael Jackson!!" the announcer said then Michael Jackson then was on stage and started singing "Dirty Dina" then as he started singing in front of the microphone Alex just watched then Alex started jumping and people where screaming like crazy when Michael Jackson was playing the song on the electric guitar then Alex had a smile on his face and then just kept watching Summer then Alex just kept on enjoying the concert then Michael Jackson then walked to left side of the stage and then jumped to the right side playing the guitar then he also playing the guitar like crazy kept screaming "Dina!" while he was playing the guitar then he jumped to left side and then he started spined around 30 minutes while he was singing then Michael Jackson then did a cart wheel then played guitar going from note to note on his guitar then sang the last part of the song playing guitar raptly fast while it was making different electric sounds then the song was over then everybody started clapping "thank you Canada!!" he yelled out to the crowd then Alex and Summer got out of the concert "wow Michael Jackson is so awesome that was such a great concert what do you think Alex?" Summer said "I loved it there is no one like him he's like superman" Alex said "so what now?" Alex said "we could stay in a hotel in Canada what do you think?" Summer said "sure I'm down for that" Alex said "I knew you would" Summer said

Then Alex and Summer then checked into a hotel in Vancouver, Canada that was really nice then Alex then as he got in the hotel room he then took off his shirt sweet shirt then Alex didn't have any extra clothes with him because they were back in Downtown Seattle his hotel there "so have you been to Canada before?" Summer asked "oh no I have not but it's really cool so far" Alex said then Summer then went on Alex and started making out with him then she stopped kissing him "I'm going to take my clothes off in the bathroom I'll be right back Alex baby" Summer said "okay Summer" Alex said then as Summer went inside the bathroom Alex then looked at the window and saw the city of Vancouver and looked so beautiful and had an awesome view "man Michael would love to be here right now and so would Owen" Alex said then Summer was back in the room with a bath robe and then she took off the bath robe and then she was naked underneath it "do you like what you see?" Summer said "oh wow I…holy crap" Alex said "you're not going anywhere Alex baby I have you right here in my arms" Summer said then Summer started taking Alex's pants, socks, shoes, and underwear off then Alex and Summer then got into the covers and then Alex felt the bed go mattress moved around "oh wow this is a water bed" Alex said then Summer started kissing Alex on the lips "this pretty far the best trip I have…ever….been on" Alex said then Summer just smooched him on the lips and then she got on top of Alex's naked body and pulled the covers over them "oh wow…yeah….okay that's my neck your kissing" Alex said then Summer's legs went around Alex's legs and the wild night began

Chapter 2 waking up in Vancouver

then as the time was 8:00AM Alex then looked at the window then Summer turned on the radio then Alex tried to get up and then as he started moving his head he then steam coming out of the bathroom and then Alex realized that Summer was in the shower then Alex got up and then Alex took a shower after Summer came out and then Alex went into the shower and then got dressed into his dark blue jeans and then put on his purple shirt and his leather jacket and got on his tennis shoes

then as Summer and Alex checked out of the hotel Alex and Summer then drove back to Seattle, Washington then as Alex was driving he then starred at Summer and she loved looking at the window and she loved looking at the leaves and green grass then Alex kept on driving then as they got back to Washington state they came back around 6:00PM then Alex drove around downtown Seattle "so where's your apartment?" Alex asked "it's over here" Summer said then Alex drove around and saw a small 5 floor building then Alex parked his car by a meter "thanks for driving me home Alex" Summer said "you're welcome Summer" Alex said then Summer then put her arms around Alex and smooched him for 30 minutes then Alex tried to whip the lip stick off his check but it was permanent then Alex kept on driving to his hotel by the Seattle aquarium then Alex parked his car by a seafood restaurant then Alex then Alex went inside his hotel then Alex got to his floor were his hotel room Alex then saw balcony then Alex went outside and then looked at the beautiful view

then Alex saw the lamp posts on the streets and then Alex started think about Summer and then about how Seattle changed since he graduated in 1984 which was last year Alex never had the chance to be there for his last 2 years because RAD was starting to go after him again just they did in 1976 Alex's Sophomore year in high school then as Alex was in his own little world he then herd a door opening then Alex saw the person go into his hotel room then Alex pulled out his PP7 and then went into his hotel room and then Alex was about to shoot but then the lights went on "surprise!!!" Michael and Owen said "happy birthday Alex!!" Michael said "wow!!" Alex said "thanks guys" Alex said "I got you this" Michael said "what is it?"Alex asked "it's a new leather jacket it's blue leather" Michael said "thanks I like it" Alex said "so what did you get him?" Michael asked "well I got him a car and an awesome ring" Owen said "really where is it" Alex asked "well it's outside then Alex and Owen then got outside out of the hotel and saw the car and it was a 1985 Lamborghini Countach and it looked the car Alex drove when Alex was in Los Vegas in 1978 "this is awesome Owen Love these cars what's the brand of the car" Alex asked "it's a 1985 Lamborghini Countach" Owen said then as the party went on back to the hotel room and hanged out Michael "hey Michael" Alex said "hey dude what's up so what did you do last night?" Michael asked "I went to a Michael

Jackson Concert last night" Alex said "with who dude" Michael said "with a girl I met at Sonics game" Alex said "do you know her name or know her number" Michael said "well her name is Summer Nightway and we went to a concert last night and then we stayed into a hotel in Canada and then we had sex that night too and them my mind just went blank from there" Alex said "dawn Alex sounds like you had huge hangover" Michael said "yeah I did" Alex said "do you think you will see her again" Michael said "hopefully" Alex said then later that night Alex, Michael, and Owen then went home Alex and cleaned up then as Alex was done cleaning up he then thought about Summer and where she could really be then as Alex slept in the hotel that night he then dreamed about Summer and then for some reason Alex then woke up around 5:58AM and then he took a shower and packed all of his things in his suitcase and also got dressed and got on dark blue jeans, a brown long sleeves and then got on his black leather jacket and then he got on his tennis shoes and then he headed off to Sea-Tac airport

then as Alex got there he then Summer walking to ticket checking and then as Alex saw her Alex then looked at his citizen eco drive sliver watch and started looking at the security cameras from his watch so he could find Summer then as Alex then went to an old school computer and then Alex hooked his watch to pay his plane ticket and then the watch controlled the cameras and saw Summer heading to the east gate then as Alex got his ticket and then he started running then Alex got on metro transit train that goes to east side of the airport then Alex got off at that stop and then Alex was still looking around to see if he could find Summer anywhere then as Alex got to gate number where Summer was going he then gave his ticket to the flight attendant and head to his cabin number row in the plane

then as Alex got on the plane he then sat in cabin number 604 and he was sitting on the 3rd seat in the row he was then staring at Summer as she was about to get in her seat then Alex fell asleep as the plane was about to take-off Alex was thinking about Summer and there was nobody in his row then Alex looked at his window and then as Alex was about to go to the bathroom then as Alex got out of the bathroom then a random double agent showed up and he was wearing a suit and he also had a gun "MUAHAHAHAHAHAH GOOD EVENING MR.AUSSMEN!!!" the agent said "NOW MOVE OR A SHOT IN THE HEAD!!!" the agent said then as Alex was moving he then looked at the person gun from in back of him "KEEP MOVING!!" he yelled then a lot of people on the plane where looking at Alex and they were scared then Alex was taken to the pilots room then a man with a cane then looked at Alex "hello young man Alex Aussmen if that's right is it not" he said "great that you can join us get his ID" the old man said "put her hands in your pockets" the agent said then as the agent was looking at his ID then Alex then whacked the agent in the face then Alex ducked and used right forearm and body slammed the agent then Alex then punched him in the face then Alex grabbed his ID and started running "STOP HIM!!" the old man yelled then the two agents started shooting pistols at Alex then Alex got out his PP7 gun and hid in back of a row and started shooting back them then Alex hid a again then the old man went up to Alex and grabbed Alex by the neck and slammed against the floor "I HAVE HAD ENOGUH YOU

STUPID RESOUESE AGENT NO MORE GAMES YOU STPUID SPEAICL ED.STUDENT FROM TAHOMA NOW DIE!!!!" he yelled then the old man was about punch Alex in the face and then Alex then grabbed his riest and twisted his arm "AHHHHHHHHHHHHHHHHH!!!" he yelled then Alex punched him in the face and he was knocked out then Alex noticed that emergency door was open then Alex grabbed a par shot and jumped out of the airplane then Alex was sky diving then Alex was falling down through the sky Alex then started falling faster and faster and then as Alex was falling out of the skies and then Alex noticed that he was going to land in a backyard with a swimming pool and a hot tub and also a yard too then Alex started yelling

then Alex then landed as he pulled the shot Alex then landed in the back yard and fell flat on his face then Alex got up and wondered where he was and then Alex looked around and then Alex with no common sense went around lock rooms even the girl's look room and then as Alex got out Alex found a photo then Alex grabbed the photo and it was a picture of Fran Tarkenton in his Minnesota Vikings uniform "HOLY SHIT!!!!" Alex yelled in shock "WHAT THE HELL ARE YOU DOING IN MY HOUSE!!!!!" a loud voice said then Alex turned back "you better have some answers young man" he said "Fran what's going on down there?!" his wife said "nothing honey" Fran said "you have to get out of here quickly son" Fran said then Fran and Alex got of Fran's house and Fran drove Alex out of the neighborhood like he was never there in the first place "anyway son usually I would call the police on people who broke into my house you seem like a nice guy what's your name dude" Fran said "Alex Aussmen" Alex said "I like your last name it sounds adventurous" Fran said "so how in the hell did you get in my house" Fran asked "well sir I was on my way to Chicago and then some double agents or something like almost kidnapped me and so then I had to escape by jumping out of the plane with a Para shoot and then I landed in your house sir and I'm so sorry sir please don't press any charges" Alex said "so where are you from Alex" Fran asked "well sir I'm from Seattle, Washington" Alex said "I know that city it's pretty nice but rainy to" Fran said "that's why they have the Kingdome" Fran said "wait the Kingdome?" Alex said "yeah where Seahawks play football at I played football myself but I played for the Vikings in the 70's and the 60's too" Fran said "so where too" Fran said "well first of all where we are?" Alex asked "well we just left Benson and now heading to Minneapolis" Fran said "okay Mr….." Alex said "Trakenton" Fran said "wait are you Fran Trakenton?" Alex asked "yeah" Fran said "it's such an honor to meet you sir can I have your attagraghic?" Alex asked "sure son" Fran said then as he was signing a football in the car they then as they got to Minneapolis Fran then dropped off Alex around a hotel "thanks sir" Alex said "don't mention it" Fran said

Chapter 3 finding Summer

Then Alex then looked at the hotel and the hotel was very tall then Alex checked into the hotel and then Alex got a suite in the hotel then some strange thugs there

former Tahoma transition where spying on Alex by using Security and there were 3 of them one was skinny and had brown hair, one was tall and muscular and had black eye and the last one was scarred up and didn't even look anything like other Transition students he looked very scary for a transition student he had eye glasses and had zits on his forehead and had a Mexican mustache and he was leader of the group and then the other one was had brown hair and he was skinny but he looked more normal then the rest "we have targeted Mr.Aussmen" one of them said "GREAT NOW FIND MR.AUSSMEN AND BRING HIM TO ME ALIVE AND WE WILL TORCHER AND KILL HIM!!!!" the scary one said "but McClues what floor does he stay on" the one with brown hair said "around 9th floor" he said then as Alex got to his hotel room he then started thinking about Summer then Alex's hotel phone started ringing then Alex answered the phone "hello?" Alex said "oh hey Alex it's summer so whats up" Summer said "oh nothing much where are you?" Alex asked "oh I'm St. Paul do you want to go out to dinner with me tonight?" Summer asked "sure I'll be there" Alex said "awesome" Summer said "I'll see you in a little bit Summer" Alex said then Alex hanged up the phone and Alex bought a white suit with a sliver tie and sliver shoes and then Alex then called for a taxi and Alex headed to St. Paul Minnesota then Alex saw a fancy restaurant in the capital then found the restaurant and got out of the cab and started waiting for Summer "hey Alex" Summer said then Alex saw Summer in a blue dress and she had red lip stick on then Alex kept on staring at Summer "wow" Alex said then Summer ran up to Alex and hugged him and kissed him on the lips then Alex and Summer went into the 360 restaurant in Minnesota then inside there was dinning and then in the 2nd floor there was dancing then after they ate Alex and Summer went to the 2nd floor and then Alex started dancing and spinning around and he did his disco moves on the dance floor and they where playing "baby be mine" by Michael Jackson then Alex jumped in the air and then Alex started shaking his body and then Alex clapped once then Alex snapped his fingers and moved his hands then Summer danced with Alex then Alex grabbed her hand and spined Summer then Summer moved her long brown hair back and forth and then Summer moved her hands and then she did disco moves then Alex did the tango then Alex spined Summer again then Alex spined 3 times and then Alex lowed Summer "atta boy man!!" the crowd yelled then Alex and Summer did a kiss sign to end the dance then crowd on the dance floor started clapping "wow boy that was bad-ass!!" the DJ said then Alex and Summer headed off the dance floor and to a bar table "that was some impressive dancing" the bartender said "thanks sir" Alex said "so what can I get for you two" the bartender said "2 beers please" Alex said then the bartender brought them 2 beers for Alex and Summer and then Alex and Summer drank the beers "that was so amazing how can you do that?" Summer said "I don't know Summer it just comes natural to me" Alex said then as Summer had a couple of drinks and then Alex got out of the Nightclub and then Alex called a taxi and then Alex and Summer got to the hotel Alex was staying in then Alex and Summer got to Alex's hotel room then Summer started smooching Alex on the lips then Summer then took off her dress and then Summer then took her bottoms off and then Alex kept on kissing Summer then Summer then put her arms around Alex then Summer was feeling Alex's back like crazy then Summer then rest her head on Alex's right shoulder then Summer kept on kissing Alex and still kept smooching him "oh Alex baby" Summer said

Chapter 4 the FRAD group

then Alex got up Alex then went to take a shower and then as Alex got out of the shower then Summer was still sleeping then as Alex was getting dressed Alex then found a piece of paper that Summer and Alex where invited to a party in Chicago, Illinois then Alex kept on looking at it

then as Alex was looking at the invitation then 4 Transition thugs where spying on Alex looking at the paper then Alex wrote a note to Summer that he was going on a walk then Alex went downstairs and then one of the doorman told Alex that his Lamborghini Countach was here then Alex went into the car and then as Alex left then one of Transition thugs then used a taser and tasered the doorman and stole his car and then they went to go fallow Alex then as Alex was driving to St. Paul then as Alex was driving he then noticed that the hotel car has been fallowing the car then Alex started speeding and then Alex started driving really fast and then Alex took a right turn into Minneapolis then Alex started driving faster and then Alex locked back and then the 3 transition thugs started shooting ZMG guns at Alex then as Alex was driving he then pressed a button by his radio in his car and Alex then pressed the green button and then machine guns started firing back at them then Alex took a right turn into downtown in Minneapolis and started driving around downtown and around the city too then Alex then took a U turn and then his car went off a ramp and then as the car went off the ramp then Alex then drove by the capital judge house then Alex parked his car by court house and headed inside the court house and got out his PP7 gun and started shooting at the FRAD thugs "boss Aussmen is escaping" the thug with brown hair said "I'll lock up the court house" McClues said then Alex headed inside and then Alex started running he then kept shooting back then Alex looked at his watch and noticed that Michael was trapped in court room about to get sent to Tahoma Transition by a FRAD agent then Alex found out what the number of the courtroom was then Alex used a code disable clock to crack the code on the door then Alex sneaked in and pulled a ZMG gun and then hid behind a wall

then as Michael was hand cuffed by the FRAD agents in the courtroom then a FRAD agent was walking out of the courthouse then Alex punched him in the face "IT'S AUSSMEN KILL HIM!!!" the FRAD agent said then Alex shot all the agents with his ZMG gun and they where all dead then Alex ran to Michael "are you okay Michael" Alex said "I'm fine Alex thanks for saving me bro" Michael said "what the hell did those guys want with you Michael" Alex said "I don't know I was sleeping back in Seattle then the next thing I knew I was kidnapped in a sliver container and I was stuck in there for 2 days" Michael said "well lets go dude" Alex said then Alex and Michael then started running then more FRAD thugs started showing up then

Alex pulled out his ZMG gun and started shooting at the FRAD thugs then Alex and Michael started running then Alex and Michael got outside and go into Michael and then Alex started his car and then back out and then he put the car on drive and then started driving and he also started speeding then the FRAD agents chased Alex then Alex pressed a button in his car that got out the machine guns that fried at the FRAD cars then Alex took a right turn into Minneapolis, Minnesota then Alex started driving "there catching up Alex" Michael said "just hang in there Michael" Alex said as he was driving then Alex the took out his ZMG gun and started shooting at the FRAD thugs then Alex took a right turn into Minneapolis then Alex pulled out a grenade and threw the grenade at the FRAD car and then 5 FRAD agent cars exploded then Alex kept on driving and then Alex then found a parking spot by the hotel he was staying in

then Alex and Michael then got out of the car and then they started inside the hotel then they went inside an elevator and then as Michael and Alex were in the elevator Michael then pressed a button in the elevator "so what floor do you stay on" Michael asked "on the 7th floor dude" Alex said then as Michael and Alex where waiting the elevator then stopped at the 7th floor then Alex and Michael then got out of the elevator and then got into Alex's hotel room then as they walked in Summer was still asleep "is that the hot girl you where with 4 days ago?" Michael said "yeah thats her" Alex said "wow awesome Alex she is hot" Michael said then Michael then took a shower because he really smelled from being looked in the FRAD cell in their hideout

then Michael got out of the shower Summer then got up "Alex oh my god I haven't seen you all day so what where you doing all day" Summer said "it's a long story" Alex said then Michael came into the room "anyway Summer this is my friend Michael, Michael this is Summer" Alex said "pleasure to meet you Michael" Summer said "Michael you gotta tell us how you got kidnapped from this group and what did you do to them" Alex said "I don't know what they wanted from me but one thing that was really bad is that they wanted to kill you Alex and they want to kidnap your friends such as me" Michael said "so where did they lock you up" Alex asked "well when I was in the hotel in Seattle the group I think they where called the "FRAD" group and then they gave me a shot and then I don't remember anything else but I do remember this though I remember getting up and they where talking about you and saying that they wanted to steel your identity and your worse then FRAD and there also responsible for putting you in Special Ed. when you where in high school and Alex you're not a Special Ed. kid" Michael said "WHAT!!!!?" Alex yelled "so my high school Special Ed.life was a total lie!!!!....I doesn't believe this Michael I've been running from RAD for nothing just because they wanted to lock me in Transition just because my hospital file was a fake this is terrible Michael we have to do something!!!" Alex yelled "don't worry Alex where going to get this set right" Michael set "well where is this FRAD group?" Alex asked "their headquarters are in Chicago you can try to sneak into their hideout once we get there but knowing your luck FRAD will find you" Michael said "but what about you Michael" Alex asked "no I'm just like you" Michael said then later at night time Alex, Michael, and Summer then drove to Chicago to go find the FRAD building then as they got there Michael then found a basement then Alex and Michael set everything else and the computers there as well and Alex and Michael where all set

Chapter 5 the party in the FRAD headquarters

Then as night time came the next day Alex and Summer went to the FRAD party to find any information about FRAD and see what they were hiding and what their plans were then as Alex and Summer came into the party Alex had a suit with a black suit jacket, and a gold tie and his disco shoes then as Alex went in a person said he could come in then as Alex was looking around as he was in the party then he notices some people that where there were in their 30's and Alex noticed that Summer and him where only the ones that where youngest couple at the party then as Alex was looking around then McCracken came in he then found Alex "oh Mr.Aussmen such a pleasure to meet you" McCracken said "nice to meet you too Mr. McCracken" Alex said "I have herd soooooo much about you Mr.Aussmen" McCracken said "so who do you work for Mr.Aussmen?" McCracken said "it's a secret" Alex said then McCracken then looked up stairs "it was a pleasure to meet you Mr.Aussmen" McCracken said then he went to one of his thugs "look in his files and see if this is the real Alex Aussmen" McCracken said "I'm on it boss" the thug said

Then Alex started dancing as people started dancing and doing his old disco moves and then Summer started dancing with Alex then Alex did the tango then Alex snapped his fingers and then started spinning around in circles then Alex did a back flip then raised his number one finger then Summer ran to Alex then Alex spined her then Alex jumped in the air and then did a cartwheel and moved his hands left and right and he also moved his feet then Alex clapped his hands and then rolled his hands then did his disco moves and then lowered himself and pointed a Summer and sharked his body and then started spinning around for minutes and then the song ended and then everybody in the party started clapping "ah very good Mr.Aussmen I see you're a great dancer" McCracken said and I see you have a really beautiful girlfriend as well I know you had many over the years" McCracken said "what?" Alex said "oh I know a lot about you Alex" McCracken said then Alex and Summer then got some Champaign then as Alex was drinking his Champaign Michael then talked to him on his ear phone "talk to me" Alex said then back at the basement Michael was on his computer looking at the hole party "Alex I got some news McCracken is having a race in downtown Chicago you should try to go there and find out why he doing that" Michael said "don't worry I will" Alex said

Then the next day Alex then went to downtown Chicago and found a raceway then as he looked at the raceway and saw all the cars going on the track then Alex saw McCracken with his thugs loading up bombs to his hideout then Alex found racing car then Alex pulled out his PP7 gun then opened the door and then punched the racer in the head and shot him with his PP7 pistol then Alex started driving then he got into McCracken's hideout then Alex got out of the car and then Alex realized he was in an elevator then as the elevator stopped Alex then sneaked into the lobby and then Alex realized that a guard was coming by then Alex then took out his PP7 gun and shot him and then Alex started running and he wanted to find out where McCracken's office then Alex noticed that some of the thugs where heading to 12th floor in the building then Alex went to the 12th floor and then Alex found out what McCracken's evil plan was to steal money from hospitals and making fake files on new born babies and fake details and the worst thing he was trying to do create a bunch of copy cats of Alex running around stealing money from the state of Illinois and also the worst of all McCracken is also responsible for putting Alex in Special Ed. in middle school in 1972 and Alex wanted revenge then Alex noticed that the money was going into a safe and also McCracken also wants to create fake military equipment for destruction

Then Alex started running then some of the thugs found Alex and started chasing him "CODE RED!!!! AUSSMEN IS IN THE BUILDING!!!!" the FRAD agent said then Alex kept on running then Alex slided through under a thug and shot him in the face then Alex started running faster and faster than Alex reloaded his pistol and started shooting at more thugs then as Alex was in the elevator then without knowing McCracken then walked into the elevator "hello Alex" McCracken said them McCracken then took out a gun and shot a tranquilizing gun and shot Alex in the arm then Alex's body then started shaking and Alex fell a sleep

Then minutes later Alex then woke up tied up and then McCracken was starring at Alex with an evil smile "good evening Mr.Aussmen muahahahaha" McCracken said "I should of known it was you the hole time" Alex said "correct Alex "so what are you using the money for?" Alex asked "just using to destroy major cities with Military equipment and using them to destroy file holders in the nation's capital and steel social security numbers and in short Mr.Aussmen make a lies just like I did with you muahahahaha" McCracken said "your insane that will never work McCracken!!" Alex said "then I will use the destruction and make my own raceway that will burn the buildings and already one is heading to our hometown Seattle, Washington and NOW IS TIME TO FINSH YOU OFF ALEX AUSSMEN!!!" McCracken yelled then McCracken then tried stab Alex with a knife then Alex untied himself and then Alex kicked McCracken in the face and then started running out of the entrance "GET HIM!!!!" McCracken yelled then bunch FRAD thugs started going after Alex then Alex remembered that the shoes Alex where roller skates then Alex pressed a button that made the wheels rise up then Alex started to skating he then got out a rocket launcher and started shooting it at the thugs then everybody and everything started exploiting then as the place started fallowing apart then Alex found the garage and then Alex pressed a button on his watch that powered the car then Alex's car started driving itself but then Alex didn't know was that Michael was driving the car with a remote back in his hideout Alex and him where in then as the car showed up Alex got into the car then Alex pressed the button on the shoes that made the shoes hide skating the wheel then Alex pressed the pedal and then started driving and then Alex pressed a button in his car that fired machine guns at the FRAD thugs then Alex took out his rocket launcher and then blew the door down and then Alex started heading back to his hotel then Alex's screen was ringing then Alex pressed the button and then McCracken appeared on Alex's screen "Mr.Aussmen I'm afraid you have 19 million things that belong to me" McCracken said "I don't owe you anything YOU JACK ASS!!!!!!" Alex said "oh really Mr. Aussmen well you have 2 things my hotel and Summer Night way and oh yes I know all about her Mr. Aussmen" McCracken said then his screen went off and Alex kept on driving

Chapter 6 the Runaway Nightway

Then as Alex got back to his hotel in Chicago he then took the elevator to his hotel room and then Summer then was laying on Alex's bed "hello Alex" Summer said "hey" Summer said then as Summer went up to Alex she then put her long arms around Alex and then started smooching him on the lips and then Summer took off Alex's shirt off and then she took off Alex's pants off as well then Alex took Summer's strap dress off and then the next morning their clothes and their underwear where on the floor and then Summer laid on Alex's chest and kissed him everywhere "Alex do you like being in Seattle" Summer asked "It okay sometimes" Alex said then Summer got up without putting on a towel to cover her nudity and then she took a shower then as Alex was on the bed Alex was starting to think then Summer then did a come here sign with her finger then Alex then started heading to the shower then Alex went inside the shower then Summer pressed the button that turned the shower then Summer started making out with Alex in the shower and started touching Alex

then as Alex and Summer where making out then some FRAD thugs broke into their hotel then Alex started realizing it then Alex loaded up his gun and started shooting the gun at the FRAD thugs "Summer duck!!" Alex yelled then Summer ducked and hid in back of the dead and then Alex kept on shooting at the thugs then Summer was getting grabbed by the thugs "Alex help me" Summer said "Summer!!" Alex yelled then Alex even with no clothes on he kept on shooting at the thugs and started shooting at the thugs then one of the thugs then knocked out Alex and Alex was knocked out and was butt naked then as Alex got up he then stole some clothes in closet in the hotel room he was staying in then Alex went back to his hotel room and started packing his clothes and then Alex checked out of the hotel in Chicago then as Alex was driving he then saw the the FRAD thugs put Summer in the trunk and she was naked in the trunk of the car then Alex pressed a button that started shooting at the car then Alex started fallowing the car then the FRAD car started going on a freeway that Alex had never seen before and it was called "the runaway Nightway" then Alex put the pedal to the medal and started speeding and went on that freeway and the freeway was heading to Downtown Seattle then Alex started going faster and faster then started shooting at the other FRAD cars he was chasing then without realizing it Alex was started getting chased by more FRAD cars then Alex pulled 4 grenades and threw them in back at them and blew up the rest of the FRAD cars then Alex chasing the FRAD car that had Summer in the car then Alex started going faster then in 34 minutes he was in Montana then Alex didn't know how he was going past the states so fast then Alex found out that he was in fast force field that was making the cars go faster to like 400 miles per hour then Alex kept driving he then saw the space needle and then Alex saw the thugs where about to get off of the Runaway Night way freeway then Alex looked 10 seconds head and then Alex then a sharp turn into downtown Seattle and then started heading to McCracken's lair in downtown Seattle

then Alex parked his car around McCracken's building then a bunch of FRAD thugs started shooting at Alex then Alex got out an A33 riffle and started shooting at the FRAD thugs and hid behind a wall then Alex started shooting at them crazy then Alex started running to the elevator and then Alex pressed the 34th floor in McCracken's building and then as Alex got to the floor he then started looking for Summer

then as McCracken entered the building the FRAD thugs took Summer to McCracken's office "hello Mrs. Night way so where's Mr.Aussmen" McCracken said "I will never tell you" Summer said then McCracken went up to Summer "do you know what plan will be Miss Nightway" McCracken said then McCracken then pressed a button that showed downtown Seattle "you see Miss Nightway I plan will be to destroy downtown Seattle cause medical Farad on new borns braking into their birth certificates and writing disabilities that our lies and then I will also steel money from hospitals around the country even in Canada and build military equipment that will brake into federal files placements in Washington D,C and no one will stop me" McCracken said "your insane" Summer said "oh yes I am miss Nightway muahahahahahah" McCracken said "so what do you want with me?" Summer said "I believe you have someone name Alex that belongs to me" McCracken said

then Alex started running to find Summer and Alex found McCracken's office and then Alex broke into his office "Summer!!" Alex yelled "Alex! Are you alright" Summer asked then McCracken then pulled at knife and then started heading towards "ALEX LOOK OUT!!" Summer yelled then Alex ducked and then got punched in my face "I WILL FINSH YOU OFF THE WAY I BEGAN WITH YOUR PATHIC HIGH SCHOOL LIFE YOU STUPID SPEICAL ED. SECERT AGENT SON OF A BITCH!!!" McCracken yelled then McCracken then started whacking the knife at Alex then Alex ducked then Alex punched McCracken in the face then kicked him in the face and then grabbed him and then threw him against the wall "YOU FOOL I WILL KILL YOU ONCE AND FOR ALL MR.AUSSMEN!!!" McCracken said then McCracken then then started doing fight moves and then Alex avoid his attacks as much as he can then McCracken then jumped in the air and then Alex was then looking around to try to find him then as Alex was looking around then McCracken then tackled Alex from behind and slammed on the ground and then pulled out his knife "YOUR TOO LATE AGAIN MR.AUSSMEN!!!! IT'S SUCH A VERY BAD HABIT TO FAIL WHEN YOUR FIGHTING AND I WILL BE SUCH A BLAST!!!" McCracken said then Alex found a wire on the ground "I believe your about to meet your end McCracken" Alex said then Alex punched him in the face and then grabbed the electric wire and started electrocuting him for 10 minutes then Alex grabbed Summer "come on" Alex said

then Alex and Summer started running after the building then Alex set a building then Alex cared Summer in his arms and then Alex took an elevator then Alex found an elevator and Alex broke into an elevator and then he pressed a button his watch that disabled the money transferring to McCracken's building and then not only that but then Alex in a way to make sure that there was no more medical Fraud anymore and also Alex cleared his files and his name

Chapter 7 the party in downtown Seattle

Then as the building exploited Alex and Summer then hid behind Alex's car and then headed off to a hotel in downtown Seattle then as Alex and Summer got into the hotel they then found cash in their trunk then later that day Alex then had a party and had a bunch of friends and there was dancing there aswell then Alex looked around he then found Michael and Owen and hanged out with them then as he was with Michael and Owen he then saw Summer in a golden dress with golden heels and she had red lip stick "you want to dance Mr. Aussmen" Summer said then Alex got up and started dancing with Summer and they did the tango then as they where dancing she put her hands around Alex and then Alex picked her up and then Alex kept spinning her around and kept chuckling then she kept smooching Alex then Alex was kissing her in front of the full moon for the rest of the night "it might be time to go home in like 4 days Alex said "oh Alex" Summer said

The Stars Of Love

The Stars Of Love

By: Nelson Amador

Chapter 1 Denver Colorado 1986

 It was a very snow day in Denver and Alex was driving his 1986 Ford mustang and then as Alex was driving he then got to a hotel in the city and then Alex found a parking spot around the hotel and then Alex went into the hotel and he started heading to the lobby and then as Alex was in line Alex saw a beautiful girl that was walking through the hotel and she was wearing a very beautiful snow suit and she also had ice skates that where sliver and gold and then she started walking to her car and then she started heading towards the rocky mountains to practice ice skating then as Alex got in front of the line he then rang the bell on the conserirses table "good evening my name is Aussmen, Alex Aussmen I believe you have a resveration for me" Alex said "oh yes we do Mr.Aussmen you will be staying on the 29the floor enjoy your stay Mr.Aussmen" the doormen said "thank you" Alex said

 Then Alex took the elevator and he got to his hotel room and as he got to his hotel room he then opened the door and his hotel room was huge and there was a very nice fire place and there was 6 sofas and very big TV and there was a huge window that had a great view of city of Denver,Colorado and as Alex looked at the buildings and then Alex looked at his bedroom and he had a huge bedroom and then Alex looked at his bathroom and the bathroom was just really gorgeous and the bathtub was really huge and the shower looked awesome and then as Alex was done looking at the house he then found a snowboard in his closet and then Alex went back to the lobby and he started heading to the rocky mountains and as Alex got to the snow resort and then Alex found a parking spot and then as Alex got out of the car he then looked and he had lift pass that said his name and everything and then Alex got out of the car and he then Alex went to go look for lift chair and then as Alex was in line he then got on the lifting chair and as Alex was on the lifting chair he saw the view of the mountains and then as Alex was dropped off Alex started snowboarding on the rocky mountains

 Then as Alex was snowboarding then a couple of thugs in black snow suits started chasing Alex down the mountain and then as Alex was snow boarding he then noticed right away and then Alex did a backflip off a jump and then a missile came out of one of his boats and fired at one of the thugs and then more thugs started chasing him and then some of thugs started shooting at him with PP7 guns and then Alex dodged the shots and then Alex used his spy watch and he fired translating bullets that fired at the thugs then the thugs got knocked out then Alex saw another jump and then Alex did a very huge jump and then as Alex landed he then pressed a button his snow board and then his snowboard and then his snowboard went really fast with a very huge boast and then as Alex was going very fast then more thugs started chasing him then Alex got out a huge sniper riffle and as Alex was on the snowboard he then fired one of the sniper riffles at 4 thugs in the head and then Alex pressed the boat button and he started going faster and faster and then 4 more thugs kept on chasing Alex and then reloaded his sniper riffle and then shot the 4 of the thugs in the head and then another knife tried to whack Alex in the face but then Alex ducked and then tripped and then Alex punched him in the face and then threw him in the snow and then Alex started going really fast on his snowboard and then Alex saw a really big cliff and then Alex jumped off the cliff and then as Alex jumped off the cliff he then started sky diving and then as Alex was sky diving Alex then got out his pra shoot and then Alex started gliding down then as Alex was gliding down then for no reason there was an exploation that ricked up his sky diving and then Alex was falling really fast and "AHHHHHHHHHHHHHHHHHHHHHHHHHHHHHHH AWWWWWWWWWWWWWWWWWWWWWWWWWWWWWWWWWWW WWWWWWWW AWWWWWWWWW" Alex screamed and then Alex fell flat on his face on a flat on a para shoot rescuer device that they used in movie stunts and then Alex fell off the rescuer Matt and then fell flat on his face in the snow then one of snow rescuers went up to him "are you alright you bro?" one of the rescuers said and then Alex was still knocked out for 17 seconds without moving his entire body and then Alex started getting up and then started scratching his head and then as Alex was getting up he then saw the ice skater getting into the lockeroom in the sky resort and then Alex started fallowing her

Then as Alex got in there he then went into the men's locker room and found a bathing suit in the locker room and then Alex put the bathing suit on then as Alex was putting on the bathing suit he then saw the ice skater and then Alex saw her going in the hot tub and then Alex started starring at her and she was so beautiful she was really fit, her hair was blonde and brown and curly, and she had really sparkling sliver eyes and she also had on red lipstick on her lips and then as Alex got on his bathing suit he then dived into the swimming pool and then he started swimming under water and as Alex was swimming under water he put both of his hands behind his head like was laying down on his bed and then as Alex got his head to surface and he then got up and then sat on the cement floor the ice skater girl started smiling at Alex "that was a really awesome dive you did" she said "oh thanks" Alex said "so you do like going swimming?" she asked him "oh yes I do" Alex said "so where are you from?" she asked "oh I'm from Seattle" Alex said "oh that's really awesome I hear it's a really nice" she said "yeah it is" Alex said "I'm Hannah by the way" Hannah said "I'm Aussmen......Alex Aussmen" Alex said "awesome name I like it" Hannah said "oh thanks" Alex said "so what hotel are you staying at?" Alex asked "well I might be staying at a hotel in downtown Denver" Alex said "what about you" Alex asked " I think I might be staying around the snow resort" Hannah said "that's awesome so how long have you been ice skating" Alex asked "oh since I was little" Hannah said "oh that's awesome" Alex said then as Alex was in the hot tub Hannah smiled at Alex and then she sat by him in the hot tub "so where do you want to stay at my hotel tonight?" Alex asked "oh sure" Hannah said "so Hannah do you have a last name?" Alex asked "oh yes I do Alex it's stars" Hannah said "awesome baby it's sounds very Groovy baby girl" Alex said "oh thank you" Hannah said then as Hannah was in the hot tub with Alex then Hannah started making out with Alex in the hot tub and then as Alex was making out with her Alex then but his hands on her waist "...do you want to get out of here" Alex asked

 Then later that night Alex and Hannah then headed to Alex's hotel in downtown Denver and then as they got into Alex's hotel room Hannah really loved his hotel room "oh my god is this your hotel room?" Hannah asked "oh yes baby girl it is" Alex said then Hannah really started getting very exciting and then she started running to the bed room and then Hannah then took off her clothes till she was in her underwear and then Alex hanged up his snow jacket and then started walking to the bed room as Alex got to the bed room Alex saw hannah in his bed room in his bed and as Hannah was in Alex's bed with a huge smile on her face then Alex took off his shirt and his pants off and then went under the covers with Hannah in his underwear and then he started kissing Hannah "I'm going to see that I might go on very sparkling ride" Alex said jokingly then Hannah did a very sexy laugh and then as Alex was making out with Hannah they then fell off the bed "oooooooooooh" Hannah said as they fell off the bed.

Chapter 2 getting to know Hannah Stars

Then the next morning Alex and Hannah laid next to each other on the bed "oh my god you where wild last night" Hannah said then Alex looked at Hannah with the feeling he did something wrong "really? I didn't think I was that wild" Alex said "yeah but you were and your like a crazy wild sexy dog" Hannah said "oh thanks" Alex said then they both paused "so what are you doing today?"Alex asked "I don't know I think I might be ice skating today" Hannah said "oh really that sounds awesome are you a pro ice skater?" Alex asked "yeah a little bit" Hannah said "not to make you feel strange or anything but....I think your the most beautiful ice skater I have ever seen" Alex said "oh thank you" Hannah said

Then Hannah looked at the clock and then Hannah got up and then she took a shower and then as she was taking a shower Alex got up and then used the shower in the other room in the hotel room and then as Alex was done taking a shower Alex walked with Hannah to the lobby in the hotel "so do you need me to drive you?" Alex asked "oh yes please thank you Alex" Hannah said "your welcome baby" Alex said then as they where about to walk to the parking lot Hannah realized that she forgot her ice skates "oh shit I forgot my ice skates upstairs" Alex said "don't worry I will go get them" Alex said

Then Alex went back to his hotel room and then he found Hannah's ice skates in the hotel room by the bed then Alex went back to the lobby and then gave the ice skates to Hannah "oh thank you Alex" Hannah said then Hannah hugged Alex really tight then later that day Alex drove to Hannah to the snow resort around the rocky mountains and then as Alex got there he parked his car and then hannah got out of Alex's car and then she started running to the ice rink and then she started ice skating and then as she was on the ice rink in the snow resort Hannah started working on her tricks and then she did a lot of spins and then she did another trick where she jumped up the air and landed with one foot and then she continued ice skating and doing new tricks and then Alex started watching her ice skate with a smile on his face and to Alex watching her ice skate was like watching diamond bend done and then as Alex was watching he then took out his 1979 camera and started taking pictures of Hannah ice skating and then Alex was taking pictures of her he then saw some guys in black snow jackets go into lifting container that took them all the way to the rocky mountains and then without them knowing Alex took pictures of them and he took 4 photos of them going in the lifting container then as Alex was done taking pictures he then drove to downtown Denver to go look around the city like go in the malls, Alex also went to check out the republic pizza building and he also took a picture of the building as well and as he was also on one of the bike trails as well and as Alex was walking on the bike trail he then found a golden gem on the ground and then Alex looked at it and then Alex put it in his pocket and then took a picture of it

Then as Alex took the gem there was a camera that was spying on Alex walking around the trail and then from another building in downtown Denver there was 4 men in gold and silver suits that where in the republic building and they saw the footage of Alex "golden, we saw one of the gem steelers" one of the guards said then a man wearing all gold and even gold dress shoes went up to the computer screen and looked at Alex's face on the screen "well then we will find out who that man is and if he finds more of them we will make sure he never leaves this city alive" he said then the man walked to his desk and looked at his golden watch and then he did an evil smile and then he looked at the window with an evil look on his face

Then Alex went back to his hotel room around snow resort and then as he got there he then sat on his couch and then he found a note on his hotel table and then the note said "look at the window." and then Alex looked at the window and then Alex saw Michael climbing up the hotel and then Alex shot right up to the roof "yeeeeeeeeeeeha!!!!" Michael screamed and then Alex opened the window and looked out the window and he saw nothing and then Michael zoomed back down and then Michael fell into the hotel room and then Alex was knocked against the wall and then Michael walked to Alex "are you okay dude" Michael said then Alex pulled himself back up "Michael what the he'll are you doing in Denver?!" Alex asked "oh I just here you were here buddy" Michael said "oh that's nice Michael...say you don't know where my girlfriend Hannah is do you bro or where she went?" Alex said "oh you mean the ice skater with curly blonde hair she left around a couple minutes ago dude" Michael said "did she say on where she was going?" Alex said "well my guess Alex is that she went ice skating I think" Michael said "oh thanks Michael" Alex said "so what do you want to do tonight?" Alex asked "well I'm not sure we can go clubbing tonight" Michael said "okay sure we can do that" Alex said

Then Alex and Michael later that day went clubbing around 5:00PM and they headed to downtown Denver and they wait in line it was the new beautiful gold club and it was a big as a normal building and then Alex was wearing a red button up shirt, dark blue jeans, dress shoes and a golden leather coat with shades on his head and Michael on the other hand was wearing crazy brown 80's pants and a very crazy a purple button up shirt with a sliver neck tie, and a blue tennis shoes on and he was also wearing a big huge black and white crazy gangster coat with a big huge black white gangster hat that kind of looked like walt fraizer's hat

Then as Alex and Michael got into the nightclub Alex started dancing and he was on the dance floor dancing like he always has and then Alex was dancing he then do a cartwheel and then Alex did back flip and also Alex did a handstand that lasted 30 seconds then Alex kept moving his hands and then as Alex was dancing then Hannah was hanging out with her fellow skaters and then she saw Alex dancing and then Hannah walked by Alex "Alex?" Hannah said "oh hey what's up" Alex said as he was dancing "how did you find me here?" Hannah said "I didn't know you where" Alex said "so you do you want to dance" Hannah asked "sure of course" Alex said and then Alex started dancing with Hannah started spinning her around and then Alex lowered Hannah "wahooo" Hannah said then Alex started moving his hands and then Hannah's boots turned into roller-skates "you roller skate too?" Alex said "yeah when I don't ice skate" Hannah said "oh baby your good baby girl" Alex said then Alex spinned her around while she was roller skating and then Hannah then did a cartwheel and then their dance was starting to get noticed more and more and a lot of people in the night club started watching them and then so did Michael

Then Alex started moving his feet and then Hannah moving her hands and moving her body and then Hannah did a back flip and then Hannah then put her arms around Alex and then Hannah started moving Alex's hands as they where dancing then Alex did moving his hands and his feet as he was dancing and he also started doing the robot and the wave dance and also his head then Hannah moved her head back in fourth and Alex started moving his hands and then Alex lifted her up and then the whole crowd went nuts and then for the finale Alex did a ton of Alex dance moves and then Alex made one dance move where he did a hand stand with one hand and he spinned himself with one hand then Alex threw himself up in the air and then Alex landed on his feet and then the dance ended with Hannah putting her hands around Alex and then the crowd in the nightclub just went nuts and started clapping

And then Alex and Hannah got off the dance floor and sat a table in the nightclub and then they had a couple of beers and they talked a lot about tons of things "so how long have you been ice skating?" Alex asked "for 6 years" Hannah said "that's awesome" Alex said and then later that night Alex and Hannah started walking around downtown Denver and it was a very beautiful night and they walked on the streets and then they walked by one of the fountains that was in downtown Denver "so do you like Denver?" Alex asked "it's okay to visit but not to live" Hannah said "oh I understand" Alex said then Alex and Hannah looked at the fountain that was by one of the buildings "hey anyway thanks for hanging out with me Alex your a great guy" Hannah said "hey anytime" Alex said then Hannah smooched Alex on the lips for 20 minutes in front of the fountain in downtown Denver and then Alex then fell into the fountain and got really wet and then Alex jokingly grabbed Hannah and they started splashing each other in the water and then Hannah started laughing

But then as they where in the fountain some of the thugs where staring at Alex and then without them knowing the thugs left then later that night Alex and Hannah walked back to Alex's hotel room and then as they where walking back Alex was looking at the stars and then as they got back to the hotel room Alex and Hannah just slow danced in the hotel room "so what are you doing tomorrow?" Alex asked "I think I might be going to skating practice" Hannah said "are you like preparing for a huge game" Alex asked "well I need a ice skating partner for an ice skating rink" Hannah said "well I'm not much of an ice skater but I can try to help you" Alex said "awwww thanks your my diamond your so sweet" Hannah said then Hannah smooched him on the lips

Meanwhile back in downtown Denver Michael was exploring the downtown area as well and he looked all the exciting things and then as he was exploring a bunch of thugs shot a tranklaser at his neck and then Michael fell flat on his face and then the thugs came "tell Golden we have his friend" one of the thugs said then they took Michael in their car and he was kidnapped

And then the next day Alex and Hannah headed to the snow resort to go practice and as Alex was putting ice skates he looked on the ice rink and he started thinking about things like "what if I fail at this" Alex thought then Hannah came to him "remember baby boy just don't think just feel and keep your balance" Hannah said "okay Hannah" Alex said then Alex got on his ice skates and got his snow clothes on and headed outside on the rink

Then Alex and Hannah started ice skating and as Alex was ice skating was trying the best that he could "alright I need to lift me up as high as you can baby" Hannah said then Alex while he was ice skating Alex lifted up Hannah as high as he can and then Alex put her back down and then as Alex was about to fall Alex then did a cartwheel "that was really good" Hannah said and then the next thing they practiced was going at a fast pace and doing landing tricks when ice skating and Alex was really fast at ice skating and he had really good balance and when he ice skated with Hannah and he got most of the ice skating tricks right and when he was going to fall he always did a cartwheel and they would always practice ice skating by roller skating in parks in downtown Denver and Alex loved practicing with Hannah cause she just knew what to do and then they roller skated all around the city and Alex was roller skating and he just went faster and faster and he also jump over benches and he always landed on his feet then as Alex kept going he saw a speed bump and then without thinking Alex jumped over the speed bump and landed on his feet and then Alex started spinning around in circles "you got it your doing great" Hannah said and then Hannah kept on roller-skating and they kept on rollerskating all around downtown Denver and they started heading back to the park

As they got back to the park Alex then took his roller skating "dang that was really good Alex" Hannah said "oh thanks I really thought I was going to suck" Alex said then as Alex was putting on his shoes he herd cars come to park "Alex what is it?" Hannah said "I think someone might be here we gotta get out of here" Alex said then one of the thugs got out of the car and they started shooting at them and then Hannah started screaming "come on" Alex said then Hannah and Alex got into Alex's car and Alex started driving off and then Alex took a right turn to get on the highway to avoid the thugs and then the thugs kept on shooting at them and then Alex took out a PP7 and started shooting at the thugs "Alex what is going on here?" Hannah said "I don't know but these people are after us for some reason that I will find out" Alex said then Alex pressed a button on his car that made the car have oil slick come out of his car and then the oil was on the road and then thugs car started moving back and fourth and then one of the cars crashed into the freeway wall and then another thug took out a sniper riffle and tried to shoot alex in the head but then Alex ducked his head and then Alex took out mine bomb and threw it at the road and then the mine was stuck to the car and then the car blew up and then Alex took a right turn into rocky mountains snow resort and then Alex parked his car right by his hotel room "are you okay Hannah?" Alex said "I'm okay Alex" Hannah said "who where those guys" Hannah said "well I don't know but who ever they I think they might be after me for some strange reason" Alex said "oh baby" Hannah said then Hannah hugged Alex "alright let's just get inside" Alex said "okay baby" Hannah said

Then Alex and Hannah got inside the hotel and went up to Alex's hotel room "so can I get you anything?" Alex asked "just some hot chocolate" Hannah said "okay" Alex said then Alex went to go make some hot chocolate for Hannah and then Alex brought some to her and then Alex sat on the couch with Hannah "Alex I think your going to do really well in ice skating met" Hannah "oh thanks Hannah so when is it?" Alex asked "it's somewhere around next week" Hannah said

And then as Alex and Hannah where sitting down someone knocked on the door "I'll get it" Alex said then Alex went to go get the door and as Alex opened the door owen was at the door "hey Alex what's up?" Owen said "Owen what are you doing here?" Alex asked "oh I'm just on vacation here dude and I have been going skiing too" Owen said "so who is the hot girl" Owen said "oh this Hannah she is my new girlfriend and my ice skating partner" Alex said "oh awesome it's a pleasure to meet you" Owen said "nice to meet you too" Hannah said then as Owen was here they talked for awhile and then Owen left and went back to his hotel room and then as Alex and Hannah were still in the hotel room

Then back at the golden building headquarters in downtown Denver the gold thugs showed golden the footage of Alex in his car "we almost had him boss but for some reason he just escaped" one of the thugs said "not a problem just don't fail me again otherwise I will have other plans for you" Golden said "yes Golden" the thugs said "anyway I will get my gold tuxs ready tomorrow for the fancy party around the jewelry building around downtown Denver and while I am there you guys will look for Mr.Aussmen and bring him to me alive" Golden said "we will do that boss" the thugs said "I HOPE FOR YOUR SAKE YOU ARE RIGHT THIS TIME!!!!!!!!" Golden said "NOW GET THE HELL OUT!!!!!!!!" Golden yelled then the thugs ran out of his office and then golden looked at his golden tuxs and then he looked at his golden jewelry eye patch and then he did a very evil smile

"MUAHAHAHAHAHAHAHAHAHAHAHAHAHAHAHAHAHAHAHAH" Golden
laughed

Then back at the hotel Alex and Hannah were outside looking at the moon outside
"I love looking at the stars" Hannah said "thats awesome I know they are
beautiful" Alex said then Hannah smooched Alex on the lips and then as Hannah
was making out with Alex, Alex then put her hands on her face and Alex saw
Hannah's cute sparkling green and sparkling eyes and then they kept on looking at
the starts "Alex baby what is Seattle?" Hannah asked "oh it's really awesome even
though it's rains a lot but it's a gorgeous city" Alex said "why do you ask baby girl"
Alex said "oh I was just really wondering" Hannah said "so what do you see up
there?" Alex asked "well I like looking for the Greek gods like Hercules,Pegasus,
and alferodati, if you where going to be any Greek god which one would you be?"
Hannah asked "well I don't know I think I would be Hercules" Alex said "hahaha I
would imagine you being Hercules cause your just really sexy and you have a nice
body" Hannah said then Hannah smiled at Alex and did a sexy laugh and then she
put her arms around Alex stomach and laid her head on Alex's chest "I love you
Alex" Hannah said "I love you too Hannah" Alex said then for the rest of the night
they slept outside in sleeping backs outside of the hotel room

 Chapter 3 The star who loved me

Then the next day Alex got up and he was really cold and he took a very warm
shower and then he got on some warm clothes and then as Alex got on warm clothes
Hannah then saw Alex taking a shower and then she took a shower after Alex and
then she put on a pink snow jacket and she was wearing yellow pants and very sexy
pink 80's snow boats "so what are we doing today?" Alex asked "I don't know we
could go snow hiking today" Hannah said "sure let's go" Alex said then Alex
packed food and blankets and some money just in case they need to buy any food
and then around 1:00PM they where off

Also along the hike Alex brought ice skates just in case Hannah wanted to ice skate
and then as they where hiking that day Hannah and Alex just hiked and then during
the Hannah got really tired and then Alex lifted up Hannah and Hannah was in
Alex's arms throughout the whole hike and then as Alex carrying Hannah in his
arms Alex saw all the beautiful trees under the snow and then Alex saw the birds
flying through the air and then as Alex saw them Alex just smiled and then as they
got up the mountain Alex set Hannah on a blanket and then Alex set food and
started making a fire to cook the food Alex brought with him and then as he was
done cooking he then woke Hannah up "are you hungry?" Alex asked "oh yes
please" Hannah said then Alex gave hannah some food "thanks Alex" Hannah said
"your welcome Hannah said" Alex said then Alex and Hannah sat by the fire and

looked at the beautiful view of Denver Colorado "it's very beautiful" Hannah said "I know it is" Alex said "so do you come up here often?" Alex asked "just once in a while" Hannah said

Then Alex and Hannah where on one of the rocky mountains from 7-10PM and they started packing up their stuff "oh my god it's going to be such a hassle getting down there" Hannah said "or no it won't" Alex said "what are you talking about?" Hannah said then Alex picked up Hannah and Hannah was on Alex's back "Alex what are you doing put me down"Hannah said jokingly and then Alex's shoes turned into ice skates "what are you doing?" Hannah asked him "trust me and hold on tight" Alex said then Alex with Hannah on his back Alex started ice skating down the hill on ice "WAHOOOOOOOOOOOOOOOOOOO" Hannah yelled and then as they where getting down the hill Alex pushed a button on his spy watch to make the ice skates slow down and then got down to ski lift and then Alex hanged on to one of the metal bars and then Hannah got off Alex's back and then Alex fell on his back "Alex are you okay" Hannah said then Alex got up back on his feet "I'm okay Hannah I just fell" Alex said then Alex and Hannah ran to the hotel room and then as they where running to the hotel room Alex picked up Hannah in his arms and Hannah started laughing and then as they got into the hotel room Hannah then turned on the radio and started playing music and Alex and Hannah started dancing and rocking out and jumping on the couch and then as Alex was jumping on the couch he saw Hannah's beautiful face and then Alex landed on Hannah they just rested on each other and they started kissing on the couch

But then as they where kissing on the couch, Golden and his thugs saw Alex in his hotel room then Golden did an evil smile "kill him" Golden said then as Alex and Hannah where kissing on the couch then a bunch of thugs broke into hotel room and then Hannah screamed and then Alex turned back and he took out his PP7 gun and started shooting at them and then Alex punched on of them in the face and then as he was fighting one of them then one of the thugs grabbed Hannah and put her in a bag "Hannah!!!!" Alex yelled then another a thug whacked Alex in the face and then the thugs left his hotel room and tour up his hotel room while Alex was knocked out and Hannah was kidnapped

Chapter 4 finding Hannah in downtown Denver and meeting Golden

Then as Alex was knocked out he noticed that Hannah was gone then Alex jumped out the window and he landed on a mustang and then Alex started the car and he started chasing the car and then Alex took a sharp right turn into downtown Denver and then Alex fallowed the car into jewelry diamond and then Alex took a left turn into the garage and then Alex jumped out of the car and pulled out his gun and then a bunch of henchmen started shooting at Alex and then Alex took out an A33 riffle and started shooting at the henchmen and then Alex started running and then he shot one of the henchmen in the hand and then pressed a 69th button to get the 69th floor

Then back on the floor Golden turned back "I see you have his girlfriend" Golden said ".......let..me go" Hannah said "well hello miss stars Im really sorry about all this trouble and I will give you all the jewelry I have" Golden said "what do you want with me?" Hannah said "very good question the reason I want you miss stars is I want to destroy the rocky mountains with my jewelry that I think belongs to me my dear" Golden said then Golden did a very evil laugh with out opening his mouth "and also if you don't give it to me you will die miss stars by my men throwing into my great white shark tank and then your life will be over" Golden said "I'm doing giving it to you" Hannah said "very well..." Golden said then Golden pressed a button that grabbed Hannah by her waist and the machine tied her up and then threw her into a metal cage and then Golden started looking at Hannah's ear rings "MUAHAHAHAHAHAHAHAHAHAH oh yes finally I have this I have been looking for this for 4 decades and now it is mine muahahahaahahahahahahahahah" Golden laughed

Then Alex got to the floor and then he took out his PP7 gun and loaded it up and then saw Hannah in the cage and then as Alex was sneaking up to get Hannah out of the cage Alex got hit in the back of the head with a metal bar by a henchmen and then Alex was tied up on a metal bed "good evening Mr.Aussmen" Golden said then Alex tried to untie himself "don't bother Alex I have golden ropes that I used to take care of you" Golden said "wheres Hannah?!" Alex said "oh she is by the metal cage just about to get thrown by the sharks" Golden said "what is our plan?!" Alex said "oh it's not really much Alex I'm just going to use golden, sliver, rubies, and diamonds to make a gem bomb that will destroy the rocky mountains including the ones that you and your girlfriend went on my boy and also use the gems to bomb the city of Denver and to create a gem city so it will just be my new city and me" Golden said "this will not happen and you will not get away with this!" Alex said "oh foolish Mr.Aussmen I think I will" Golden said then Golden pressed a button that would cause the ropes to electrocute Alex "good bye Mr.Aussmen" Golden said and then the eletrecicty was about to start Alex then used his spy watch to brake through the golden ropes and then Alex got out his PP7 gun and started shooting at the henchmen and then Alex started the running and then he kept on shooting like crazy and then threw grenade and then the grenade blew up and damaged parts of the building and then Alex then took out an A33 riffle and just started shooting at the henchmen like crazy and then Alex broke through door that leads to the sharks room and then Alex saw the Hannah was not in the room and then Alex saw a jet pack and took the jet pack on put on his back and then Alex started flying through the air and then Alex put the cord nets of where Golden might be at and then Alex landed by his other headquarters back the top of the rocky mountains and then sneaked into the building

Then golden tied Hannah on a bed with a bathing suit "now you are beautiful my dear just like a gem" Golden said "you will not get away with this" Hannah said "oh Hannah my dear there is just a lot in this city and I can control" Golden said

Then Alex broke through the back room and then Alex saw an elevator and took it and then as Alex was in the elevator something was on the intercom "your too late Mr.Aussmen this is where you die" Golden said then golden pressed a button to throw Alex into a shark tank and then Alex avoid being thrown out he used his watch to be strapped on to a hook in the elevator and then Golden noticed that Alex did not fall and then Alex showed up with a gun in his hand "Alex what a pleasant surprise I was not expecting to show up" Golden said "where's hannah?!" Alex said "oh she is somewhere around here Mr.Aussmen" Golden said and then as Alex was about to shoot Golden, Golden then shot a rocket launcher at Alex and then Alex avoid the explosion and then Alex shot Golden in the head and then Golden was dead and then Alex shot Golden in the balls and then Alex grabbed his rocket launcher and shot it right at him and then Golden got forced out of the building and then Alex ran to find Hannah and then found her on the couch tied up "Alex" Hannah said "Golden?" Hannah asked "Golden is dead and we will too if we do not get out of here" Alex said then Alex and Hannah started running of the building and then Alex shot one of the controls that would blow up the city of Denver and then Alex used his spy watch to disable the bomb and then Alex and Hannah got on to a snow mobile and then Alex started turning on the snow mobile and then they started going down and then the building exploded and then Alex put the snow mobile on full blast and then Alex got a lot of air and then they landed on to the snow resort entrance and Golden and his henchmen where destroyed and then Alex and Hannah laid by the snow resort "thanks for reusing me Alex" Hannah said "your welcome Hannah" Alex said then for the rest of the afternoon Hannah and Alex laid down on the rest

Chapter 5 the ice skating meet in downtown Denver

 Then the next day was the ice skating met and Alex and Hannah were dressed up in fancy clothes and Hannah was wearing a nice sliver and green dress and then Alex was wearing a black suit with sliver and green neck tie and then they got on their ice skates and waited for their turn to compete in the ice skating dance "alright ladies and gentlemen without further adio let's here for Alex Aussmen and Hannah stars" the announcer said

Then Alex and Hannah started dancing and ice skating and they where playing "more then a women" and it was the Bee gees version and then Alex lowered Hannah as he was dancing and then Alex spinned Hannah around in circles and then Alex ice skated and then he did a huge jump and then Alex put his hands on Hannah's hips and then Alex moved his hands around and then Alex lifted up Hannah and set her down and then Alex ice skated to Hannah and then Alex spinning her around in circles 5 times and then Alex did a disco sign as he was disco sign and then as the dance ended Alex lifted up Hannah and smooched her while he was ice skating and they started spinning around and around and then the dance ended then everybody in the crowd started clapping and going nuts "give it up for Alex Aussmen and Hannah stars" the announcer said then as it was over they got first place and won and Hannah was really excited and so was Alex and then as Alex and Hannah were getting off the ice rink he then saw Michael and Owen "hey guys I'm glad you guys came" Alex said "your welcome you where great out there" Michael said "thanks man" Alex said and then Alex showed Michael and Owen his gold medal and then after Alex hanged out with them Alex then hanged out with Hannah and then as Alex went into the locker room and then Alex saw a note and it said

"look in your hotel room." the note said then Alex headed to his hotel room and then as he got there he then saw Hannah in his bed room under the covers "surprise" Hannah said "oh nice" Alex said then Alex started kissing Hannah on the lips "thanks for helping me win that gold cup Alex" Hannah said "your welcome Hannah" Alex said and then as Alex was making out with Hannah in bed he then saw a stars that where in the sky "001"

"the stars seem pretty beautiful" Alex said "they always will be with you around baby" Hannah said then Alex looked his ice skates and took his gold medal and threw it in one of his ice skates and then he kept on kissing Hannah and then Hannah started laughing and then she took her gold medal off and threw it by Alex's medal and she kept on laughing "oh Alex" Hannah said

Automatic Lover
Arena

Automatic lover

By: Nelson Amador

Chapter 1 Seattle Center 1986

It was a very cloudy and windy day in downtown Seattle people where in rain jackets or sweet shirts and some people where getting off the Seattle Monorail and some people where heading to the fun forest to go on the rides some of them went to look at the EMP theater, pacific science center, and the science fiction museum other people went to go eat food at the Seattle center food court

Then a person dressed in business clothes went into the Seattle center food court and went up to the very top floor and then he went into a room and then there was another person waiting for him "so great that you can see Mr. Kareem what brings you to Seattle center on this very unexacting cloudy day?" his boss said "well I just wanted to give you this" he said "what the hell this is a lot of money Mr.Kareem how in the world did you mange to get this?" he asked "well there is no story really boss I just knew more about your workers then ever and about your daughter" Kareem said "well my daughter is doing fine she lives in this area and she is a Seattle sonic dancer at sonic games at key arena" he said "well Owen is she seeing anyone?" Kareem said "well not that I know of but she was a seeing one of sonic players though I can't remember his name though" he said "well that's funny Owen because last I herd I was dating her..." Kareem said "wait a minute she..." he said then suddenly Kareem got out of his chair and took out a PP7 and shot him in the head and then Kareem shot another office worker in the face and stole his security key and traced the key to find out where Owen's daughter might be then Kareem ran to the elevator and headed out of the food court in Seattle center and he started running to key arena to find his daughter

Later that day the Monorail came back to Seattle center and as Monorail stopped a lot of people came out and Alex was one of them Alex then started walking to key arena for a Seattle Supersonics games and Alex was excited he was a huge sonics fan and on the day sonics won the 1979 NBA championship series Alex and Michael where at Alex's house and there was a huge sonics party at Alex's house around June 1st 1979 and about 58 people where at Alex's house for the party watching the game and when sonics won everybody in Alex's house went crazy and a lot of people where super crazy and drunk and they where drinking beer and after the game Alex and Michael that night went to downtown Seattle to celebrate with the rest of the Seattle Supersonic fans and they went into the bars and just celebrated and they got really drunk and the next day they had a huge hangover and they even went to the Seattle sonics victory parade and they were going nuts and they did more partying and then around June 3rd 1979 they went back to maple valley and headed back to Tahoma to finish their senior and the rest was history

But now it was 7 years later Alex was now 26 years old and was now an undercover secret agent but unlike other agents Alex does not work for any agency such as the CIA ,FBI, nor the NSA or ISS, and he enjoys not working for those agencies and he loves working for himself cause if when ever he solves a crime he atomically gets paid by the police as a reward and they it pays better

Alex then walked in line like everybody else to get into key arena then Alex held out his ticket and then as Alex got to the front of the line he showed the ticket guy his ticket and he went into the arena and found his seat and then he sat down and watched the sonics play

As Alex was sitting down he was watching players practice during the game and saw how they where shooting ball and sometimes when Alex was watching sonics game he would sometimes day dream about what would it be like he was a an NBA basketball player playing for the sonics and in his day dream he would dribbling the ball and scoring 3 pointers and dining through players like Larry Bird, Magic Johnson, and Michael Jordan and he also day dreamed that a lot of sonic players where saying how good he was and how he was a good team mate and they would not know what to do with out him

And then Alex got out of his day dream and then the game started up and basketball horn went off "GOOOOOOO SONICS!!!!!!!!!!!" Alex yelled and then the players intro was about start

"alright get on your feet and let's hear for your Seattle Suuuuuuuuuuuuuuuuuuuuuuuuuuuuuuuuuper sonics...STARTING FOWARD FROM WITCHITA UNIVERSITY NUMBER 34 XAVIER MCDANIEL!!!!!!!!!" then McDaniel came running down the court and getting high fives by his sonic team mates "AT CENTER FROM UTAH NUMBER 24 TOOOOOOOOOOOOM CHAMBERS!!!!!!!!!" then chambers came running on to the court "AT GUARD FROM TENNESSEE NUMBER 3 DAAAAAAAAAAALE ELIS!!!!!!!!!!!!!!!" and then Elis ran on to the court high high diving his teams "and tonight the sonics will face LA lakers!!!!!!!" and then everybody in key arena started booing at pictures of Magic Johnson on the screen "MAGIC SUCKS ASS!!!!!!! GO BACK TO LA YOU STUPID LAKER PIECES OF SHIT!!!!!!!!" one of sonic fans in the stands yelled but Alex just was standing and clapping and then the game was underway

As Alex was watching the game he saw a lot of sonic dancers practing their dance moves and Alex saw a sonic dancer with brown hair and she had a really fit body and her greats were really big and she had a red lipstick on and she was also wearing black sandex on with 80's tennis shoes and then as the sonics got a time out the sonic dancers danced in front of the crowd and started moving their hands and Alex just smiled at them and then he contained watching the game but then as Alex was watching the game Kareem was also at the game and he was staring at Alex and then he had a telescope and he saw one of the sonic dancers dancing "I found my girl" he said then she went up to one of the sonic players and it was sonics player that was I think a back up to Tom chambers and then she kissed him on the lips and then Kareem left the area he was in a disappeared

Then after the game Alex was heading of the game through the lower Queen Ann area and he was about to walk back to his house in Seattle but then one of sonic players came out of key arena out of the locker room and no one noticed probably because was not starter and he might have been a rookie and only Alex saw him "hi are you sonics player?" Alex asked "yeah I am" he said "oh awesome bro I have been a sonics ever since I was a kid and what's your name" Alex asked " I'm drew stoning I'm back up to Tom chambers" drew said "oh that's awesome bro can I have your autograph bro" Alex asked "sure man I it's always nice and actually this is like my first signing with any fan in this city your my first one" Drew said "oh wow that's an honor" Alex said "thanks bro" drew said then as drew was getting done giving Alex his autograph then Kareem took out a sniper riffle and then all of sudden Alex herd a gun shot and then drew was shot "drew are you okay bro.....Somebody help I think somebody got shot" Alex yelled then an ambulance came and then they found out that was one of the sonic players drew stoning and then Kareem was walking into the darkness and Alex saw him walking in the dark in Seattle center.

Chapter 2 Alex's new job

 The next day Alex got up the next morning and he took a shower and then as Alex went downstairs he looked at the Seattle times newspaper and saw the article about Drew's death and then Alex had look of disbelief on his face thinking "how in the hell would anybody want to kill one of the sonic player it just makes no sense" he thought then Alex made himself an egg sandwich and then he got out strawberries, bananas, ice, milk, yogurt, and some tang powered and he put it in the blender and started making himself a smoothy with his egg sandwich and then as Alex was done eating breakfast he then herd a knock at his door and then Alex answered the door and as Alex open the door it was Michael

 "hey Alex how are you doing bro" Michael asked "oh good Michael did you hear about what happened after the sonics game?" Alex said "yeah I herd one of the Seattle sonic players got shot very sad" Michael said "yeah I know I feel bad for his parents man" Alex said "hey I know dude" Michael said "but the good news is that your going to be playing basketball" Michael said "what does that mean?" Alex asked "well since drew has been shot and killed I convinced sonics head couch KC Jones to give you a basketball work out so you can replace drew" Michael said "WHAT?! Are you crazy I can't play in the NBA I'm not even that good I mean I played for fun in high school but I wasn't really good at least tell me what position I'm going to be playing" Alex said "your going to be a center" Michael said "alright cool when is practice?" Alex asked "it's around 1:00 to 5:00" Michael said "oh god" Alex said

 Then around Alex drove to the Seattle sonics practice that was in Seattle and then Alex got out of his car and then went into the locker room and then as Alex went into the locker room then Kareem started starring at Alex "I shot one of the sonics player and your next!!!!" Kareem said

Then as Alex was in the locker room he then looked for his locker and then Alex saw his locker and it said "Alex Aussmen number 31" and then alex started changing into his practice uniform and then as he was changing then the rest of the sonic players and coaches came into the locker room and then as Alex was done getting dressed he then headed to the basketball court and started stretching and then as he was stretching a lot of sonics players just saw him and they asked a lot of questions about him and then sonics head couch KC jones was on the court with his clip board and then the best players on the team just looked at him "who is this guy coach?" Xavier McDaniel asked "oh this our new back up center Alex Aussmen" he said "so where did he play college ball at" Dale Elis asked "well he didn't play college ball but he did go to the university of Washington and graduated from there in 2 years ago" he said

Then practice started with the team doing 30 laps around the court and Alex was good runner and he knew how to pace himself and then the rest of sonic players looked at him in disbelief "what the hell this guys fast" Tom Chambers said "i know bro I don't who this guy but something tells me this guy is in shape I wonder if he ran track in college? Dale Elis said then they did basketball drills and Alex was pretty okay at them but he was awesome when he was dribbling the ball and shooting the three pointers "good job Alex" KC jones yelled and then around the end of practice they had a one on one drill and Alex had to go one on one with Tom chambers the man he was backing up then the coach blew his whistle and then they started and then Alex got through chambers around the 3rd try because he was good defender and then Alex did a huge dunk on chambers and then round 2 Alex did a spin move on him just went for a field goal and then Alex won the drill and then after practice Alex started walking to his car and Alex pulled out his remote to unlock his car "dude that's nice car where did you get the car?" a voice said and then Alex turned back and it was Xavier McDaniel "I didn't buy it a friend of mine made this car it's a 1986 mustang with golden rems, very tough tires and it's also green and gold as well cause before I was just a sonics fan" Alex said "I'm really sorry about drew" Alex said "oh no brother don't mention it drew wasn't even very good and he was never going to win the starting job at center anyway" Xavier said "what about me" Alex asked "your pretty good" he said "oh thanks man" Alex said "so anyway do you want to hang out or anything we could go get a beer or something" Alex said "sure man I'm down for that" Xavier said "awesome" Alex said

Then Alex and Xavier drove to downtown Seattle and they went to a bar as they walked in they sat around the bar area "two bud lights please" Alex said then the bartender gave them two beers "are you Xavier McDaniel?" the bartenders said "yes I am" Xavier said "oh my god I am such a huge fan can I have your autograph" the bartender said then xavier gave the bartender his autograph and then Alex and Xavier had a beer and then through out the week Alex practice and he worked on his dribbling, and his speed and also Alex worked on sprints back and fourth on the court and then as time went on Alex was getting closer and closer to winning the starting job and then one practice Alex was practicing like normal and then he herd later that day that he was the starter and Alex was pretty excited but Alex also thought "this is great but how is this going to help find drew's killer" Alex thought but then after practice as Alex got out of practice court in Seattle Alex then noticed a buisnessmen go into key arena and then Alex went into his car and then got out his PP7 and then Alex started fallowing him and as Alex was fallowing him he hid behind the wall and he started loading up his PP7 and then Alex saw the buisnessmen go into the general mangers office and then Alex saw him checking it out the files and then as the buisnessmen was opening the files Alex broke down the office door "FREEZE!!!!" Alex yelled and then Alex pointed his gun at him "fine work Mr.Aussmen but not good enough" Kareem said and then Kareem threw a grenade at Alex and then alex did a summer salt and then Alex started shooting his PP7 and then Alex loaded up the gun and kept on shooting and then Alex got up and then Alex pressed a button on his watch and then his disco shoes turned into roller skates and Alex started roller skating around key arena and then as Alex was roller skating and then Alex started shooting Kareem and then Alex tackled him and then Kareem got up and then his shoes turned into skates and then Alex kept on skating and chasing him and then they skated out key arena and they headed towards to the fun Forrest and Alex kept on shooting at him and then Kareem skated into the fun house and then Alex did a summer salt and then Alex loaded up his gun and then he got up again and then found Kareem trying to skate off a ramp but then Alex tripped him from behind and then grabbed him by the neck "who are you working?!" Alex yelled "I don't work for anybody mr.Aussmen but there are people that work for me" Kareem said and then Kareem punched Alex in the face and then Alex got up and kicked Kareem in the face and then kicked him in the stomach then Alex grabbed him by the shirt and punched him in the eye and gave Kareem a black eye and knocked out Kareem and then Alex found his wallet and then Alex looked at his wallet and he took a picture of Kareem's ID and stole Kareem's money and then Alex pressed a button on his watch and Alex kept on roller skating and then Alex roller skated to his 1986 mustang that is parked by key arena

Chapter 3 going on a date with one of sonic dancers

 Then as Alex got to his car he then saw one of sonic dancers head out of key arena with her friends and she was wearing black spandex and she was also wearing blue tennis shoes and she was really tall and she looked very fit and she also had blue jewelry ear rings and she also had blonde hair and she had red lipstick on and then without thinking Alex went up to her "hey what's up?" Alex said "oh hi what's up?" she said "oh nothing I was just roller skating around Seattle center" Alex and then she seemed pretty amazed "that sounds like a lot of fun" she said "yeah it is" Alex said "I'm Susana Fawcett" she said "my name is Aussmen...Alex Aussmen" Alex said "oh pleasure to meet Alex" Susana said "so what are you doing around Seattle center Alex baby" Susana said "oh I was just got back from the practice and then I started roller skating" Alex said "oh that's awesome" Susana said "wait do you play for sonics?" Susana asked "well...yes I do actually" Alex said "oh AWESOME I always wanted to date one of the sonic players" Susana said and then Susana hugged Alex "so where did you play our college ball at?" Susana asked "well I didn't play basketball in college but I went to university of Washington" Alex said "oh that's awesome so you are from here" Susana said "yeah" Alex said and then Susana and Alex started walking to Alex's car and then as they got there ales opened one of his car doors "I hope you like mustangs" Alex said "are you kidding I love mustangs what year do you have?" Susana said "oh I have the new 1986 mustang" Alex said "oh wow that's awesome" Susana said then as they got into Alex's car Alex then started his car up and then on the radio he was playing "pop goes my heart by pop" an then Alex started driving his car "so where do you want go?" Alex asked "well I was wondering If you can take me to dinner" Susana said "then dinner it is my dear" Alex said and then Alex started speeding and then Alex started driving around Eliot bay around downtown Seattle and then took a right turn into a street that was next to Nordstrom and west lake center and then Alex speeded up again and then took a left turn into a parking garage and then Alex parked his car around the right area of the west lake center and then as Alex turned off his car and Susana was just blown away "oh Alex your car is amazing" Susana said "oh thanks" Alex said "so should we go get dinner" Alex asked "oh yes" Susana said and then Alex and Susana walked into the mall and then they went into a restraint that was really fancy

 As they got into the restraint and sat down Susana and Alex loved talking to each other "so how long have you been with the team" Susana asked "oh I have been with them for a couple of days" Alex said "so are you starter or a back up?" Susana asked "well when I started I was a back up and now I think I'm a starter" Alex said "what about you baby girl" Alex asked "well I have been on the cheer team here for almost 2 years and it's really fun I love doing all the sexy cheerleading moves and doing awesome back flips and cartwheels" Susana said "oh wow that's awesome" Alex said "I know" Susana said "so how are we paying?" Susana asked "hey dinner is on me" Alex said "oh really you are awesome" Susana said "no problem" Alex said then as they were sitting down Kareem saw them sitting down "I will destroy this area if it is the last thing I do" Kareem said

"so what do you want to do after dinner" Susana asked "well I was thinking about going dancing" Alex said "really" Susana said

 Then later that night Alex and Susana then headed to a night club around in downtown Seattle and then as they where in line everything looked really fancy and there was even a red carpet and it looked very up to the minute and then Alex was just amazed at the night club then as they were in line Alex had on Grovey 80's clothes and Susana was wearing an awesome 80's purple and gold dress with a golden bracelet and then as they got into the night club Alex just loved the music in the night club and Alex started going crazy "thanks for taking to this place Alex" Susana said "your welcome anytime" Alex said then as Alex was dancing then the song "automatic lover by dee d Jackson" was starting to play and then a disco ball showed up "you want to dance?" Alex said "sure" Susana said

 Then Alex and Susana started dancing and then Alex started spinning and twisting his body and then Alex was mixing up his 80's moves with his disco moves he did back in the 70's and then Alex started doing the disco sign and then Alex grabbed on Susana's hand and he started spinning her in circles and then Alex lowered Susana and then Alex picked up Susana and started spinning her around and then Alex put her back down and then Alex started moving his finger and his body and then Alex ended the dance with him grabbing on to Susana's hand like they where going to do the tango and then as the song ended the hole night club clapped "oh wow not only are you good basketball player but your a great dancer" Susana said "thanks" Alex said and then Susana and Alex then sat down at a table "how do you do all those dance moves?" Susana asked "well they are pretty simple they are anything I think in my head" Alex said "oh cool" Susana said "anyway do you want me to get you a beer or something" Alex asked "oh yes please" Susana said then Alex headed over the bar area to go get two beers and then as got the beers he then walked back to the table to meet Susana "here we go I got us some bud lights" Alex said "oh yeah" Susana said with an excited voice and then the two of the them lifted up their beer bottles "cheers!!!" Alex said then Alex and Susana touched each other beer bottles and they both drank but then as they where drinking Kareem sneaked into the night club without Alex knowing and then Kareem sneaked into the main club room on the 3rd floor and for some reason he knew the password to get into the vault and then as Kareem was getting the money a security guard came and then Kareem took out a magnum gun and shot him in the head and then Kareem stole the money and headed out of the nightclub and then as Kareem was about sneak out he then took out a mobile 80's phone out of his pocket "kill Mr.Aussmen " Kareem said

And then as Alex was sitting down and then one of Kareem's thugs got Kareem messages and then he pulled out DD4 gun and then he was about to shot Alex in the head and then he pointed the gun at Alex in the head "don't move Seattle boy we have orders to kill you for the buisnessmen" one of the thugs said and then as Alex was about to rest his arms on his legs then Alex punched him in the face and then Alex took out his PP7 gun and shot him in the stomach and then another thug tried to attack Alex and then Alex grabbed him by the neck and slammed on to another bar table and then Alex reloaded his gun and shot him in the head and then another thug tried to tackle Alex from behind and then Alex ducked and grabbed from the arm and threw against the wall then more of the thugs showed up and then Alex grabbed Susana by the hand "come on" Alex said and then the thugs started shooting at Alex with A33 riffles and then Alex and Susana hid behind a table and then Alex got out an ZMG gun and then Alex started shooting his gun at the thugs and then Alex shot 15 thugs in the neck and then Alex and Susana started running of the nightclub and then Alex pressed a button on his spy watch and then his 1986 mustang came to him with a touch of button and then more of the thugs came "get in" Alex said and then Susana and Alex got into the 1986 mustang and then Alex started speeding up and then some of thugs started getting into limos and then they started chasing Alex

And then Alex took a left turn into the soto area and then Alex pressed a button in his car and then limos started shooting at Alex's car and then a machine gun came out of Alex's mustang and started shooting at the limos and then Alex pressed a button and then a grenade blasted at the limos and then the limos exploded and then Alex took a turn that went on one of the freeways and then Alex got on to another road that took them back to the lower queen ann area by Key arena and then Alex parked his car by one of the restraints "are you okay Susana?" Alex asked "I think so but who were those guys?" Susana asked "well I don't know but I for some reason they were after us" Alex said "anyway thanks for the great night I had a great time at the nightclub with you" Susana said "oh sure Susana anytime" Alex said and then Susana laughed "so you don't want to stay at my house?" Alex asked "you have a house here?" Susana asked "yeah I have one in downtown Seattle it's a pen house and it's really nice" Alex said "you want to see it" Alex asked "oh yes I would love too" Susana said and then later that night Alex and Susana went to Alex's pen house in downtown Seattle and it was in one of one of buildings and it was an a fancy building and it was right between lower queen Ann and by the IREA building and then as Susana and Alex where in the elevator Susana just couldn't wait to see Alex's pen house in downtown Seattle and then as the elevator stopped at Alex's floor in the pen house building "here it is" Alex said and then Alex touched Susana by her shoulders and Susana just had an exciting look on her face "oh wow it is very beautiful Alex" Susana said and then in Alex's pen house on the left side there was a fancy kitchen and a huge black wooden table, and then a bar table, and then on the right side there was a dance area where people could go dancing on that dance floor and also there was a fancy black wooden coffee table with a fancy couch and 5 sofas and then there another table and then was an awesome flat screen TV and a huge couch and there was even a popcorn machine to make popcorn in just in case they wanted to make popcorn and then there was 4 bathrooms and one of the bathrooms had a huge bathtub and bathtub was really deep and almost as a deep as a swimming pool and you could actually swim in the bathtub and it was almost as big as a fish tank in like an aquarium and then upstairs was a master bed room and the covers were blue and purple and there was also a balcony that had a view of Eliot bay, downtown Seattle, and the space needle in Seattle center and then last in Alex's pen house there was 60 feet deep swimming pool on the top of the pen house and there was a 4 diving board, and a really tall water slide and Alex's pen house was just awesome and then there was a huge deck and BBQ a cooler to store drinks like soda,beer, and vodka

"so what do you want to do first?" Alex asked "well I was thinking about going swimming " Susana said and then Susana went upstairs to the swimming pool and then Susana was heading upstarts she started taking her clothes and then Alex started staring at her with his fist on his check and with a childish smile on his face and then Susana dive into the swimming pool butt naked "WAHOOOOOOOOOOOOOOOOOOO!!!!!" Susana yelled in excitement "oh my god the water feels great what's the tempter of the pool" Susana asked "I think it's around 71 degrees I guess" Alex said "oh come in the water Alex it feels great" Susana said and then Alex just smiled and he just took of his clothes and then he dived into the swimming pool butt naked with Susana and then as Alex was in water Susana started laughing and started splashing Alex in the face and then Alex went under water and Alex started tickling Susana's naked body and then Susana started laughing and then Susana started going crazy and then Susana jumped on Alex and she started kissing Alex on the lips and then as Susana was smooching Alex then Alex picked up Susana in his arms and he started spinning her around 4 times and then Susana started laughing and then Alex pressed a button that made his swimming pool made hot table bubbles "oh baby" Susana and then Alex and Susana started swimming pool and then Alex started kissing Susana under water and then as they were kissing in the water then Alex pressed a button under water that made the roses make rose pelts that made a shape of a heart

And then later that night as Alex and Susana got out of the swimming pool she started running to the master bed room and then Alex ran after her and he started playing with her and started kissing her on the lips and then they landed on the bed and then they started making out under covers and as Alex was making out Susana she just had very beautiful arms and her feet were always moving around and then Alex and Susana got out of the covers and then they started making out on the bed like crazy and then Alex put on some music while he was making out Susana and then for the rest of the night Alex was making out with Susana for the whole night.

Chapter 4 the game against the Boston celtics at key arena and finding out Kareem's plan

Then the next day Alex looked at his clock by his bed and then Alex got out of bed and then Alex walked to his bathroom and then he went into the shower and he started taking a shower and then as Alex got out of the shower and then he got on some clothes on and then he put on some dark blue jeans, and then Alex put on red tennis shoes, a green sweeter, with a blue leather jacket and Alex was also wearing a scarf that was yellow and then Alex went into his laundry room and he got his sonics uniform and his tennis shoes and then Alex went into his mustang and then he started driving to key arena and then as Alex was driving there was 4 cars fallowing him and they kept telling him to pull over and then one of the drivers of the car then pulled out a sniper riffle and then Alex started speeding up and then the other cars started speeding up and then they started shooting at Alex's car and then a car chase started and then Alex started speeding around lower queen Ann and around downtown Seattle and then the other cars tried to crash into Alex's car and then bumped the other cars back and slammed into the buildings and then one of the thugs started taking a ZMG guns and started shooting at Alex and then Alex looked at one of his buttons in his car and then Alex pressed a button and then the button made the car do a spin flip and over the gun bullets and then as the car went back on it's wheels Alex then pressed another button as he was driving and he shot a rocket launcher at 2 of the cars and the car blew up and then Alex pressed a button and then Alex drove by TJ Mchughes restraint around Seattle center and then Alex drove into a parking garage in Seattle center and then Alex found a parking spot and then Alex turned off his car and then Alex got out of his car and then as Alex got out of his car Alex started hearing foot steps and then more thugs came up from out of nowhere and then they started shooting at Alex and then Alex started running as fast as he can to try to get himself to key arena and then Alex pressed a button on his spy watch and then his tennis shoes transformed into roller skates and then Alex started roller skating around Seattle center and then Alex kept on roller skating and then thugs were also roller skating and then they got out DD4 guns and they started shooting at Alex and then Alex avoid the gun bullets and then Alex ducked and he got out his PP7 gun and he started shooting at the thugs and then Alex shot down 3 thugs and then more thugs kept on shooting at Alex and then as Alex was going faster and faster on his roller skates he was getting around the key arena area and then alex saw the doors open for the players and he saw the door that the players came into and then as the door was open to get into the sonics locker room and then without thinking Alex then did a huge dive into the sonics locker room and then Alex hit his shoulder really hard on the door and then Xavier herd the sound of the door getting "AHH" Alex said as he hit his shoulder and the Xavier came "boy what the hell are you doing we have a game to play and your out here roller skating come on dwag" Xavier said and then Alex started getting up "dude you don't understand there was guys trying to kill me and that's why I was wearing roller skates" Alex said "wait a minute hommie " Xavier said and then Xavier picked up Alex's secret agent ID "wait so your a secret agent" Xavier asked "yes I am but listen to me bad things are going to happen and there is buisnessmen trying to steel money from Seattle center and downtown Seattle and his thugs were after me" Alex said "but why you boy?" Xavier said "well reason why they are after me is because one of his thugs killed drew" Alex said "what?!" Xavier said "and I was there when drew died he was shot by key arena and then the next morning my best friend wanted to help you guys cause we were big fans and he made me play for you guys to replace drew" Alex said and then Xavier looked and his ID and then back at Alex "I believe you boy because it just makes sense the mustang, the clothes you wear, the watch on your riest" Xavier said "look Xavier as my favorite player can you please not tell anybody that I'm a secret agent please?" Alex said "sure hommie" Xavier said "thanks man" Alex said and then Alex changed into his sonics uniform and then he got on wristbands on

And then the sonics players went on to the hardwood and went to their bench and set their stuff down and then Alex started warming up and then as Alex was warming up on the hardwood he then looked up into the stands and he saw a lot of people in the stands and he even saw Michael in the stands and then Susana was with her dance team "piss....Alex" Susana whispered and then as ales was done warming up he went over to Susana "hey what's up?" Alex said "oh nothing anyway Alex I just wanted to say I love you and I hope you have a great game" Susana with a smile on her face "yeah thanks" Alex said and then Alex looked his team "anyway I gotta go" Alex said and then as Alex was getting ready to leave Susana grabbed Alex by the wrist and she started smooching Alex on the lips and she was kissing him for 10 minutes and then as they were done kissing Alex started running back to the locker room "go get em baby" Susana said

Then as Alex was heading back into the locker room Kareem was staring at Alex going into the locker room "once I have his little smochie I will destroy lower queen ann and downtown Seattle and Alex Aussmen will be dead NOTHING CAN STOP ME NOW!!!! BRAHAHAHAHAHAHAHAHAHAHAHAHAHAHAHAHAHAHAHAHAHAHAHAHAHAH AHAHAHAHAHAHAHAHAHAHAHAHAHAHAHAHAHAHAHAHAHA MUAHAHAHAHAHAHAHAHAHAHAHAHAHAHAHAHAHAHAHAHAHAHAHAHAHA HAHAHAHAHAHAHAHAHAHAHAHAHAHAHAHAHAHAHAHAHAAHAHAHAHAHA HAHAHAHAHAHAHAHAHAHA" Kareem laughed and then Kareem walked away

And then as the sonics got out of the locker room they sat on the bench and then lights were shut off and then the sonics intro was about start "ALRIGHT SONICS FAN STAND UP AND GET ON OUR FEET FOR YOUR SEATTLE SUUUUUUUUUUUUUUUUUUUUUUUUUUUUUUUUUPER SONICS!!!!!!!!!!!!!!!!!!! AND HERE ARE TONIGHT'S STARTERS" and then the crowd starting going nuts "STARTING FOWARD FROM WITHCA UNIVERSITY XAVIER MCDANIEL!!!!!!!!!!!!" then Xavier started out and high fiving people "AT GUARD FROM TENNESSEE NUMBER 3 DAAAAAAAAAAAALE ELIS" and then crowd just staring screaming "AND FINALLY AT CENTER FROM THE UNIVERSITY OF WASHINGTON NUMBER 31 ALEX AUUUUUUUUUUUUUUUUUUUUUUUUUUUSMEN" and then Alex started running like crazy and high fiving all of his sonic teammates and he was going crazy "AND YOUR HEAD COUCH FOR YOUR SEATTLE SONICS KC JONES!!!!!!!!" and then Alex went into a huddle break "ALRIGHT LISTIN UP I KNOW ITS MY FIRST YEAR BUT ARE GOING TO LET LARRY BRID AND HIS CELTICS TAKE OVER OUR PLACE?!" Alex yelled and his teammates resounded with "NO!!!" they said "NO IS RIGHT LET'S SHOW THESE BOSTON BOYS HOW ME PLAY BALL IN THE PASFIC NORTHWEST LET'S GO SONICS ON 3 123" Alex yelled and they all yelled "SONICS!!!!!

And then the game started and the game started with Larry Bird dribbling up the court and alex was defending him like crazy and then he threw a pass to former sonic Dennis Johnson and then Alex rejected the shot and then Alex started dribbling up the court and he did a lay up on Larry Bird and key arena was going nuts and then Larry bird got the ball again for anybody that was open and then Alex ran up to him and he stole ball away and Alex crated a turnover and then as Alex was dribbling the ball he passed to ball to Xavier and then Xavier did a really sweet drink and then in 2nd quarter Dennis Johnson was trying to score by doing a lay up and then Alex blocked the lay up and then Alex got the ball and then he made a pass to Dale Elis and then dale Elis scored 2 points for the sonics and then as Larry Bird was trying to shot a 3 pointer for the Celtics then the basketball went off the rem and Alex grabbed the ball for the rebound and he started dribbling the ball and then Alex did a huge dunk on Dennis Johnson and then all of Celtic players were looking at Alex in disbelief and then all of the sonic players started to high five Alex and celebrating "good job homme!!!" Xavier said and then Xavier gave Alex a bro hug and then by halftime it was 36 to 28 the sonics were leading in the game

And then as sonics and Alex were heading into the locker room they were just really happy and Alex was just having fun and then as Alex was about to go into e locker room at half time then a trap door and went open and Alex fell into the trap door "AHHHHHHHHHHHHHHH" Alex yelled and then Alex fell on a chair in a strange room under key arena "oh my god what the hell" Alex said and then the lights went on in the room "good evening Mr.Aussmen muahahahah" Kareem said "it's you" Alex said "oh yes it is me Mr.Aussmen and I was watching the game and wow a lot of dunks Larry bird way to kick ass hommie" Kareem said "what the hell do you want?!" Alex said in a very angry voice "oh muahahah I know you would ask that question Mr.Aussmen I want you to loose Alex so I can blow up this hole dump here in Seattle center" Kareem said "is that why you wanted to get money just so you and your thugs could blow up this beautiful place just to create a junk yard in this city?!" Alex said in a pissed off voice "you are half correct Mr.Aussmen not only will I blow up lower queen Ann but I will also blow up downtown Seattle with mines that are set around the city and around lower queen Ann and there is one that is located right here in key arena that disables all of them but not enough time to get them all MUAHAHAHAHAH" Kareem laughed "I'm not going to loose and I will stop you!!!!" Alex said "eu I can't wait for you to do that Alex so this dump could be happy and so I can be the automatic lover to Susana hhehehehehe" Kareem laughed "Susana has nothing to do with us!!!!!" Alex said "oh that's were your wrong Mr.Aussmen you see I have a lot of history with myself trying to get money to do this and yes I did have to kill some people including your former center you know play for" Kareem laughed "wait a minute so it was your the one that killed drew and the owner of Seattle center you piece of shit!!!!" Alex said "your correct Mr.Aussmen and not only that but I also killed Susana's father and stole his money to do this operation and the best part is nobody around this place knows about it MUAHAHAHAHAHAHAHAHAHAH" Kareem laughed and "catch you later jack Sikma junior huahahahahahahahahahahahahahahahahahahah" Kareem laughed and then Kareem pressed a button and that got Alex back to the locker room and then Alex headed back with the team and then as they got out of the locker room Alex then started looking around to see if there is anything strange in key arena but it didn't stop Alex from playing in the game and then as Alex was playing a lot of sonic dancers were cheering "go Alex go" they cheered and then Alex kept on getting points on the board for the sonics and the Celtics were just mentally out of it and then the final horn went off and the sonics won the game and all of Alex's teammates told him how great he did

Chapter 5 disabling the mine bombs in key arena, the car chase in lower queen Ann, and the fight with Kareem

 And then as Alex was getting on the bench he then saw one or the mines are around crowd "STOP THAT CART RIGHT NOW!!!!" Alex yelled "....THERE'S A BOMB IN THERE!!!!" Alex yelled then key arena starting going nuts and then a security guard came and opened the cart there was mine in there "who are you and how did you know your just NBA basketball player" the guard told him "I'm not an NBA player my name is Alex Aussmen I'm Secret agent from Seattle" Alex said and then Alex showed the security guard his ID "alright go head son" the guard said and then Alex starting trying to disable the bomb and it was 14 seconds in counting and then Alex disconnected one of the wires and then countdown stopped and the everybody blew a sign of relief and then all of sonics players looked at him "dude you saved our lives bro" Xavier said "yeah no problem dude" Alex said and then as everybody in key arena was celebrating but Alex knew that fight was not over yet

 And then as Alex got out of the locker room after he was done changing Alex then saw Susana waiting for alex in front of of key arena and then as Alex was walking up to her then a black limo came up to Susana and grabbed her and pulled her into the limo and Susana started screaming and then Alex started running and then Alex knew he didn't have enough time and then as Alex was running his tennis shoes started transforming into roller skates and Alex started roller skating after the limo and then Alex pressed a button on his spy watch that made his roller skates go a lot fast like as a car and then Alex started catching up to the limo and Alex started going faster on his roller skates and then the limo took a left turn on to the freeway in Seattle and then as Alex got on the freeway with his roller skates Alex put on full blast on his roller skating and then ales started blasting a huge amount of flames that made Alex got faster and faster and then one of the limo drivers saw Alex and then as Alex was roller skating he then took out an A33 riffle and started shooting at the tired on the other limos and blew up 4 limos as Alex was chasing the one with Susana and then Alex pressed another button on one of the livers he was holding in his hand and it made blast up in the air and then Alex landed on Kareem's car and then Kareem saw Alex and then Kareem took out a knife and he tried to cut Alex in the head with his knife and he tried to cut him 5 times and then Alex head-butted Kareem and then Kareem's driver then took a right turn into one of his buildings in downtown Seattle and then Alex was still holding on to the car and then car crashed into the window that went into his sweet and then Kareem grabbed susana by the arm "GET OUT!!!!" Kareem yelled and then Kareem tried to get free from him and then Alex went up one of the elevators to get up Kareem's sweet

As Alex was in the elevator he then got to sweet room and then Alex saw Susana trapped into a room and then used one his gadgets to get Susana out "Alex!!!" Susana said "are you okay?" Alex said "yeah I'm just glad your here" Susana said and then as Susana was hugging Alex then Kareem grabbed Susana from behind and then Susana screamed and then Kareem took out a ZMG gun and pointed at her and to a ledge "NOT SO FAST MR.AUSSMEN WE STILL HAVE STILL UNFINISHED BUISNESSMEN!!!!" Kareem said and "LET HER AGO KAREEM YOU ALREADY LOST NOW LET HER GO!!!!" Alex said "IT WILL NOT BE SO EASY IN LESS YOU WANT TO GRAB.....THIS!!!!"

Kareem said and then Kareem took out the last bomb remote and then Alex tackled Kareem and then Alex kicked Kareem in the face and he started punching him in the face and then Alex grabbed him by the shirt and the shoved him against the wall and then Kareem punched Alex in the face and then Alex blocked one of Kareem's punches and then Alex whacked Kareem in face "FRIST I KILL YOU AND THEN I BLOW UP THE CITY!!!!!!!" Kareem yelled and then as Kareem was about to stab Alex in the face then Alex kicked Kareem in the balls and then Alex got right back and then Alex kicked Kareem in the face and then Kareem set his sweet on fire and then the building was getting covered in flames and then Alex started running and then Kareem tried to stab him with his knife and then Alex ducked by his bar table and then Alex saw Kareem's guns in his room and then Alex loaded up one of Kareem's rocket launcher and then without thinking Alex fired Kareem's rocket launcher at Kareem and then Kareem got blasted by his rocket launcher and then Kareem fell off one of the ledges and then his hole place was starting to burn up and then Susana was watching Alex then Susana started slipping and then she grabbed on the ledge "Susana hold on" Alex said and then Alex was running then Kareem came out of nowhere and whacked him with a metal bar and Kareem's face was all burned up and so was his body "YOUR TOO LATE MR.AUSSMEN AGAIN AND NOW WITH MY BOMB I STILL HAVE IN MY HAND I WILL BE ABLE TO BLOW UP DOWNTOWN SEATTLE AND LOWER QUEEN ANN AND IT'S GOING TO BE SUCH A SONIC BLAST" Kareem said and then Kareem grabbed Susana and pointed his knife at Susana and she was screaming and then without fear Alex pointed the rocket launcher at Kareem "DROP TO KNIFE KAREEM AND BACK AWAY FROM MY GIRLFRIEND!!!!!" Alex said and then Kareem did an evil smile and then he thew one of his mines at Alex and then it broke the rocket launcher "noooooooooooooo" susana screamed "GO,GO,GO AUSSMEN!!!! HEHEHEHEHEHE" Kareem laughed and then Alex got out and looked at Kareem and then Kareem took out his knife and he was about to stab Alex "Alex look out!!!!" Susana and then Alex did a backflip and then Alex looked at the celling and then Kareem punched Alex in the face and gave him a black eye "it's all over Alex you loose I have won and your girlfriend is mine and so is Seattle MUAHAHAHAHAHAHAHAHAHAHAHAHAHAHAHAHAHAHAHAH" Kareem laughed and then Alex had a angry look on his face "I think we also have other unfinished buisnessmen Kareem!!!!...." Alex said and then Alex punched Kareem in the face and kicked Kareem's knife out of his hand and then started grabbing Kareem's wrist really hard "YOU FORGOT THE FRIST REAL BUSINESS AND RULE NUMBER 1 NEVER MESS WITH SONIC FANS!!!!" Alex yelled and then Alex threw Kareem against the wall and he picked up his rocket launcher and shot him with his rocket launcher and then Kareem started faking off the building with flames covering him "AHHHHHHHHHHHHHHHHHHHHHHHHHHHHHHHHHHHHHHHHHHHHHHHHHHHHHH HHHHHHHHHHHHHHHHHHHHHHHHHHHHHHHHHHHHHHHHHHHHHHHHHHHHHHH HHHHH" Kareem yelled as he was falling off the building with flames on him

And then Alex helped Susana get up "we got to get out of here" Alex said and then Alex and Susana and the building starting to burn up real bad and then Alex found one of the elevators that w still working and then Alex and Susana were in elevator and then as they got out of the elevator the building was really starting up to burn up and then Alex found one of the limos his thugs left behind and then Alex went into the limo and he started driving the limo and then as Alex and Susana left Alex used his spy watch and he hacked into Kareem's bomb remote and disabled Kareem's remote and the mines the city of Seattle was saved

 Then as Kareem was laying down on the ground burned up then a pile of burning bricks came down on Kareem and then pretty soon the whole building exploded and the pieces fell on Kareem
"AWWWWWWWWWWWWWWWWWWWWWWWWWWWWWWWWWWW WWWWWWW!!!!" Kareem yelled and then the bricks fell on Kareem and and then the hole building did and Kareem was dead

Chapter 6 the automatic lover of Seattle

Then the next day Alex went back to sonics practice in Seattle and returned his sonics jersey and he gave it back to him "here is my jersey back coach" Alex said "and I'm sorry if I made you guys look foolish by being the first secret agent on your basketball team" Alex said then KC Jones looked at Alex "no Alex it was a pleasure having you on this team and I wish you the best and also I hope we found another basketball player just like you kid" KC jones said "thanks couch" Alex said and then Alex hugged KC Jones and then Alex got out of the building and then he drove back to his pen house in downtown Seattle and then Alex looked at his window of the view of the space needle and then the next day Alex went to another sonics game against the trail blazers and he watched the game like a fan like everybody else and then he saw some of the sonic dancers dancing and Alex starting feeling like Susana forgot about him and then Alex got out of key arena and he went back on the Montreal train back to his pen house in downtown Seattle and then as Alex was on Montreal train he then saw a girl with blonde hair walking towards Alex on the train and then she sat by Alex on the train "hey baby" Susana said "what are you doing here?" Alex asked "well I just wanted to see you" Susana said "Susana Im not an NBA player the reason I was because I was on a huge case and I'm pretty sure you like someone else" Alex said in with a depressed voice "no I love you Alex I don't love anybody else but you" Susana said and then Susana kissed Alex on the lips and then on the train they started kissing for 30 minutes

Then Alex and Susana went back to Alex's pen house in downtown Seattle and then Alex grabbed Susana's hands and then they laid on the couch together "Alex I love you" Susana said "I love you too Susana even though I only played one year in the NBA but I brought best part of that time back with me" Alex said "awwwww thats sooo sweet" Susana said and then Alex and Susana smooched each other on the lips "hey do you want to go swimming" Susana asked "oh my god yes" Alex said and then Alex and Susana took off her clothes and went into the swimming pool butt naked and then Alex went into the pool with his bathing suit and Alex put on "automatic lover by Dee D Jackson" as they were swimming in the pool and then Alex started tickling her from head to toe and then they started kissing and laughing and then Susana started kissing Alex for the hole night and then as Alex was making out with Susana in the swimming pool Susan then took off Alex's swimming trunks and kept on making out in the swimming pool "oh Alex" Susana said

The Winds Of Change

The winds of change

By: Nelson Amador

Chapter 1 Toronto,Ontario, Canada 1987

 It was a very cold and windy day in the Toronto city area around in Ontario and the stores were very busy and people were hanging around with friends and they were drinking coffee or hot chocolate or even a cup of tea and then around downtown Toronto then a metro Toronto came around one of the district areas around the city and then a person with a suit and a long fur black jacket came off the bus and the person had a camera and then as the person was walking he starting to take pictures of the beautiful buildings in Toronto and then as the person kept on walking he then saw another building and as the person walked into the building and as the person walked into the building he walked into the Toronto eaton centre and then the person started walking around the mall and he saw all the awesome clothes and then there was a poster of girl that was wearing Victoria secret underwear and then the person took a picture of the poster with his camera and then the person reloaded his camera and he took more pictures and then as the picture was taking pictures of the Victoria secret poster around that area, then there was a girl that was wearing a dark purple dress, she was also was wearing red high heels and she had really beautiful brown 1980s style hair and she was also wearing a really nice necklace that was made of gold and the necklace had blue,pink, and purple rubies on her necklace and then the girl smiled at the person that was taking pictures of the victoria secret poster and then she started walking to the person but then the person kept on walking around the Toronto Easton centre and then as the person was done walking in the mall the person in the suit and long black coat sat around the food court in the building and then as the person was sitting down then the girl in purple dress saw the person sitting down and she sat next to him "hi..." she said in very happy voice "hey what's up?" the person said "oh not much I just saw you taking pictures of the Victoria secret poster in the mall are you tourist or something?" the girl asked "kind of yes why do you ask?" the person asked "oh I'm just wondering" the girl said "is this your first time in Toronto?" the girl said "well not really I have been to Canada before back in 1985 and I went to go to Vancouver" the person said "oh wow what's awesome I'm Victoria Simmons what's your name?" Victoria asked "my names Aussmen....Alex Aussmen" Alex said "oh love that name it's so interesting" Victoria said "so where are you staying at?" Victoria asked "oh I'm staying at a hotel in downtown Toronto do you want to come with me" Alex asked "oh YES!!!!! I would love to come with you" Victoria said and then after they went shopping around Toronto then Victoria and Alex then headed back to the hotel room that Alex was staying in

Then as they got to the hotel they then took the elevator and they walked into his hotel room "oh wow your hotel room is so beautiful it even has a great view of the city" Victoria said "I'm really glad you like it" Alex said "so do you have wine in this hotel room?" Victoria asked and then Alex walked over to his fridge in the hotel room and then he found some red wine in his hotel room and then he found a bottle opener and then he opened the bottle of red wine and then Alex got out two wine glasses out and he poured 2 glasses of red wine and Victoria drank a lot of the red wine and then she started laughing and then she put her head on Alex's shoulder and then Victoria started kissing Alex on the checks 3 times "I can give a great ride" Victoria whispered in Alex's ear and then Alex started making out with Victoria on the bed and then as Alex was making out with Victoria he then turned on the radio and then the song "crush on you by the jets" started playing while they were making out and then Alex unzipped Victoria's dress off and her underwear "oh yes" Victoria said and then Alex kept on making out with her a lot more and more and the night was really, really wild

Chapter 2 the trip back to Seattle with Victoria

 The next day Alex got up he took a shower and then after he took a shower he then got dressed and then as Alex was getting dressed Victoria just smiled at Alex "that was a really wild night" Victoria said "I couldn't agree with you more" Alex said "so what are your plans for today?" Victoria asked "well I'm thinking about going home back to Seattle" Alex said "oh wow your from Seattle" Victoria said "yeah I'm from there it's a really awesome city it's not as nice as Toronto or New York but it's a little bit like those places" Alex said "awesome when do you leave?" Victoria asked "well my flight leaves around 3:00PM" Alex said "oh that's awesome can I come with you?" Victoria asked "um sure do you have a passport?" Alex asked "oh yes" Victoria said and then Victoria got out of bed and then she took a shower and then she put on lip gloss and make up and then she put on a very beautiful dress and then she also put on pink heels and Victoria also had a really awesome purse and then later that day Alex checked out of the hotel Victoria and him were staying in and then Alex and Victoria caught a Toronto metro bus that took them to the airport and as they got to the airport they then got their tickets to get on their flight heading to Seattle and it was a one way ticket to and then as they got on the plane Alex started listening to music on the plane and he started rocking out and he was shaking his head "do you like rocking out music?" Victoria asked "oh yes I sometimes like to enjoy the heck out of the music I listen to" Alex said "oh that's awesome" Victoria said and then as Alex was rocking out to his music then Victoria looked at the window and she started looking at the sky and as she was looking at the sky she started seeing a lot of different things and she saw a cloud that was a shape of a flower and then Victoria smiled

Then as they were on the plane then food came around allies around lunch time and then a flight attendance came by "can I get you people anything?" the flight attendance asked "sure I'll have a doctor pepper please" Alex said "and what about you miss?" the flight attendance asked and then Victoria turned back "I'll have some champagne please" Victoria said "I will get those for you guys right away" the flight attendance said and then as she left Alex then started looking around the plane by moving his head around and then as Alex was looking at some things he then saw a person with a gold suit on looking at a magazine "Alex, where do you live in Seattle do you live like around the city?" Victoria asked "I live around Seattle center it's kind of around were the Seattle Sonics play basketball" Alex said "oh wow so do you live like in an apartment or something?" Victoria asked "not exactly I actually live in a pen-house around the REI building in Seattle center" Alex said "oh that's awesome I really can't wait to see it" Victoria said "so do you have any friends you see in Seattle?" Victoria asked "well I do have a best friend I see sometimes every day" Alex said "oh that's awesome" Victoria said and then around 5:00PM west cost time they landed into sea-tac airport and then as they got off the plane Alex and Victoria then started heading to the baggage clam and they went to pick up their suitcases

 As Alex and Victoria were picking their suitcases some thug in a blue suit saw Alex and Victoria getting their suitcases and he was wearing avatar glasses and he also was wearing a pair of headphones on his head "I see the girl she is with a young gentlemen with long brown 1970s hair" the thug said "what does the gentlemen look like, like what is he wearing?" his boss asked and then the thug back around baggage clam took another look at Alex "he is wearing a red slacks, black disco shoes, a blue,red, and sliver disco shirt, and a silver suit jacket" the thug said "well find out where the girl and him are going and I will find out who this person is" his boss said "yes sir" the thug said and then thug hid behind one of the carts and he started spying on Alex and Victoria as they were getting their suitcases

 As Alex and Victoria were getting their suitcases then Alex saw a blue 1980s mustang and then on the car there was a poster and the poster said "welcome home Alex!!!!!" and then Alex looked on the poster "oh no..." Alex said and then Michael showed up and Michael was really excited "Alex your back!!!" Michael said and then Michael hugged Alex and then Michael gave Alex noggie "so how was your trip to Toronto?" Michael asked "oh it was really awesome I got to see the city I and sailed on one of the boats up there and I even got to go shopping as well" Alex said "that's awesome man" Michael said "anyway you didn't mess up my place while I was gone did you?" Alex asked "oh no of course I didn't man I would reck up your place" Michael said and then Michael started loading up Alex and Victoria's suitcases "so who is the beautiful lady?" Michael asked "oh this is Victoria I met her on my trip and I met her at one of the malls around the city" Alex said "dude that's awesome Alex" Michael said "anyway let's get the hell out of here" Michael said and then Michael, Alex and Victoria got into Michael's car and then as they got into the car Michael started up his car and then he started speeding "WAHOOOOOOOOOO OH YEAH!!!!!!" Michael yelled as he was speeding

As they got into downtown Seattle Victoria was so amazed at downtown Seattle "Alex Seattle is beautiful" Victoria said "yeah it's awesome but it's kind of little too" Alex said and then Michael took a right turn into Seattle center and then Victoria saw the pen house Alex lived in "Alex is this were you live it's amazing" Victoria said "oh I'm glad you like my dear" Alex said and then Michael parked his car in the parking garage under the pen house and then Alex and Michael unloaded all of Alex and Victoria's suitcases and they brought them to Alex's pen house and then Alex set his suitcase around his couch by his TV and as Victoria got into the pen house she was so amazed "Alex your pen house is very beautiful and even has a beautiful view of the space needle" Victoria said "so what do you want to do right now?" Alex asked "I mean there is a swimming pool, hot tub, and then there is also a pool table upstairs and bar as well" Alex said "that's awesome" Victoria said then Victoria went upstairs and she saw all the fun things that were in Alex's pen house and not only did she saw all the pool tables but there was also a disco area and a stereo system and Alex also had a record player as well upstairs and then Victoria looked at the records Alex had "how many records do you have Alex?" Victoria asked " I think I have 3,000 records from all the 70s including the disco records as well" Alex said "oh wow that's a lot of records" Victoria said "oh yes and I also have some 80s songs as well put their mostly like pop, 80s disco, and some rock and roll" Alex said and then as Victoria was looking around she then found the song "cruel summer by bannarama" and then she put the song on and then she started dancing to the song "oh wow I didn't know you had songs by bannarama" Victoria said and then Victoria started dancing to the song and snapping her fingers and she was also shaking her head as well and then Alex started dancing and moving his hands and then Alex did a handstand and then he started moving his arms and making disco dance moves and then as Alex was dancing then he pressed a button by his lamp "you want to see something cool" Alex said "sure" Victoria said and then Alex pressed a button and then the dance floor started raising up like 3 inches off the ground and then the floor started spinning "oh wow this is awesome" Victoria said and then as they kept on listening to the song Alex and Victoria were having a great time and then as the song was done then Alex pressed the button and then the dance floor went back to the floor and then Alex laid down on his back and then Victoria laid on Alex's body and she laid her head on his right shoulder "oh Alex that was really fun" Victoria said "so what do you want to tomorrow?" Alex asked "I don't know why do you ask?" Victoria said "I'm just wondering cause I was wondering if you wanted to go the mall?" Alex asked "oh yes that would be very awesome I would love to go to the mall" Victoria said and then Victoria kissed Alex on the lips and then as Victoria was kissing Alex then Alex started smooching really hard

Chapter 3 spending the day with Victoria and Michael

Then the next day Alex got up the next morning and then he took a shower and then as Alex took a shower he then put on some music as he was taking a shower and then as Alex got out of the shower he then put on dark blue jeans, a dark red tee shirt, a sliver watch, then he wore a pice necklace, and then Alex put on a brown leather jacket, and a scarf and then Alex put a pair of socks on and then he put on red 1980s style tennis shoes

Then as Alex was getting dressed then Victoria showed up and she was wearing a yellow strap shirt, and dark blue jeans, and she was also wearing a golden bracelet and then Victoria was wearing a black leather jacket and purple high heeled boots "oh wow Victoria you look very beautiful" Alex said "are those clothes new?" Alex asked "oh no sexy boy I brought these clothes with me from home" Victoria said "oh that's very incredibly hot" Alex said and then Alex and Victoria got out of Alex's pen house and they started walking to pacific place mall and then as they got into the mall they both looked around the mall and looked at all the clothing departments in whole mall and then Alex and Victoria went down to the basement and then they went into barnes & Noble and they looked at a lot of books and magazines and then as they were looking then they got some coffee around a coffee place that was in Barnes & Noble and then Alex and Victoria sat around a table in the coffee shop

"so Alex were did you go to college?" Victoria said "I went to the university of Washington and I graduated in 1984" Alex said "oh wow that's awesome were did you go to high school?" Victoria asked "I went to Tahoma High School and I graduated from there in 1979" Alex said "that's awesome so did you like college or high school?" Victoria asked "well I liked college better cause my high school life was really complicated and there was a lot of uncertain things" Alex said "why is that were you a nerd in high school" Victoria asked "well no I wasn't a nerd it's just that it was just really bad and I had a lot enemies" Alex said "oh you poor baby" Victoria said "it's alright Victoria said....but anyway I don't want to talk about it let's do something else today...do you want to go to the fun

Forrest?" Alex asked "were is that?" Victoria asked "it's in Seattle center but well stop around west lake center and its on the way there" Alex said "oh sure yeah thanks Alex" Victoria said "hey no problem anytime" Alex said

Then Alex and Victoria started walking to west lake center and as they were walking a thug in a suit was fallowing them and then as the thug was fallowing them then he got out a pair of benkncolers and started spying on Alex and Victoria while they were heading into west lake center and then thug got on the phone with his boss "king I have the girl and gentlemen she is with and they are heading to Seattle center" the thug said "I will be in Seattle in your hideout by tomorrow and then we will find out who this strange charming gentleman is and kill him" his boss said "yes sir" the thug said and then the thug hanged up the phone

Then Alex and Victoria started heading to west lake center and then as they got there then they went on the monorail train that led them to Seattle center and then as they got on and Alex and Victoria sat around by the window and as they were sitting down Victoria started getting really excited and Alex was pointing at the really awesome things that where really awesome and Victoria got more and more excited and then as they got to Seattle center Victoria and Alex went to the fun Forrest and they started going on the rides and they even went on roller coaster and then as they were done going on the rides then Alex and Victoria started sharing cotton candy together and then they went inside one of the fun Forrest game room and they started playing a couple of games and then they even saw a rollerskating rink "you want to roller-skate?" Alex asked "oh sure I would love to" Victoria said and then Alex and Victoria started rollerskating and as Victoria was roller skating Alex just skated with her and teaching her how to roller skating and every time she fell Alex would always catch her and then just roller skated 7 times around the rink and they stopped around the 7th time and then they got off the rink and they started taking off the roller skates "Alex that was so incredible" Victoria said "oh do you know how to skate that good?" Victoria asked "I use to ice skate" Alex said "you where an ice skater?" Victoria said "well not exactly but I was a partner with an ice skater in Denver" Alex said "do you still see her?" Victoria asked "no not really" Alex said

Then Alex and Victoria started walking around Seattle center and around the Seattle fountain and Alex even told her the story on how he was a back up center for the Seattle sonics "wow that's super cool" Victoria said and then Alex and Victoria took the Montreal back to Alex's apartment and then as they back to the apartment Alex just rested on his bed and he started day dreaming in his bed room and then Victoria came into Alex's bed room and sat on Alex's huge bed in his apartment "so how do you like Seattle center?" Alex asked "oh Seattle center was wonderful" Victoria said and then Victoria just hugged Alex and then as Victoria was hugging Alex then Michael came into the apartment "hey guys how was Seattle center?" Michael asked "oh it was great man" Alex said "hey guys there is new night club opening tonight in sodo do you guys want to go" Michael asked "sure I'm in" Alex said "I'll go" Victoria said and later that night Alex and Victoria got on some different clothes and they took a metro bus to the sodo area and then as the three of them got on the bus Alex just looked at the window and Victoria just put her arms around Alex's arms and laid her head on Alex's shoulder and Michael was standing and hanging on the rail on the bus and then as the three of them got to the soda area there was a huge line to get into the night club that was in the sodo area and Alex, Victoria, and Michael got in line but as they were in line then some dudes in red suits with avatars on saw them in line

Then as Alex,Michael, and Victoria were in line Alex just started shaking his hand "do you always do this when you go to a night club?" Victoria asked "all the time" Alex said "you got to see him when he is in the dance floor he is crazy as hell" Michael said and then the three of them got into the sodo night club and then saw all the dancers and then without knowing Alex just started dancing and moving his hands and he started doing 80's dance moves and moving his hand and then Alex started spinning around 10 times and then Alex did a handstand and then did a back flip and then Michael joined in the fun and he started dancing and going crazy and then Victoria was not a huge dancer and then Alex grabbed her hand and he started spinning her around and then she started moving her hands and shaking her hand and then Alex lowered her down with his arm and lowering her down as down as he could go and then Alex and Michael started to roll move and then they did thumbs up and Alex and Victoria kept on dancing and just kept on grooving like there was no tomorrow and Alex took it to the floor a couple of times and then Alex did a cartwheel and he Spin Victoria and then the dance was over "that curl summer by bananarama" the DJ said and then Alex, Michael, and Victoria sat down at a table after they were done dancing "wow that was really awesome I had tons of fun" Victoria said "so you do want me to order some beers" Alex asked "HELL YEAH ALEX!!!!" Michael said in excitement "sure" Victoria said and then Victoria, Michael and Alex had a couple of drinks and drank a lot of beers and Victoria drank 3 cocktail drinks and then after the night club they took a cab back go Alex's apartment in lower queen Ann and then Alex and Michael slept around the couch and Victoria just slept by Alex but then as they were sleeping one of the Canadian thugs saw Alex sleeping on the couch with Victoria and took a picture of him and sent the photo to his boss "boss I got the photo of the American his name is Alex Aussmen an autistic secret agent from Seattle,WA" the thug said "well find out where else he is going and then fallow those fools and bring the girl to me alive" the boss said "yes sir" the thug said and then he disappeared and he was gone

Chapter 4 the road trip to Vancouver, British Columbia and the camping along the woods

Then the next day Alex,Michael and Victoria woke up from a very wild night in sodo and they all took a very long shower and they all got dressed "man last night was very wild" Alex said "oh yes it was man" Michael said "so what do you want to do tonight?" Alex asked "well we could go shopping but I'm starting to run a little low on cash" Michael said "I know what we could do we can go camping" Alex said "when man?" Michael asked "like around tonight at 6 we could go on a road trip to Vancouver and go champing" Alex said "where hell are we going to get gear?" Michael asked in a con fussing mater "well there is the REI store by my apartment I could go get some sleeping bags,tents, lamps, and a compass" Alex said "oh don't forget some "off spray" as well man" Michael said "what about swim suits?" Alex asked "Alex we are going to be in the forest so I think we will live without swim trunks when we go swimming I would guess" Michael said Alex then thought about it for a couple seconds but then came to a conclusion with "nah" Alex said and then around the afternoon Alex and Victoria went to the REI store and they got tents, sleeping bags, and lamps, and a compass and they also got new clothes as well "I'm so excited to go champing" Victoria said "same here we are going to have so much fun" Alex said and as they were done shopping they headed back to Alex's apartment in lower queen Ann and then they went up to Alex's door and there was a note and it said "went to go get a surprise back around 5" the note said Alex then grabbed the note and looked at it for a couple seconds and then put in the recycle and then Alex and Victoria waited for Michael and then around 4:50PM Michael showed up a 1980s style RV and it was really new and it looked awesome "so what do you think?" Michael asked as he showed up in the driver's seat "I thought you said you had no cash with you" Alex asked "yeah that was a lie I said that as a joke" Michael said "damn it Michael" Alex said and then Alex and Victoria went inside the RV and Michael did all the driving and Victoria and Alex were laying down in the bedroom "we are on are way" Alex said "oh yes we are baby" Victoria said and then Victoria started making out with Alex on the bed and then they went under the covers and started making out like crazy but then as Michael was driving the RV then a couple of thug cars were spying on the RV

Then as Michael was driving he then started driving really fast and then Michael turned on the radio and the song "the winds of change by Alec costindinos" was playing on the radio and then Michael turned on a highway that kept on going to I-5 north to Vancouver ,British Colombia and then as it got really late and it got to 11:00PM Michael made a left turn into a random camping site that was around a waterfall and it was by grass and Michael drove down the hill and he went down really slowly and then as they got down Michael parked the RV around the camping site by the river and where the waterfall was and then as Alex looked out the window he saw the beautiful water and the water was really beautiful and blue as the ocean and it shinned like the stars and then Alex saw the waterfall and the water coming down like shinning stars and then Alex and Michael set up champ and the tents and Michael didn't really like tents so he slept in the RV and Alex and Victoria slept in the tent they got at REI and just like in the RV Alex and Victoria just really enjoyed spending time with each other and they slept in the tent throughout the rest of the night

Then the next day Alex and Victoria got up and Alex took a shower in the RV and then as Alex got in the RV Michael was sleeping on the bunk bed in the RV and then as Alex got out of the shower he noticed that there was not a lot of food in the RV "Michael? Did you buy food?" Alex asked and then Alex noticed that Michael was still sleeping "wake the hell up!!!" Alex said and Alex started shaking Michael " I DON'T HAVE AIDS!!!!!" Michael screamed as he thought he was having a very bad dream "WAH,WAH AHHHH..." Michael yelled and Michael fell off the bunk bed and landed flat on his face "oh it was just a dream" Michael said and then Alex started cracking up like crazy "but dude did you buy food?" Alex asked again "well there is some food in fridge" Michael said and then Alex looked in the fridge and there was just a couple of snacks "DUDE YOU NEED TO BUY FOOD NOW HOW THE HELL ARE WE GOING TO SURVIE!!!..." Alex yelled "we could find a grocery store" Michael said "where the FUCK are we going to find a grocery store!?" Alex yelled again and then Alex got of the RV devastated and he headed back to his tent and then as Alex was sitting down he saw some people on a dock by another piece of land "what in the hell?" Alex thought in his head and then Alex saw 3 people swimming in the water and then as Alex was looking then Victoria walked up to Alex "hey Alex" Victoria said "oh hey what's up?" Alex said "oh nothing what are you looking at?" Victoria asked "oh nothing just some people swimming in the water" Alex said "do you want to go swimming?" Victoria asked "sure I don't really have a bathing suit though" Alex said "it's okay I don't have a bathing suit either" Victoria said then without Alex knowing Victoria started taking off her clothes and started striping down intel she was butt naked "oh you are serious" Alex said and then Victoria then went in the water "come on Alex the water feels great" Victoria said and then Alex started taking off his clothes and then went into the water butt naked and Victoria and

Alex started swimming in the water and then they started swimming to dock and then as Alex was swimming in the water he went under water and saw all the beautiful things in the water and all the beautiful fish and then Alex and Victoria went underwater and he went really,really deep and then Victoria started swimming with Alex in the water and then they got to the surface of the water and then as the two of them got to the dock then the two of them looked around "something is wrong I don't see them" Victoria said and then as Alex was on the floating dock on the water then Alex saw the waterfall "I see something they are over there" Alex said and then Alex and Victoria dived into the water and then they started swimming water and Alex was just fascinating with the water and he loved going swimming even when he was not wearing a swimsuit he still loved going swimming and then as the two of them got closer and closer to the waterfall then Alex and Victoria started climbing up the waterfall and Victoria could not really climb so she had to ride on Alex's back and let Alex do all the climbing and then as Alex was climbing they got to the top and then they dived into the water and the water in the upper level was just as deep as the lower part of the forrest "I wonder how far we went?" Victoria asked "I don't know it sounds like we are on the top of the waterfall and then as Alex were in the water they kept on going and swimming and then they dived under water and they found themselves in giant river currant and then they started going really fast and as they were on the currant then Alex grabbed a hold of Victoria's hand and then Alex and Victoria started climbing and then saw a shallow part and then they kept on swimming and then they dived under water again and then they found a tunnel and then they started going down the tunnel and started sliding down the water tunnel and going through a lot of caves and then Alex and Victoria went down the tunnel and they fell off another waterfall and then they splashed into the water and then the water was really cold and Alex and Victoria started swimming and then they saw another dock that was right by another wall "Victoria grab on" Alex said and then Victoria and Alex grabbed on to the dock and then they started climbing up the dock and avoid getting fallen off another waterfall "now where are we?" Alex asked "I don't know I think we might be lost cause I don't see our camp sit anywhere and hopefully we find some people that can help us and give us some clothes" Victoria said but then as Alex were sitting on the dock and as Alex was trying to warm Victoria with his warm arms then something coming out of the water and Alex and Victoria started getting really scarred that something was moving the dock and then the two of them really held their breathes and the dock kept on shaking and shaking but then as Alex thought it was something moving the dock then out of nowhere 2 naked women came out of the water the first girl had a very fit body and her arms looked beautiful and her legs looked very healthy they shinned like the water and she had blonde and brown hair the other girl had dark brown hair and she had a very beautiful cute face and she had brown eyes and she had a very skinny body and her hands and arms where very light and her legs were very skinny but very beautiful "are you two alright?" the girl with brown hair said "yeah were fine we thought something was wrong with the dock" Alex said "oh nothing is really wrong with dock it was just us coming if you know what we mean" the girl with blonde hair said and then the two ladies started giggling and saying how cute Alex looked "by the way what's your name sexy baby boy" the girl with brown hair asked "Aussmen...Alex Aussmen" Alex said "I'm penny and this is Jenny it's very nice to meet you Alex" penny said "oh this is my girlfriend Victoria" Alex said and then penny and Jenny got excited and they hugged Victoria like they were all friends "wait you know them" Alex asked "yeah we all went to college together in Vancouver" Victoria said "that's awesome anyway do you guys have a camping site that's close?" Alex said and then the girls giggled "yeah we do it's really close just swim with us we will get there" Jenny said

Then Alex and Victoria and the girls started swimming to another unknown champing site around that area and then Alex, Victoria, Jenny and penny waked to their champing sites and their camping sites looked very down to earth and looked like a normal champing site and there was just tents,food, and a hippie van and then as they got down to the site Alex and Victoria just sat around the site "Swyan we got guests" Jenny said and then out of nowhere a naked man with black hair and a little bit of facial hair jumped off the hippie van "hey about time you fine ladies showed up and who's the disco boy and this beautiful work of art" Swyan said "oh I'm Alex Aussmen and this is my girlfriend Victoria" Alex said "hi" Victoria said and then Victoria shake Swyan's hand "do you guys have any clothes we can wear" Victoria said and then Jenny, penny, and Swyan paused for a couple seconds and then the three of them started cracking up like drunk monkeys "what's so funny?" Victoria asked "....we don't wear clothes when we go champing my dear cause we don't want to get any clothes dirty just to save money" penny said "so you guys just don't wear any clothing what so ever when ever you guys go champing?" Alex asked "that's right sexy boy" penny said "well....you know what this is awesome I'm in this is how champing should be after all we are in Forrest right" Alex said "there you go man" Swyan said and then throughout the rest of that night Alex and Victoria stayed with Jenny, Penny, and Swyan and they ate some food and they stayed with them for a couple of 4 days with them and it was really fun but Alex started getting a little worried about Michael and how he was doing but Alex knew Michael would be just fine and Victoria and Alex had a lot of fun champing and they went swimming a lot and also Jenny and Penny had a very big huge crush on Alex and sometimes when Victoria was gone Penny would always try to flirt with Alex and so did Jenny and it was pretty wild and they would always start making out with him in the hippie van and it would get crazy but Victoria never really found out and she knew that they were always like that to a lot of guys they met and then after 4 days of camping in the woods with no clothes on Alex and Victoria went into the hippie van with Swyan, Jenny, and Penny "so are you guys heading to

Vancouver?" Swyan asked "yeah we are heading to Vancouver is there a shot cut to get there?" Alex asked "yeah if we just keep on going on I-5 north we should be there in a couple minutes" Swyan said "oh and yes we will get some clothes in Vancouver for you guys to put on and the same for us as well" Jenny said "oh wow thanks" Victoria said "yeah no problem we do this all time" Penny said

Then as they got to Vancouver they didn't have to show passport and they got in really easily and then as they got there Swyan parked the van around a really fancy store in Vancouver and Swyan just walked in the store like his nudity was no big deal and then Jenny and Penny got out of the RV and Alex and Victoria realized that Canada's laws were much different from the US laws in America and so without thinking for too long Alex and Victoria got out of the RV with no clothes on and went into the store but then as they went in the store the thugs that were in Seattle spying on Alex saw Alex and Victoria going in the store "the two of them are in the store king" one of the thugs said "good now when you get a chance drug them" his boss said on the walke talkie "yes sir" the thug said and then the thug in the suit went into store and he started looking for Alex and Victoria

Then as Alex and Victoria were done looking for clothes they went to the casher to pay for their new clothes they got and then casher looked at Alex and Victoria "so are you guys streakers or something like that yeh?" the cashier said "no were not streakers" Alex said "well around we have a lot of streakers in canada so no need to be assumed mates" the cashier said "oh okay thanks what do I owe you" Alex asked "oh your money is no good here since you guys are streakers you guys have 900% discount" the casher said "900% discount?" Alex said "yeah for streakers that come into this store it's always free" the cashier said "wow thanks man" Alex said "no problem mates are you guys from America?" the cashier asked "we I'm in American I'm from Seattle, Washington but my girlfriend is from Toronto" Alex said "oh nice well you Americans have a good day and if you ever loose your clothes your always welcome to come here mates" the cashier said "wow that's awesome thanks again man" Alex said and then Alex and Victoria left the store and they started back to hippie van but unfrogently they did not know what they were about to get into it was too late

Chapter 5 the ambush and drugged up by Canadian thugs

As Alex and Victoria were walking out of the store Alex was starting to think about Michael and how he was holding up "hopefully I will be able to find a pay phone here somewhere cause I think I really need to call Michael and tell him that we are okay" Alex said and then as they kept on walking Alex then saw a pay phone around where the hippie van was but for some reason the van was gone "what the hell? What happened to the van?" Alex said in shock "maybe they went to go find parking" Victoria said "well oh well at least there is a pay phone right there" Alex said and then Alex walked up to the pay phone and he started dialing the number to call Michael and then the phone starts ringing but Michael did not answer the phone "that's weird Michael always answers his phone I don't get it" Alex said "oh yes you don't get it Mr.Aussmen..." a voice said and then Alex and Victoria turned back and then the thug shot a medicine gun at them and then Alex and Victoria started falling a sleep and they were drugged and Alex and Victoria passed out "we got both of them king and we are going to take them to the headquarters right now" the thug said "good I would love to meet Mr.Aussmen and finally get my hands on that girl he is with HAHAHAHAHAHAHAHAHAHAHAHAHAH" the king laughed then the two thugs but Alex and Victoria's naked bodies in back of the car they were driving in and Alex and Victoria did not know where they were getting taken to but it was too a very dark place but as the thugs got there the building looked like a hotel and it was painted gold and sliver and it was located north of downtown Vancouver and as the thugs parked their car they got out of the car and put Alex and Victoria in a bag and they brought them into their boss's office "we got the secret agent from Seattle Washington king" the thugs said then their boss started walking out of their darkness and he was wearing a gold suit with gold dress shoes and he was also wearing gold leather gloves and a gold eye patch "good put them in a cage and then when they wake up bring them robes and bring them to me" their boss said "yes sir" the thugs said and then the thugs put Alex and Victoria in a cage that was metal and it looked like a jail cell and then Alex got up from a very long drugged up sleep "oh my head" Alex said and then Victoria got up as well "what happened to us?" Victoria said "I don't know I think we got kidnapped" Alex said and then Victoria looked around and she was very scarred "how are we going to get out of here?" Victoria asked "well another thought is how we are going to clothes" Alex said then their cage cell opened and the thugs brought Alex and Victoria golden robs that would cover their naked bodies "our boss would like to meet you Mr.Aussmen" one of the thugs said "yeah I do see that" Alex said and then Alex and Victoria started walking up the stairs and as they were walking Alex noticed that they were heading upstairs into the top floor and then as they kept on walking they then just stand and saw the man in the golden suit come into the area "please let them sit down" their boss said and Alex did not know how to act whether to think he was a bad guy or dude that wanted something from him "Alex Aussmen so glad to meet you for the first time allow me to introduce myself I am Wilson Winds and this is my building you are in" Winds said and he sounded like a younger man and he had blonde hair and he looked very slim and he also had a gold cane with him as well "I see you have my ex girlfriend with you Mr.Aussmen I have been looking for you for a couple of days" Winds said "you know him?" Alex asked "yeah we went out a couple of times while we were dating but then I got board and I started heading to Toronto and that's where I met you" Victoria said "and Mr.Aussmen you also has something that belongs to me" Winds said "and what the hell would that be" Alex asked "well my plan is destroy to pacific northwest including Vancouver, Portland and your hometown Seattle and my men and I know all about your naked hippie friends back in the forest as well" Winds said "what have you done with Michael?!" Alex said in rage "nothing I didn't know you had another friend with you but here is the deal you will give me 8 million dollars to destroy the pacific northwest and if you don't..." Winds said and then Winds pulled out a remote that brought up Penny,Jenny and Swyan and they were tied up in ropes and had duck tape on their mouths "your friend and your girlfriend will die in my hot,hot hot tub that can get hotter then a hot shower and burn them" Winds said and then one of the guards grabbed Victoria by the wrist and then Alex punched one of the guards in the face and then Alex grabbed a wine bottle and then the other guard pointed a gun at Alex "that is 1763 wine bottle it would be very upsetting if you broke it" Winds said "clumsy Mr.Aussmen you disappoint me" Winds said and then Alex put the bottle down "in 24 hours I will be destroy the pacific northwest and you people will never see your beautiful states again and they will be mine forever and so will your girlfriend...take the girl to my room and kill Mr.Aussmen HEHEHEHEHEHE AHAHAHAHAHAHAAHAHAHAHAHAHAHAHAHA" Winds laughed and then the guards grabbed Victoria and started pulling her into an evaluator "Alex,Alex, Alex!!!!!" Victoria screamed and then as guards were going to put Alex in jail then Alex punched of the thugs in the face and pushed them against wall and then Alex grabbed a PP7 gun and he started shooting at 9 thugs in the head and Alex started running to rescue Victoria and the others that were captured and then Alex was going up the stairs more thugs were shooting at Alex but then Alex hid behind a wall and he kept on shooting at Alex but then Alex un hid and started shooting at the thugs in the head and killed 34 thugs and Alex just started running to the elevator and then Alex pressed the up button to get to the top of the floor and then as the elevator was going up Alex noticed that the elevator was breaking down and then Alex climbed up to the other part of the elevator on the outside and then without thinking he took off his rob and he used his rob as rope and he started climbing up to the other floor and then as Alex was climbing he just jumped off his rope and then his rob fell and he failed to catch it but without thinking he knew what was in important was that he had to save Victoria from Winds before he destroys the pacific northwest

Chapter 6 The winds of change

And then as Alex got to the floor Alex knew he had to hide from the thugs and then as Alex was hiding he then found a PP7 gun he shot one of the thugs with the gun and then Alex pulled the dead thug and he stole his jumpsuit and his boots and then Alex kept on running to find Victoria

Then as Alex was looking for Victoria, Victoria had her rob removed and she was butt naked and Winds "you know my dear it was such a mistake to leave me for that Alex Aussmen fellow and you want to know something my dear" Winds said as he was kissing her "this place will be mine and yours" Winds said and then as Winds was kissing Victoria then Victoria noticed that Alex was almost in the room somehow and then Victoria started playing along with Winds and started pretending that she loved being kissed "oh I do love your gold outfit and I think your very charming Wilson and I love your gold" Victoria said and then as Wilson's phone started ringing then Victoria started smooching him on the lips just to distract him and then Alex went into the other room "I will have to take care of some business" Winds said and then Alex hid behind a table and he had a PP7 gun in his hand "you are too late Mr.Aussmen your girlfriend is just getting started with me and your Seattle will be destroyed just like you will" Winds said and then without Winds knowing Alex showed up from behind and whacked Winds in the face with his PP7 gun "think you did a good job with the lines" Alex said and then Alex pointed his gun at Winds "where's Victoria?!" Alex said "she is in my room Alex soon as I get my money she will be ours" Winds said "you know Mr.Aussmen if you did let me destroy Seattle I would have named a state after you but you just want to be part of the world like always" Winds said and then without knowing Winds threw a grenade at Alex and then the grenade exploded and Alex for forced against the wall and then Alex got up back on his feet "AHAHAHAHAHAHAHAHAHAHAHAHAHAHAHAH it's time to a play game I would love to call "the winds of change" Mr.Aussmen" Winds said and then Winds grabbed Alex by the neck and started chocking him and then ales punched him in the face and then Winds tried to punch him in the face and then Alex ducked and then did a summer salt and then Winds got out a staff and he tried to whack Alex with the staff and then Alex grabbed the staff and then punched Winds in the face again and kicked Winds in the face and then as Alex was fighting Winds then Alex forced Winds against the wall and then Winds took out a gold cane and whacked Alex in the face and then Alex got up and punched Winds in the face "it's time to die Mr.Aussmen" Winds said and then Alex noticed while Winds was trying to kill Alex with his golden cane Alex then used his watch to try to electrocute Winds and then Alex grabbed Winds by the wrist and then Winds started getting electrocuting him and then Winds was dead

Then as Winds was dead Alex started running to save Victoria and then Alex braked the door down "Alex" Victoria said "Winds?" Victoria said "Winds is dead and we are going be too if we don't get out of here" Alex said and then Alex and Victoria started running of the headquarters and then Alex pressed a button on a control panel that would let Penny,Jenny and Swyan go "thanks Alex" Swyan said "your welcome dude" Alex said and then Alex and Victoria went down an elevator to the entrance and then Penny, Jenny and Swyan came along as well and then Alex found one of the cars that one of the thugs were using and then Alex went into the car and then he used one of his gadgets that Michael gave him to start the car and then Alex started the car and then they started getting out of the headquarters area and then as they were driving the building started exploiting in flames and Winds's plan was destroyed and the pacific northwest was saved for good

Chapter 7 meeting up with Michael and heading back to Seattle with Jenny,Penny, and Swyan

 Then as Alex, Victoria, Penny, Jenny, and Swyan got back to Vancouver they then headed back back to downtown Vancouver and Swyan, Penny, and Jenny, finally found some clothes to put on and they stayed in Vancouver for a couple of days and then after 2 days the 5 of them then went on a cruise to Seattle and then as they were on the cruise Alex started thinking about where Michael and then as Alex was sitting on the chair by the swimming pool and then he saw some dude that looked like Michael and then the person jumped off the highest diving board in the whole swimming pool and then the person jumped off the tallest diving board "AHHHHHHHHHHHH!!!!" the person yelled and then Alex realized that it was Michael and then Alex walked to the swimming pool "Michael?" Alex said and then Michael got his head to the surface and saw Alex's face "Alex dude your back" Michael said "I know man how where you able to hold up" Alex asked "well I bought some food around Vancouver and I stayed in a hotel while you and Victoria were gone" Michael said "you will have no idea what we had to go through dude" Alex said "dude you got to tell me bro" Michael said and then Penny,Victoria, Jenny and Swyan "hey Alex is this your friend" Swyan asked "yeah this is Michael" Alex said and then all of them just talked about a lot of things and about the while things that happened along the trip and then as they got back to Seattle,Washington around lower queen Ann then there was a huge party and there was a huge dance party and there was even a lot of loud blasting 80's music and then Swyan and Michael were just diving into Alex's swimming pool and then Alex was watching then Victoria came up to Alex "how did you like the trip?" Alex asked "of I loved it baby" Victoria said "oh same here" Alex said and then Victoria just started smooching Alex on the lips for 20 minutes "you want to go for a swim" Alex asked and then Victoria started striping into a bathing suit and she was wearing a blue bikini bathing suit "wow..." Alex said "now that is very sexy baby girl" Alex said said and then they just kept on kissing and making out and then as they were making out Swyan and Michael pushed both Alex in the swimming pool and they both fell into the swimming pool and then as they got into the swimming pool and then they just started laughing and then Alex just left up Victoria and they just started making out in the swimming pool and they were kissing as the space needle was in the background and then they just kept on laughing and joking around for the rest of the night "oh Alex" Victoria said

The Woman With Venus Eyes & Eye Lashes

The Woman With Venus Eyes and Eyelashes

By: Nelson Amador

Chapter 1 Bellevue, Washington 1987

it was a very windy and sunny day around the east side of Washington and a metro came around Bellevue Transit train and then Alex walked out of the metro bus and he started walking to Ear's restraunt in downtown Bellevue "hi welcome to Earl's" the waitress said and then the waitress seated Alex at a table and then Alex started looking at the menu "what can I get you to drink Mr.?" the waitress said "Aussmen...Alex Aussmen" Alex said "and I will have a bud light please" Alex said and then the waitress went to go get Alex a bud light "thank you baby girl" Alex said "can I get you anything to eat?" the waitress asked "yes a beacon cheeseburger please" alex said "okay I will get you that sir" the waitress said and then the waitress went to go get Alex his food and then as alex was waiting he then saw a women in white trench coat and she was wearing a Carmen Sandiego style hat and Alex really curious and then Alex put on his spy sun glasses he had in his coat pocket and as he was looking through her clothing she was a blonde women that looked like she was in her late 30's or early 40's but she looked very heathy but she was wearing a lot of expensive clothing as well and then as Alex was spying then the waitress came with Alex's burger "heres your food" she said "thank you" Alex said and then Alex started eating his food and then as Alex was done eating his food then he staired at the women again and then the women started coming to Alex and then Alex started turning away but it was too late "hello young man my name Monica Lights and you must be Alexander Aussmen secret agent from Seattle,Washington" Monica said "yeah that is very true" Alex said "so what are you doing here?" Monica asked "I'm just having lunch" Alex said "oh well Mr.Aussmen I have a job for you" Monica said and then Monica handed Alex a photo of a girl in a Carmen Sandiego type outfit but only this time she was wearing a red,purple, green, and blue trench coat with her hat being the same colors and the same type of hat Monica was wearing "what the?!...is this a joke?! this girl looks like Carmen Sandiego I have no time for childish jokes" Alex said "young man this is no joke I will sure you that...this is Rebecca Monroe a New York assassin that has been killing tons of people here in the east side of the state of Washington and here in Bellevue and she is a man eater and kills any man she is making love to and don't her sex appeal fool you Mr.Aussmen she is beautiful...but very dangerous" Monica said "where can I find her?" Alex said "no one knows where she will be she goes to Bellevue square here in this area you will probley find her but be careful Mr.Aussmen she is a good smeller and loves the smell of cologne and I would be careful" Monica said "alright I'm in how much do I get paid?" Alex asked "saying 60,000$ if you can find her alive and turn her into our agency" Monica said "alright I'm going to go look for her right now" Alex said "you go do that Mr.Aussmen" Monica said and then as Alex left to go to Bellevue Square then in the shadows the girl that Monica was talking about was in the shadows and then the girl pulled out a cigarette and she lit

"I will find you Mr.Aussmen and you will not resist or escape" the girl said and then girl walked away in the shadows and then the girl did an evil women laugh

Chapter 2 finding the so-called "Venus killer"

 As Alex walked into Bellevue Square that same day he just started looking around the men's area and then as Alex was looking around men's department and then as Alex was around that area he noticed a lip gloss mark around and then Alex found the lip gloss stick and then Alex looked at the lip stick very close and he noticed that it was a part of a clue and then Alex took out his 1979 camera and he took a picture of the lip gloss and then Alex threw the lip gloss in the trash and then Alex kept on looking around and then Alex started walking into Bellevue Square and then as Alex walked into Bellevue Square then the girl with the trench coat started fallowing Alex without Alex even noticing and then as Alex went into a store he then found another clue and then as Alex went into that same store the same girl then hid around bushes and then as Alex was in the store he noticed that the next clue was another stick of lip gloss and then Alex took a photo of the other lip gloss and then Alex put the photo in his pockets and then as Alex got out of the store then girl with the trench coat then took out a sniper riffle and she then started loading the riffle and she tired to shot Alex with the riffle and then as Alex herd the gun shot Alex ducked and the bullet missed him and then Alex looked around to make sure he was not shot anywhere and then Alex kept on walking and then as Alex was walking he noticed that one lip gloss was green and the other one was light red and Alex knew that this girl that Monica was talking about was not an ordinary girl Alex would see most of the times and this girl was actually just like Alex and it appeared that finding this girl was trying to find himself and without him knowing he was looking for his match

 Then as Alex came back to his apartment in Seattle he then went to his desk in his pen house and he looked under a microscope and looking at the lip glosses and he noticed that both lip glosses where different brands and then as Alex kept on looking at the lip glosses again he then noticed that they had some sort of silver in them that made the colors of the lip gloss shine and then Alex took out a cell phone and he started calling Michael "hello?" Michael said "yes Michael this is Alex I need you to come over to my apartment tomorrow" Alex said and then Alex hanged up the phone and then the next day Michael came over "hey Alex what's up?" Michael said "hey man yesterday was crazy this women approached me giving me a case to go look for a killer know as "the Venus Killer" and I found her lip glosses in Bellevue square last night" Alex said and Alex hands Michael the lip gloss and Michael takes a look at them "wow so where do you think girl can be now Alex?" Michael asked "well Monica did say that she was always hanging around Bellevue and her agency has been searching for her for awhile and she is a killer" Alex said "damn Alex sounds like you are taking this case very seriously" Michael said "well yeah but I don't get one thing...how come this Monica women approached me and hired me when they have good agents looking for her right now?" Alex said "you know that is a very good question Alex my man" Michael said "so when do you go back to Bellevue?" Michael said "well around later tonight around another mall thats there" Alex said "well good luck and hope you crack this case alive" Michael said and then Michael left Alex's apartment and Alex started thinking to himself for a while and he kept himself busy by swimming in his swimming pool and watching TV

then around night time Alex got on a red suit on with red suit pants with a blue neck tie and Alex drove his 1985 Lamborghini Countach around Bellevue and he parked his car around another mall in Bellevue and then Alex walked into the mall and then he started looking around and then as Alex was walking around the mall an older gentlemen with blonde hair and eye glasses saw Alex "stop young man that's a trap" the man said "wait what?" Alex said in shock but it was too late and Alex fell into a trap door from the floor and Alex started sliding down a slide like he was going down a water slide in a water park and then Alex fell flat on his face on the ground "ahhhh...shit" Alex said as he was on the ground and then Alex got up back on his feet and then Alex herd an evil women laugh "well hello and good evening I am Rebecca Monroe and you must be Alex Aussmen I have herd so many wonderful sexy things about you" Rebecca said and then as Alex was on his feet he noticed that the girl was in a chair wearing a red,green, and purple trench coat and both of her eyes where both different colors and so were her eye lashes and the women was honey blonde and she had medium length of hair but she had a very fit body and her breathes where very huge "so Mr.Aussmen I see you do a lot of spying if that's correct" Rebecca said and then Rebecca pressed a button on her remote that brought down a huge TV screen and then the screen showed a lot of places Alex was in including Bellevue Sqaure and him finding the lip sticks "I see you are a very gifted and very smart secret agent Mr.Aussmen we both have that part in common how we both seduce people and do a lot of spying but only difference between you and me is that I have more clothes to wear so no one finds me while you just blind in with the crowd but another thing we both have in common Mr.Aussmen is that we both wear very expensive clothing" Rebecca said "what are you planning anyway I know Monica Lights contacted me to find you and to take you in" Alex said and then Rebecca started laughing for 17 minutes and she would just not shut up "oh you are funny Mr.Aussmen but Monica is a liar and you won't find that out now but you will later Mr.Aussmen" Rebecca said "what the hell are talking about?" Alex asked "come with me Alex and I will tell you everything..." Rebecca said and then Rebecca pressed a button on her remote went down another trapped door and Alex started hearing another evil woman laugh and then Alex was on another water slide like slide that was taking him up and then going straight down really fast "AHHHHHHHHHHHHHHHHHHHHHHHHHHHHHHHHHHHHHHHHHHHHHHHHHHH HHHHHHHHHHHHHHHHHHHHHHHHHHHHHHHHHHHH...."Alex yelled and then before he knew it Alex flew out of air vent down and landed flat on his face again and then Alex got back on his feet "what in the hell?" Alex said and then as Alex was getting up he noticed he was now in Pen House in Bellevue and he noticed a lot of things this one that were a lot different from his pen house in Seattle there was huge living room,kitchen, swimming pool, an upstairs, and a gym and the room was painted red and pink "how do you like my pen house Mr.Aussmen?" Rebecca said "it is really nice" Alex said and then Alex started looking around for anything that looked strange and then Alex noticed she also had a record player as well and it looked like she tons of money just like Alex did and Alex felt like for the first time he was looking in a mirror and seeing a women version of himself and that women version of Alex was Rebecca in a lot of ways and it seemed like Rebecca had the same personality that Alex had very fun to be around, very nice,very sexy and very crazy "why don't you come outside Alex" Rebecca said and then Alex went outside on her porch and Alex then herd a huge splash and Rebecca was in her swimming pool butt naked "why don't you come in...it's very cold but you will make it a lot warmer if you come in" Rebecca said and Rebecca had a very beautiful smile and then Alex started taking his clothes off and then he went into Rebecca's swimming pool butt naked "wahoo" Alex said and "you know there is something about you that just turns me on..." Rebecca said and then Rebecca started touching Alex in a tons of areas including his pennis and his back area and around his apps as well "oh your apps are just so very fit" Rebecca said and then Rebecca just kept on kissing Alex on the lips and then Alex just caught up in the moment and then Alex slept with Rebecca and had sex with her

Chapter 3 meeting William Rivers and Dennis Castillo

 Then the next day got up and he was butt naked and then without covering his nudity he started looking for his clothes and Alex could not find them "where the hell are my clothes?" Alex asked "oh I'm sorry Alex but I burned them" Rebecca said and then Rebecca just started laughing like crazy "Jesus christ!!!" Alex said and then Rebecca just kept on laughing and then as Alex tried to get out of his bed then Rebecca grabbed Alex's arm "no your not going anywhere Mr.Aussmen" Rebecca said and then Alex tried to get free but Rebecca was just really strong "let go of me" Alex said and then finally when Alex got free Alex just started running but then as Alex was trying to run out of the Rebecca's room but then Rebecca pull out a claw gun and then the claw grabbed Alex's ankle and then Alex tripped and then Rebecca got out of bed without covering her nudity and she went on top of Alex "oh you think you can hurt me baby boy" Rebecca said and then Alex tried to get free again by trying to spread Rebecca's legs but her thighs where very strong and then as finally got free again Alex then picked her up and threw her off the pen house room and instead of screaming she just started laughing while she was falling down and then as Rebecca was falling she then grabbed a hold of metal bar that was close to ground and then as Rebecca got to ground then Rebecca started streaking around and started running around the city butt naked "catch me if you can Alex Aussmen" Rebecca said and Rebecca took off running and then Alex ran out of her pen house and then stole a man's suit that was a white suit jacket with a black button shirt with a British style scarf and then Alex saw a 1987 mustang then Alex hopped into the car and then Alex started speeding and then Alex saw Rebecca on a motorcycle speeding around Pioneer square "you have your car, I have my motorcycle" Rebecca said and then as Alex started speeding up in his car and then Rebecca pressed a button on her motorcycle that blasted a oil slick at Alex's car and then Rebecca just started laughing and then Alex whipped the oil slick with his car whippers on the wind shelled of the car and then Rebecca took a left turn around eliot bay in downtown Seattle and then Alex kept on falling her and they where both going really fast and then as Alex was gaining on Rebecca then pulled out some glasses that has lasers on them and then Rebecca fired a laser at Alex's tires and then Alex's tires started getting worn out and Rebecca just kept on laughing like crazy and then Alex jumped out of the car and hoped on Rebecca's motorcycle "STOP THE BIKE!!!!!" Alex yelled "or what I know your not going to arrest me...Mr.Aussmen" Rebecca said and then Rebecca "catch you later sexy boy..." Rebecca said and then Rebecca pressed a button that was an ejector seat and then the seat blasted off "AHHHHHHHHHHHHHHHHHHHHHHHHHHH..." Alex yelled and then Alex landed flat on his face and then Rebecca "bye,bye Alex Aussmen" Rebecca said and then Rebecca just started laughing in crazy laughter and then Alex got up on his feet and then Rebecca got closer and closer to the eliot bay and then she turned off her motorcycle and she took off her clothes and she dived into the ocean butt naked and started swimming and the cops never caught her and then Alex watched in total shocking amazement and then as Alex was about to walk away then a truck pulled up and grabbed Alex and kidnapped him and Alex tried to get free but then as he tried to get free one of the thugs in the car gave Alex a shot that put him a sleep and then an agent group broke into the truck and rescued Alex

then later around night time Alex was laying down on a bed and then Alex got up from sleeping and he noticed he was somewhere else "are you okay dude?" a voice said "yeah I am who are?" Alex asked "I'm Dennis I'm a field agent we noticed you were in trouble and we saved you" Dennis said "oh thanks the names Aussmen...Alex Aussmen" Alex said and then an African American that looked like she was in her late 20's showed up "hey sugar are you alright" the women said "yeah I think I am" Alex said "do you need us to give you ride home?" she asked "no I thank I can walk home...where am I by the way?" Alex asked "your in lower queen ann" another voice said then a much older man in his late 30's and early 40's showed up and he had blonde hair with a bald spot on his head and he was wearing blue and black eye glasses and was wearing a piece necklace and was wearing red jeans with white dress shoes and a hippie shirt "good evening Mr.Aussmen I am William Rivers head of Lower Queen agencies and I see you meet Jamie and Dennis one of our agents but you can call me Will" William said "how did you know who I was?" Alex asked "who doesn't know who you are you Alex Aussmen one of most heavily respected private investigator and secret agent in the city of Seattle and you also graduated from Tahoma High School in 1979 we know who you are in a lot of good ways" William said "awesome" Alex said "alright anyway thanks for your hospitality but I gotta go home" Alex said "don't you want to eat some dinner first before you leave?" William said "who was I kidnapped by?" Alex asked "you where kidnapped by a Venus truck and they are posing as a make-up company but really they are trying to make fake make-up products to kill people with them and their factory is in Portland, Oregon and Rebecca Monroe the girl you where chasing is working for them and is highly dangerous killing thousands of college students in

Bellevue and in the east cost as well" William said "yeah she was hard to chase down it just seems she knows all my moves and just took them to another level" Alex said "do you know who her boss is?" Alex asked "well we are trying to get that point but we do know that their factory is in Portland,Oregon so thats all we know" William said "oh thats a very good start" Alex said "anyway do you wants us to get a cheeseburger for you Mr.Aussmen?" Dennis asked "yes please" Alex said and then later that night Alex and this agency group talked more and more

then around night time Jamie drove Alex home back to his apartment in Seattle Center "anyway thanks for driving me by the way" Alex said "your welcome Alex anytime" Jamie said and then Alex walked out of Jamie's car and started heading into his apartment and then as Alex was going into his hotel room then the security camera got hacked and then from somewhere else Rebecca and Monica where spying on Alex and "what a stupid man how we hired for nothing once he finds out the truth about our little evil make-up product plan" Monica said "oh yes Monica Mr.Aussmen will never be able to stop us and the make-up world will be in total chambulls and nobody can stop us" Rebecca said "that is very true" Monica said and then Monica started doing an evil women laugh

Chapter 4 the trip to Portland with Dennis, Jamie, and William

 Then the next day Alex got up and he took a shower and then he got on a suit with red jeans with some 1980's tennis shoes with a belt and then Alex was wearing a yellow button up shirt with a orange tie and Alex was wearing a red suit jacket and then Alex started packing his clothes into a suitcase and he also brought his wallet and Alex put into his wallet into his suitcase and then Alex walked out of his apartment and he started heading towards his bus and then as the express bus came Alex then started going on the bus and Alex sat on one of the high seats on the metro bus and the bus was heading to Portland, Oregon and then as Alex was on the bus as the bus was heading south of the state of Washington and Alex saw the city of Tacoma and Tacoma was just an awful city and was very awful looking compared to Seattle but the good news though was that Alex saw Olympia the state capital of the state of Washington and then as the bus went more and more south Alex started notching was getting a lot more and more warmer and sunny and then as the express was going across the Colombia river Alex knew that he just arrived in Portland and Alex was just fascinated with the weather in Portland and then as the bus got to downtown Portland the bus got dropped Alex around one of streets in the city but unlike Seattle Portland seemed like a very small city compared to Seattle and Alex didn't have too much trouble finding his way around and then Alex was walking in the city he saw a lot of small coffee shops and stores and then as Alex got into more of downtown Portland he saw a mall that was in Portland and then without thinking Alex went into the mall and then as Alex got into the mall Alex just started looking around and the clothes in Portland where just really awesome looking and Alex noticed just like with everybody else was that there was no sales tax in Portland and Alex right off the bat bought a lot of awesome 1980's style clothing in the mall

then as Alex was done shopping he then found a hotel room in downtown Portland and then as Alex walked into the hotel room a women wearing a gold trench coat and hat saw Alex go into the hotel room and the girl was Rebecca and Rebecca did a very evil girl smile then Alex walked to the lobby "good evening my name is Aussmen...Alex Aussmen do you have an able hotel room?" Alex asked "oh yes we do Mr.Aussmen there is a suite that is one the 43rd floor sir" the door man said "awesome I will take it" Alex said and then Alex was handed the key and then Alex walked to the hotel room on the 43rd floor and then as Alex saw the hotel room and the room just had a very awesome view of the city and there was even a huge swimming pool and the pool looked very beautiful and then just without thinking Alex started digging into his swim trunks and he put on his swim trunks and then Alex took the elevator to the swimming pool and then as Alex got to the swimming pool he then jumped into the water and Alex started swimming in the pool then as Alex was swimming he saw a women a very green and yellow bikini and then Alex saw a very tall and beautiful African American girl and the girl looked like Jamie but Alex just tried to focus on her and he kept on swimming and then as Alex was done swimming Alex then grabbed a towel and he started drying himself off and then Jamie turned her head to Alex as she was tanning "nice swimming moves for a secret agent" Jamie said "oh thanks" Alex said "how did you know I was here?" Alex asked "your very noticeable because of your sexy 1970's hair-do sugar" Jamie said "that is very true" Alex said "so hotel number are you staying in sugar?" Jamie asked "well I'm on the 43rd floor in this hotel you?" Alex asked "just a floor lower then you sugar do you stay in a normal room or a suite?" Jamie asked "it's a suite" Alex said "oh my god you are kidding..." Jamie said "I'm not kidding" Alex said "damn sexy boy you have good spy skills and your hella rich damn sugar" Jamie said "so is it just you here then?" Alex asked "yes Dennis is staying in another hotel with William" Jamie said "oh nice" Alex said "you want to come see my suite?" Alex asked "hell yeah sugar of course I would" Jamie said "don't you need to shower first" Alex asked "i'll shower in your room you don't mind...do you?" Jamie asked "no go head you can use anything you want" Alex said "thanks sugar" Jamie said and then Jamie kissed Alex on the check

then Alex and Jamie started heading to Alex's hotel room and then as Alex opened his hotel room door and Jamie stood there in a amazement on how Alex's hotel room looked very nice "damn Alex your hotel room is hella nice" Jamie said "oh thanks Jamie" Alex said "well I better want to go shower" Jamie said and then Jamie went into Alex's bathroom in his hotel room and she took her bathing suit off in Alex's bathroom and she went in the shower and she started taking a shower and then as Alex was waiting for Jamie to get out of the shower then suddenly the shower just stopped and Jamie came out of Alex's bathroom with a towel covering her nudity and then as Alex was sitting on the bench on the balcony of his suite then Alex noticed some clothing on his bed and it was Sonic's jersey, a pair of blue 1980's jeans, blue socks, a wristband and that was it "I'm not going to be an undercover NBA player am I...cause I was one of my missions 3 or 2 years ago" Alex said "no your not sugar it's just disguise sugar" Jamie said "oh thank god" Alex said "anyway dress me..." Alex said "really?" Alex said "okay" Alex said and then Alex stripped Jamie's towel off of her and Jamie was butt naked in front of Alex and Jamie didn't do anything "now you" Jamie said and then Alex took his clothes off and butt naked in front of Jamie "I think your body of work should be fine now lets put some clothes on we don't want to go the game butt naked sugar" Jamie said "game?" Alex asked " that's right we are going to a trail blazers game Rebecca Munroe and her thieves are going to be there" Jamie said "got it" Alex said and then Jamie handed Alex a PP7 gun "your going to need that" Jamie said "sweet" Alex said and then Jamie and Alex started getting dressed and Jamie was wearing silver jeans on wearing a Trail Blazzers jersey without wearing a bra and she was also a wearing some 1980's style shoes with some socks and then her DD4 gun was in her pocket and she was also wearing a silver watch and a wristband "you ready sugar" Jamie asked "I was born ready" Alex said

Chapter 5 spying on Rebecca and her master thugs at the trail blazers game

 Then as Alex and Jamie got to Trail Blazers arena they found a way to get tickets into the game and then Alex and Jamie found Dennis and William sitting around the lower area of the arena and then all four of them including Alex started watching the game "you see anything Alex my man" William asked and then Alex pulled out binoculars and looked on the other side of the arena and then Alex suddenly saw Rebecca and Monica at the game "yeah I see her Will" Alex said "alright Alex you go chase Rebecca and Jamie and the rest of us will hack into the suites and see if there is any stolen cash in the suites in the arena" William said "I will do that Will my man" Alex said "do you have a gun?" Dennis asked "oh yeah" Alex said "what do you see next Alex baby boy" Jamie asked Alex then looked into them again and saw her with one of the trail blazers cheerleaders " I see her...she is giving a fake eye lash to a cheerleader...uh oh she is running..I gotta go chase her!!!" Alex said and then Alex suddenly got out of the stands and he started running to find Rebecca around the walking areas of the arena and Alex knew he had to step up his chase and then Alex saw Rebecca running "STOP RIGHT THERE!!!!!!" Alex yelled and then Alex pulled out a PP7 gun out of his pockets and tried to shoot at her but his bullets missed her and Alex kept on chasing her and then Rebecca climbed onto a ladder and then Alex started climbing to catch her but then as Alex got to the top Rebecca was gone and Alex just started looking around but then suddenly then Alex got punched in the face and it was by Rebecca and then Alex tried to kick her in the face "don't you ever give up Mr.Aussmen" Rebecca said and then Alex avoid one of her punches and then Alex did a cartwheel and loaded up his PP7 gun and shot her in the arm "AHHHHH..." Rebecca yelled and then Rebecca fell against the ground and Alex slapped her in the face "where is your boss and the eye lashes?!" Alex yelled and then Alex loaded up his PP7 gun again "if you don't tell me you will either get a shot in the head or I take you the police NOW TALK!!!!" Alex yelled "I will never talk no matter how many times you catch me Mr.Aussmen and your little secret agent group of yours will never catch me and my frad business and you will never know the truth about Monica" Rebecca said "oh yeah try me god damn it!!!" Alex yelled and then loaded up his gun again but it was too late and then William, Dennis, and Jamie showed up and arrested Rebecca "this ain't over Mr.Aussmen" Rebecca yelled "oh yes it is" Alex said and then Alex started running to the trail blazers cheerleaders locker room and saw the girl with eye lashes "DON'T PUT THAT ON!!!!' Alex yelled "but it's makeup though the cheerleader said "no it's not..." Alex said and then as the cheerleader dropped the eye lashes then the eye lashes fell into a puddle of water and then eye lashes start spreading around the puddle of water and then the cheerleader started getting really scarred "is that poison oh my god..." the cheerleader and then she got really scarred and then she hugged Alex "yes it was poison and that was going happen to your body if you put that on" Alex said "thank you...you saved me Mr.?" the cheerleader asked "Aussmen...Alex Aussmen" Alex said "thank you Alex" the cheerleader said

 Then as Alex and Dennis, Jamie, and William got out of the arena in Portland then to celebrate that they caught Rebecca they went to a restraunt in downtown Portland but they went in there the restraunt was above a thugs basement and then one of the thugs saw Alex coming "he's coming Mrs. Lights" the thug said "good I want you to make sure he sits on the trap seat and gets brought to me" Monica said

 Then as Rebecca was in prison in Portland then for some reason she was able to escape by using some sort of gadgets that she had and then she even killed one of the police officers and she stole a car and headed to that same location Alex and the group he was with and Alex was walking into a very huge trap

 Chapter 6 the truth about Monica Lights in the basement

 Then as Alex,Jamie,William, and Dennis walked in they then sat down "so what are you drinking Alex?" Dennis asked "I don't know yet Dennis my man probley a bud light I guess" Alex said "same here dude" Dennis said "what about you Will?" Alex asked "probley scotch" William said and then as the night went along just fine they all ate pizza and drank tons of beer but then as they got then a random band started playing "Summer Madness by Kool & The Gang" but then as they kept on playing then some metal cups grabbed Alex's legs and the chair tipped over and threw Alex into a slide that was going down "ALEX!!!!!!..." William yelled and then as Alex going down then a couple of thugs pointed guns at Jamie, Dennis, and William "hands up Seattle people and we will take good care of Mr.Aussmen you Seattle shit-heads!!!!!" the thugs said

"AHHHHHHHHHHHHHHHHHHHHHHHHHHHHHHHHHHHHHHHHHHHHHHHHH HHHHHHHHHHHHHHHHHHHHHH!!!!!!..." Alex yelled as he was sliding down and then Alex fell on a chair and then cups showed up on the chair and locked on Alex's wrists and then Alex herd an women laugh and then a women in a gold dress with white gloves with gold high heals "Alexander Aussmen agent 001 I'm really glad you can join us" Monica said "wait a minute your not a CIA agent your the one thats behind all this!!!" Alex yelled "oh correct you are Mr.Aussmen I knew you would fall for my nonsense so I used you to chase after Rebecca so I could see you die in action but it turns out you are very hard to kill Alex" Monica said and then Rebecca showed up with an A33 riffle "your not going to get away with this Monica!!!!!!!" Alex yelled "oh what the hell are you and your Seattle secret agent going to do to stop me and my plan from succeeding Mr.Aussmen and tons of women buying eye lashes only to realize they are poison" Monica said and then Monica started laughing "your going to kill millions of women in the country thats a very sad thing to do" Alex said "oh it is Mr.Aussmen but I'm afraid you never got to find that out as quickly as you would of loved to if thats right" Monica said "Rebecca won't you be a good barbie doll and kill Mr.Aussmen" Monica said "with pleasure" Rebecca said and then Rebecca took Alex's clothes off intel he was butt naked put him on a slider to slide him into very cold ice water that 400 degrees below 0 "you know Alex we could have been very talented and awesome lovers but you choice to be the good guy and I choice to make make-up better and make tons of money doing it" Rebecca said "how does that sound Mr.Aussmen" Rebecca said and then Alex noticed some sort of rope and then Alex grabbed on to the rope and kicked Rebecca and then Rebecca tried to attack Alex with a knife but then as she did Alex ducked and then Alex saw a green liquid run that hatched to a hose and then Alex turned the hose on and then as Rebecca was about to attack Alex then Alex spread the hose gun at her and then as Alex was spraying the green liquid started eating up her clothes and Rebecca was butt naked and then Alex threw a rock over her head and then Alex tackled Rebecca and then Rebecca started sliding down the slide
"AHHHHHHHHHHHHHHHHHHHHHHHHHHHHHHHHHHHHHHHHHHHHHHHHH HHHHHHHHHHHHHHHHHHHHHHHHHHHHHHHHHHHHHHHH!!!!!!!" Rebecca screamed and then Rebecca froze into an ice cube "try to out heat that" Alex said and then as Alex escaped his clothes where distorted and Alex saw a thug walking by and then Alex beat up the thug and stole his clothes and then Alex found a way to get back to the top floor and then as Alex got to the top floor he then met up with Jamie and Dennis and Alex got back to his hotel room and Alex knew he had to stop Monica and Rebecca from getting those eye lashes on the market and fast

 Chapter 7 the break into the eye lashes factory

Then as Alex got back to his hotel in Portland he then told the gang about Monica's plans "so where are they going to sell the product?" Jamie asked "I don't know yet but I know they are going to see if they can get those eye lashes on the market and we need to stop them and quick" Alex said "I agree with you Alex" William said "do you have the address of the factory?" Dennis asked "well not yet but we got to get it and fast" Alex said

Then the next day Alex and his group went to go look for this factory but then as they all looked on the map it was not on the GPS in William's rented car and they realized it was in one of the mountains really high "so what do you purpose we do Alex?" Dennis asked "well Jamie and I get some snow clothes and see if we can get the top" Alex said "what about us?" William asked "you guys come with us but go through the back of the mountain and we will take the front" Alex said and then Alex and Jamie went into a North face store around the mountain and then Jamie and Alex got on some clothes and then Alex saw one of the guards come near them and then as they saw them they pullled out laser guns "YOU GUYS HANDS UP!!!!!" the guards yelled and then Alex took out a PP7 gun and shot him in the head and so did Jamie "come on" Alex said and then Alex and Jamie jumped on to the snow mobile and then they started going up the mountain really fast and then as they where going really fast then a couple of thugs started chasing them "Alex we got company" Jamie said and then Alex pulled out a PP7 gun and then he started shooting the thugs but the thugs started shooting back "STOP OR YOU WILL BE SHOT!!!!!" the thugs yelled but then Alex threw a grenade from his spy pack he had and threw it at the thugs and then thugs's snow mobile blew up in flames and then as Alex and Jamie got up to the top then they got to the top and just saw nothing "now what do we do?" Jamie asked "I'm thinking of something" Alex said and then as Alex was thinking then Alex came up with a solution and then Alex saw a weak part of the mountain and just thought of an idea "I got it but we got to stand back" Alex said then Alex used one of his grenade and then shoved the grenade into the mountains pitts and then the grenade exploded in flames and then as the grenade Alex and Jamie saw a hole and then Alex and Jamie jumped into the hole and then they started sliding down and then they fell into a huge eye lash factory that was just huge and had tons of convarelbelts

then suddenly Jamie tripped and fell off one of the ledges and she screamed "JAMIE!!!" Alex yelled and then another object hit Alex from behind in the back and then Alex and Jamie went on separate belts in the factory and then Alex did a bunch of summer salts to avoid the knives that where trying cut the fake eye lash hairs and then Alex jumped to another converal belt and then Alex tried to get back on the ledge as fast he can and then Alex started slipping and then Alex tried to keep his balance and then Alex noticed a lot of ice coming down on the eye lashes coming down and then Alex did more summer salts to avoid the hits then more thugs went to attack Alex as he was on the conferral belts "GIVE UP MR.AUSSMEN YOU ARE DOOMED!!!!!!! AHAHAHAHAHAHAHAHAHAHAHAHAHAHAHAH"

Monica laughed as she was on the screen in the factory "FUCK HIM!!!!" Monica screamed and then thugs tried to attack Alex and punch him in the face and then Alex avoided all the hits and punches and then Alex noticed some of the bars by him and then Alex whacked one of the metal bars in thug's face and then another thug tried to whack and knife and then Alex defined himself with a metal bar and whacked him in the face then Alex noticed more things in the factory coming right at him and then Alex noticed that they where about to go into a liquid shooting that made the eye lashes fashionable and then jumped up in the air and to avoid the shots but then Alex as he was not looking then a eye lash gun shot at Alex's arm and then Alex was stuck to the converell belts and then Alex as fast as he could tried to get free and Alex noticed he was coming into freezer that where going to freeze the eye lashes into a special freezer and then more thugs tried to attack Alex with a kitchen knife and cut him in the head "IT'S TIME TO HAVE SOME FUN YOU AUTISTIC SEATTLE MOTHER FUCKER!!!!!!!" one of the thugs yelled at Alex as they where trying to stab him in the head and then Alex got himself free with one of heat gadgets he had in his pocket and then unfreeze his arm and then kicked one of the thugs in the face and punched the other one in the stomach and then more thugs came at Alex as he was on the belt and then Alex tackled one of the thugs and knocked him out and then another thug tried to stab Alex but then Alex but then Alex turned back and then kicked the thug in the face and the thug fell off the ledge

 Then Jamie was really scarred and then she tried to run on the belts to avoid the hits and knives coming down on her but then just like with Alex she got hit by an eye lash gun and Jamie tried to get herself free but then Jamie used her strength to get free and then Jamie pulled out a laser gun and she started shooting at thugs that where trying to attack her but then a random attacked Jamie from behind "get off me" Jamie said and then Jamie fell of the belt and then she fell into a huge eye lash pan and it was pouring ice water and then Alex saw the gun about to pour down on Jamie but then Alex took out a sniper riffle from his pack and shot the riffle at one of the wires to disable to gun and Alex started running to Jamie "Jamie hang on" Alex said and then Alex held on to Jamie's hand and brought her up "are you okay?" Alex asked and then Alex got shot in the neck by a tranquilizer gun and Alex passed out "ALEX!!!!!" Jamie yelled and then more thugs showed up and they had a A33 riffle guns in their hands and Jamie and Alex where captured "DON'T FUCKING MOVE SEATTLE AGENTS TAKE THEM AWAY!!!!!!" the thugs yelled and then Alex and Jamie where handcuffed and then they where taken upstairs into the royal part of the factory and there was Monica's desk all iced up she even had a frozen office chair and then as she was sitting down she then saw Alex and Jamie handcuffed "good evening Mr.Aussmen and I see you brought your girlfriend with you" Monica said and then Monica did a very evil women smile and then Monica went up to Alex and just slapped him and made a scare on his check "you see Alex I'm making the best make-up in the world and the whole world will know of my product" Monica said "give it up Monica nobody will never buy those lashes you have" Alex said "wrong Mr.Aussmen young man my work will be defined in a lot of ways and it will change to make-up industry as we know it" Monica said and then Monica pulled down on a lever and then some of eye lashes came down on some of the female workers and then the eye lashes started killing down and then Monica just started laughing like an evil cheerleader and laughing like a complete bitch "that was the most fucked up thing I have ever seen" Alex said and then as Monica stopped laughing she then took out an iced cigarette and she then started smoking "it's too late to save your other fellow agents Mr.Aussmen cause my thugs have captured them as well" Monica said and then Monica pulled out a remote and showed Dennis and William tied up in ropes "so what is it going to be Alex your friends or the mission to stop me?' Monica asked and then as Monica asked then Rebecca showed in a yellow jumpsuit "and this time you will not get out of my sight Alex" Rebecca said and then Alex headed butted one of the guards and unhandcuffted himself and then Alex punched one of the guards then Monica punched Alex from behind with her fist in the back "YOUR TOO LATE AGAIN MR.AUSSMEN!!!!! AND YOUR FRIENDS ARE GOING TO DIE!!!!!" Monica yelled and then Jamie handcuffed herself and then Jamie kicked Monica in the face "think again you old eye lash bitch!!!!!!" Jamie yelled and then Jamie got up and then she took out a dart gun and shot Jamie in the arm and then Jamie passed out "NOOOOOOOOOOO!!!..." Alex yelled "ahahahahahahahah there is nobody that can help you Mr.Aussmen..." Monica said and then Rebecca suddenly took off yellow jumpsuit and Rebecca was butt naked underneath the jumpsuit and then Rebecca started chocking Alex with the jumpsuit and then Monica pulled out a DD4 gun and loaded the gun and Monica pointed the gun at Alex's head "its a shame such a cramming man like you has to die Mr.Aussmen and nobody not even you will stop me" Monica said and then as Rebecca was chocking Alex then Alex head butted Rebecca and then Rebecca without putting her jumpsuit back on then she tried to Alex but then Alex picked up a huge ice cube bar and whacked Rebecca in the face with the bar and knocked her out and then Monica got out a huge ice staff and she tried to personally fight Alex in staff combat and then Monica tried to stab Alex in the stomach but then Alex summer salted and then he picked up a small kitchen knife he found the ground and then Monica tried to whack Alex in the face and Alex avoided all of Monica's attacks and then Monica whacked Alex in the face and then Alex had a black eye and then Monica tried to whack Alex again with her ice staff but then Alex kicked Monica in the neck and then Monica fell on her back and then she got back on her feet "you cannot break me Alex cause I'm very strong and very beautiful" Monica said and then Monica tried to stab Alex in the head but Alex dodged the attack and defined himself with his kitchen knife and then as Alex kept on defending himself then Monica whacked the kitchen knife out of Alex's hands and then Alex picked up a small metal bar then Alex defended himself with a metal bar but then Monica whacked Alex in the face again and then Monica whacked Alex in the stomach and Alex was just beaten up like crazy from Monica's ice staff and Alex was just tried and egsausted "you have interfered with my plans for the last time Mr.Aussmen!!!!!" Monica yelled and then Monica tried to hit Alex in the face but then Alex barley avoided the hit and then Alex saw a fire gun that was by him and then "it's time to die Mr.Aussmen now say good-night!!!" Monica yelled and then Alex did a very huge gulp and then as Monica was about to attack Alex then Alex kicked Monica in the wrist and then Alex as fast as he could pulled out the fire gun and then Alex started shooting a flame gun at her dress

"NOOOOO... MY DRESS IT'S BURNING!!!!!!!...NOOOOOO!!!!" Monica screamed and then Monica's dress started burning up in flames and then so did her ice high heels and her ice clothing and they started melting and then Monica was butt naked "noooooooooooo my beautiful clothing I don't want to be naked" Monica said and then Monica got really angry and then she tried to attack Alex but then Alex whacked her in the face with his metal bar and knocked her out "the only thing your getting is a pass to jail!!!" Alex said

 Then Alex ran to Jamie and then Jamie got up and she started coughing "Jamie are you okay?" Alex asked "I'm fine Alex" Jamie said "common we gotta save the others common" Alex said then Alex and Jamie started running as the eye lashes factory was just going crazy and then Alex and Jamie saw Dennis and William in a jail cell "Alex" William said "hey guys Monica is dead is there a way to crack this open" Alex asked "right here my man" Dennis said and then Dennis opened the jail cell "are you guys alright?" Alex asked "I think where fine you saved us dude" William said "your welcome Will dude" Alex said and then Alex,Jamie, Dennis, William started running out of the eye lashes factory and then Alex opened a helicopter door "get in" Alex said and then Jamie, Dennis, and William got into the helicopter then from out of nowhere Rebecca appeared wearing an ice jumpsuit "Alex watch out behind you" William and then Alex turned back and Rebecca used an A33 riffle and she hit Alex in the face and then Alex got up and then Rebecca grabbed Jamie by the wrist and pointed the A33 riffle "don't get up Mr.Aussmen or I kill your girlfriend and your friends" Rebecca said "it's all over Rebecca let her go..." Alex said and then Alex noticed some sort of weak spot on Alex's jacket and then threw one of his grenades and threw it around the piles of snow on the mountain and then snow fell on Rebecca and then Alex did a summer salt and saw a hose and sprayed the hose at Rebecca "AHHHHHHHHHHHHHHH!!!!..." Rebecca yelled and then Rebecca pulled out a kitchen knife from her jumpsuit and then she tried to stab Alex in the stomach and then Alex dodged one of Rebecca's attacks and then Rebecca bitch slapped Alex in the face really hard and then Alex got really quickly and jumped in the air kicked Rebecca in the face and then as Rebecca was on the ground then she got up and she tried to punch Alex in the face and then she got out a huge double ice sword and tried Alex in the face with the sword and Alex did a backflip cartwheel and then as Rebecca was about to hit Alex in the face Alex then grabbed the sword to protect himself and Rebecca tried to stab Alex in the head but then Alex was grabbing on to the sword Alex kicked Rebecca in the stomach and then Alex slapped her in the face and then as Rebecca was on the ground then she got out a taser and then Rebecca tried to taser Alex "I owe a very painful death Mr.Aussmen" Rebecca said and then as Rebecca was about to taser Alex, Alex noticed a branch on the mountain and then Alex jumped to hang on the branch and then Alex kicked Rebecca in the face for the final time and then the taser came out of her hands and then Alex grabbed the taser and then took out one of taser bullets and put into his PP7 gun and then as Rebecca was about to attack him Alex shot one of the taser bullets at Rebecca's shoulder and then Alex started electrocuting Rebecca
"AHHHHHHHHHHHHHHHHHHHHHHHHHHHHHHHHHHHHHHHHHHHHHHHHHHH.

...." Rebecca screamed and then Alex bitch slapped her in the face "Rebecca Monroe you are under arrest for criminal and henchmen activity and for murder and committing FRAD YOU ARE GOING TO SPY JAIL!!!!!!!!!!!" Alex yelled "NOOOOOOOOOOOOOOOOOOOOOOOOOOOOOOOOOOOOOOOOOOOOOO OOOOOOOOOOOOOOOOOOOOOOO!!!!!!! THIS IS NOT THE END OF IT I WILL COME BACK AND GET YOU ALEX AUSSMEN I WILL KILL YOU, YOU SON OF A BITCH!!!!!!!!!!!" Rebecca yelled and then Alex put her on the helicopter in handcuffs and so was Monica and Alex both took them to jail locked up in the CIA jail cell in Seattle and make-up industry was saved

Chapter 8 the date with Jamie and the reward from Nordstrom

 Then as Alex, Jamie, Dennis, and William got back to Seattle the Nordstrom was really proud of Alex and his fellow Seattle agents and then there was even a ceremony and Alex was given 35,000$ for not only saving the make-up industry but for also saving the Nordstrom business as well and also Alex was given a men's Nordstrom shinny ring and in the crowd Dennis, William, and Jamie where really happy for Alex "oh Alex we are really proud of you" William said "oh thanks guys but I didn't do it we all did it" Alex said "yeah that fight with that blonde chick was very epic my man how did you know how to fight her?" Dennis asked " cause I knew her too well Dennis my man" Alex said "so we got celebrate big time I'm ready to party" Jamie said and then in a fancy house in a Seattle neighborhood there a huge party and Alex was doing crazy dance moves there was a even a crazy swimming pool and the song "He's my man by the Supremes" where playing at the party and Dennis was also having some fun as well as he was having fun and then Alex was dancing Jamie "wahooooo" Jamie said and then Alex spin Jamie in circles "oh you are very wild Mr.Nordstrom Aussmen" Jamie said "oh I have more bag of tricks then that baby girl" Alex said and then Jamie just did a little girl laugh and then Alex kissed Jamie on the lips "oh we want to congratulate Mr.Alex Aussmen for saving Nordstrom industry" William said to the crowd and then crowd started clapping and then Alex lifted up Jamie "Alex put me down" Jamie said in joking matter and then Jamie started laughing and then Alex kissed Jamie under the moonlight "oh Alex" Jamie said

The Beauitful Girl in the Shinning Moonlight
001

Chapter 1 Paris, France 1987

 It was a very sunny day in Paris, France and a lot of people where doing tons of fun things and the people in France love do things that are really fun particularly in the summer but then a girl with brown hair went into a cab in Paris and on her trip she then got to France airport and she had red lipstick and she was wearing some fancy 1980's clothing and she looked like she was a lot younger then she looked she looked like a girl that was 18 years old but it was only because she was really fit but as she got through the terminal she then pulled a necklace out of her purse and then the girl went on a plane that was heading to Boston, Massachusetts and as she was on the plane she then looked at her passport checked off a couple of things that she needed to have and then as she was going through costumes in Boston she got through costumes really well and then she got on a city bus in Boston that was heading to downtown Boston and then with her money she got a really awesome apartment in the city and as she was in her apartment she just looked at the window and as she was in the moonlight her necklace started sparking and then her lipstick started shinning as well like lip gloss and then she put on some music and then she started to the song "Lotta Love By: Nicolette Larson" and she just started dancing and spinning herself around in circles and doing a lot of dance moves and she started singing the lines in the song and the girl just had a very beautiful singing voice and the girl spoke really, really good English and through out the whole night she just kept on dancing and dancing to the that same song through all most the whole night

Chapter 2 the man on the northwest side of the west cost

 The next day in Seattle in an apartment in Lower Queen Ann in downtown Seattle Alex got up from bed and then Alex took a shower and got on a suit a 1980's style suit and tie and was wearing some fancy shoes and then after Alex brushed his teeth and put Cologne on and then he went into the garage and started his 1987 mustang car he had and then Alex started driving to his new agency he worked for called "Seattle agencies" in Lower Queen Ann and also Alex never really thought he would work for a secret agency group other then himself and also since 1976 he has always worked for Michael but Michael moved out of Seattle and he now lives in San Francisco, California and now Alex has a new boss "William Rivers" William met Alex for the first time when Alex was involved in the Monica Malone case a couple of months ago and William hired him for a secret agent job and if he got hired he would be their top agent in their agency and so it was kind of the same how Michael used Alex but a little different and Alex also had a new alley name "Dennis Castillo" he was a little bit like Michael but unlike Michael Dennis was very edgy and very demanding but in some ways he always managed to treat Alex like Michael treated him by being a good friend and a good partner as well

  Then as Alex parked his car into a parking spot, Alex turned off his car and then Alex got out of the car and then Alex started walking into the SAB building in Lower Queen Ann in downtown Seattle and then Alex went into the elevator and he pressed the top floor which was like the 49th floor in the building and then as the elevator reached the top floor in the building, Alex got out of the elevator he then got to the main floor and then a women that was about Alex's age looked Alex in very sexy way "do you have an appoint Mr.?" the women said in her sexy voice "oh yes I'm here to see Rivers the names Aussmen...Alex Aussmen" Alex said "oh Alex Aussmen I will page Rivers right now" the women said and then as the women was about to page rivers she then looked at Alex and then she just started laughing and giggling at Alex "so is this your first day working here? cause I began to love you alright Mr.Aussmen" the women said "call me Alex" Alex said "Alex Aussmen is here Will" the women said "send him in" William said and then William hanged up "you better want to go in...it was nice to meet you Mr.Aussmen" the women said "same here I'll see you later darling" Alex said

then as Alex got into William's office Alex walked to William's desk "good evening sir" Alex said "hello 001 I'm glad you where able to find the place Alex" William said "well it was pretty easy cause I live in the same area" Alex said 'oh very funny Mr.Aussmen" William said "so what is my mission William" Alex asked "well I will run a slide show and tell you Alex my boy...dim the lights" William said then the lights where dimmed and then William started showing Alex some footage of the girl that entered into Boston airport "a couple of hours ago a girl from Paris,France entered into Boston, Massachusetts and the reason she went to the US was that she was getting chased by an evil Paris Raffia organization that wants to kill her and get her money and her fortune...I want you to find her and protect her and then I want you to find this organization and find out who their leader is before they get the girl's money and if they get control of her money they will destroy all the banks in the country and commit fraud...here is your one way ticket to Boston first class...good luck Alex and I hope you come back alive" William said "don't worry I will William" Alex said and then Alex started walking out of William's office and started heading back to his pen house in Lower Queen Ann in Downtown Seattle

then as Alex gout of William's office, Alex came across the secretary again "so where are going disco boy...did you get a mission yet?" she asked "yes I did I'm going to Boston tomorrow morning and my flight leaves around 6:00 in the morning" Alex said "oh wow that sounds very exciting I would love to go to Boston is sure sounds very beautiful" she said "whats your name by the way?" Alex asked "oh Im Jennifer Vetoer but you can call me Jenny" Jenny said "So what are you doing after work?" Alex asked "well nothing why" Jenny asked "well I was wondering if you wanted to have a drink before I leave" Alex said "sure I would love to where and when?" Jenny said "my pen house in Lower Queen Ann I think you will like it" Alex said and then Alex walked away and then Alex started going home

as Alex got home he then went to his apartment door and he opened his door and then as Alex got into his apartment he then threw himself on the couch and then as Alex was watching TV in his pen house he then started hearing some sort of noise upstairs in his bedroom and then Alex went upstairs and there was blasting music in his bedroom and Jenny was in his room and was she was butt naked under the covers "hello Alex care to join me" Jenny said "How did you get into my apartment" Alex asked "I you left me a key" Jenny said "anyway it doesn't matter" Alex said and then Alex took off his clothes and then Alex and Jenny started making out on Alex's bed and Jenny started laughing and giggling and throughout the whole night Jenny and Alex where making out throughout the night

Chapter 3 the one way trip to Boston

Alex got up around 4:00AM and then took a shower, got dressed, ate some breakfast, brushed his teeth and then as Alex got out of his apartment Alex started heading to west lake center to catch a metro bus that was heading to Sea-Tac airport and then as Alex got on the bus he started thinking about things and then Alex got out a piece of paper and Alex wrote down a list of what to ask if he was going to ask any questions to people on his mission and then as Alex got to Sea-Tac airport, Alex asked for his ticket and then Alex got his airplane ticket and caught the gate that was heading on a one way to trip to Boston and then as Alex was on the plane he just looked out the window and just looked at the clouds like any normal person would and then as Alex was sitting down in his seat, as Alex was sitting down, Alex saw a beautiful girl that had very long brown hair, she had a very fit body and her breathes where very huge and round and she was also wearing a pink 1980's style dress and she was wearing 1980's style jewelry like rings, bracelet on her left wrist, and she also was wearing a necklace that had had a diamond around her beautiful neck and as she was walking she sat in first class and Alex just eyed her and then as the plane landed in Boston around the Boston airport and as Alex got off the airport he started heading out the door of the airport and Alex noticed a lot of honking from cars and Alex noticed right away that the people in Boston where very rude and Alex looked in his pocket and felt his gun and thought in his head "thank god I brought my gun just in case somebody messes with me" Alex thought in his head and then Alex caught a bus that took him to rental car but without knowing the girl with the pink dress starts fallowing Alex and she also had a spy watch system in her bracelet and then she started talking into to it "Mr.Aussmen is in Boston" she said and then she turned it off and then she got on the bus without Alex realizing it as Alex got on the bus he sat around one of the high seats and Alex just looked out the window and Alex looked another way and then as Alex was looking the other way, the girl from the plane sat right in front of Alex "good evening I noticed you where eyeing me on the plane here" the girl said and then Alex turned his head to her "oh I just like to look at things" Alex said "oh yeah I can see that" the girl said "I'm Selina Pierson" Selina said 'I'm Alex Aussmen" Alex said "so what brings you to Boston Alex?" Selina asked "oh I'm just on a mission" Alex said "oh mission that sounds very exciting are like a spy or something" Selina asked "some what like that" Alex said "so where are heading to?" Selina asked again "well I think I might be staying in a hotel in downtown Boston" Alex said "oh very fun" Selina said "oh yes" Alex said "so where are you heading to" Alex asked "oh well I just need to meet a friend that lives in downtown as well" Selina said "very exciting" Alex said then the bus stopped around a rent a car place in downtown and then Alex got off "it was to nice to meet you Mr.Aussmen" Selina said "yeah same here Selina" Alex said and then a couple of seconds as Alex got off the bus stop Selina got off another stop that was in the same area and then she hid behind a wall and then she took out a camera and then as Alex was done paying and financing the car to get it Alex went into garage and he got a 1987 mustang and then without Alex noticing Selina hide in one of the walls and she took a picture of Alex's license plate on his rented car

 Alex started driving to downtown Boston heading to a very nice hotel that was in downtown and Alex took a left turn into the city and Alex started driving around the city to look at the awesome landmarks in the city and then Alex took out his 1979 camera and he started taking pictures of the landmarks in Boston and then as Alex was done taking pictures he then went to a hotel that was in downtown and then Alex found a parking spot and then Alex started heading into the hotel lobby and went to the front desk "hello my name is Aussmen...Alex Aussmen I was wondering if you have any free rooms" Alex asked "oh yes we do we have a suite that is on the top floor enjoy your stay Mr.Aussmen" the front desk said then as Alex got to his suite he just was wowed at the view of the city and looked at the window for 30 seconds and then Alex looked at a book that had all the awesome things you can in downtown Boston and then Alex started writing down a list of where this evil organization criminals and thugs might be and Alex started writing down the places that where in the entertainment district and then Alex set his suitcase in his room and then Alex started exploring the city and he started looking for the women with brown hair and from Paris,France and finding out where she is

 Then later that day Alex headed to the entertainment district in Boston and he started looking in all the malls that where in downtown Boston and all the stores were really nice and very fancy and Alex was able to buy a couple of new shirts and new jeans and some new shoes and then as Alex was done shopping he then went back to his hotel room and put his new clothes in his closet in his hotel and then Alex looked at a magazine and found out there was some sort of party at another hotel in downtown and since the party was a really fancy party Alex knew what he wanted to wear and he wore his Seattle style suit to the party with his green neck tie, black button-up shirt, and black suit pants and then Alex got out of the hotel with

Seattle style suit on and he got his car out of garage and Alex started driving to the party

Chapter 4 the party at the Atlantic hotel

 Alex got to the hotel in his 1987 mustang and the hotel itself was around the east cost around downtown Boston and Alex parked his car and Alex started walking into the party and without knowing, Selina saw Alex in a pink long dress and she was also wearing red lipstick and then she started fallowing Alex into the party

 as Alex was in the party he started looking around and walking to a lot of different spots and there was also Casino tables and Alex was not much of card player but he would watch and he was good at a few card games like 21 and some other games as well but not as skilled as like secret agents like James Bond or any of the other agents in either pop culture or real life then Alex walked to a bar and Alex got a beer and as Alex was drinking his beer he saw another women that had same brown hair that the girl from france had and Alex saw her sitting down and Alex gently taped and touched her shoulder and then she turned back "hello can I help you?" she asked "oh no I just like your dress that your wearing" Alex said "oh thank you" the women said "the names Aussmen...Alex Aussmen" Alex said "I'm Miranda Flotuite" Miranda said "so where are you from Mr.Aussmen? If I may ask?" Miranda asked "I'm from Seattle,Washington it's on the west cost here" Alex said "oh thats very wonderful Alex this is my first time in the states so I'm still trying to get the fallow of things" Miranda said "oh Im sure you will" Alex said "oh thank you Alex" Miranda said "so what do you do for a living?" Miranda asked "well that is a little bit of a secret baby girl" Alex said "oh I love the way you talk and I love your style of clothing" Miranda said "oh thanks" Alex said and then Miranda looked away for a half a second and then she turned back to Alex "hey do you want to get out of here?" Miranda asked "sure what did you have in mind?" Alex asked "well what about a nightclub?" Miranda asked "oh yeah I love nightclubs" Alex said and then Miranda giggled and did a very sexy laugh and then Miranda and Alex left the hotel and they started heading to nightclub in downtown Boston

as Alex and Miranda got to the nightclub there was a very huge line and Alex and Miranda got in line and then Alex and Miranda got into the nightclub and then Alex and Miranda started dancing under nightclub disco ball "you are very good dancer Mr.Aussmen" Miranda said "oh thanks" Alex said and then Alex started doing a lot funky dance moves and spinning around 4 times and doing ducking dance moves and then Alex spinned Miranda in circles 4 times and Alex and Miranda kept on dancing in the nightclub then as Alex and Miranda where dancing in the nightclub then a couple of guards came into the nightclub and they started looking for Alex and Miranda and they looked like the evil Raffia group that was after Miranda and the group that William was talking about and then one of the members of the raffia group broke into the 2nd floor of the nightclub and they got out a sniper riffle and they aimed the gun at Alex as he was dancing with Miranda and then as Alex was dancing he noticed that one of the men in the group was coming towards him and Miranda and then one of the members got out a gun and pointed the gun at Alex's head "don't move Mr.Aussmen" one of the raffia thugs said and then Alex back punched him in the face and then Alex and Miranda started running to the 2nd floor in the nightclub and the thugs where chasing them "KILL HIM!!!!" the lead thug yelled and then the thugs started shooting at Alex and then Alex got out a PP7 gun and started shooting at them and Alex shot 3 raffia thugs in the head "Come on" Alex said and then Alex and Miranda ended up in one of the rooms in the nightclub and it was like the lounge areas in the building and Alex and Miranda hid in the rooms and as they hid in the room, one of the thugs came into the room and without him knowing, Alex punched him in the face and kicked him in the balls and then more thugs came and they started shooting at Alex then Alex reloaded his gun and started shooting at them even more and then Alex and Miranda ended up on the balcony of the nightclub and then Alex got out his grabbing hook gun out of his coat pocket "hold on" Alex said and then Miranda went on Alex's back and then Alex jumped off the nightclub building and then as Alex was sky diving he shot his hook gun at one of the other buildings by the property and Alex started lowering the two of them to the ground with the gun and they both ended up on the ground and then Alex saw a 1987 motorcycle and then Alex and Miranda went on the motorcycle and Alex turned on the motorcycle and Alex started going full blast on the bike and Alex started going really fast on the motorcycle and then more thugs started coming after them in cars and then they started chasing Alex and shooting at him and Miranda and Miranda was starting to get scarred and then Alex got out a spy machine gun and put the gun on the machine gun and then Alex pressed a button on the gun that made it power up on the bike and then Alex started shooting the thugs cars with the machine gun "AHHHHHHHHHHHHHHHH!!!!" the thugs yelled and then Alex went on the highways in downtown and more thugs started coming at them and then Alex reloaded the machine gun on the motorcycle and Alex turned the motorcycle around and he started blasting the thugs cars with full weaponry and shooting at their wind-shields, tires, and gas tanks and then there was one more thug car left "Alex there is one more car on us" Miranda said and then Alex put a grenade in the machine gun and then Alex shot the grenade bullet at last thug car and then around 4 minutes or so the car exploded in flames and Alex started heading back to the Atlantic hotel where they might be a little safer

as Alex and Miranda got back to the Atlantic hotel in Boston they headed right back into the party and just sat down at a table that was there and without knowing Selina saw Alex and then Selina turned back "hello Alex how did you get in this party?" Selina asked "I was invited actually" Alex said "oh thats awesome Alex..so who is your friend" Selina asked "oh this is Miranda" Alex said "oh it's very nice to meet you" Selina said "oh yes same here" Miranda said "so how do you like Boston so far?" Selina asked "oh it is very beautiful" Miranda said "oh I'm glad you like your trip so far" Selina said "well anyway I will see you around Alex" Selina said and then Selina started leaving and then after the party Alex and Miranda started heading back to Alex's hotel room in downtown Boston and as they got into the hotel room Miranda just really loved Alex's hotel room and she started looking at the window and the view of the whole city "wow your hotel room is very beautiful Alex" Miranda said 'oh thank you" Alex said and then as Miranda was in the hotel room she started looking at the moonlight "the moon is very beautiful" Miranda said "oh yes it's always very beautiful at night" Alex said and then Miranda kept on looking at the moon and then she started dancing and then spinning around and started dancing in the moonlight and then Alex started dancing with her as well and then as Alex was dancing with her, Alex noticed that Miranda was wearing fancy diamond ring and and it was really shinny and beautiful "where did you get that diamond Miranda?" Alex asked "oh I bought in Paris and shines when ever your under the moon" Miranda said "oh wow that is super cool" Alex said "oh yes" Miranda said and then later that night Alex was making with Miranda on his bed in the hotel room and they where making out under the shinny moonlight "so have you been to Paris before Mr.Aussmen" Miranda asked "no I haven't what is like there" Alex asked "well it's very beautiful there and you would love it Alex" Miranda said "so when do we go?" Alex asked "does tomorrow sound really good" Miranda asked "oh yes sounds really awesome" Alex said and then Miranda and Alex kept on kissing on the bed

the next day Alex and Miranda got up really early and then they caught a plane that was heading to Paris, France and as they where on the plane Alex started looking at the window and Alex saw the efflel tower and then Alex just slept on the plane for the remainder of the flight but as Alex was sleeping, Selina was on the same plane and she was with a couple of thugs in suits and Selina started taking pictures of Alex and Miranda and then Selina turned on a spy watch that she was wearing and then she started into it "hello Selina baby how is everything going?" her boss said "well everything is going well and I know where the french girl and Mr.Aussmen are going sir" Selina said "well did Mr.Aussmen leave any clues in Boston last night?" her boss asked "well he was at a nightclub in Boston and then a couple of thugs chased him but failed" Selina said "well it doesn't matter Selina baby girl Alex and the girl are getting closer and closer to the headquarters her in Paris and Alex Aussmen must die and we must get a hold of that girl with the moonlight ring has and use it for world domination and then we will kill the girl and Mr.Aussmen" Selina's boss said "don't worry we will" Selina said "good...Uv Wah" her boss said in French and then her boss hanged up the conversation on Selina's watch and without Alex or Miranda knowing Alex and Miranda where getting flowed by the Raffia thugs which was not good at all

Chapter 5 the arrival into Paris

 As the plane landed in Paris, Alex and Miranda got off the plane alright and found their bags and then they started looking for a cab that would take them to a hotel in Paris and Alex did not know Paris very well and the last time Alex was on a mission outside the US was back in 1979 when he was 1st year post-grad after graduating from Tahoma High School and he went to Nicaragua to take down the evil organization known as the "the evil Bulga" and Alex was able to take them down just fine and get back home to Seattle very safely

Alex and Miranda where able to catch a taxi to a hotel and as Alex and Miranda where in the car, Alex started looking at the famous landmarks in Paris and then Alex took out his 1979 camera and Alex started taking pictures "so do you like taking pictures?" Miranda asked "oh yes I sometimes do it from time to time" Alex said "when did you get that camera?" Miranda asked "well for my birthday" Alex said "oh thats wonderful Alex" Miranda said "so what hotel are we staying in?" Alex asked "oh we are staying in really nice hotel" Miranda said and then the taxi drove into a really fancy hotel that was in the heart of Paris and as Alex got out of the car, Alex started moving his head around just looking at the people and how lovely they looked and their styles as well and Alex was just fascinated and then Alex and Miranda went into the hotel lobby and they checked into the hotel "bo sur one kind of room will you lovely couple will be staying in" the doorman asked "just one suite please" Miranda said "alright here is your key and I hope you two enjoy your stay uv wah" the doorman said

Then Miranda and Alex went into the elevator and they started heading into their hotel suite in Paris and Alex loved the suite and everything in the suit was gold and it seemed like they where in a treasure chest or something thats how beautiful it was and just the hotel room in Boston it had a great view of the city and country of France and Alex and Miranda unpacked their clothes and put them into drawers in the hotel room "so what do you want to do tonight?" Miranda asked "well I would love to go out to dinner tonight and then maybe walk around if thats okay" Alex said "of course Alex anything for you darling" Miranda said and then Miranda and Alex started kissing on the bed for the entire afternoon

Then around nighttime Alex and Miranda got on some fancy clothes and they went out to dinner in Paris and then they found a place that was around the heart of Paris and where they were there was also a nightclub so the area was kind of

entertainment district in the city as Alex and Miranda went into the restraint, the both of them where seated and they ordered food that was from France and they both loved their meals and also loved the wine they drank as well "so Alex how do you like Paris so far?" Miranda asked "its very wonderful so far I love it" Alex said "very fantastic Alex but I will take you somewhere were you will really have fun" Miranda said "really what place would that be" Alex asked "well there is a really nice nightclub you will really like" Miranda said "really thats awesome I love dancing" Alex said and then after dinner and before they went dancing Alex and Miranda walked around Paris together and Miranda had her arms around Alex while they were talking around Paris but as they were talking around a couple of raffia thugs where spying on them "we will see if we can abduct the girl and take her to the boss and get her money" the thugs said and then Alex and Miranda where heading towards the nightclub in Paris and things where about to get really wild

Chapter 6 the abduction

 Then as Alex and Miranda finally got into the nightclub the whole club itself was really modern and 1980's looking and people where dancing and the French girls where moving their long hairs a lot and then without thinking Alex started dancing "get into the grove By: Madonna" and Alex started making a whole bunch of dance moves and jumping up and down and Miranda just started dancing with him Miranda started doing other dance moves and Alex started spinning Miranda in circles 5 times and Alex spin his whole body 3 times and started snapping his fingers and then Miranda found a fedora hat and she happily put the hat on Alex's head and Alex just started getting it down and the stereos where getting louder and louder as Alex just kept on dancing and dancing and moving his arms and his hands and then a random french guy really liked Alex's dancing style and he threw a rose at Alex and then Alex caught the rose with his mouth and then Alex grabbed Miranda's hands and he started doing the tango with her and spin her and then Alex kept on moving his body and then Alex lowered Miranda really,really low and then Alex brought her back up and then Alex started spinning his body around and around moving his hands and then Alex did one of his famous dance moves and then Alex did a cartwheel and did a backflip and Alex ended the song with him shaking his whole body break dancing and moving his hands and then Alex and Miranda ended the song with Miranda about to kiss Alex on the lips and putting her hands around Alex's neck and then people in the nightclub started clapping and cheering and then Alex and Miranda sat down at a table "you sure have some really sexy dance moves Alex" Miranda said "oh thank you" Alex said "I knew you would have tons of fun at this place" Miranda said "you choice the best place" Alex said and then a waiter was coming towards them and then Alex ask the man for a beer and then the waiter brought Alex a beer and he also brought Miranda a Migrate as well and then Alex and Miranda started drinking and talking while they where at their table and then as they where talking then Miranda just really loved talking to Alex and then Miranda just kissed Alex on the lips "so where do you live Alex?" Miranda asked "I live in a pen house in downtown Seattle" Alex said "that sounds like a very exciting life you live Alex baby" Miranda said "yeah it gets really crazy from time to time" Alex said "I would bet" Miranda said "oh yes" Alex said and then Alex and Miranda kept on talking then the song "Everything Jody Watley" came on "you want to dance?" Alex asked "sure I would love to" Miranda said and then Miranda and Alex started slow dancing on the courtyard in the nightclub and as they where dancing Miranda put her head on Alex's left shoulder and then put his hands on Miranda's hips and they danced really slowly for the entire song

then as Alex and Miranda were slow dancing then a couple of thugs from out of nowhere broke down one of the stereos and then they started shooting people in the nightclub and then Alex herd gun bullets and Alex knew that they where in trouble big time and it was the raffia group "Miranda we got get out of here" Alex said and then Alex and Miranda started running out of nightclub and then a couple of thugs showed up "you are not going anywhere Mr.Aussmen" the thugs yelled and then Alex got in rage and kicked the thugs in the face and then Alex got into a fight with 5 thugs raffia "run Miranda run" Alex said and then Alex kept on fighting the thugs and one of the thugs tried to punch Alex in the face and then Alex ducked and whacked the thug in the face then another thug tried to kick Alex in the face and then Alex body slammed and and punched the thug in the face and gave him a black eye and bloody lip "it's time to kill you Seattle agent MOTHER FUCKER!!!!!!!!!!" one of the raffia thugs yelled and then Alex grinned his teeth with rage and grabbed the thug by the button shirt and threw against the wall then another thug tried to grab Alex but then Alex dodged his attack grabbed his knife and stabbed the thug and stabbed the thug in the head then another tackle tried to tackle Alex from behind and then Alex did a back flip and Alex grabbed on to the chains and let himself go from the the chains and then Alex got back to the ground and the same thug tried to do multiple punches attacks on Alex but Alex dodged all his attacks and then Alex whacked the thug in the face and then Alex did a spin kick and kicked the guy in the face and the last thug tried to stab Alex in the neck and then Alex did a very epic dodge and grabbed a metal chair and whacked the thug in the face with a metal chair and killed him

and then as Alex was breathing very heavily suddenly a random man in a suit whacked Alex from behind and pushed him from behind and slammed against the wall "good evening Mr.Aussmen my name is Alistair Jamison and I know all about you and your agency Mr.Aussmen" Jamison said "where is she?!" Alex said in a very mad voice "oh the girl she is with us cause she has some resources that we want Mr.Aussmen like her jewelry for example and her cash Mr.Aussmen" Jamison said "you are not going to get away with this" Alex said "oh I think we will Mr.Aussmen and it's time for you to die" Jamison said and then Jamison took out a silenced PP7 gun and pointed the gun at Alex and then Alex got in rage and got up and punched Jamison in the face and gave him a black eye and kicked him in the balls and then before Alex went back to his hotel room he stole Jamison's money and Alex stole 900$ from his wallet and then Alex went back to his hotel room and he saw just a note on his bed and it said this "hello Mr.Aussmen if you want to see your girl again meet us in Philly back in the states or your girl is in deep trouble" the note said and then Alex started backing up his suitcase cause he knew that Miranda was in deep trouble and then suddenly Selina showed up in very sexy underwear clothing "hello Mr.Aussmen" Selina said "Selina how did you know where I was staying?" Alex asked "oh I know a lot of things Alex" Selina said "well Selina I would love to stay but Miranda is missing and she just got kidnaped and I have to find her and..." Alex said and then Selina interrupted Alex and then Selina put her arms around Alex and then Selina started kissing and licking Alex "I know how I can turn you on baby" Selina whispered in Alex's ears and then Selina stopped kissing Alex and then Selina started taking her robe and her underwear off of her and Selina was butt naked in front of Alex "do you like what you see baby boy?" Selina asked in a very sexy voice and then in Alex's nature Alex got very overwhelmed and tempted by Selina and then Alex started making out with Selina like "sure why not" in his mind and then Alex and Selina started making out on Alex's bed and Alex and Selina started having sex on Alex's bed throughout the whole night "so how many women have you slept with?" Selina asked "I don't know I usually don't keep up probley like 13 women" Alex "oh my god you are such a stud baby boy" Selina said and then Selina kept on making out with Alex throughout the whole night and Alex was about fall into the biggest trap of his life without knowing it

Chapter 7 the chase out of Europe and back into the states

 As Alex got up the next morning he took a shower and then without him expecting Selina took her clothes and Alex and Selina started making out in the shower for 40 minutes and then after Alex and Selina took a shower and then Alex got on some causal 1980's clothing and Selina got in some awesome causal 1980's clothing "I had really great night Alex and don't you worry I'm pretty sure Miranda will be alright" Selina said "yeah I hope so" Alex said and then as Alex was all ready to go, Alex opened the door and then Alex opened the door and he noticed right away that there was a thug of raffia standing in front of the door and then Alex shut the door really hard and then as Alex was about to pull out a PP7 gun then Alex herd another gun bullet getting loaded and it was Selina's gun "oh I got you good baby boy and I know where Miranda is Alex baby" Selina said and then the thugs came into Alex's hotel room "don't you see Alex baby boy Miranda has some of our resources that belong to us and Alex we cannot let you save her and if you do we can kill you" Selina said "well baby girl...I don't like women that kill people" Alex said "well say goodnight...baby boy" Selina said and then Alex took out a gadget that William gave to him and it was sleeping dart and then Alex loaded the dart into his spy watch and without Selina knowing Alex fired the dart at Selina and the dart put

Selina to sleep and then Alex started running out of his hotel room and then a couple thugs started chasing him and then as Alex was running the door man saw Alex running away from the thugs "sir I need my money" the man said and then Alex threw a toy grenade at the door man and then toy grenade exploded on him and it was a 5,000$ check "thank you sir" the door man said and then Alex got outside and without thinking Alex stole a motorcycle and then Alex started riding a motorcycle and then the raffia thugs started chasing him and Alex started heading to the France airport and then as Alex got to the airport he parked the motorcycle and he started running to the runaway and Alex saw a helicopter and then Alex used passport that had a key hacking code to hack into planes into helicopters and then as the door opened the thugs saw Alex getting into the helicopter and they started shooting at him and then Alex got into the helicopter and Alex turned on the helicopter and the helicopter started going up into the air and Alex started flying it an airport that was in the states but as Alex flying the helicopter then more helicopters started chasing him and firing machine gun bullets at him and lucky the copter had some rocket launchers and then without thinking Alex fired the rocket launchers at the other copters chasing him and then Alex switched to machine gun bullets on to the copter and then more raffia copters showed up and then Alex fired machine gun bullets at the raffia copters and then Alex switched back to the rocket launchers and then Alex fired the rockets at 5 last other raffia helicopters and the helicopters exploded into flames and fire and copters fell out of the sky and then Alex started heading on his way back to the east cost to save Miranda from the raffia organization before they get their hands on her jewelry and fast

as Alex got back into the states, Alex landed in Philadelphia airport and Alex found a way to sneak out of the runway and then as Alex was around the departure street around the airport he saw a couple of thugs get into a car and they were wearing very evil red suits with gold neck ties and Alex knew right away that those where bad guys and Alex then found out right away that William also put some special skating wheels in his tennis shoes and then Alex pressed a button and this wheels came out of his shoes and then Alex pressed a button on his spy watch and then Alex started flying on his skating tennis shoes and Alex started chasing the raffia car "WAHOOOOOOOOOOOOOOOOOOOO" Alex yelled in excitement and then Alex noticed that he had levers that controlled the skate wheels in his tennis shoes that controlled how fast they went and then Alex pressed a button that made the shoes go really,really fast and then the raffia thugs noticed Alex chasing them and then they started shooting at Alex and Alex did a lot roller skating moves,tricks and jumps avoiding gun bullets and then Alex fired a missile out of his spy watch and then raffia car started going really fast and Alex ended up on the highway heading to downtown and then Alex jumped on to the car and Alex pressed a button on his spy watch and broke the bad guys windshield and electrocuted the raffia thugs and then Alex punched them in the face and then Alex was able to stop the car on the highway and Alex looked inside the car and he found a lot things such as where the raffia headquarters is and a map of Philly and 38,000$ in cash and Alex put the cash in his backpack and he started heading to the raffia headquarters

Chapter 8 the break into the raffia headquarters in Philly

 As Alex got into downtown Philadelphia he saw the raffia building in downtown and it was a very tall and very black looking building with red and silver on it and Alex knew he had to find a way to get into that building and save Miranda before it was too late and Alex found a way to get into the parking garage and as Alex was in the parking garage he found a door that led to the elevators and as thugs came to guard the door Alex took out a PP7 gun and shot the thugs in the head and stole their money out of their wallets and then Alex headed into the elevators and knew that the last floor was guarded by a code of some sort and then Alex looked at his spy watch and he started hacking and getting the code and then Alex typed the code and he found a way to get into the last floor in the building and then as Alex was on the last floor he started looking around and Alex noticed that the raffia group was steeling money from the government just like what William told him before his mission started and then as was spying spying around Alex hid around the walls and noticed Jamison and his thugs walking and they where walking into a secret room and then without thinking Alex used a hook-lock door opener that held the door open and then Alex went into the room and Alex noticed he was a special part of the building and everything was really shinny and there was a lot jewelry on the walls and a lot of diamonds as well and then Alex saw Miranda in a very large jewelry dome-like room and then Alex jumped off one of the ledges in the room and Alex got out his hock shot and lowered himself down and Alex started running to save Miranda and then there were guards guarding the door and then the guards saw Alex and they took out their PP7 guns "HEY MOTHER FUCKER YOU ARE TRESPASSING!!!!!!!!!!" the guards yelled and then Alex whacked the guards in the face with his hock shot gun and Alex slammed the guards against the wall and then Alex took the guards money and got one of their keycards and Alex got into the dome-like room

then as Miranda was looking at the window in the room, Alex ran to Miranda and Miranda ran up to Alex and hugged him "Alex!!!" Miranda said "are you alright?" Alex asked "yeah I'm alright I'm glad you came to save me Alex" Miranda said "no problem" Alex said "lets get out of here" Alex said and then as Alex and Miranda where about to escape, Selina showed up she had a green jumpsuit with silver strips on it and then she took out a very huge A33 riffle with machine guns "oh I don't think so Aussmen baby it sounds like you and your girlfriend might have to be taken to Alistair for questioning...GRAB THE GIRL!!!!!!!" Selina yelled and then Selina tried to shot at Alex's head and then Alex ducked and then Selina grabbed Alex threw against the wall and punched Alex in the face and then more guards came and grabbed Miranda "Alex!!!..." Miranda yelled and then Miranda just kicked Alex in the face and then she took off her jacket and Selina was topless under her jacket and then she started chocking Alex really hard "poor Alex Aussmen it's shame you had to come to Philly to die cause Alistair and I will be able to use these jewels to destroy the US and you will be no more" Selina said in a very sexy evil voice and then Alex noticed he had his electric watch that William gave to him and then Alex pressed a red button on his watch and he electrocuted Selina and then Alex got free and Alex took out a fire gun and tried to spray fire at her out a gadget gun and then Alex kicked Selina in the face and then Alex got behind her and Alex took out a spy knife and started cutting her clothes off "no,no my clothes noooo" Selina screamed and then Alex threw her clothes on the ground and Selina was butt naked and then Alex grabbed Selina from behind and locked her up in an ice cube freezer "no,no let me out I will play nice,let me out" Selina said and then Selina's body started freezing in the freezer as Selina was butt naked "talk shit the cops will arrest your ass pretty soon" Alex said

then Alex started to the 2nd floor to save Miranda and then as Alex got to the 2nd floor Alistair punched Alex from behind and whacked Alex with a metal cain "good evening Mr.Aussmen...I see were able to get to my jewelry and diamond just fine my boy" Jamison said "where is she?!" Alex said "oh she is here Mr.Aussmen...but I think you will never live to see her get frozen my boy" Jamison and then a guard showed up and pointed a PP7 gun at Miranda's head "what do you want with her?!" Alex asked "oh my men where always after her not only for her money but she just resources to make our plan work to make a new diamond and ruby world that will destroy the US and turn into a stone country Mr.Aussmen and with the fluids in her purse we will be able to blow up the world and make a new city with no damage Mr.Aussmen" Jamison said "oh and by the way I have something i want to show you..." Jamison said and then Jamison shot himself with his own gun and then his eye started growing back into a jewelry eye and the big part of his eye was a diamond and the moving circle inside was a moving green gem "MUAHAHAHAHAHAHAH BRAHAHAHAHAHAHAHAHAHAHAHAHAHAHAHAHAHAHAHAHAHAHAHAHAH AHAHAHAHAHAHAHAHAHAHAHAH!!!!!!!!!!!...."Jamison laughed "you are one very sick man" Alex said "that is very true Mr.Aussmen...but if you accuse me Mr.Aussmen with my Miranda's money and her jewelry I will be able to turn Philly into a gem city and I will be really close to taking over the world....GOOD-BYE ALEXANDER AUSSMEN!!!!!!!!!!!" Jamison said and then Jamison got out a DD4 pistol gun and pointed the gun at Alex's head and then Alex identified Jamison's weakness in the gun with his autistic brian and then Alex twisted Jamison wrist really hard and then Alex in rage head-butted Jamison and kicked him in the face and then Alex did a summer-salt and more of Jamison's men started shooting at Alex and then Alex grabbed the guard that held Miranda hostage and punched him in the face "come on we have to get out of here" Alex said and then as Miranda and Alex where running to try get out of the building, the jewelry building started to get torn apart and flames started to burn the whole room and the thugs and guards where getting burned and then Alex turned back "listen I need to get out of here and what ever you do just run Miranda GO,GO!!!!!" Alex said and then Miranda started running of the building trying to escape from the jewelry building as fast as she could

then Alex went back around the jewelry and diamond chamber that is controlling jewelry melting and then Alex started climbing up the ladder and then Alex took out his spy watch and then Alex pressed three or six buttons on his watch to disable the chamber from getting active and then Alex got done disabling the machine, then suddenly out of nowhere somebody whacked Alex in the head from behind and it was a metal contraction bar "AHHHHHHHHH..." Alex yelled "YOU ARE FUCKING TOO LATE MR.AUSSMEN!!!!!!!!!..." Jamison yelled "I just set a timer that is has made my jewelry chamber active again and I will steel money from banks and it will be a very grand ride and now it's time for you to die Mr.Aussmen" Jamison said and part of Jamison's face was burned and scratched by and his lips where frozen and then Jamison picked up the metal bar again and tried to whack Alex in the head, but then Alex got up and he battled Jamison one on one and then Jamison tried to punch Alex in the face 6 times and then Alex dodged all of Jamison's attacks and Alex tackled Jamison and threw him against the diamond chamber and Alex took out his knife and stabbed Jamison in the arm but his blood was solid ice "MUAHAHAHAHAHAHAHAHAHAHAHAHA YOU CANNOT KILL ME I'M FROZON!!!!!!!!!" Jamison said and then Jamison tried to kick Alex in the face and he also tried to whack Alex in the face with another metal bar and then Jamison tried to hit Alex in the face, Alex grabbed the bar to protect himself and then Jamison whacked Alex in the face and gave Alex a bloody lip and a black eye "poor Alex Aussmen and now your gadgets will never work now and it's time to kill you and your girlfriend and my raffia thugs will rule the world and there will be nothing you can do" Jamison said then Alex loaded up his gun and whacked Jamison in the head with his PP7 gun and then Alex started shooting 17 gun bullets at Jamison's head and blood started coming out of his head and then Jamison was dead and then Alex kicked Jamison off the ledge and then Alex jumped off the ledge where the diamond chamber was and Alex started running to get to the elevator and then as Alex got back to first floor a gun that was pointed at his head "DROP THE GUN MR.AUSSMEN OR I KILL YOUR GIRLFRIEND!!!!!!!!!!!!!" and it was Selina and during the explosion she was able to escape the freezer Alex put her in "it's over Selina your boss dead now let Miranda go" Alex said "alright Alex time to get shot in the fucking head...say good-night baby" Selina said and then Selina loaded new bullets in her gun and then she started shooting at Alex and then Alex jumped up in the air and then Selina tried to punch Alex in the face and then Selina punched Alex in the stomach and then Alex got up and Selina tried to whack Alex with a metal bar and then Alex avoided the hit and grabbed on to the bar and then Selina with no common sense tried to kick Alex in the face but then Alex grabbed Selina and flipped her on her back and then Selina went behind Alex and then she started chocking him "is there anything you want to say before you die!!!!" Selina said and then as Selina was chocking, Alex noticed a taser gun on her belt and then Alex whacked Selina in the stomach and then Alex took the taser and then Alex started electrocuting Selina like crazy "yeah I got one word....BITCH!!!!!!!!!!" Alex said and then Alex bitched slapped her in the face and then Selina was dead and her body was left in the sand and then Miranda went up to Alex "Alex are you alright?" Miranda asked "oh I'm fine Miranda but I think it's time to get out of here come on" Alex said

then Alex and Miranda started running to Alex's car as Jamison's building started explode in flames and then Jamison's building was destroyed and Miranda and Alex made out very safely

Chapter 9 Alex's trip back to Seattle

 as Alex got back from Philly and with another successful mission, Alex headed back to Lower Queen to debrief his mission with William and it was very positive "well done Alex on your mission the raffia thugs have been taken to Prison and Jamison and Selina have been killed as well...job well done 001" William said "thank you William" Alex said "so where is the girl?" William asked "she is in my apartment" Alex said "you know she has to go back right" William said "yeah I know she will go back sir" Alex said

 then as Alex was about to walk out of William's office William then shouted "001,.." William said and then Alex turned back "...your pay check" William said and then William threw Alex's pay check at him and then Alex caught it and it was in a plastic case and the check was for 19,000$ "thanks William" Alex said "no problem 001" William said and then Alex walked out William's office and he started heading home

Then as Alex got home he started looking around and then a bunch of people showed and there was a huge party and with a lot of people at his apartment and then Miranda showed up in a 1970's style disco dress that was silver,blue, and white with white hippie boats "oh you are good Miranda baby" Alex said and then Miranda went up to Alex and then they started kissing each other on the lips "do you want a dance?" Alex asked " of course I would Alex baby boy" Miranda said and then Alex and Miranda went up to the rooftop and Alex pressed a button on his rooftop and the stereos appeared out of the roof of the apartment and then Alex took his suit jacket off "what song are we going to dance to Alex?" Miranda asked "you will see" Alex said and then Alex went up the radio set up on the roof and then he put on the song "lotta love by Nicolette Larson" and then as the song started playing Miranda noticed it right away " I love this song how did you know this was my favorite song?" Miranda asked "you talk about about it all the time" Alex said and then Alex and Miranda started dancing on the rooftop and the moon and the moonlight was above and Alex started spinning her 5 times and then Alex lowered her and then brought her back and as they started dancing Miranda's dress started shinning and sparking in the moon light and then Alex and Miranda kept on dancing and then Alex lowered Miranda again and then Alex started smooching her on the lips and then Miranda put her arms around Alex "I really love your dress you are very beautiful as the moonlight" Alex said "I'm glad you like it Alex baby" Miranda said and then Alex and Miranda kept on kissing and Miranda kept on laughing as Alex kept on kissing her and they kept on dancing under the shinning moonlight "oh Alex" Miranda said

On Seattle's Doom Mission
001

Chapter 1 Sonora, Mexico 1987

 It was around a beach in Sonora and there was a party going on there where some Mexicans and Americans going into a beach house and then there was a mariachi band playing "LaBamba" and there where people dancing to it and some people where drinking and then a Mexican lap dancer came and was dancing and the men in the beach house where going very wild and screaming "YAHOOOO!!!!" And "Iei ei" they yelled and some men danced with other women in the beach house and dirty dancing as well and most of the men in there where acting like whole gins and crazy people and then a young man with long blonde hair he looked very fit and he had blue eyes was wearing a 1980's style bathing suit and then he walked to the bar "hola senior quto ago?" The person asked "uncervisa por favrido" the blonde young man said in Spanish and then the man gave him a Cora light and opened it for him and then he began to drink it and then as he was drinking it he then noticed a surfer coming in and then the blonde young man out on some sun glasses and looked him in spyish way and then as he was looking at him then the blonde young man looked at his watch and then from gulf of California a boat was coming in and then the boat was parked around the dock and then from out of nowhere another man with a 1980's style bathing suit with a Hawaiian shirt on with aviators and he had brown long hair and then as the man parked his boat he then started walking on the sand he then walked into the beach house and then the man with brown hair just sat on a couch that was in the beach house then the Mexican dancer walked up to the young man with brown hair and then all the Mexicans started saying"vela,vela,vela" they all chanted and then the man with brown hair started dancing with the Mexican dancer and then the man with brown hair had arose in his mouth and then he spin the girl 5 times and he also lowered her as he was dancing with her and then the Mexicans and Americans in the beach house all cheered and raised their beers and then the man started doing salsa dancing with her and doing dirty moves as the man was dancing her and then everybody in the beach house was clapping 34 times and then the man grabbed a sum burro and started doing silly dance moves and moving his left finger and moving both of his arms and his hands and then the man then grabbed the Mexican dancer and raised her and then the man lowered her again and made a kiss sign and then everybody in beach house was clapping and saying "WAHOOOOOOO!!!!!"and "iye candmba muchichio" and then the man with blonde hair watched and started walking up to him and saying "tu vala my bien que tunombra?" He asked in Spanish and then man turned back he was wearing a sumburro "mi nombra es Aussmen...Alex Aussmen" the man said"Alex?!...Damn it Alex" Michael said "what?.." Alex asked "you made you made a huge entrance...you never told me you where heading to Mexico" Michael said "well it's because I just want to get away from Seattle for a little while" Alex said "so what hotel are you staying at Michael?" Alex asked "well I'm staying in one that is in the town I think" Michael said "dude did you see my dance moves that was awesome" Alex said "I think you might have shocked the country of Mexico dude" Michael said "common Michael that is not the sprit we are in Mexico for beaches, hot girls, Mexican food, and great hotels and nightclubs and also surfing as well" Alex said "oh yeah there was a surfer that came into the beach

house earlier" Michael said "oh that's kind of shocking" Alex said "well anyway I have hotel Sonara if you want to come" Alex said "no I'm okay Alex I will stay here" Michael said and then Alex started walking to his hotel room but then he stopped at a couple Mexican stores and bought himself a hamic and then as Alex got back tohis hotel and then as he opened the door to his hotel room he saw the Mexican dancer butt naked "hello" Alex said "you a great dancer I was wondering if I can stay with you for a while" she said "and I know your not Mexican..." She said and then the girl laughed "now that part is true baby girl I'm not" Alex said and then Alex walked up to herand then Alex started making out with her and smooching her on the lips and then Alex and the girl fell on Alex's bed and then the girl started taking Alex's clothes off and then they both started laughing

Then later on that Alex the girl just put her arms around Alex and then she started kissing him on the lips "you are very beautiful man" the girl said "oh thank you" Alex said and then Alex got up from bed and he started looking at the moon and then the girl got up without covering herself "what are you looking at Alex?" She asked "I don't know" Alex said "Mexico is so beautiful just like you are" Alex said "awe your so sweet" she said and then Alex and the girl kept on making out in Alex's hotel room but then as they kept on making out some sort of special evil gang started recording Alex and the girl making out in his hotel room and then in another place or so then a man with a blue and black suit on started looking at the camera and looking at footage "I'm am very sure Mr. Aussmen will never get-out of here alive and I have been waiting for this moment and so Alex Aussmen and his friend Michael will be no more!!!!!!!!" The man said

Chapter 2 the great Mexican escape

 Then the next day Alex got up from bed and then he took a shower and then girl that was in bed with him started walking him and then she went into the shower with him and then Alex and the girl started making out in the shower and then as they both got out of the shower Alex's watch started beating "oh shit not again I gotta go baby" Alex said "no mi amora stay with me" she said "no I can't I have to go" Alex said and then Alex started getting his clothes on and then later on that Alex checked out of his hotel room and then Alex started to heading to Michael's hotel room south of Sonara and Alex road in some car down there was from the 70's but Alex loved it "oi amigo es tu cadro"the man said to Alex "si" Alex said in Spanish and then Alex road in his car and then Alex got to Michael's hotel room and his hotel was around the beach around the gulf of California and then Alex parked his car and then he set his car around the building and then Alex went into the building "hello can I help you?" The conserguige lady asked "yes my name is Aussmen...Alex Aussmen is there a person name Michael staying here? "Alex asked "oh yes he is staying in the other tower" the lady said "thank you" Alex said and then Alex started walking to the other tower and then Alex went into the elevator and he tapped on the 6th button and then as the elevator got to the 6th floor Alex then got out of the elevator and then started looking for Michael's room number then Alex found the room number and then Alex knocked on the door and then Alex waited for a couple seconds and then all of a sudden then Michael opened the door "Alex what's up dude?" Michael asked "oh nothing very much Michael I just wanted to come to see you my man" Alex said "oh that's really good...so how did last night to with that really hot chick?" Michael asked "oh yes it went really good the sex was just fantastic" Alex said "atta kid" Michael said "oh yeah" Alex said "so how long have you been here for Michael?" Alex asked "well Alex I just needed a fresh start cause you know I need to be more presentable and so I then was here for a couple months and last a whole ass load of weight and grew my hair out as well" Michael said "congrats dude" Alex said "best part of all if you ever have a mission maybe in the near future I'm more fit to go with you and help you" Michael said "yeah that would be great cause working alone can get very boring at times" Alex said "and also too I have been working on my Spanish as well" Michael said "that's awesome...you want to make coffee or something cause I have not eaten breakfast yet" Alex said "oh sure that would be awesome go for it Alex "Michael said "so how are things with Seattle Intelligence with your new boss "William" is it good" Michael asked "it's alright I have just not been assigned anything in a while and so William told me I can have 2 weeks off from work and clear my head" Alex said "dude you the man" Michael said "oh yeah" Alex said and then Michael hi fived Alex and then Alex and Michael sat down at bar table in Michael's hotel room and then Alex and Michael sat down "dude I might getting too old for this shit and I'm 27 now and I just feel old" Alex said "what the hell are you talking about that is still young" Michael said "yeah it's just not that same as it once was back when we where in high school back in the 70'sand all those missions we went on and we where young and reckless" Alex said "oh yeah I love those times and yeah I looked so different back then" Michael said and then Alex poured 2 cups of coffee and then both Alex and Michael did cheers "here's for more years for spy work" Alex said "oh yeah" Michael said

Then suddenly some guys in suits sneaked into the hotel through the back door and then they had sniper riffles "we are in the building Romnitka" one of the thugs said "good now I want that Alex Aussmen captured and brought here alive "Romnitka said and then more of thugs where going up the stairs and then got tothe 6th floor and then Alex and Michael heard some of the notices happening "did you hear that?" Alex asked "hear what my man?" Michael asked and then more thugs came on to the floor and then as Alex opened the door then Alex closed the door very shut and "dude we got a problem" Alex said "what's going on Alex?" Michael asked and then Alex pulled out aDD4 pistol and then Alex started shooting at the thugs and then Alex killed 6thugs "dude we gotta get out of here my man" Alex said and then Michael and Alex started running to the top of the roof and then more thugs started coming towards them and then Alex reloaded his DD4 pistol gun and then started shooting at more and more thugs surrounded them "so what do we now?" Michael said "I got one thing" Alex said then Alex pulled a garbling gun out of his pocket and then shot the gun then a hook shot came out of it "hold on buddy" Alex said and then Michael hung on to Alex from behind and then Alex jumped off the building and then Alex and Michael started gliding through the garbling wire and then Alex dropped the gun and then Alex pressed a button on his watch and then his watch turned into a climbing cuffing and then Michael started climbing up the building and then as Michael and then as Alex and Michael got to the top they started running down the stairs to the 1st floor and then Alex and Michael got to the 1st floor and then and Alex started looking around "do you have another plan?" Michael asked and then Alex saw a 1978 thunderbird and then Alex and Michael ran to the car and then hoped into the car and then Alex found the car keys and then Alex started the car "it's going to be a bumpy ride" Alex said and then Alex started speeding on the road and then Alex got on the road that was heading north of Sonara, Mexico then Alex kept making a lot of sharp turns and then more and more of thugs started gaining on them and shooting at them and then Alex was coming across a ramp and then Alex went off the ramp"WAHOOOOOOOO!!!!" Michael screamed "HERE WE GO!!!!!" Alex yelled and then the car landed on its tires and then Michael started looking in the back and then suddenly Michael found a rocket launcher in the back of thecar "yo dude I found something" Michael said "what is it?"Alex asked "I just found a rocket launcher" Michael said and then Michael looked up and then got out of the car and then he fired a lot of rocket launcher bullets "SAY HELLO TO MY LITTLE POWERFUL FRIEND MOTHERFUCKERS!!!!!!" Michael yelled and then Michael fired 7 rocket bullets and then a lot of thugs cars got blown up in flames and a lot thugs where blown up into pieces "is that the last of them?" Alex asked "I think so Alex my man" Michael said "dude I think we better want to get out of here cause I think they might Coyote thugs" Alex said "that's impossible cause they would not have guns like that in their cars" Michael said "dude every thug has those kinds of weapons" Alex said "oh I forgot" Michael said and then Alex and Michael drove back to Alex's hotel room and then went to Michael's hotel room and checked out of there as well and then Michael and Alex started driving to the US border and then they got passed the border really easy "so where do we go first?" Michael asked "San Diego, California" Alex said "for what?" Michael asked "cause it's part of our road trip back to Seattle that's why "Alex said "oh I thought we were going there because of a lot of hot girls there" Michael said and then Alex kept on driving and Alex knew him and Michael had a really long way home

Chapter 3 surfing in San Diego

 As Michael and Alex got to San Diego the whole city was hopping and there was surfers and people where playing 80's songs from there radios and then Alex found a parking spot around a hotel building in the city and then all of sudden Alex saw a women that was topless running across the street and Alex just did a very silly smile "amigo I think we are here Michael my friend" Alex said and then after Alex and Michael got out of the car and then Alex and Michael walked into hotel lobby and then Alex and Michael got separate hotel rooms and then Alex and Michael put their bags in their hotel rooms "do you think there are more of those thugs that chased us back in Mexico" Michael asked "I don't know Michael my man but who ever they are working for I think they want to us" Alex said "so what do you want to do tonight?" Michael asked "I don't we could go look for some hot chicks or something "Alex said "yeah that really sounds like a really awesome idea lets go" Michael said then Alex and Michael started heading to Pacific beach in San Diego and Alex and Michael put on some 1980s style swimsuits and they started looking around and then Alex spotted some girls going suffering "yo dude check it out those girls are surfing lets come with them "Alex said "so you surf?" Michael asked "well no but I can learn" Alex said and then Alex walked up to some surfers "so where you guys heading to?" Alex asked and then all of a sudden 4 people showed there was one young man that was tall and skinny, the other boy was short and he looked a California skateboarder, and then there were 2 girls with blonde hair the 1st blonde was wearing a red bikini, the other blonde was wearing a bikini that had pink stripes, and was also yellow with miller beer on the bottoms "what up Dwags" the young man with black hair said "oh yes is it okay if we surfing with you guys" Alex asked then the young man turned back at his group "sure we could use some more people we are planning on going on the islands over there on the coast you guys want to join?" The man asked and then Michael and Alex looked at each other in a dumb founded way "sure we will go surfing with you guys" Alex said and then the man with black hair handed Alex and Michael some sort boards and then the rest of the group started laughing at them with great and humorous joy and then the group fallowed them and then as Alex and Michael got into the ocean "dude the waves are strong" Michael said "yeah no shit" Alex said and then Michael and Alex went farther and farther into the ocean and then the rest of the group fallowed them "yo guys are you guys safe out there?" The young man said, "oh no everything is fine" Alex said "yo man did you see a way yet?" Michael asked "I don't think so dude" Alex said and then Alex and Michael surfing then Michael all of a sudden saw a really big wave coming at them "um Alex we got a huge ass wave at 12 a clock" Michael said and then Alex and Michael started standing on the surf boards and then Alex and Michael started surfing on the waves and then Alex surfed on the waves "WAHOOOOOOOOOOOOOOOOOOOOOOOOOOOO"Alex yelled and then Alex surfed on the waves and then all of a sudden Alex fell into the ocean "Alex!!!!!" Michael yelled "Alex are you alright?!" Michael said and then Alex was in the water and bubbles started coming out of his mouth and then Alex started swimming to the surface and then he was able to get back on his board "oh shit" Alex said "Alex are you okay?" Michael asked "yeah mane I'm alright" Alex said and then Michael and Alex kept on surfing and then found themselves on some sort of island and the island looked really awesome it had gold sand and there were palm trees which was really cool and then Alex and Michael started looking around the island and then Alex jumped into the water and started swimming "do you know if the other suffers know that we are on this island? "Michael asked "I don't know Michael but so far this island does not like bad" Alex said and so then Michael and Alex where on the island for an hour or so and then as Alex was walking around Alex then found a motor boat "um Michael your going to love this dude" Alex said and then Michael ran to Alex "what is it?" Michael asked "I think's its a motorboat" Alex said "awesome" Michael said and then Alex and Michael went into the boat and they started looking around on the boat and they suddenly found the keys to the boat and then Alex started the boat and then the went back to the shores of San Diego "dude that was such an surf my man" Michael said "yeah I agree Michael. Say where did those suffers go?" Alex asked "I don't know Alex maybe they went back to their hotel rooms" Michael said and then as Alex and Michael where walking they then saw some sort of party going on in one of the hotels in the downtown area and I think it was happening around the top suite in that hotel room and then Michael and Alex checked out the hotel and suite

then Alex and Michael went to the suite and the suite was just hopping and there was dancing, people in the swimming in the pool, some people where playing arcades and playing billiards and darts "this looks like such an awesome party Alex my man" Michael said and then also they where people cards and gambling "I will go look for some chicks" Alex said "okay buddy "Michael said and then Alex started looking around the whole suite and then all of a sudden Alex saw this girl that was kind of short but she had curly blonde and brown hair and she was holding a bud light lime and then Alex stood next to her and he just checking a whole bunch of women at the party and then the girl with bud light lime looked at Alex "having fun checking up people "she said "oh yeah I am" Alex said "so do you like California girls Mr.?" she asked "Aussmen...Alex Aussmen" Alex said "I'm Jasmine double" Jasmine said "it's a pleasure to meet you miss Double" Alex said "so what brings to a wild party Mr. Aussmen" Jasmine asked "I don't I'm here with my friend Michael and we are just here on a trip" Alex said "oh wow that is really awesome Alex" Jasmine said "yeah today Michael and I where surfing on the coast here and we ended up on some sort of island of some sorts" Alex said "oh that island that is owned by Romatika" Jasmine said "uh that is interesting what does he do on that island?" Alex asked, "I don't know. Nobody really knows what he does there or why he bought it "Jasmine said "well I think that is going to change pretty soon I think" Alex said and then Alex and Jasmine went into the suite and then they started looking around then as Alex was with Jasmine, Michael was swimming in the swimming pool and having a lot of fun and then as Michael was swimming in the pool then the man with black hair caught up with him "yo buddy how was that surf?" he asked "oh it was great" Michael said and then the 2 blonde girls showed up "where did you guys go?" he asked "well we found this strange island and what was really funny is that we stole this motor boat from there as well" Michael said "oh my god that is just way too funny my man" he said "oh yeah I'm Trevor by the way this is Amy and Paula" Trevor said "oh awesome glad to meet you guys" Michael said "that is really cool that you went all the way to that Island over there" Amy said "oh thanks" Michael said "say you guys want to join for a road trip we might be going to a mountain in Russia I think" Trevor said "oh yeah that would be awesome "Michael said "yeah not problem guys" Trevor said

Then the next day without Alex and Jasmine knowing, Michael and Trevor went on an airplane and they went to the mountains of Russia and then the plane landed on a runaway and then Trevor, Michael, Amy, and Paula got off the plane and then they saw the mountains and then the group got on their skies and then they went on the ski lifts and then Michael started skiing and he had a headset on his head and then Michael and Trevor just skied down the very huge hill and Amy and Paula fallowed them "wow this is a very beautiful mountain" Michael said"yeah it's very beautiful but the USSR keeps the mountain very guarded with a whole bunch of Communist guards" Trevor said "oh my god" Michael said and then as the group kept on going down the hill, Michael used a hook shot gun and then Michael put the gun on his waist and then Michael an Trevor swing into the headquarters and they broke one of the windows and then as Michael and Trevor got in there they both got out flash lights and they saw the factory and the factory was making a lot of weapons "oh wow that is just insane "Michael said "yeah I know I have investigating this mountain for a couple of months now" Trevor said and then Trevor and Michael hid behind one of the walls and they saw a lot of guards that where coming into Romatika's office "did you find Mr. Aussmen?" Romatika asked "no doctor we have-not found him yet but we will really soon" one of the guards said "you better get Mr. Aussmen otherwise you will face the really deadly consequences" Romatika yelled and then he banged on his desk with his fist" that's him that Dr. Romatika he is behind an operation called Doomsday and this plane involves him and his goons to destroy the whole west cost with laser weapons" Trevor said "oh my god that is just insane I gotta tell Alex" Michael said and then as they both kept on spying Michael used a special bug to track down the rest of the goons and then Michael and Trevor and the rest of their group was able to get out of the headquarters just fine but then one of the security guards saw tape of both Trevor and Michael escaping from the headquarters and then as they escaped, Michael and Trevor stayed in hotel that was by the mountains and as they got into their hotel room Michael then called Alex on the phone "Alex you better pick up the phone "Michael said

Then back in California Alex and Jasmine where in a beach house on the cost and they where making out on the bed and Jasmine was wearing a gold dress "I love your dress and your beautiful house" Alex said "oh thanks Alex" Jasmine said "so what college did you go to?" Jasmine asked " I went to University of Washington" Alex said "oh wow that is really cool I hear that is really nice school" Jasmine said and they kept on making out on the water bed but then as they kept on making out on the bed then a person that looked very model like had a pistol in his hand and then Alex noticed the gun right away "duck!!" Alex said and then Jasmine ducked her head and then Alex punched him in the face and then knocked the gun out of his hand and then the gun tried to whack Alex in the face, then Alex tackled the guy and punched him in the face and then threw against the wall and then Alex got up and then guy took a Russian sword and tried to cut Alex in the neck but then Alex kicked the guy in the face and knocked out his front teeth and blood started coming out of the thugs' mouth and then the thug got up he tried punch Alex in the face again and Alex dodged all of the attacks and then Alex whacked the thug in the neck and kicked him in the stomach and then Alex grabbed him by the neck and whacked him in the face and gave the thug a black eye and then thug grabbed a kitchen knife and he tried to stab Alex but Alex then did a backflip and then he hanged on the a piece of wood and then Alex saw a sharp little piece of wood and then Alex threw the sharp piece of wood at the thug and then Alex jumped from hanging on the wood rope and then Alex kicked the thug from behind and then Alex pushed the guy and kicked the guy in the face and then he was on the sand and then Alex threw a rock at his face and then Alex threw the kitchen knife at the Russian thug and stabbed him in the neck and blood started coming out his neck "try to heal from that you communist" Alex said and then Alex walked back inside "are you okay Jasmine?" Alex said, "who was that guy?" Jasmine asked "that is what I'm trying to ask myself" Alex said and then all of a sudden the phone rang and it was Michael and then Alex answered the phone "hello?" Alex said "hey Alex this is Michael I'm in Russia right now and Trevor and I found something really weird in the mountains of Russia you have to come here ASAP" Michael said "wait didn't we saw something very similar to that on that one island 3 days ago" Alex said"yeah but this place is a lot bigger and more complex" Michael said "I will send some pictures" Michael said and then Michael fax the pictures to Alex's hotel room and then Alex picked up the pictures and then he started looking at them "oh my god this is crazy" Alex said"yeah I know they are planning on making laser weapons" Michael said "oh my goodness that is really bad. Yeah Michael I will be there as soon as I can" Alex said, "okay thanks Alex" Michael said

Then later that week Alex and Michael started heading to Seattle and Alex went to go see William at Seattle agencies around Seattle Center and then as Alex walked into his office William was throwing darts in his office "oh hey Alex I thought you where on vacation" William said "well William I was. But I think we have a huge situation on our hands" Alex said, "Wait what do you mean? "William said "well my friend Michael and I got some pictures of some Russian guy name Romatika and Michael was able to break into his fortress in Russia with other agents" Alex said and then Alex showed William the pictures of the weapons "oh my god that is insane what kind of man would do something like this" William said "do you know the places he is going to hit?" William asked "no sir" Alex said "but I think he is going to hit Mt. Rainer and strike at the mountain" Alex said "oh no not Mt. Rainer that is terrible, Alex I want you and Michael and investigate that mountain and find out if that Romatika is doing any sort of plan he is up to" William said "I'm on it sir and I'm on the case William" Alex said and then Alex walked out of the office "Michael get the RV ready" Alex said "Don't worry I will Alex my man "Michael said

Chapter 4 The Dangerous mission of climbing up Mt. Rainer

Then later that day Alex drove his 1978 Lamburgeni and he started driving to Michael's apartment was around Montlake around University of Washington and then Alex kept looking at his GPS system in his car and then Alex kept on driving and then Alex finally found Michael's apartment and his apartment was not even an apartment it looked like a mini secret agent building that looked like it blended right in with the UW campus and then Alex got out of the car and then Alex went to go knock on the door and then as Alex knocked the door opened and it was an elevator and then Alex went inside the elevator and then the elevator started going down and then as Alex got to the basement floor then Alex noticed that Michael's room looked very 1980s ish it had a huge spinning circle bed, a couple of posters of Michael Jackson a 1980's apple computer, and then Michael showed up "hey dude how do you like my place?" Michael asked "I like it dude it's really awesome your room is very hi-tech" Alex said and then Michael opened up his closet and he had a lot of 1980's style clothes and also some70's clothes in there as well and he even had a Michael Jackson style outfit "wow this looks awesome Michael" Alex said "anyway reason I came here Michael is that my boss at Seattle agencies said we had the okay to go up to Mt. Rainer to investigate possible laser attacks and I was wondering today if you wanted to go to REI to get some camping gear" Alex said "oh hell yeah I will go Alex my man of course dude" Michael said "hey do you want to have something eat before we go there?" Michael asked, "no thanks Michael I'm fine" Alex said

Then Alex and Michael headed off to REI to get some camping clothes and then as they got other Alex started getting all sorts of clothes and then as they got out they then headed back to Michael's agent house in Montlake and then Alex and Michael then started putting their camping clothes in Michael's RV and they also put some food, drinks and beer inside the RV and then as Alex and Michael where done packing, Alex got a call from Jasmine telling him that she was coming along with and then Jasmine started driving to Michael's house and then she parked her car around Michael's driveway and then Jasmine got out of her car, she then started walking to Michael's front door but then she saw a note on the door that said "we are in the RV" and then Jasmine walked to the RV and then she knocked on the RV door and then Alex answered the door "hey"Alex said "hey how long have you been here?" Jasmine asked "I think a couple of hours" Alex said and then Jasmine walked into a bed room "so what's the plan going to be?" Jasmine asked "well Michael and I will get to the mountain and see if Romatika and his goons are planning any sort of dangerous activity up there" Alex said "that sounds very exciting Alex I've always wanted to go up a mountain" Jasmine said and then Jasmine put her arms around Alex and then they started making out in the bedroom in the RV and then around 7:00PM Michael then started up the car and then RV started heading to Mt. Rainier the next day as they started heading more and more south Alex noticed as he was getting up from bed that they wherein Enumclaw, WA "oh Enumclaw...I hate this place" Alex said Alex never liked Enumclaw because it was country like and that it smiled really bad but it was his mission to go to Mt. Rainier and he would have to get past Enumclaw and then Michael was driving he noticed the sign saying that they where getting really close and it started snowing, Michael then turned on the whippers and then they got to the tip of the Mt. Rainer parking lot and then Alex parked the car and then Alex started getting some hiking clothes and gear on him "how cold is it?" Alex asked "it's around 10 degrees but I think we are going to be just fine" Michael said and then the three of them got out of the car and then got the ropes out and then Alex, Michael, and Jasmine started hiking up the mountain

As Alex was climbing up the mountain they got some of the edges of the mountain and with snowing blowing in their face, Alex took out a hook shot gun and then Alex started zooming to the top and then Alex held on really tight and then Alex fell on the snow and then as Alex was standing on the snow he noticed that some of the snow was not melting "hey guys I think you might want to take a look at this" Alex said and then Michael and Jasmine climbed up to that same spot where Alex was "what is it?" Michael asked "for some reason the snow around this area is not melting" Alex said and then Michael started feeling the snow "damn that is just too weird" Michael said and then Michael used a laser gun to shoot the spot and then he realized that it was a door he was trying to open and then Michael used his watch to crack open the door "my god what the hell do you think would be down there?" Alex asked "I have no idea" Michael said and then Jasmine came up to the same spot and then Alex, Jasmine, and Michael climbed down the door and noticed they where in some sort of cave and also an office area "I don't think this place is a cave" Alex said and then they got to the main lobby of the complex and then they noticed guards in suits walking around and then they hid around hiding places in the headquarters and then went into an elevator and then they started heading up to the 4th floor in the complex

Then as Alex and Michael got to the 4th floor in the building noticed some of the workers working special bombs and then Alex started taking pictures of the projects they were working on "what kind of bombs do you think they are?" Michael asked "I don't know but I think they are the most dangerous bombs I have ever seen" Alex said and then Romatika walked into the room "so any word on Mr. Aussmen" Romatika asked "no sir no word about Mr.Aussmen"one of the guards said and then Alex started running out the factory and then as he was about to run Romatika noticed with one of his eyes "that's Aussmen kill him!!!!" Romatika yelled and then a couple of guards got outA33 riffle guns and then they started shooting at Alex and then Alex kept on running and then a couple of guards started coming after him and then Alex took out a laser gun and he started shooting at the guards and then another guard grabbed Alex and then Alex grinned his teeth really hard and then Alex punched the guard in the face and gave him a bloody nose and then Alex kept on running and then Alex grabbed on the keycards "STOP HIM HE HAS

THEKEYCARD!!!!" Romatika yelled and then Alex kept on running for his life and then Alex made a really huge leap of faith and then as he jumped out of the factory he then landed on the snow of the mountain and then Alex pressed a button on his watch and then skies came out of his shoes and then Alex started going down the mountain in ski and more guards where starting to ski down the mountain and chasing Alex down the mountain and then as they were shooting at him, Alex turned back and took a DD4 pistol gun and he started shooting at the thugs that were chasing down the mountain and then Alex kept on going down and then Alex took out his headset "hey Michael I have a couple of thugs that are on my tail I need a an escape route out of this chase" Alex said "oh okay Alex I will see if I can come up with something my man "Michael said and then Alex kept on going down the mountain and then Alex jumped off of a lot of ramps and then Alex did a lot of backflips and then as Alex was getting more and more down, he noticed there was a lot of more trees and noticed that the snow was snow was melting and then all of a sudden Alex Tripped on a piece of wood and then Alex's skis came off of him and then Alex started yelling "AHHHHHHHHHHHHHHHHHHH!!!!"and then Alex started for something in his pockets that would prevent from falling to his death and then as Alex was falling then there was a parachute platform that caught Alex and then the platform put Alex in Michael's car "dude are you okay Alex my man? "Michael said "yeah I think I am my man, that chase was very intense "Alex said "you got the key card?" Michael asked and then took out the key card from his pockets "right here my man" Alex said and then Alex handed the key card to Michael "interesting I will see if I can take a look at this through the computer" Michael said and then Michael drove Alex back to his hotel room and then Jasmine was with Alex through out the whole night while Michael was looking at the key card and where this card leads to then as Michael was looking at the key card he kept on looking at the numbers on the card and then Michael scanned the card again and then the computer screen showed a submarine that was silver and red and then Michael was really shocked and then Michael went to Alex's hotel room "Alex!!" Michael said and then Alex answered the door "hey man what's up?" Alex said "I found out where the key card leads to "Michael said "oh wow that is really wonderful Michael and what did you find out" Alex asked and then Alex sat down on his bed "dude this is going to blow you away" Michael said and then Michael scanned the card and then computer that Michael had with him powered the projector that Alex had and then Michael started showing him pictures of the submarine and saw that was in Union Bay in Seattle "oh my goodness that is one huge sub Sean "Alex said "Yeah I couldn't believe it when I saw it too my man "Michael said "but how do you know that the card leads to this place? "Alex asked "well because the number led me to this sub and I'm thinking that Romatika is planning on something really big by blowing a the whole bay and also lake Washington and then with that explosion he will use the weapons to destroy Hawaiian Islands and then he will destroy Alaska" Michael said "oh my god that is really awful Michael. So do you have any wet suits that me and Jasmine and I can use?" Alex asked "yeah I have some stuff you guys can use" Michael said "alright that is good Michael" Alex said and then Michael walked out of Alex's hotel room and then Alex went back to his hotel room and then Alex started having thoughts that maybe Romitka might be working for someone other than himself and maybe that there might be another person like Alex that has the same disability and the same type of knowledge as him

Chapter 5 The Huge dive into Union Bay

 The next day Alex, Jasmine and Michael got out of Southern Washington and then they started heading back to the Seattle area and Alex started drawing up really huge plans on how he was going to attack this submarine and also he was thinking about if this Romatika person was working for someone and Alex really wanted to tell William and he also wanted to tell Dennis on how he was going to do this special plan and then Alex and Michael started looking around for a special place around union bay and then after 2 hours of looking Michael and Alex found a spot that was Iver's seafood restaurant "so do you got the submarine missile that you built?" Alex asked "yeah it's done and it's in the truck "Michael said and then Michael pressed a button and then truck had a huge claw and then the claw came out of the truck and the submarine was placed into the water and then Alex went into the water and he put on a jump suit and then Alex went inside the missile and then Alex started powering up the missile "am I good Michael?" Alex asked "your good Alex" Michael said "good luck Alex" Jasmine said "thank you" Alex said "in 5, 4, 3,2, 1 and GO!!!!!!!" Michael yelled and then missile blasted into the ocean and then missile was going about 90 miles per hour and then Alex started seeing the radar bullet pointing at features that were inside the bay and Alex saw a lot of fish "Alex do you see the Romatika's submarine?" Michael asked "not yet Michael but it's hiding somewhere in the ocean" Alex said and then missile kept on going really fast and then out of nowhere then a turbo bullets started coming after Alex "Michael, I got bullets that are chasing my tale" Alex said "try to dodge them Alex" Michael said and then Alex pulled a lever inside the missile and then Alex's missile back flipped and then the bullets crashed into coral reef and then out of nowhere, the submarine came out from the ground and it was a huge submarine and it was as huge as a cruse ship "Michael I found the submarine and it is really big" Alex said and then Alex pushed a button and then Alex was ejected out of the missile and then Alex started swimming to the submarine and then Alex was able to break into the submarine and then Alex was around the locker room and then Alex put on one of the uniforms that was in locker and the uniform looked dark blue and then the paints looked like purple jump suit pants but Alex put on the pants and then as Alex got out of the locker room Alex hid in back of a wall and then Alex used his autism perspective vision and prestige and then Alex pulled out a colt 1911 pistol and then Alex saw Romatika looking at the huge window "so when is the final missile going to get launched?" Romatika asked "it will get done in about 30 minutes or so" one of his guards said "30 minutes?! That is way too late I want that missile done right away no buts!!!!!!" Romatika said "yes sir" the guard said and then Alex put on his army style hat and then Alex started looking around and then of the guards saw Alex "what is your assignment??" The guard said "I'm here just to check over this control panel" Alex said "well Romatika already said that he wants top lace the submarine now get back to work" the guard said "okay "Alex said and then all of a sudden the same guard noticed Alex's face "he you look very filmier" the guard said "are you new here?" The guard asked "no I'm not" Alex said and then as Alex was about to walkaway then the guard pointed a gun at Alex and then flick the hat off of his head "hey it's Alex Aussmen!!!!!" The guard yelled and then everybody stood up and then "oh we are going to kick your ass really bad Seattle boy!!!!!" The guards said and then with rage Alex pulled out his pistol and then Alex started shooting the guards in the head and then Alex started running and then guards started chasing him and then guards started firing A33riffles at Alex and then Alex started firing back at the guards and then Alex jumped up in the air and then Alex hanged on to a rope and then Alex started climbing up the rope and then Alex started climbing to the 2nd floor and then as Alex got to the 2nd floor Alex just kept on running and then as Alex got to around Romatika's office Alex then used a mine bomb to blow up the door "freeze!!!!!!!" Alex yelled and then Alex started looking around and he saw a lot of gold in Romnitka's office and then Alex saw the gold map that Romatika was using to track Alex down and then just kept on looking at it and then all of a sudden Romatika had a pirate sword in his hand and he dressed up as Captain Hook "salutations Mr. Aussmen it's a shame you will have to die and you have melted with my plans for the last time!!!!!!!" Romatika yelled and then Romnitka tried to whack him with a sword and then Alex did acart wheel and then Romnitka kept on trying to cut Alex and then Romatika punched Alex in the face and threw him against the wall and then Alex kicked Romatika in the face and then kicked him in the nut shack and then Alex punched Romatika in the face gave him a black eye and then Alex grabbed a metal bar and whacked Romnitka in the face and his mouth started bleeding and then Romnitka punched Alex in the face and then Romatika gave Alex a cut on his arm and then Romatika did an evil laugh and then Alex kicked Romatika in the face and then Alex punched him in the stomach and Alex grabbed him by the shirt and then Romatika saw the nuclear remote and then Alex forced him against the wall "DONT EVEN THINK ABOUT CAPTION SHIT HEAD!!!!!!!!" Alex yelled and then Romatika just started laughing "you have already lost Mr. Aussmen and in 60 minutes the biggest nuclear bomb is going to blow up this bay and you are agents will never stop it" Romatika said and you will never stop my boss Mr. Aussmen" Romatika said "who are you working for?" Alex asked and then Romatika got up and then all of a sudden he electrocuted Alex and then Romatika kicked Alex in the face and then he grabbed his pirate sword "well Mr. Aussmen this is a perfect way for you to die because with all my smarts I can be able to blow up this bay and create another missile crises and you will see my plan succeed" Romatika said and then Alex just looked at Romatika and then Alex fired his gun at Romatika in the head and then Romatika was dead and then Alex ran to the remote to try to decode the bomb and then Alex noticed that the wiring was around the back of the submarine and then Alex found a way out of the submarine and then Alex started swimming to the front and and then Alex was looking in his pocket and then Alex found a hook gun and then Alex shot the gun at the submarine and then submarine started catching on fire and then as submarine was catching on fire, Alex went back into the submarine and then he grabbed the keycard and then the submarine blew up inflames and then Alex found away to get alkali beach in Seattle and then a couple of solders that were working for Romatika and then Alex electrocuted them "you guys are under arrest" Alex said and then Alex handcuffed them and then Michael drove to alki beach and picked up "are you okay Alex?" Michael asked "yeah I'm fine thanks for picking me up "Alex said "your welcome Alex anytime" Michael said and then Michael drove Alex back his house and then as they got into the house, Jasmine was waiting for Alex and then as Alex opened the door Jasmine saw him "Alex!!!" Jasmine said, "Are you okay?" Jasmine asked "yeah I'm fine and I also got the keycard to give to William" Alex said and then Jasmine then hugged Alex really tightly and then Alex started kissing her on the lip and Alex kissed her really passionately but then all of a sudden then Romatika showed up and then they both turned back at him "I'm glad that was able to find Mr. Aussmen" Romatika said "you really think blowing up my submarine will really stop me. No it will not Mr. Aussmen and now there is a missile heading to this house as I speak and you have interfered with my plans for the last time Mr. Aussmen!!!!!!!" Romatika said and then Romatika pointed the gun at Alex "PUT YOUR DAMN HANDS UP YOUSTUPID AMERICAN!!!!!!!!" Romatika yelled and then as he was pointing the gun at Alex, all of a sudden Alex whacked the gun out of his hand and then Alex kicked him in the stomach and then Romatika had a hook hand and he tried to cut Alex in the face, then Alex ducked and then Alex tackled Romatika and punched him in the face 13 times and then Romatika tried to do a spinning punch on Alex but then Alex defended himself and grabbed his wrist and twisted his wrist really hard but then Romatika grabbed Alex by the neck and "so what are you going to do disco boy!!!!" Romatika said and then Alex noticed his hook hand had gasoline and then Alex tried to reach out a lighter and then Alex lit Romatika's hook hand and then fire burned his face"AHHHHHHHHHHHHHHHHHH!!!!!!!!" He yelled and then all of a sudden his face just started burning up and his eyes started turning black and the fire burned up his whole face and Romatika was dead for good "that is what happens when you a captain at sea for a very long time" Alex said and then Alex found the controller in Romatika's pocket and then Alex found the button to disable the missile and then missile blew up and then Alex ran to Michael's room and then Alex untied Michael "oh my god what happened? What did I miss?" Michael asked "you didn't miss much but captain Romatika go this face blown off so he is dead" Alex said and then Alex walked to Jasmine "darling should we get out of here?" Alex said

And then later that night Alex and Jasmine went to eat dinner at the space needle to eat dinner "after all the years I have been living in Seattle I always wanted to live in Seattle" Alex said "so Alex how do you all the stuff that you do?" Jasmine asked "well I like saving the world my dear and keeping the world safe" Alex said and then Jasmine and Alex smooched each other on the lips and then Alex put his hand on jasmine's face and he started kissing her really passionately "there will be always be on Seattle agent "Jasmine said and then Alex kept on kissing her "oh Alex" Jasmine said

Bellevue Assault & Notebook Franchise

001
Bellevue Assault & Notebook Franchise
By: Nelson Amador

Prologue

It was a really sunny day around the east side of Western Washington right around Seattle and Bellevue. And in the summer there is a lot of people in Bellevue and Seattle in the summer time that are always either having a lot of fun or working during the science. As the day reached around 3PM while a lot of people where shopping at Bellevue Square and buying a lot of 1980's clothing and also other products as well. People where listening to cassette players and a lot of people on the streets where wearing a lot of 1980's style clothing and people had a lot of funny hair. A lot of the teenagers were trying to impress the girls by dancing in front of them and also trying to dance like Michael Jackson. Some teenage girls were talking to the girlfriends and talking the cutest guys in their school. And a lot of yuppies in Bellevue where in fancy places like playing golf, at country clubs, playing tennis, on their boats on lake Washington, and also most of all they were in their mansions having fun or having fun in different places. During the day there was a group of teenagers that went down to Maydenbaur park around downtown Bellevue and they had on a lot of a 1980's style swimsuits and they were talking about how happy they were that school was finally out. Some of them were hitting on each other and flirting as well.

But as this was going on, all of a sudden there was a young man that had slick back hair and he was spying on the teenagers. As the man was at the park, he looked at his watch and then he walked on the dock of Maydenbaur park and he approached one of the teenage boys that were in the group. "enjoying the sun?" he asked "yeah it's always really great to see sun to this area because a lot of people think this place rains a lot" one of the boys said "oh really is that so?" he asked again "well I hope you boys enjoy your summer" he said and then he just walked away. And then as he walking away, a beautiful woman in her early 30's or late 20's started walking on the dock, and she had tan skin, her breathes were really huge and she was wearing a very beautiful golden bikini and it was shinning a lot. And a lot of guys just stopped and staried at her. As she was walking on the dock, the same guy started fallowing her and the woman started looking at the boats and then all of a sudden she dived into lake Washington and she started swimming out in the open water and the same guy started swimming after her. As she got to middle of the lake, the young man was able to catch up to her "wow you are a very athletic swimmer" he said "oh thank you" she said "I really love your hair by the way. How do you make it like that?" she asked "well I just went to this really fancy salon that is here in Bellevue" the woman said and then all of a sudden there was something in the water and she started feeling something was touching her right leg "uh oh something is touching me" the woman said "oh don't worry miss you won't feel a thing real soon…" the man said and all of a sudden he got out a medicine gun and he gave her a shoot that knocked out her. The man then grabbed the women and he started dragging her underwater to a submarine that was in the water. As the man was in the submarine, a lot of his thugs showed up and they started warming up the girl and they even took off her bikini and but her in a steam room. The man changed into a blue suit jacket and he spiked up his hair using an old spice hair product and he looked like some sort of crazy character from a video game. He went inside a room that was in the submarine and the woman was tied up in the spa room "good evening…it has really come to attention that you have something that we really want miss Thomas" he said "what do you want with me??…" she cried "well I was looking at the newspaper and I want to steel your husband fortune and become the richest man in Bellevue and you are going to tell where the money is" he said "I will never tell you where it is" she said "oh well that's a really huge shame because I would really hate to kill such a beautiful girl like yourself…but then again I do love money!!!!" he said and then all of a sudden there was a swimming pool that -99 degrees below zero "put her in the ice pool" he said "no,no please I will tell you where it please don't kill me…" she cried and then all of a sudden the guards threw her into the ice pool with no clothes on and her body started getting really weak and her skin was turning blue and all of a sudden the woman was dead. The thugs grabbed her body put her body in Lake Washington her dead frozen body started sinking deeper and deeper "rich people in Bellevue…not anymore…soon with my lawyer skills that I have working on so much…I will be able to frame people and making sure that the wealthy people in this state loose their money and their fortune…" he said then all of a sudden he pressed a button on his remote that had a picture of the woman's husband that died "soon I will be able steel all of Red McLeod's money and soon there will be a new rich man in Bellevue and I will steel everything that is in his name, I will get all the things that he loves so much, including all the women that he use to date and most of all his billions of dollars!!!!! Nothing can stop me…..MUAHAHAHAHAHAHAHAHAHAHAHAHAHAHAHAHAHAHAHAHHAHAHAHAHAHA HAHAHAHAHAHAHAHAHAHAHAHAHAHAHAHAHAHAHAHAHAHAHAHAHAHAHA HAH BRAHAHAHAHAHAHAHAHAHAHAHAHAHAHAHAHAHAHAHAHAHAHAHAHAHAHAH AHAHAHAHAHAHAHAHAHAHAHAHAHAHAHAHAHAHAHAHAHAHAHHAHAHAHAHA HAHAHAHA!!!!!!!!!" he laughed and then as he was laughing, the women's gold bikini was inside of a glass container locked up

Chapter 1 Lower Queen, Seattle, Washington 1987

The next morning it was another beautiful day in Seattle. As the day progressed, a young man with brown hair and a suit started walking to Seattle Center. The guy was constantly looking at his watch and he just kept on walking. As he got around Seattle center, he looked up at the Seattle Agencies building and he went inside the building and he took the elevator and the elevator started going up. The elevator reached 18th floor in the building and a beautiful girl with brown hair smiled at the young man "hey Alex how was your weekend?" the girl asked "oh my weekend was really wonderful Jenny. Michael and I went to Brazil and we had a really interesting experience. Michael got really wasted and he drank around 55 beers and I had a hard time getting him back on the plane" Alex said "my god. I guess that guy really loves to have a good time" Jenny said "oh you have no idea. Is Rivers in his office?" Alex asked "yes he is. I will call him right now" Jenny said "Will, Alex is here" Jenny said "alright send him in" Rivers said "I really need to take you somewhere sometime soon Jenny" Alex said and all of a sudden Alex put her hands Jenny's shoulder and Jenny put her head on Alex's chest "….oh I would really love that…" Jenny whispered "well I better want to get going. You want to my apartment later today?" Alex said "yeah sure thing baby" Jenny said and then Alex went into Rivers's office "good morning zero, zero, one. Take a seat we have a really huge problem on our hands" Rivers said "what's going on Will" Alex said "well yesterday afternoon around Bellevue a woman was killed in lake Washington and nobody knows how she died or who killed her. The Bellevue police department was able to get some footage of what happened by Maydenbaur park" Rivers said and all of a sudden, Rivers started showing Alex some of the footage on a VHS of what happened and showed her drowning in the water "that just seems really wrong" Alex said "you got that right Alex" Rivers said "your 1st mission is going to be investigate what happened at Maydenbaur park and then also we suspect someone name Wilson Trybee a western Washington attorney will be able to help you and also try to get some information out of him" Rivers said "yeah I will go Bellevue tomorrow to investigate Will" Alex said "oh I know you will Alex" Rivers said Rivers handed Alex documents of Trybee's records as a lawyer and Alex headed out the door.

As Alex went out the door, Jenny smiled at Alex "so how did it go?" she asked him "well it sounds like Lake Washington might not be the best place to go swimming at" Alex said "why do you say that?" Jenny said "it's mostly because there was a killing that happened yesterday" Alex said "oh that's not good." Jenny said "yeah tell me about it. There is a lot of crazy people in this world" Alex said "like you?" Jenny said "….yes like me but I'm just really crazy mainly because I'm really goofy" Alex said "and you are very sexy" Jenny said "yes and that too" Alex said and then Alex headed out the door and he started heading back to his pen house apartment in downtown Seattle. As he went inside, Alex turned on his really huge TV in his apartment and he started drinking a bud light and he was watching king 5 news and on the news, they were talking about the murder that happened around Lake Washington. All of a sudden as Alex was watching TV, Jenny knocked on the door "come in" Alex said and Jenny opened the door and she walked towards Alex and she put her arms around him "I always love coming to your apartment Aussy baby" Jenny said "yeah my apartment is really nice." Alex said and Jenny started kissing Alex everywhere on his face and Alex pressed a button and he started playing the song "no more love on the run" and then later that night, Alex and Jenny went swimming in Alex's swimming pool.

Chapter 2 Rich Part of Bellevue

The next morning Alex got up from bed and he noticed right away that he wasn't wearing anything at all and he saw a note from Jenny that said "I had the best time with you last night" Alex got on his feet and he put the note on his desk, he took a shower, got dressed and he wore a 1980's style suit and tie and he brushed his teeth and he also put on some cologne and he took the elevator to the garage and he got into a 1987 Acura Integra that Michael sent him. Alex got into the car he noticed right away that Michael put a lot of gadgets and weapons into the car and Alex smiled and Alex pressed a button and a GPS map showed up. Alex typed up the address as a 1980's Mac keyboard showed from under the steering wheel. Alex started up the car and he just started driving to Bellevue from his pen house apartment. As Alex got to Bellevue, he noticed how beautiful Bellevue really was and Alex has been to Bellevue many times but every time he would go there, Bellevue always looked really different and there was always a new building in the city. Alex kept on driving and he started heading to a neighborhood called Clyde Hill and there was a lot of mansions everywhere as Alex was driving. Alex parked his car that was by a red and sliver mansion that was a 2 story house and the owner around 3 fancy cars in his drive way. Alex got out of the car and he walked up to the front door and he knocked on the door. All of a sudden a man with brown and spiky hair answered the door "awwwe Mr. Aussmen I'm glad you are here" he said "yeah I'm glad I am able to come see you." Alex said "come in" he said. As Alex was in the house, he noticed a lot of fancy things that were in the house, a lot of paintings, a lot of silverware and other fancy elements in the house "can I get you a drink Mr. Aussmen. Juice, coffee, sparkling cider, whisky?" he asked "it's funny back when I was growing up, my parents never drank alcohol in the morning" Alex said "yeah it's the life of the rich Alex. Being rich is good" he said "so I hear that you are an attorney. The reason I came here was I wanted to ask you if you knew anything from the killing that happened at Maydenbaur park?" Alex asked "oh how very awful. Yes, I herd about that on the news. I feel very sorry for that girl" he said "me too Alex, she was a very beautiful girl" he said "so what do you do for a living Mr. Aussmen?" he asked "well I'm a private investigator" Alex said "oh yeah that's a really good job" Wilson said "I feel like we are not so different you and I, we both deal with laws of this country" Wilson said "yeah. I also herd that she is the wife of Red McLeod" Alex said "oh yeah the richest man in Bellevue. A lot of people are always really jealous of his life-style" Wilson said "I don't know maybe if I got to know him, he wouldn't be that bad of a person" Alex said "oh you are too young Mr. Aussmen how some rich people are very bad and very selfish" Wilson said "well I don't know Mr. Trybee I'm going to go see him later today and talk to him" Alex said "really? I would really hate for you to go. We have so much in common" Trybee said "yeah I think like you, I also have work to do" Alex said "well good luck on finding the things that you need" Trybee said "thanks" Alex said and then Alex headed out of Trybee's house and he went back into his car, some of Trybee's thugs showed up from behind him "you know that young man sure asks a lot of questions" one of his thugs said "yeah he sure does. That's why we have to fallow him because he is one of those secret agents. And we must kill him" Trybee said "yes sir" the thugs said

As Alex drove away from the house, Alex knew from the visit that something really wasn't right and knew that maybe some people in Bellevue that are rich are not all bad people and also Alex didn't believe what Trybee said and Alex right away called Rivers "did you find any information about the killings?" Rivers said "I sort of did. I found that Trybee knows nothing about the killings but I can really tell that he was lying." Alex said "just try to spy on him as much as possible Alex" Rivers said "yeah I will do that" Alex said Alex hung up the phone and he started driving to Bellevue Square and he parked his car in the garage and he started walking into the stores. As Alex was in the mall, some of Trybee's thugs were fallowing Alex as Alex was just going into the stores that he really loves going into and some of thugs were able to hide in different places and spy on him using a sniper riffle in the mall. Also when Alex was in the mall, Alex saw a very beautiful girl that had brown hair and she was working at American eagle. Alex started going into the store and he just looking at random men's clothing. The beautiful girl with brown hair noticed Alex right away and she also had very beautiful blue eyes. "is there anything that you are looking for?" she asked "oh well not really I'm just looking around" Alex said "oh okay. Well if you need any help, just let me know" she said "I really love your eyes by the way" Alex said "oh thank you Mr.?" she asked "Aussmen...Alex Aussmen" Alex said "well Alex I can point you into some clothes that might fit you. If you want to see them." She said "oh that would be really great. Thank you." Alex said the girl started walking to the latest clothes that just got delivered to the store and Alex was just smiling and really fascinated "I never really got your name" Alex said "I'm Megan Ryan" Megan said "it's a pleasure to meet you Megan" Alex said as Alex kept on talking to Megan, more of Trybee's thugs started getting closer and closer to Alex and Alex really started feeling their presence. And then all of a sudden one of the thugs shot one of the American eagle workers that was working and then all of a sudden the people started screaming in terror and in fear and Megan was really scarred "come on!!!!" Alex said and Alex right away grabbed Megan and they started running to find a way to get out Bellevue Square. As the assignation happened in the mall, Bellevue Square was in lock down mode and all of a sudden the thugs pulled out their guns and they took out Beretta model 93R machine pistols and they started firing the guns at Alex and Alex got out a colt MEU Semi Automatic service pistol gun and Alex started firing 4,000 bullets at the thugs and trying to kill them. Alex was able to kill around 5 thugs and Alex and Megan ran up to the 2nd floor in Bellevue Square and Alex loaded up his pistol gun with more bullets and more thugs showed up. Alex started firing more bullets at the thugs. As the thugs were firing at Alex, Alex dodged the bullets by summersaulting and dodging to objects and hiding behind objects. Megan also noticed that some thugs were coming after Alex. Megan all of a sudden grabbed Alex to turn him around and Alex started firing at the thugs that were coming after him and Alex was able to kill them. All of a sudden, one of the thugs were able to throw a grenade at both of them. Alex and Megan ran away and the grenade exploded into flames. Alex right away noticed that there was a thug that had a sniper riffle and Alex re-loaded his gun and Alex fired his pistol and he shot the thug that had the sniper riffle and killed him. Alex and Megan were able to get into Nordstrom and noticed that more thugs were in Nordstrom looking for Alex. Alex was able to hid behind walls and he shot the thugs and the head and killed them. Alex and Megan found a secret way to get out of the Nordstrom and to get outside. "who were those guys??" Megan asked "I don't know but I'm going to find out" Alex said "that is really crazy that you know how to use a gun" Megan said "yeah the first thing you know about me is that my job is protect people from guys that were trying to kill us" Alex said "is there a safe place that we can go?" Megan asked "yes, I will take you to my apartment and we will be safe there" Alex said

Alex and Megan ran to the Bellevue garage and they got into Alex's car. Alex started up the car and Alex started driving out of the garage and he was looking for a road that would get him on the highway. As Alex was driving, there was a lot more thugs that were on motorcycles and they started chasing Alex. Megan noticed this right away and she got really scarred "Alex they are starting to come after us" Megan said and all of a sudden, Alex pressed a button in his car and a rocket launcher came out of the roof of the car. Alex pressed another button and the rocket launcher on top of the car started firing at the thugs that were chasing after Alex. Alex fired around 55 rockets at the thugs at the motorcycle and causing 44 explosions in downtown Bellevue and people were going crazy. Alex then put the car on reverse and Alex turned his head back and he saw the Bellevue park. Alex put the car on forward and Alex started driving really fast and then more thug cars started coming after him, as Alex was going really fast, Megan got more scared "don't worry Megan we will find to get out of here" Alex said and then Alex pressed another robot and he started firing a grenade launcher at the cars and Alex ended up blowing up 22 thug cars in flames. And Alex ended up on the road and Alex was going around 70 miles per hour and Alex took a right turn on to I-405 and Alex started heading north and he went on to another high way to downtown Seattle and Alex drove Megan to his apartment and parked his car. "who in the hell where those guys?" Megan asked "well I don't know who they are. But whoever there are, they must be working for Trybee" Alex said "you will be safe in my apartment" Alex said

Alex and Megan then started walking up into Alex's pen house and Alex started calling Rivers on his phone and Rivers answered the phone. "hello?" Rivers said "yeah Will, I was in Bellevue Square and Trybee's thugs ambushed but thankfully though I was able to destroy their cars" Alex said "that's great

Alex. Good job!!!" Rivers said "thank you sir" Alex said "Alright well your next task is to meet with Red McLeod and just talk to him" Rivers said "yeah I will do that sir" Alex said "he lives in Kirkland, Washington" Rivers said and then Alex hung up the phone and Megan laid down on his couch "you must have a lot of money to live in a place like this" Megan said "well I just choose to save my money and I like the Seattle skyline" Alex said "it's really beautiful" Megan said "thank you" Alex said

Then later that day, Trybee was in one of his rich boats on lake Washington and he was drinking 5 shots of wisky and he had 2 beautiful girls around him and he had 1980's aviators on him and 2 of his henchmen came into the door and Trybee was watching the footage of what happened in Bellevue on TV with a very pissed off look on his face. All of a sudden Trybee through a wisky bottle at the TV and broke the TV and he screamed in anger "I want you to kill him!!!!!!!" Trybee yelled "kill who boss?" one of his henchmen said and then Trybee took out a pistol and he killed one of his henchmen "what do you fucking think?! Alex Aussmen!!!!!!! He killed 99 of my thugs and on top of that, he is embasoul that thinks he can just kill my boys. I will make sure that little fox gets a very bloody death" Trybee said and then he banged his fist on the coffee table "I will make sure that Aussmen is killed and make his life a living hell" Trybee said

As the day went on Alex and Megan started spending some time together and they were sitting on the coach "so have you always done this?" Megan asked "yeah throughout my life. I have been doing this ever since I was 16 years old" Alex said "wow that is a really long time" Megan said "but I can really tell that you are really good at what you do" Megan said "oh thanks" Alex said "Megan can I ask you question?" Alex asked "do you want to help me track down the person that is trying to kill you?" Alex said "Alex I don't know if I would be really good but I think I really trust you and I will help you" Megan said

The next day Alex took a shower and he got dressed and he headed over to Kirkland to meet up with Red McLeod in his house. Alex parked his car around the drive way and Alex got out of the car, Red opened his front door and he was a man in his early 40's, he had blonde hair, and was wearing 1980's business clothes "Alex welcome to my home. Come in" Red said and Alex walked into the house and he was amazed at all the photos that he had "do you want me to fix you a drink?" Red asked "yeah coffee would be really awesome. Thank you" Alex said "now anyway sir, I just wanted to ask you a couple of questions" Alex said "like what kind Alex?" Red asked "well for starters, Red I know that your wife is gone and me and a lot of other agents are going to find who did it" Alex said "oh you herd, yeah I was really sad when she died Alex and I just don't know who the hell would do such a thing" Red said "yeah me neither sir" Alex said "do you know who could be behind the killing of my wife?" Red asked "well yesterday I was in Bellevue and all of a sudden, there was a couple thugs that chased after me and they had a lot of crazy weaponry. I feat that there might be a terrorist group in the east-side" Alex said "are you serious Alex?" Red asked "sadly I am" Alex said "oh my god" Red said but anyway as Alex and Red are talking in Red's house then more of Trybee's thugs saw from out of the shower and they took out riffles and they aimed the riffles at Red's head and then as Red was talking, Alex noticed the thugs outside and saw them loading up the guns "Red we have to get out of here right now!!!!" Alex said "what?! What's going on Alex?!" Red said in shock and then all of a sudden it was too late, one of the thugs shot Red in the head and then all of a sudden leaned on Alex's body and blood started coming out of the back of his head and Red was dead. And then all of a sudden without thinking, Alex started running and he broke through a glass window and landed around the backyard and then Alex reached out of his pocket and he found a Beretta 92 gun and he started shooting the thugs with the Beretta 92 gun. Alex started dodging a lot of bullets and taking cover from behind the trees from the bullets firing, Alex turned back and he shoot 8 bullets at Trybee's thugs shooting him and Alex ended up killing 6 of his thugs. Alex started running to Red's front door and then he got to his car and then he started driving out of the drive way and then more of the thugs got on motorcycles and they started chasing Alex in Kirkland. Alex then took another turn and then he started driving to Bothell and a lot of thugs started firing a lot of rocket launchers at him and blowing up 5 buildings in flames

Alex pressed a button on his car and then a couple grenade launchers came out from both sides of his car and he started firing the grenades at the car and blowing up the cars chasing him from behind. And then Alex started going really fast in his car and then Alex went off a really huge ramp on the high way and he landed on the rooftop of Totem Lake Mall and then Alex pressed another button and a rocket launcher came out from the top of the car and thugs started firing ZMG guns at and Alex started firing a rocket launcher by bulling the lever back like it was a coin shooter machine at an arcade. Alex ended up blowing up 22 of the thugs that were on the motorcycles and killing them. Then all of a sudden a helicopter showed up and then Alex started driving really fast and then started going on the highway south towards Bellevue "it's all over Alex. You must surrender by the same of the Trybee organization!!!!" the helicopter said and then the helicopter started firing a lot of misses at Alex's car. Alex started drifting the car really fast and he drifted the car and Alex turned the car around and Alex pressed another button and the same rocket launcher. Alex fired the rocket launcher at the helicopter chasing him and he blew up the helicopter and then 4 more helicopters showed up and then Alex fired four more rockets at the helicopters and blew up 5 of them in flames and then Alex started driving really fast and then he took a left turn into Overlake and he called Rivers on the phone "Will, McLeod is dead, more of the same thugs started coming after me" Alex said "damn it" Rivers said "well it's okay Alex. It sounds like this is going to be a really tough mission. You're going to need some big time help" Rivers "yeah for sure sir" Alex said "How is the car?" Rivers asked "the car is fine but the thugs did a lot of damage to McLeod's house back in Kirkland" Alex said "good god!!!!!" Rivers said "yeah I know it's terrible and they were able to get to his property through swimming across lake Washington" Alex said "sweet Jesus!!!!!! Alright well that is shame McLeod is dead but we will see if we can do a lot more digging on this case because it just sounds like whenever we get close, his thugs are right there. It just makes you think this guy could be anywhere" Rivers said "yeah" Alex said "well anyway Aussmen out" Alex said and then Alex turned off the phone in his car and he started heading back to his apartment. As Alex got back into his apartment, he then started writing down a lot of notes on the thugs and all the things he was noticing. One of the things Alex wrote down was technology and lot of jumpsuits because he noticed from the file of the mission that most of these thugs were killing a lot of rich people on the east side and they just killed the McLeod a moment ago. And then all of a sudden Alex realized that he couldn't do this mission like the others ones he did in the past alone and that he had to assemble a team of agents to check out a lot of areas.

Chapter 3 Operation Notebook Franchise

As Alex came back to his apartment in Seattle, He started writing down a couple of names of agents that could work with him. One of the people Alex wrote down was Jenny because she was really smart and she knew how to really handle herself with technology and she also knew how to shoot a rocket launcher. And then as Alex was at his desk, he then got a phone call and Alex answered the phone. "hello" Alex said "Hey buddy Rivers told me about your operation and I'm in" the voice said on the phone "Who is this? Where can I meet you?" Alex asked "I'm around South Center if you want to meet me" he said and then he hung up the phone. Alex then started heading to south Center in his car and as he found himself a parking spot, he then turned off his car, and he started going inside the Nordstrom that was there. As Alex was inside, he just started looking around the store and he was looking at the latest men's fashion and looking at all sorts of clothes. But as he was looking around, there was an African-American gentlemen that was wearing a Don Johnson style outfit and he came to him "Mr. Aussmen?" he asked and then Alex turned back and he saw him "It was not that hard to find you man. I'm Deshaun Ford. Rivers sent me to find you and meet with you" Deshaun said "Yeah I'm glad because I really think we are going to need all the help we can get in this mission" Alex said and then during the day Alex and Deshaun were walking around the mall going into different stores and they were talking about the case and then after they did so, they then started eating Philly Cheese steaks sandwiches in the mall. "so what do you need me to do Alex?" Deshaun asked "well right now I'm just setting up a team to take down Trybee and we have to hit in a place where he will not expect us to be in" Alex said "yeah I think that is a really good plan man" Deshaun said "who else is on yo team?" he asked "Well there is also Jenny as well" Alex said "alright well I'm in buddy" Deshaun said "so what's this operation called?" Deshaun asked, "I'm going to call it…operation Notebook franchise" Alex said "Now that is a really good name hommie" Deshaun said

As Alex left south Center, he went into his car and he saw his phone ring inside the car and he answered the phone "hello." Alex said "Alex, this is Rivers and we found word that Trybee might be having a party around Kirkland at a mansion that is there. I want you and your team to get to that party" Rivers said "got it Rivers we will do that" Alex said and then Alex hung up the phone and he started his car and he started heading back to his pen house apartment in Seattle and he just started watching TV and he started red mountain dew.

Then the next day Alex started jogging around Seattle and he started running to the Seattle Agencies. Alex entered the building and he took the elevator and he went into Michael's office "well sounds like you had a really fun run" Michael said "yeah I did and I think ended up burning around 2,000 calories" Alex said "Now this is a very no invention that I did and this will help you turn your tuxedo jacket into many different colors" Michaels said "That's really cool Michael" Alex said and then Alex grabbed the jacket and he put it on and Alex started pressing the buttons and the tuxedo jacket started changing into many different colors "I really like it already" Alex said "I'm really glad that you like it Alex" Michael said "And then this is also a new watch that can shoot lasers and get you out of trouble. So just in case you don't have a gun with you, you can use this watch to kill bad guys in laser shot" Michael said Michael gave the watch to Alex and Alex started shooting the lasers from the watch and shooting them at target boards "Nice shoot man" Michael said "thanks buddy" Alex said "I hope these gadgets will be able to help you on your new mission buddy" Michael said "I'm sure they will Michael" Alex said and Alex grabbed his two new gadgets and he started heading to Jenny's office in the building. Alex got into the office and Deshaun and Jenny were in black jumpsuits "man these suits are dope man" Deshaun said "Yeah I'm really glad that you like them" Alex said "so anyway the reason I called you guys here is because we are going sneak into Trybee's mansion in Kirkland and it's not going to be easy. Because they have security around that area like crazy. And there is also a security wall around the dock. So here is the plan we will start scuba diving from Renton and then swim to the house because that way nobody will see us. And then get in through the back area of the house" Alex said "that sounds like a really great plan Alex" Deshaun said "and then also we have clothes to change into once we get to shore and Michael and Rivers also created really fake invitations and nobody will know the difference once we get there" Alex said and then later that night, Rivers was in front of Alex and the rest of his team "Alright guys, you know I don't have to say much, but good luck and find any sort of information that you can" Rivers said and then the agents and Alex were in a van and they got dropped off by a park that was in Renton and they got out of the van and they started running towards the water and then they jumped into Lake Washington and they swimming really deep into the water and then Alex pressed a button on his wet-suit and Alex started swimming really fast underwater and Deshaun and Jenny did the same thing and they also started swimming really fast. Alex then looked at his water-proof watch and he started looking at the map of Lake Washington and he noticed right away that they were getting close to the mansion and Alex pressed the button again and they started slowing down and they got to the dock.

Then one of the guards noticed that there were people in the water "hey man there are people in the water" one of the guards said and then they saw bubbles in the water and then took out PP7 guns and the bubbles stopped bubbling "what the hell?!..." one of the guards said and then Alex, Deshaun, & Jenny got out of the water and Alex grabbed on the of thugs from behind and Alex punched one of them in the face and then punched him in the stomach and knocked him out. Jenny avoids another punch and she kicked another guard in the face and bitch slapped him in the face and electrocuted him. And Deshaun punched the last guard in the face and kicked him against the stomach and forced him against the wall and the guards were dead "I think that is the last of them" Deshaun said "oh okay good" Alex said and then Alex took the guards keycards "Here is the keycards to access the building" Alex said "thanks man" Deshaun said "oh yeah this mission so far is one of the best missions with you Alex" Jenny said "we can flirt later Jenny but we have a mission to do" Alex said "oh I just love when he talks to tough. It makes me more attractive to him even more" Jenny said "alright lets get on different clothes" Alex said and then Alex, Deshaun, and Jenny started changing into different clothes and Jenny started changing into a golden and sparkling dress and Deshaun started changing into a white tuxedo and Alex started changing a green suit with a golden button up shirt with a blue neck tie and Alex was wearing a blue flower on his suit and Alex was wearing sliver dress shoes "yo man you looking good Alex my man" Deshaun said "thanks Deshaun" Alex said "you also look very handsome Alex" Jenny said "thank you Jenny. Alright let's go stop this guy" Alex said and then Alex, Deshaun, & Jenny started getting in line and there was a lot of fancy people getting into the party and they were playing "no more love on the run" and the guards were checking invitations and then as the line was going along, the guards came to Jenny, Alex, and Deshaun "hey man. Name please." The guards asked him "the name is Aussmen...Alex Aussmen" Alex said "can I see your I.D. Mr. Aussmen?" the guards asked "oh yeah sure my man." Alex said, "there he goes, Alex is always very smooth saying that" Jenny said and then the guards started looking at Alex's I.D. card "alright you are good. Go on in buddy" the guards said and the rest of the guards started checking on Jenny and Deshaun and the guards starting letting them in.

As Alex, Deshaun, and Jenny got into the party, they saw a lot of people drinking fancy drinks and wearing really nice outfits and people were talking and checking out the beautiful and stunning view of Lake Washington "man this party is really hopping" Deshaun said "oh yeah it is my man. Alright we are going split up and just network and mingle with people" Alex said "alright we are really good at that" Jenny said "I know you are Jenny my dear" Alex said "And what are you going to do Alex?" Deshaun asked, "I will seeing if I can find any clues myself. If you guys have any questions just reach me through my spy-watch" Alex said "sounds good" Deshaun said and then Deshaun, Jenny, and Alex split up during the party and as they did this, Alex started walking outside and she started fancy drinks "mountain dew teeny please" Alex said "yes sir" the bartender said and then the bartender started making him a mountain dew teeny drink and then as he was done, he then gave the drink to Alex "Here you are sir" the bartender said "thanks man" Alex said and then as Alex was drinking, he saw a beautiful girl with a red dress and she was wearing red lip-stick and then Alex started walking towards without really thinking and the girl was drinking champagne out of a glass "Hello beautiful" Alex said and the girl turned back and it was Jenny "Alex. How did you get into this party? Don't you know not a lot of people were invited to this party" Megan said, "yeah I know that's why my fellow agents and I came to this party" Alex said "man you are a new kind of crazy" Megan said "Oh I don't think you really mean that Megan" Alex said "then why were you invited to this party?" Alex asked and then Megan paused and she couldn't come up with an answer "yeah I thought so" Alex said and then all of a sudden, Trybee showed up and he saw Alex "Ah Mr. Aussmen I am really glad that you were able to come here" Trybee said "yes you really have a very beautiful mansion" Alex said "it must have cost you a fortune to get this place" Alex said "oh not really Mr. Aussmen. I have my ways of making money." Trybee said "so do I Trybee" Alex said "Also I didn't really know you had a dance floor. Do you like to dance yourself" Alex asked right out of nowhere "Yeah I do Mr. Aussmen it's a blue one" Trybee said and then Trybee, Megan and Alex started walking towards the balcony and they saw a lot of people dancing "I really like it so far" Alex said "I was really wondering if you wanted to dance Megan" Alex said "oh yes I would love to" Megan said and then Alex and Megan started dancing to the song "Sailing" and they started slow dancing and Megan put her arms around Alex's arm and they started dancing in front of the beautiful and stunning view of Lake Washington in Kirkland "you are a really good dancer" Megan said "oh thank you" Alex said and then Alex and Megan kept on dancing and then Alex lowered her and then Alex pulled her up again and they started spinning around in circles. And then as Deshaun was in the party himself he then broke into the D.J. office and he knocked out the D.J. and he started turning on a red heart light and he started flashing the light on Megan and Alex and then Alex span Megan in circles 4 times and Alex slowly put his hands on Megan's waist and then Alex did his old disco move that he use to do where he would expand his arms and then Megan and Alex span around in circles again and Alex lowered Megan to the ground as the song ended and the song ended and Alex ended the dance doing a kissing sign. And a lot of people during the party saw Alex dancing and they started clapping and cheering and even Deshaun was clapping and Jenny was even watching Alex dancing "wow I didn't know you were a very passionate dancer Alex" Megan said "Yeah there is a lot of things that you don't know about me Megan" Alex said

Then later that night, Jenny started going upstairs and she saw a secret room that was in the mansion. Jenny took out the keycard and she sided the card and she was able to open the door. Jenny got into the room and at first she was just a master bedroom but then she went into a bathroom and she went into a secret elevator and the elevator started going down and Jenny ended up being in the submarine room and she saw a lot of subs in this secret room. Jenny started taking photos of the subs and she started sending them to Alex. Alex started getting the pictures of the subs through his spy watch and Alex saved them on his watch.

As Alex kept on taking pictures, More of Trybee's men started looking around the room, Alex without hesitating, went inside the closet and they also had hand guns in their hands. They started looking around but they didn't see Alex anywhere and then they went out of the room. Alex then turned on his spy watch and he started contacting Deshaun and Jenny "Alright guys I was able to get blueprints of the submarine. Lets up and get the hell out of here" Alex said "Alright we hear you bro" Deshaun said "Sweet Aussmen out" Alex said and then Alex turned off his spy watch and more thugs were looking around. Meanwhile back at the party, Trybee started getting really upset "What is wrong sir?" one of his men asked "I have disgusting feeling that we might rats in this party!!!" Trybee said with a very mad tone of voice "Well we always set rat traps everywhere sir" the henchmen said "NO that those kinds of rats you idiot!!! I mean like spies" Trybee said "I want to look for them and also capture them as well!!!" Trybee said

And then more of Trybee's men started looking around the party and then one of the men caught Jenny and Deshaun "hands up!!!" the henchmen said and then all of a sudden, Jenny started firing laser gun and she started kicking them in the face and then she punched another thug in the face. And then Deshaun dodged a couple of punches from the other henchmen and he kicked another one in the face and knocked him out and then he took out a DD4 gun and he shot another in the face and killed him. "Come on lets get out of here baby girl" Deshaun said and then Deshaun and Jenny started running away from the guards and Deshaun kept on reloading his gun and he kept on shooting more of the henchmen. Then Jenny started throwing grenades at them and causing a lot of explosions around them.

Then some of the guest at the party started hearing the noise "What the hell is going on?!...Nobody fucking leave this party!!!" Trybee yelled and then Alex was walking around the party and he saw Deshaun and Jenny sneaked out of the party. And then more guards saw Alex "It's one of the spies. Kill him!!!" one of the guards yelled and then they took out guns and they started shooting at Alex. Alex then hid behind a wall and he took out a pistol and he started shooting at the guards and he shot them in the head and killed them and Alex started running away and Alex started climbing on a rope and Alex swing on the rope and he kicked more henchmen in the face and knocked them out. Then another henchmen tried to punch Alex but Alex dodged the punch and Alex punched the henchmen in the face and kicked him in the balls and Alex grabbed the henchmen very aggressively and he reloaded the gun and he kept shooting at the thugs and Alex ended up killing around 15 henchmen and shooting them in the head. Alex kept on running and saw a cliff and Alex jumped off the cliff and Alex dived into the water and Alex started swimming to a motorboat. Alex got on the boat and Alex started the boat and Alex started driving the boat really fast and a lot of Trybee's henchmen started chasing him and they were riding on other motor boats and they started firing a lot of rocket launchers at Alex. Alex dodged the attacks and he took a lot of turns on the boat and Alex got out a riffle and Alex started firing a sniper riffle at the henchmen and Alex started shooting at them and killing more of his Trybee's thugs on the other boats and Alex got out a grenade launcher and Alex started firing the grenade launcher and Alex started firing the grenade launcher and the other motor boats started exploding in flames and Alex kept on riding into the night. As Alex kept on riding the boat he then saw Deshaun and Jenny on another boat as well "Dude that was so awesome. Way to go bro" Deshaun said "good job Alex" Jenny said "thanks guys but sadly more of those people are out there and we really need to stop them," Alex said "anyway lets just get out of here" Alex said and then Alex, Jenny, and Deshaun started heading back to downtown Seattle.

As Alex headed back home, Alex then started drinking 4 Budweiser and 4 cornea beers. And then Alex turned on the TV and he started watching TV. Alex kept on watching TV Intel around mid night and then Alex went to bed and before he went to bed, he also set an alarm to 8AM and Alex went to sleep. As Alex was sleeping, Alex typically dreams about a lot of different women, some his age, some a little bit younger then him, and also strangely sometimes older women. But there are times when Alex does dream about his past including when Morella use to take care of him back when he was a teenager and also dreamed about Sabrina Fiorina as well.

Alex got up the next morning and he took a shower, then he headed back to his bedroom in his apartment and Alex took off his towel and he stood in front of the window butt naked and he did this to see if any girls saw him or he sometimes would do it just so that there was like a mother and her daughter saw and then she would right away cover her daughter's eyes and she would started screaming and this would sometimes Alex laugh a lot. Alex then got dressed and he made himself some breakfast and got a cup of coffee and Alex started eating breakfast. Alex after breakfast got out of his apartment with some clothes on and he started heading to a lot of stores in downtown Seattle including department stores, electronic stores, just any sort of store that guys would go into it. Also sometimes in the stores, Alex would sometimes would start checking out a lot of different women walking and checking them out from head to toe. But then as Alex was in the store, he then saw a very random beautiful girl and Alex just started fallowing her and she was heading towards Elliot bat in downtown Seattle. As Alex kept on fallowing her, she then started taking off her clothes and she was in a 1980's bikini bathing suit and she dived into the water and Alex ran to the dock and Alex just being very lucky, started stripping off his clothes and he was wearing a bathing suit himself as well. Alex jumped into the water and as he was underwater, Alex saw a submarine and it was really huge. Alex managed to sneak into the submarine and as Alex got into the submarine there was a lot of people wearing purple jumpsuits and even some of the men working in there were also wearing purple jumpsuits. Alex then hid behind a wall and he saw one of the henchmen walking by and Alex suddenly kicked the henchmen in the face and he stole his clothes and he threw his dead body into a huge garbage can and Alex started putting on the purple jumpsuit and Alex saw the henchmen that he killed had a pistol and Alex grabbed the gun and he loaded up the gun and Alex started looking around the submarine and he saw Trybee's office in the submarine and he was talking in his office. Alex then saw him talking in his office and then Alex jumped on a moving cart and Alex discovered more of Trybee's evil plan and Trybee wants to break into the biggest bank in Washington DC and Alex also discovered that Trybee wants to use a missile to fire at it. "Oh my god I have to tell the others" Alex said and then as Alex was on the cart, more of the henchmen saw Alex on the cart. "It's Aussmen kill him!!!" they yelled and then Alex punched 3 of them in the face and kicked another one in the face. Alex shoved another one against the wall and whacked in the face really hard.

And then one of the henchmen saw the whole thing happening and pulled the alarm in the submarine and then the submarine started going off like crazy "Introducer, Introducer!!!" and then Alex grabbed one of the riffles and he started shooting with the riffle in his hand and firing 44 bullets at the rest of the henchmen shooting at him and killing them. Alex kept on running and more bad guys were firing at Alex and Alex would jump and avoid more bullets and Alex reloaded the gun and he kept on firing and killing them. Alex started running to get to the top of the submarine. As Alex was around the top floor dodged more attacks from bad guys that didn't have guns and Alex punched 3 of them in the face and body slammed other henchmen as well. Alex then saw Trybee's office and Alex started running to the office and Alex right away kicked Trybee in the face and slammed his head against his desk really hard "Sounds like you have found out my master plan Mr. Aussmen" Trybee said "I don't care what your plan is, I think out of anything, the way you killed that one girl was really shameful!!!" Alex said "well I do like killing rich people Mr. Aussmen. And since your rich, I might as well kill you as well" Trybee said and then all of a sudden, Trybee had king staff that was in his office and all of a sudden, he whacked Alex really hard with staff in his hand and Alex got slammed against the wall and then Trybee threw more attacks at Alex and Alex was able to dodge the attacks but then Trybee punched Alex again in the face and slammed him really hard "Damn you Aussmen!!!!" Trybee yelled and then Alex punched Trybee in the face and punched him again in the fight jaw and Alex grabbed Trybee's wrist really hard and slammed him against a glass window and Alex grabbed him from behind and body slammed him to the ground and then Alex grabbed the king staff and whacked him in the head with the staff and killed him. And then Trybee fell to his death and then as much as Alex was glad that he killed him, Alex felt really puzzled and then all of a sudden, there was a woman with blonde hair that showed up and she had massive beatings on her "Good evening Mr. Aussmen!!!!...I have been...Expecting you!!!" she said in a Ukraine accent "It can't be. Victoria Borodina!!!!" Alex said in complete shock "Oh yes Alex. I remember the last time I saw you, you were just a little boy and you were 16 years back in 1976 when I last saw you" Victoria said "so Trybee was just a decoy then?" Alex asked "right, and you are a smart young man. I too have also changed as well..." Victoria said and then Victoria pressed a button on her watch and all of a sudden her hair started changing into multiple different colors and her eyes started changing into different colors as well "you see Mr. Aussmen, after you defeated me, I suffered many different bruises and surgies and they had do a lot of operating on me and sure I might not look as beautiful like before, but I just want to kill you once for all Alex" Victoria said "good bye Alex!!!" Victoria said and then Victoria's finger nails started getting longer and they started sliver and Victoria started throwing many different attacks at Alex and Alex dodged all of the attacks and Victoria gave Alex a huge around his chin and Victoria punched Alex in the face and then Alex head butted Victoria in the face and Alex jumped in the air and kicked her in the face really hard and Victoria threw more attacks at Alex and she started shooting flames out a flaming machine that is strapped on to her and Alex dodged the attack and he summersaulted on the ground and then Victoria punched Alex in the face and grabbed him by the neck "You still are a pathic fighter after all these years!!!" Victoria said in complete anger and then Victoria threw more deadly attacks at Alex and then Alex dodged the attacks and bitch slapped her in the face and kicked her in the stomach and then Victoria grabbed a chair and she tried to whack Alex from behind with a metal chair. Alex gets hit with the chair and Alex kicks Victoria in the face and Alex grabs a gun from a dead henchmen and Alex shoots at her hand "AHHHHHHHHHHHHHHHHHH!!!!!!!" Victoria screaming and then Alex punched her in the face and then Alex jumped out of the office and he landed on the ground, Alex took out the gun and shot the door look and Alex started heading out of the submarine "STOP HIM HE IS GETTING AWAY!!!!" Victoria yelled and then Alex kept on running and he started fighting more henchmen and killing them with basic hand to hand combat and killing around 10 henchmen. Alex then found an open crack in the submarine and Alex went into the water and Alex started swimming to shore and Alex got to the dock and he was wet.

Later that day, Alex headed back to his apartment and he started calling Rivers on the phone "hey Alex what's up?" Rivers asked him "Yes Rivers this is Alex, I think I really found out who is really behind all of this" Alex said "Whom?" Rivers asked "...Victoria Borodina a former Ukraine assassin. I will tell you guys everything first thing tomorrow" Alex said "Alright okay Alex" Rivers said and then Alex hung up the phone and then as Alex headed back to his room, Victoria was spying on Alex "And now finally I will be able to kill you Alex and this time Morella and Sabrina are not here to save you and I will make sure to make your death very painful" Victoria said and then Victoria walked away into the shadows.

Chapter 4 Mt. Rainer Attack

The next day Alex drove his car to lower queen Ann to meet up with Rivers and the rest of his team. Alex got into the building and as he got to the final floor, Alex went into Rivers's office and Alex in his hand, had all of Victoria Borodina's records. "What in the world is this?!" Rivers said "this all the records of Victoria Borodina. She came here in 1976 and she wanted to kill me back then and I just don't know how in the world she survived" Alex said "well do you know where is going to strike again?" Rivers asked "That I don't know sir, but it does explain why there has been killings of rich people in Bellevue and also steeling money from them" Alex said "but also there is another mission that you, Jenny, and Deshaun should go on, I don't it's related to Borodina, but we saw like a bass that was on top of Mt. Rainer. And I think you guys should check it out" Rivers said "Yeah sure we will sir" Alex said and then Alex started getting out of Rivers's office and then Alex started heading downstairs for lunch and Jenny and Deshaun saw him "yo man what happen to you?" Deshaun asked him "It's a very long story but I just got word that we might not need to go to Mt. Rainer for a mission" Alex said "oh wow that's really awesome, I love going to Mt. Rainer it's always really nice up there" Jenny said "oh yeah it is Jenny" Alex said "dude I'm down bro, lets go" Deshaun said

And then later that day, Alex, Deshaun, and Jenny then went to a sports store that was in downtown Seattle and the three of them started looking around and they all bought snowboards. As well got some snow gear and then after they bought the equipment, they then headed to Alex's apartment and they started loading up the gear into his car. As they got done putting all of the gear into the car, they all got inside the car and they started driving to Mt. Rainer. Alex started driving on the highway and they started heading south to Mt. Rainer and it got colder and colder. And the drive itself took around maybe an hour or 45 minutes. Around 3:00PM, Alex, Deshaun, and Jenny were able to get to Mt. Rainer and once they got there, it looked like a very peaceful snow day and so Alex and Deshaun they started snowboarding around the mountains and they kept on going down the mountains and Alex and Deshaun didn't really see anything. Jenny also went on a different mountain slope but she didn't see anything either, also as Jenny was snowboarding she would sometimes like Alex, she would also check out a lot of handsome guys around her and she would also check them out head to toe. Around 4:00PM, Alex, Deshaun, and Jenny didn't really see anything and they started drinking hot chocolate. "man so far we haven't really found anything" Deshaun said "yeah same here" Jenny said "well what If the base is not around the slopes, then maybe it has to be on the top of the mountain" Alex said "but isn't it dangerous to climb up Mt. Rainer?" Deshaun asked, "well it is but I think we will be okay" Alex said "I also think that I have some rope that should help us climb especially around the restricted zones of the mountains" Alex said "Alright sounds really good my man" Deshaun said and then after they were done having hot chocolate, Alex, Deshaun and Jenny started heading to Alex's car and they started getting the ropes and Alex put the ropes inside of his backpack and then they started going up the slopes around the mountain. As they got off, Alex turned his head to the left and he saw a restricted zone "it's over there you guys" Alex said and then Alex, Deshaun, and Jenny started snowboarding down and they saw the fenced area and Alex used his laser on his spy watch and he started opening and cutting the fence. Alex was able to open the fence and they started heading into the restricted zone. As they got into the zone, Alex pulled out a IWI Mini-UZI Submachine gun pistol out of his backpack and he started walking around the snow and they started running to the top. Alex then noticed a little pit of fake snow that was around the factory and Alex got out the rope and was throwing the rope around 4 times in the area and he threw the rope on to an area where the hook of the rope would be able to get attached to the area that he was aiming for. The rope was able to get caught and Alex and Jenny and Deshaun started climbing up the rope and then as they got to the top, they also got out handguns themselves. Then they saw the fake snow and Alex shot a bullet at the snow and then Alex discovered that it was actually a lock on the door and Alex broke the door down and they started heading inside and it was another factory that was similar to the factory Alex saw in the submarine "Alex what the hell kind of place is this?!..." Deshaun asked, "I don't know buddy but what ever is happening here, is really bad news" Alex said and then the rest of the group including Alex started seeing a lot of weapons and other uniforms being made. And people started getting liquid shots into their bodies and the liquid started brainwashing people like crazy and also making them fall asleep. "We have to try to blow up this factory before these people start attacking many different places" Alex said "Yeah hommie you got that right" Deshaun said

Alex, Deshaun, and Jenny started running and they started finding cover and then all of a sudden they got caught by another guard and the guard started screaming at them and speaking Ukraine language. And then Alex right away punched the guard in the face and shot him in the head and then he reloaded the gun and he shot some other guards in the head as well "Come on!!" Alex said and then they started shooting at more thugs and they started running and Alex started firing his pistol like crazy "You go find some other controls, I will go find Borodina!!!" Alex said and then Alex kept on fighting more henchmen and thugs and punching them in the faces and kicking them in the stomachs. Alex kept on running and he started running up the stairs and he started getting to the top of balcony and then Alex took out his gun and then

Alex got whacked in the face with a rocket launcher and Victoria grabbed Alex by the neck and threw him against the wires of the fence of the balcony really aggressively and Victoria started walking towards Alex "it's time for you to die Mr. Aussmen!!!" Victoria said "And you can't destroy my franchise that I built, but I can destroy yours just like at Tahoma!!!" Victoria said, "what are you talking about!!!?..." Alex asked, "You really think RAD was really working for Victoria Sennott and Sergio Finland. No not true, they were working for me and I was the one that truly set up the RAD organization and soon RAD will really rule the world and the Russians will rule the western part of the world!!!!" Victoria screamed and then Victoria yelled in anger and she took out a Ukraine sword and she tried to stab Alex and she threw 5 different sword attacks at him and Alex got a cut on his check and got punched him in the face really hard. Alex got kicked in the face and then Alex summersaulted on the ground and he got back up again and Alex threw 6 punches at Victoria and punched her in the face and jumped in the air and kicked her in the face and it forced her to the wall. "Don't you ever learn from your foolish mistakes!!!!" Victoria yelled and then Alex kicked Victoria in the face again and head butted her again and slammed her against the wall "Why you little brat!!!" Victoria yelled and then Alex kicked her in the face again "No matter how hard you hit me. You will always be that week 16 year old little boy from 1976!!!" Victoria yelled, "You will never win Victoria!!!!" Alex said in a mad tone of voice "oh I think that is where you are wrong Alex!!!" Victoria said and then Victoria pressed a button and then a really huge explosion in the base started happening and then Deshaun and Jenny started shooting more bullets at more henchmen and killing them "come on Alex lets get out of here" Jenny said and then Alex started running away from the base with Jenny and Deshaun and more henchmen started coming after them and more explosions started to happen and then Alex, Deshaun, and Jenny got outside and then Alex saw a couple of snowboards and they started getting on the snowboards and they started sliding down Mt. Rainer really fast. But as they did this, a lot of other henchmen in snow mobiles started chasing them down the hill and Alex took out his pistol and he started shooting 44 bullets at the henchmen and killing them and Deshaun started doing the same thing "We just have to get back to the main ski area and that way they don't find us" Alex said and then they kept on going down and Alex started off of huge ramps and as Alex was in air, he started doing a lot of flips and shooting more bullets at bad guys. Alex was able to land on his feet just fine but then he saw a helicopter that had communist colors on it "You will never get away from me that easy Alex and I'm sure I will start destroying all the things that truly matter to you" Victoria yelled through intercom of the helicopter "MUAHAHAHAHAHAHAHAHAHAHAHAHAHAHAHAHAHAHAHAHAHAHAHAHAHAHA! !!!!" Victoria laughed and then the helicopter started fly off into the sky

Alex, Deshaun, and Jenny got to the rest of the ski slop area and they started running to Alex's car. Deshaun hoped into the back seat and Jenny took shotgun and Alex started turning the keys in his car and he started turning on the car "Everyone hang on!!!!" Alex said and then Alex started driving the car fast down the hill and Alex started going around 140 miles per hour and Alex pressed some buttons in his car and they started firing at Victoria's helicopter and the helicopter started shooting at them and Alex started firing back and a rocket launcher came out of his car and Alex started firing a lot of missiles from the car and Alex shot around 3 missiles out of the car and Alex ended up firing his 4th missile at the helicopter and Victoria's helicopter started getting really hit really hard "NOOOO!!!! The helicopter is losing control!!!! I will get you Alex Aussmen!!!!" Victoria yelled and then the helicopter started going down and Alex kept on driving his car down the hill at normal speed. "So do you think that Borodina is dead Alex?" Deshaun asked, "I don't think so Deshaun, I think she was able to para-shot down so I don't know if she is dead my man" Alex said "So where do we go now Alex?" Jenny asked, "Well we just have to head back to Seattle and tell Rivers what happened and see if we can find out where Borodina is. And I have a feeling that she is going to strike Bellevue because she is planning killing a lot of rich people" Alex said "But where in the world is she going to be able to do something like that?" Deshaun asked, "There might be some sort of party happening and we have to find out when it is" Alex said and then Alex and Deshaun started heading back to downtown Seattle and it took them around 45 minutes to get them back there. Alex was able to drop off some of the snowboarding equipment back at the headquarters in Lower Queen Ann in Seattle and they all started heading back to their apartments.

As Alex headed back to his apartment in downtown Seattle, Alex opens the door and he set all of his stuff down. And as Alex did this, Alex started going through some old pictures that Alex kept and they were pictures of him back in 1976 when he was a teenager. In the pictures, there was a lot of pictures of him with Morella and then also with Sabrina Fiorina as well. And then Alex saw another picture and it was the picture that he took of Victoria back in Whippy Island. Alex started looking at the pictures and he started flash backing in his head to all those events and Alex put down the pictures and he started watching TV in his apartment and he also started drinking soda as well.

As Alex went to bed that night, he suddenly knew in his head that there might be more to this mission then he anticipated. And Alex went to sleep that night and he started dreaming about his time at Bellevue College back when he was 16 years old. And Alex just knew that he had to head back to Bellevue College.

Chapter 5 Returning to Bellevue College

Alex woke up the next morning and he took a shower and he got dressed and he put on some 1980's style clothes. But this time though he didn't make himself any breakfast and instead he went out for breakfast and he drove to a dinner that was in Bellevue and after he ate, he went into his car and he started driving to Bellevue Community College. And as Alex was driving, he found a parking space and he also paid for parking. Alex then turned off his car and he started looking around the campus and right away it hit Alex that this campus has truly changed a lot since 1976. As Alex kept on walking he saw a lot of the counter culture things that he saw back in the 1970's and instead there was people dressed up in high fashion 80's clothes and people were listening to Walkmans and the girls were spandex outfits and some where roller blading around the campus. Alex then started heading into the ASG room where Alex use to go and there was a lot of main-stream America and very left wing propaganda in there and posters of Ronald Reagan and they drew beat up marks and on him and they wrote on the posters saying "NOT MY PRESIDENT!!!!" And then Alex saw the same desk that Trygave Bowerson use to sit in and Alex closed his eyes and he started flash backing again. Alex kept on looking around the room and then Victoria built robots inside the classroom and they tried to attack Alex and then Alex dodged the attacks and grabbed the robots and slammed them to the ground and they blew up in flames and then Victoria showed up and she started walking towards Alex "It seems like you have gotten really strong Mr. Aussmen!!!" Victoria said, "I always remember different things that are from the past" Victoria continued and then Alex pulled out a pistol gun "Don't come any closure to me!!!" Alex said in complete anger and then Victoria pulled out an assault riffle and she pointed the gun at Alex "it's time to blow your head off Mr. Aussmen!!!" Victoria said and then she fired the gun and Alex dodged and ducked from the attack and Alex got up right away and shot one of his guns at Victoria but the bullet went through her head and was only a hologram and then the whole ASG room went on lockdown "5 minutes Intel explosion of Bellevue College!!!" the intercom said and then Alex ran out of the ASG room and he was able to use a mine bomb and he was able to blow up the door and the alarm around the campus was going off like crazy and more of the students were running out of the building. And Alex all of a sudden saw a lot of helicopters full of henchmen inside the copters and Alex started running out of the campus and the helicopters started chasing him and firing bullets at him. Alex took out another gun out of his pocket and he started firing the gun at the helicopter but the gun was not having any sort of effect what so ever. And then Victoria started yelling at Alex in Ukraine language and then she started firing a lot of misses at Alex and also causing a lot of damage around the Bellevue College Campus and setting a lot of things on fire. And then Alex saw his car and then Alex started running to his car and Alex open the car and he started the car and he started driving really fast and the helicopters kept on chasing him. The copters kept on firing a lot of bullets and weaponry at Alex and Alex pressed a button inside of his car and a missile launcher came out of the back of the car and Alex pressed another button and Alex fired the missile and it hit one of the copters and blew the copter up in flames and the helicopter started coming down in flames and it crash landed on one of the buildings around the Bellevue College Campus. Alex kept on driving and he started going around 500 miles per hour on the highway. Victoria's helicopter kept on chasing Alex and Alex kept on firing a lot more missiles at Alex. Alex while he was driving started going off a lot of ramps and he would land on the ground and he would keep on driving really fast. Alex then drove into downtown Bellevue and as he was driving, he then drove into a parking garage and he started driving really fast Intel he got to the top, Alex pressed another button and Alex started firing a lot of machine guns at the helicopter and then one of the bullets that Alex fired his the glass window of the helicopter and killed one of the pilots and then the helicopter started going down and it crashed into Lake Washington. Victoria and her henchmen survived but Alex then started driving back to downtown Seattle. As Alex was driving back, he then pressed another button in his car "Rivers, this is Alex Aussmen, I was heading to Bellevue College and I was ambushed by Borodina and her henchmen" Alex said "oh wow that is really crazy Alex. Where they killed?" Rivers asked, "no they landed in Lake Washington and survived" Alex said, "well I'm glad you are okay man. I just need you to head back to headquarters right now and we will talk about your next mission" Rivers said, "I will do that sir" Alex said "just get here when you can my man" Rivers said and then Alex kept on driving.

Alex got to the Seattle Agency building in lower queen Ann and he started running up to the building and as he got to Rivers's office, Alex opened the door "I am glad that you are here Alex" Rivers said "yeah me too sir" Alex said "well yeah what did you found at Bellevue College?" Rivers asked, "well one thing is for sure, it has really changed, and then also they don't like clean people" Alex said "yeah I can really tell that in a lot of ways this Borodina person really wants to kill you Alex" Rivers said "yeah you got that right boss" Alex said "But to help you out man, I just discovered that in Bellevue that Victoria Borodina and her henchmen are heading to a fancy party that is in downtown Bellevue and I will send Jenny and Deshaun with you on your mission" Rivers said "yeah that's a really good idea. Because I'm going to need all the help I can get" Alex said and then Alex walked out of the office and he stopped by cafeteria there and he also got a bite to eat. As Alex was eating, Deshaun caught up to him "yo man we just herd about the next mission and I'm all in" Deshaun said "yeah it's going to be a really crazy mission but I think we will be able to do it" Alex said and then as Deshaun and Alex were talking, Jenny also saw Alex them and she also sat by them as well "so what happened at Bellevue College Alex?" Jenny asked, "well sadly I was ambushed by Borodina and her henchmen and they also sadly blew up the campus as well" Alex said "Oh my god that is really terrible" Jenny said "yeah I know and it was. And they even had helicopters chasing me too" Alex said "oh you poor baby" Jenny said "But yeah hommie, we are coming with you" Deshaun said "Thanks man" Alex said Alex kept on eating his food around Deshaun and Jenny and then after he ate, Alex then drove back to his apartment and as he walked in, he started swimming in the swimming pool that was in his apartment complex and then he started playing pool in his apartment as well. And then after that, Alex started playing on his arcade and then as Alex was playing on his arcade, Alex really started to wonder about one thing in particular and it was his notebook. And Alex closed his eyes and he started to remember that he use to draw trees and other sorts of nature inside the notebook. Alex then stopped playing one of his arcade machines and he started looking through all of the books that he has in his apartment, and he couldn't find his drawing notebook anywhere.

And then later that night, Alex got on a 1980's style suit and tie and he started heading to a nightclub that was in downtown Seattle. And inside the club they were playing a lot of songs and Alex saw a lot of people doing a lot of really cool and fascinating dance moves. And then for the heck of it, Alex just started dancing even with wearing a suit and tie and a lot of people where cheering him on and Alex was dancing with 4 different young women and they started touching him everywhere and also touching his face as well. In a lot of ways Alex always really enjoyed dancing with a lot of girls. Even when they got really close to him. As Alex kept on dancing, it really just so happens that Megan was also in that same nightclub and there was a lot of music just being blasted. And Megan started heading to the bar section of the nightclub. "So what can I get you baby girl?" the bartender asked, "I will just have an apple tini" Megan said and then the bartender got her that drink and the bartender gave it to her. Alex kept on dancing and then he saw Megan around the bar and then Alex started walking up to her and Alex without really thinking, he sat by her "Hey I didn't know you were going to be here" Alex said "yeah same here" Megan said "what will you have sir?" the bartender asked "I will have a Budweiser" Alex said and then Alex started drinking a bottle of Budweiser "so is this what you do when you are not being a secret agent?" Megan asked him "Yes" Alex said with only answering the question using a one-word answer "that's really awesome...you are really good out there" Megan said "thanks" Alex said "you should dance with me" Alex said "no I'm a terrible dancer" Megan said and then another song came and then Megan and Alex started dancing on the dance floor and Alex and Megan started dancing really close to each other and then also Alex lowered her and then brought her back up and Alex started spinning around as he was dancing.

And then as both of them had a lot of drinks, Alex and Megan started heading back to Alex's apartment and they started making out with each other. Alex then started taking off her clothes and her underwear. And Megan did the same thing and she started kissing Alex on the lips and taking off his button shirt and his suit and tie. And then Alex was on the bed and Megan was on top of him. And Alex started heaving sex with Megan in his apartment and it was really wild and really crazy but Alex being Alex just enjoyed the heck out of it. As things started to slow down, Alex just laid next to Megan and Megan put her arms around Alex and Alex started kissing her from head to toe.

Chapter 6 Alex's Notebook

The next day as the sun started to rise, Alex was sleeping in his bed and he was sleeping next to Megan in his bed and Alex started kissing her on the lips and the forehead. And then as Alex woke up, Alex and Megan then took a shower together and then as they got dressed, Alex then made Megan some breakfast and both of them had coffee. And then Alex looked at the window and he saw a ferryboat that was on the Puget Sound and it was heading to one of the islands. And then as both Megan and Alex were done eating breakfast, Alex and Megan started walking around Seattle and they started looking through many different stores and Megan started trying on a lot of different clothes that were in the store. As Alex was in the store, He started seeing some guys that were in suit and ties and Alex saw them heading over to the check stand and right away, Alex knew that something was really wrong. And then Alex went to spy on these people and they started speaking Russian and they even had watches that they were talking into. And Alex knew that they were talking to Borodina. Alex and Megan started walking away from the henchmen and as Megan left Alex's apartment and went home, Alex then knew he had to go on another investigating trip. And this time he had to go to Victoria's old apartment to look for clues. Alex then went into his car and he started driving to the old apartment. Alex got there and it just so happened that the building was closed because it was for a party. And it really hit Alex that this was where the party was going to be. And Alex looked at more of the papers and Alex headed back to his apartment and he got one a blue suit wearing a gray button up shirt and a green necktie. As Alex was done getting dressed, he then met up with Deshaun and Jenny around the apartment entrance and they got into Alex's car and they started driving towards the party. And as they got there, they parked in a parking garage. Alex turned off the car as he found a parking space and they got out of the car. They then went inside an elevator and Alex pressed a button on to the main floor and the elevator started going up. The elevator stopped at the floor they pressed on and they got out of elevator and right away they saw a lot of people "So Alex what's the plan man?" Deshaun asked "well we just have to look for some clues and then also find out where all the money is that Borodina stole" Alex said "That's a good plan" Jenny said

The three of them all started going their separate ways and Jenny started talking to a lot of handsome guys that were at the party. Deshaun was also talking to a lot of beautiful ladies. And Alex was doing what Deshaun was doing as well but overall, he was looking for Victoria and finding out where she was. Alex during the party noticed Victoria in a very gold dress with purple strips on it and she started going into the elevator. Victoria pressed a button to go up and Alex hid behind a wall to avoid other henchmen from seeing him. Alex then started walking quickly but not really running and Alex pressed a button and the elevator started coming down and the elevator opened and Alex went in it and he pressed the very top floor and the elevator started going up. The elevator stopped at the floor that Alex wanted and Alex got out of the elevator and all of a sudden, the elevator door shut tight very closed and Alex looked back in shock and then Alex knew that something was not right and right away, Alex pulled out a pistol out of his coat pocket. And then Alex kept on walking and as he kept on walking, he noticed that Victoria's pen house apartment also changed and most of the counter culture stuff from the 1970's was all gone and it was replaced with Soviet Union propaganda and also posters of Ronald Reagan getting beaten up. "Oh Jesus Christ!!!" Alex said, "That is very right indeed Mr. Aussmen" Victoria said and then Alex turned back and Victoria was right there and she had henchmen with riffles in their hands "you might snaked into my party. But you will see the destruction of your own country. Because in a matter of minutes I'm going to use all the money and gold that I stole to start blowing up the islands and Downtown Seattle with a laser

001
Computadora Salido Mal

001:
Computadora Salido Mal Y los Muertos
By: Nelson Christian Amador

Prologue 1 The New Hispanic Kid at School, Tahoma High School 1976

It was a normal day at Tahoma High School in the Maple Valley, WA. But during this particular period, Alex had gone through a lot of hell, He saw a lot of important people die including Emily Romney, Sabrina Fiorina, and Ms. Larter. Though Alex at the time stayed with Matthew and Emmy Lewis, as they become Alex's new parents. But also in 1976, Alex had to face off against two evil communistic people in Victoria Sennott and Victoria Borodina and not only where they part of the evil organization RAD, but also they identified themselves as communist. But as Alex Aussmen kept on going to school at Tahoma High School, He also noticed that Victoria Sennott was not banned from coming to Tahoma High School. As Alex noticed a lot more that people in his generation where really becoming really brainwashed by communistic people in the teachers unions. One day as Alex was walking to the bus stop, Alex didn't get on the bus and he noticed more of them inside of meetings and they had tattoos of the USSR symbol on their arms. This really caused a lot of great concern on Alex a lot and sometimes he would even to go to Principal Storm's office to talk to her about it and really show concern. But during the talk, Principal Strom assured Alex that things were going all right. But as Alex left her office and behind closed doors, there was an electric wire that was hooked on to her through her back and while she was talking to Alex, it felt like she was reading off of a script. And outside and behind the building there was 2 thugs that had on blue jumpsuits giving her details on what she should say, and if she went off script, they would start electrocuting her really bad. And then as nighttime approached and as it was time for Principal Strom to go home, the thug and all of a sudden a blue and yellow 1970's limo approached the school. And the car opened up and then all of a sudden Victoria Borodina came out of the car and she had a Rottweiler puppy in her arms and the puppy itself did not look very friendly and it also had red dark eyes as well. "You didn't tell Alex about our secret operation did you Principal Strom?..." Victoria said in her Ukraine accent "No I didn't. Just please don't harm the boy. He just really wants what's best" Principal Strom said, "Oh I will harm him and I will make sure my thugs and my soldiers go after Mr. Aussmen. Because he has ruined all of my operations especially with what happen in Nicaragua and in Mother Russia as well. And also he is responsible for defeating my ally Victoria Sennott and I will make sure that he pays!!!!!" Victoria said "And then I also have a henchmen of mine that is also from Nicaragua that will help me as well" Victoria said. And then all of a sudden, there was a 16 year old boy that showed up and he got out of the car, the boy himself looked really muscular, he looked very mean looking and he had a scare by his right eye as well. "This is Cruz Manuel who is from Nicaragua and I learned while I was down in Nicaragua that he could hack into any new computer and process information more so then a normal American boy and is a lot more smarter then Alex Aussmen" Borodina said "I can't have this boy in my school, he is a criminal!!!..." Principal Storm said and then all of a sudden Borodina pulled out a taser and electrocuted Principal Strom on the grounded and she started screaming "You will do what I say otherwise your punishment will be a lot worse" Borodina said Victoria and Cruz went back into Borodina's limo and the limo drove into the darkness of the woods of Maple Valley and Principal Strom got back up on her feet and she was really torn apart because she really loved Alex a lot but at the same time, she knew that know the US government was under an known source that was telling the Federal School system what to do from Ukraine and possibly controlling parts of the United States government.

The next morning as Alex was in school, Alex went to two of his classes and he was flirting with girls and talking to them as usual. But at the same time, he also noticed that something in the classroom was wrong. And he noticed that there was a Hispanic kid in the classroom and he looked normal and he was wearing normal 1970's clothes. But what really got Alex's attention was really scare on his face and his eyes were bright red. In the classroom, he was introduced and he sat by Alex. But Alex didn't really ask him any questions "So what do you like about the United States so far?" Alex asked him while he was whispering, "I really do not like anything about your fat country you fucking GRINGO!!!!!!!" Cruz said and then him saying that word really got Alex really scarred because he knew he was not up to no good. But Alex being Alex he minded his own business and he kept on working on his assignment in class.

Then around lunchtime, Alex then sat by himself and he started spying on Cruz. Alex kept on spying on him and he was able to finish his lunch and then he noticed that Cruz was heading towards the high school library. Alex then started walking very slowly and he walked into the library and he started looking around at the many sections of the library and looking at the many books. But then as Alex was looking at one of the books in there, He noticed Cruz around one of the 1970's computers and he logged on to the computer. Typically, on a school computer, there were a lot of restrictions on students getting access to some parts of the computer. And some parts are really blocked off from one of the students. But all of a sudden, Cruz was able to hack into the main parts of the Tahoma School computer of the 1970's and he started hacking into the computer and inside of Cruz's head he was able to access Teacher files, Student information, and most importantly the main high school bank account. As Alex saw all of this happening, Alex then walked over to him and grabbed him behind and threw him against the wall and then Cruz got out a Mexican hand gun and a lot of people went really nuts and got really scarred in the library and everybody started screaming. "You come towards me Gringo and a lot of people die!!!!!" Cruz yelled, "Who are you working for?!..." Alex said, "I will never tell you!!!" Cruz said and then all of a sudden, Cruz pulled out a remote and he pressed a button and he blew up around 5 bombs that were inside of Tahoma High School and a lot of people started going crazy and explosions started to happen. Cruz then started running out of the school and Alex started chasing him and Cruz would turn back and start shooting gun bullets at Alex. Alex was able to dodge the bullets and dive under lunch tables to protect himself. Alex then got back up on his feet and he kept on chasing Cruz and Cruz started running towards Principal Strom's office. Cruz then went into the office and he grabbed Principal Strom and pointed a gun at her head. Alex then came into the room and the door all of a sudden slammed shut really tight and all of a sudden, there were evil Sandinista thugs inside the office and they ran up and attacked Alex. But Alex jumped up in the air punched both of the thugs in the face and kicked another one in the stomach and grabbed another one by the wrist and twisted the wrist really hard and broke it. Alex grabbed the thug's gun and shot more thugs in the head and killed them. Cruz then slammed Principal Strom against the wall and he was able to hack into the main safe and he was able to steel around 900,000$ in cash and it was in a blue and gold briefcase. Cruz then broke one of the windows and he started running towards a car and Cruz ended up steeling a car and he drove off going around 100 miles per hour. Alex then found a motorcycle and he went on the bike and he put the bike into full gear and all of a sudden Alex started going really fast and he started chasing after Cruz.

Alex started chasing after Cruz and Cruz kept on going really fast on the road and Cruz turned back with his head and started firing a lot of machine guns and riffles at Alex. Alex was able to dodge the gun bullets coming at him and Alex got out a gun out of his pocket and he started firing around 99 bullets at Cruz and then Alex also while on the highway also threw around 5 grenades at Cruz and causing a lot of explosions in the process. The chase kept on going and Cruz end up going on the highways that was heading towards Bellevue and around one of the main freeways in Western Washington. Cruz kept on firing more bullets and throwing more bombs at Alex and Alex kept on going and Alex then went really fast on his bike that he went off of some broken cars and Alex got a lot of serious air and landed on the ground and Alex kept on going really fast on the freeway going around 125 miles per hour on the motorcycle. Alex then reloaded his gun and with anger and rage he fired around 200 bullets at Cruz and one of the bullets shot Cruz in the back of the neck and then another bullet fired in the back of his arm. Cruz then started going really fast and he started heading towards Bellevue, Washington. Cruz got off of the highway and Alex on his tail; Cruz then went through a lot of red lights and going through a lot of speed limit signs as well. Cruz then jumped out of the car and the car itself got into a car crash causing a huge explosion around one of the Bellevue buildings and doing a lot of property damage in the process. Cruz then started running to one of the elevators and Alex then stopped his motorcycle and he started to catch Cruz and he started running up the stairs and little did Alex know, they were inside of the IBM buildings in Bellevue. Alex then was able to get to the main floor of the building which was really shopping and dinning area of the building were a lot of the rich and upper class people spent their time. More people were getting scarred and they screamed out of the building and Cruz all of a sudden got out a rocket launcher and he started firing the weapon at Alex and causing 5 explosions in the process. Alex summersaulted and dodged the attacks and Alex reloaded his hand gun and he hid behind one of the walls and as Cruz kept on firing his rocket launcher at Alex, Alex then started firing more gun bullets at Cruz. And then Cruz kept on running and he started heading to the top of the building and Alex kept on going after him. But as Alex was doing this, he noticed that there was a helicopter that had a Sandinista flag on it and Cruz started running to the helicopter and Alex with all his might started chasing him but it was really too late and Cruz was on the copter. As Alex was on the roof himself he then saw jet pack and then Alex started putting on the jet pack and Alex then pressed a button and Alex started blasting off into the air and Alex saw the helicopter was heading south and Alex started going really fast on the jet pack and Alex started firing a lot of missiles at the Sandinista helicopter and then the helicopter started firing a lot of bullets and rockets at Alex and Alex was able to the dodge the attacks as he was in the air. And then Alex pressed another button that on the jet pack that fired another rocket missile at the helicopter and causing a lot of damage to the copter as well. And then the helicopter started going down and going down really fast and a lot of the thugs and the henchmen on the helicopter started screaming and the helicopter landed on the highway causing a really huge explosion and causing a lot of people to get really scarred. Alex then landed on the ground and he took off the jet pack and then he pulled out a gun and as the Sandinista thugs were coming out of the plane and were about to shoot Alex, Alex right away shot 77 bullets at the Sandinista thugs and shot them in the head and in the stomach and also in the eyes and in the neck. Alex then saw Cruz escaping and Alex punched Cruz in the face and jack kicked him in the neck "GET THE FUCK UP!!!!!" Alex yelled in complete anger and rage "Where are the codes that you stole?!..."Alex yelled "Oh I have them senor Aussmen but I already gave them to my leader that I believe you already know who my leader is" Cruz said and then Alex grabbed Cruz by the neck and he hung him over a ledge "If you don't talk I'm really going to blow your fucking head off!!!!" Alex yelled "You will never destroy the power of my huge brain and that I have the ability to access and hack into new computer Mr. Aussmen!!!!!" Cruz said and then all of a sudden, Cruz then started laughing and then Alex with all his rage and fire he threw Cruz over the ledge and Alex murdered him and Cruz landed on the ground and he landed on a car and a lot of blood came out of his back and also blood was coming out of his mouth as well. And then Alex started walking away and he then grabbed his jet pack and then he started flying back to Bellevue and returning it as well. Alex then also started heading back to Maple Valley but because he was really tired and beat up from the chase, Alex then just went home and more then ever, Alex really was concerned at the situation and how Alex knew that RAD have now infiltrated the federal school system and from there on even with going to Tahoma High School in the coming years in 1977, 1978, and 1979, Alex truly was never the same with his school and by the end of Alex's senior year in 1979, Alex and Principal Storm were barley speaking to each other.

Also even though Alex went on a lot of other secret missions and adventures from 1976 to 1979 while going to Tahoma High School. After graduating from Tahoma he really noticed in his mind that was really an evil communist cancer growing at the school and a really evil dark cloud was also hovering the school as well. And also the district really didn't care Alex was doing and didn't show much concern for him as well especially when he was gone and things just went on like normal. Also during the incident with Alex going after Cruz, Alex then really started to notice a lot of his classmates where getting brainwashed by a lot of ant-America propaganda and Alex and Michael sometimes even stopped going to school because of it for a while. But Principal Storm because she was controlled by Victoria Borodina just really didn't care about Alex anymore and by 1979 the relationship completely fell apart and by 1979, Alex was very angry and upset that Principal Strom never gave Alex a straight answer on the matter and also grew very disillusioned with her that she let all of this craziness and all this crazy nonsense drag on. Alex also during this time when he was not going on secret missions or going to school at Tahoma, he was often staying at him and reading a lot of books that Emmy and Matthew had in their house. He also worked for Emmy doing mailing related tasks that Alex really enjoyed a lot and he would get paid around 10$ an hour which was more then any other Tahoma High Student working in a job back then. Emmy and Matthew also really tired their best to clam Alex down and they were also outraged by all this stuff as well.

In the end, Alex ended up getting his high school diploma and graduating just like everyone else. But he felt very completely empty in himself because when Alex meet Morella in 1976 before moving to Maple Valley and getting new parents after Morella's death, Alex just felt even worse about himself that he came all this way in his life only to end up hating his new school because of how they radically changed as well and it became more noticeable by 1978 and 1979. Alex also remembered the true words of wisdom and that Paul Millet said to him back in Montana where he said that Victoria Borodina is coming back and that she is slowly coming out of the shadows of darkness and that Victoria Borodina is not truly dead like Alex thought and believed. Alex ended up leaving Maple Valley in 1979 for good and he started heading to college to the University of Washington but he didn't start going to school there Intel 1980. But there was more awful and horrible things coming up for Alex as well that would also have to do with Victoria Borodina and her evil henchmen Cruz Manuel.

Prologue 2 The Safe and Secret Places At the University of Washington, University of Washington 1980

Now as Alex Aussmen got to the University of Washington, he had a lot more classes then he ever did at Tahoma High School. Also him reading a lot of books also helped him in his classes as well. And Alex was able to ask really good questions in his classes; Alex took science and economics and also criminal justice as well. And then also Alex took art and painting just to keep him busy. But also Alex noticed that there was more ant-America propaganda at the University of Washington and sometimes in his classes, there would be a lot of ant-America people that would sometimes a lot of dumb arguments and a lot of stupid statements as well. Alex always made sure not to say anything because he knew that these kinds of people have a lot power especially in a very liberal city like Seattle. And of course Alex would have parties a lot at the UW and they were really great parties and Alex always had the time of his life as well. Even when he was going on secret agents around that point of life in the 1980's, he always was really tired and he would always drink a lot as well while watching TV. He also did some other fun things as well in Seattle and he was always spending time with a random girl and always taking that girl to dates and stuff like that, But also during this time without, Alex really knowing, there was a lot of RAD agents that fallowed Alex Aussmen everywhere he went even during his secret missions and always taking photos of him. And the photos that took would be sent through an old fax machine and the fax machine sent the photos all the way to Ukraine. And with all those photos especially in the 1980's before Alex found out that Borodina was alive, Borodina would use the pictures as target practice and throw darts and knives at pictures of Alex Aussmen. But also during that time even during the missions Alex went on, Victoria Borodina's appearance started changing and changing as she highlighted ever part of her hair a different color, Victoria also got rid all of her outfits from the 1970's and her heels and her beautiful dresses as well. And she looked more like a an evil female terrorist an evil social justice warrior combined into one, her finger nails also got really long with also having every color painted on her finger nails as well. Her puppy also grew and Victoria used a very special potion to make her dog age just like a human and not like a normal dog and in-fact causing the dog she had to age slower and more like human. And her bedroom inside of her castle in Ukraine just became a ant-American bug pool full of hate and her bedroom became even more nasty and ugly looking as well.

Also during the 1980's when Alex really wanted to get away from the school, he always tried to look for places where he could socialize with people. One day as Alex was done with one of his classes, he then saw a club where there were consertive students there. And it was a much different world then what he was saw in the 1970's both in Edmonds and also in Maple Valley as well. When he walked in they were really nice and really kind to Alex and they really didn't care that he had a disability as well. And overall there were much happier people as well. And Alex throughout the 80's Alex hung around this group a lot and most of them became Alex's really good friends as well and they often did a lot of fun things together and even watched TV with them as well. And sometimes whenever President Reagan was giving a speech on TV, Alex would hang around them a lot and have a beer or a soda and watch the speech with them. And it was there was Alex would cancel out any noise that he had.

Alex had to miss parts of going to University of Washington but while he was gone on his missions, he was able to find ways to turn in his work through the mail. This was really true when he was in Miami, New York City, and also in Los Angels as well. And during that time especially in Los Angels, Alex was able to rent out the house he was staying in as well. Alex ended up going back to University of Washington to finish off his college senior year at UW and graduate from there. As he was done going to school, he then was getting ready to get an apartment in Seattle.

One day after the ceremony was done, Alex then was packing up all of his things and all of his photos and his clothes and every little and big item that he had. While Alex was doing this, all of a sudden, Tony knocked on the door "Who is it?" Alex asked "Hey hommie, It's Tony How are you doing bro?" Tony asked, "I'm doing good my man" Alex said "Oh that's good. Are you ready to see your new apartment?" Tony asked, "Yeah I'm ready Tony" Alex said "good because that is just what I want to hear" Tony said "Man it's really been a long time since I last saw you man. You were just 16 years old now your like man now" Tony said "Thanks Tony" Alex said "Also sounds like you really been through a lot as well. But I guess you get a lot of money from all your missions as well" Tony said "Yeah but it's also taken a beating on me a lot" Alex said "But you still look very healthy and a lot more stronger then you did back when you were a teenager" Tony said "Come on, lets get to your new apartment. I'll drive you" Tony said

Then after Alex was done packing up all his things, he then put all of his boxes inside of Tony's car and they started driving off to Alex's new pen house apartment that was in downtown Seattle. They got out of the car and they started bringing Alex's things to his apartment. And they as they got there and opened the door, they saw a lot of movers putting in a lot of things in the apartment itself and they were able to get everything all in there by around 5PM. As they were all done, Alex and Tony started sharing a drink and they started drinking whisky and bourbon at Alex's bar table that he had and Alex started telling all the stories of his missions and adventures to Tony both the good and also bad and really sad parts. "Man I am really sorry that happen to you Alex" Tony said "Yeah it's okay man" Alex said "So do you ever believe you will join a private agency in the Seattle area" Tony asked "No I don't think I will my man" Alex said "I don't know buddy they can really sure use someone like you in the future" Tony said "I don't know I will think about it" Alex said and then during that night, Alex and Tony kept on drinking and they then watched a movie that was on TV that was in Alex's apartment building and while Alex was hanging out and watching TV with Tony, he then started flash backing to all of the missions that he went on back when he was a teenager in the 1970's and he knew at the time, a cloud of darkness was shadowing him and it was a strange and dark invisible object.

And then meanwhile while Alex and Tony were hanging out, there was a submarine that was in the Puget Sound and it was in Whippy Island and it was heading towards downtown Seattle. "Soon I will be able to take control of Seattle just like I did all those years ago. And this time, Alex Aussmen won't be able to stop me and I will know Alex's every move and I will hit him where it truly hurts the most!!!!!" Victoria said and then out of the shadows inside the submarine was the not quite dead Cruz Manuel and Cruz Manuel looked very different from what he looked like in 1976, and he had very strange 1980's like hair, he wore a red and black jumpsuit with had a Sandinista flag and then also inside of his mouth, he also had red, purple, and sliver, and gold teeth "I will make sure when I see that Gringo again. I will make sure that I beat the living the shit out of him!!!!!" Cruz said, "I really love that plan Manuel" Victoria said "And I know that we have a lot of things to do and this evil plan of mine will be able to defeat Alex Aussmen and destroy the United States of America!!!!!!!!....MUAHAHAHAHAHAHAHAHAHAHAHAHAHAHAHAHAHAHAHAHA HAHAHAHAHAHAHAHAHAHAHAHAHAHAHA!!!!!!!!!!!!!!!!!!!!!" Victoria started laughing as she was inside of the submarine and without really knowing, Alex was really going to be in a lot of trouble and now with all the demons that Alex had because of Victoria Borodina and because of what Paul Millet said to him in Montana, Alex now was in grave and was in complete moral danger now more then ever.

Chapter 1 Heading Back to Maple Valley and Heading Back to Tahoma High School 1988

The year was now 1988 and it's been one year since Alex stopped Victoria Borodina on Whippy Island. And it was really normal day in Seattle, Washington, and the day itself resembled Alex's first day at Tahoma High School all those years ago, with Alex coming out of the car, girls checking him out, Alex saying his opening catch phrase to one of the THS staff. But that was the past, Alex now was in his apartment and it was around 10AM, Alex was playing the old Nintendo counsel on his big TV and he practically bought almost every game on the original counsel with his own money. And then during that day, Alex got out of his apartment and he was working out at a gym and lifting weights and doing cardio workouts. And then also on the same day, Alex went on a jog around North Seattle and around some of the parks especially around Golden Gardens and Alki beach as well. Alex also took a bus and he went to mall that was in Seattle and then he also went to a mall that was in Bellevue and he looked around those places and he went into a lot of different stores. But then also Alex went into Nordstrom's as well. But then as Alex was walking out of the mall, Alex then saw a couple of new computers from the 80's that were both created by Apple and Microsoft. And even though

Alex did have an Apple at his apartment, Alex just went in there and he started looking around and he also looked some of the headphones that they might have as well. Alex then got out of the store and he then started heading back home to his apartment. As Alex got to his apartment, he then went swimming in his swimming pool in his apartment and he looked at the view of downtown Seattle and he saw that the sun was going down and then after Alex was done swimming around 100 laps in the pool, he then got out of the pool and he grabbed a towel and then he started drying himself and Alex looked back at the sun and then he went back into his apartment and he took a shower and then he got some fresh clothes and he started making himself some dinner and he made himself a burger that ranch and lettuce and tomatoes and onions inside of the burger as well. And then as Alex was eating the burger, Alex then herd a knock at the door and Alex got on his feet and he answered the door and it was Michael. And Michael looked very different and he also had 1980's crazy hair while wearing a yellow Miami Vice suit while wearing a white T-shirt "Hey man what's up? How are you doing?" Michael said, "I'm doing good Michael. Man I just realized today was very similar to when I started going to Tahoma High School" Alex said "Yeah I know both of us looked very different" Michael said "But there was also some bad things that happened there as well" Alex said in a constructive like tone "Yeah I know buddy but there are just some things are out of your control" Michael said "No Michael, There was a lot I could of done but I am really sad and mad and really confused at the same time and RAD took everything from me. And Paul was right about everything. And...Victoria Borodina sadly did come back. And I feel we must go after her!!!" Alex said "Sounds like you still have a lot of questions and you want them answered" Michael said "I think at this point, we need to go back to Tahoma and meet with Principal Strom. Look as much I am very mad at her for a lot of things she did. I will go back and see her" Alex said, "When do you plan on doing that?" Michael asked "Maybe tomorrow." Alex said "But what about work?" Michael asked again "I think Rivers will understand" Alex said

And then the next day, Alex and Michael drove in one of Alex's new cars and they started car-pooling back to Tahoma High School. And as they were driving and kept on going more and more south. They started noticing more and more that Maple Valley really changed a lot since 1976 and there were more businesses and more places to go. Alex then took a turn and they started riding on a road and kept on going at a really good speed limit. "Alex? Do you think anybody there still knows who we are?" Michael asked, "I don't know Michael. Probably not" Alex said and then as they got there, Alex saw the parking lot and he was able to find a parking spot and Alex parked his car and he turned his car off and then Alex and Michael got out of the car and they started heading inside of the school. As they got inside of the school, they also noticed that the school was really different and it looked like Tahoma really adapted with the times and it looked very 1980's like. And then as they were in the building, they also noticed that a lot of the students had on 1980's clothes and other 1980's trendy clothes. "So what now Alex?" Michael asked,

"We have to get a staff member" Alex said and then Alex and Michael then walked into the attendance office and the office looked very up to date and there was even a picture of President Regan and Vice president Bush. And the main reason this was really important was because it was a very fresh tone of peace from when Alex came back to BC and there was very liberal and very anti America stuff in the torn up BC classrooms. One of the attendance people came up to Alex Aussmen and she looked like a very staff person that looked like she was Alex's age "Can I help you gentlemen out?" she asked "Yes I'm here to see Principal Strom. I'm an old student that went here and I'm Alex Aussmen" Alex said, "Do you guys have an appointment?" She asked, "Well no we do not have sadly. But is it okay if we make one for later today? Alex asked "sure thing. For what time?" she asked "Is 3PM alright?" Alex asked again "Sure" she said and then later that day, Alex and Michael while they were waiting went to go to Taco Bell and they got themselves a burrito and some soda and some chips and Tatar tots as well. "Man I just sure as hell hope that when I go there, I hope she is not reading off a script and hopefully nobody is controlling her" Alex said "what do you mean Alex?" Michael asked, "I'm saying that when I last saw her, she was hooked on to a electric wire and I can tell from that day, she was reading off a script that someone really awful and evil gave to her" Alex said "Well buddy even though socially back then I was not really aware of my social surroundings, I did notice some fishy stuff going on around school. I just can never put a finger on it" Michael said "That finger would be teachers unions, and anti-America and global people as well." Alex said, "How do you know?" Michael said "Because I have seen it before many times before I met you Michael and especially when I went to Russia and Nicaragua and then also went to Nicaragua again as well after stopping Sennott" Alex said "What about Ms. Larter?" Michael asked "Sadly I really wouldn't be surprised if she was killed in the cross fires of all this madness. And it also goes to show buddy that liberalism and socialism are a big cancer and big time disease" Alex said "And also Socialism is also like a drug as well" Alex said "I do not like the sound of all of that" Michael said "Yeah me neither Michael" Alex said And then as the clock stroke around 3PM, Alex and Michael then started driving back to Tahoma High School. They got back into the building and they started going to Principal Storm's office. Alex quietly knocked on the door "Come in" Principal Storm said and then Alex and Michael walked through the door "Alex..." Principal Strom said "Hello Principal Strom!!!..." Alex said "Alex it's been a long time since I saw you and you were just a 16 year old little boy and now you're a man and you are very muscular and have a little facial hair as well" Principal Strom said "How are you doing?" Alex asked "I'm doing okay, I know I have gotten older since I last saw you" Principal Strom asked "Principal Strom, I need to know more about what was going on back in 1976 and I need see what was going on and I need to ask you if there was any files on Victoria Borodina coming here" Alex said "Alex, I cannot revel that information to you it's private. And I really didn't want her to hurt you Alex. So I had to keep it a secret" Principal Strom said "Alex there is really nothing you can do about it, the government is just getting bigger and bigger and teacher's unions are getting bigger as well" Principal Storm said "No there is always an answer for everything. Your not hooked on to anything are you?" Alex asked, "no Alex I am not" Principal Storm said "Oh okay well at least that's good" Michael said, "I don't believe you. And I believe you are lying to me just like back then" Alex said "I need the files right now!!!!!" Alex said "I can't give them to you Alex!!!!" Principal Strom said, "I see, I should of known this was happening!!! Borodina is paying you millions of money to keep all the secrets of the communistic teachers unions!!!! You are traitor to your own country!!!!!" Alex yelled "Alex, come here!!!!..." Michael said "Dude I think a micro-chip is planted in her!!!!!" Michael said and then Alex ran to Michael and all of a sudden they noticed there a microchip planted in back of Principal Storm's neck and the microchip had a Sandinista flag on it "Oh my fucking god!!!!!!....." Alex said in a very angry and shocked and pissed off mood and then Michael got really scarred and made a scarried noise "what happen to her?!...She is still alive?!..." Michael asked in a very scarried voice and then all of a sudden Principal Strom got electrocuted and then all of a sudden Cruz walked into the office wearing a red and black suit "Buenos días Sr. Aussmen!!!!" Cruz said and then Alex and Michael turned back and Michael got really scarred because of the suit Cruz was wearing "Manuel!!!!!!! This can't be!!!!" Alex said "oh I am very alive and very well Sr. Aussmen and I can already imagine that you know that my boss señorita Borodina is now my leader and she is also paying the Sandinistas a lot of money including myself for future technology that will be more futuristic then what Silicon Valley and Redmond, Washington will produce!!!!" Cruz said, "You are one brain-washed stupid person!!!!!" Alex said with anger built in him "Oh that's a really big time statement Alex" Cruz said and then all of a sudden, Cruz took out a gun and it was a magnum gun "You really should of have really killed me when you had the chance!!!" Cruz said and then all of a sudden, while having the gun in his hand, Cruz then turned off the microchip using a remote that he had in his hand and then all of a sudden Principal Storm was knocked out and then all of a sudden as Alex saw Principal Storm knocked out, Alex then got really mad and then he reached into his pocket and he right away threw a sharp pocket knife at Cruz and stabbed him in the left arm and then Alex kicked Cruz in the face and Cruz all of a sudden landed on the ground on his back but then Cruz was able to grab the pocket knife out of his arm and get back up on his feet "You know Alex, There are more Sandinista thugs everywhere in the United States more then before and we have people everywhere as well" Cruz said and then Cruz did a really evil smile and then he started doing a very soft evil laugh and then all of a sudden, Cruz then threw a bomb at Alex and Michael "Get down!!!!!" Alex yelled and then there was a huge explosion and the Principal's office blew up and then after the explosion, Alex and Michael survived the explosion and he saw a 1980's car drive off "Alex, he's getting away!!!" Michael said "We will worry about him later...We have to get the Lewis house" Alex said and then Alex and Michael got back up on their feet and they started running out of the school and they started running to Alex's car.

Alex then started the car and Alex then started driving to the Lewis House really fast.

Alex and Michael then took a right turn and they entered into the Lewis House. And before that, Alex parked the car and he turned the car off and Alex and Michael started running inside. As both Michael and Alex got into the house, Alex right away noticed that the house was just completely destroyed and everything was a huge mess, there was some spray paint graffiti that has the Sandinista flag painted on the wall, there was some burned up wood and the house looked like it burned up over night "Emmy, Matthew!!!!" Alex yelled "Oh good God!!!!!!!" Alex also said as he saw the mess in the house "This is really not good Alex!!!" Michael said, "Yeah It's impossible, how in the world did the Sandinistas found out where Emmy and Matthew lived?" Alex asked "I think maybe I believe Borodina has hijacked the Sandinistas and used her own money from Ukraine to sadly make them more powerful" Michael said "I really do not like the sound of that" Alex said "So what do we do now Alex?" Michael asked and then Alex started thinking about for maybe around 60 seconds and then Alex then was able to offer an idea "I think we are going to have to go to every American state that has a high number of Hispanic population and gather some allies just like what I did when I was a teenager and just like when I faced them the 1ˢᵗ time" Alex said

Alex and Michael left the broken and burned up Lewis House and they started driving back to downtown Seattle and back to their homes. Alex then packed up all his clothes and a lot of other gadgets as well. Alex then was able to write a letter to Rivers telling him that he was on his own secret mission that involve going down to Nicaragua. And Alex and Michael's first stop was Miami, Florida. Alex and Michael both took cabs to get to Sea-Tac airport and they were able to catch a United flight that was heading to Miami. On the plane Alex then started sleeping and in his mind, he just really hoped that Emmy and Matthew were both all right and that nothing bad has happen to them. But then as Alex was flash-backing to all of his missions that he had that did involve going after the Sandinistas both in 1976. Especially with going after Kramer Quinne and Diego Chavez and taking on Sebastian Hooper who also fell into bed with Sandinistas as well. But this time this mission was a lot more personal and Alex's brain and his mind was really steaming and really burning him as well.

Chapter 2 Infiltrating A Miami City Council Office building in Miami

As the plane landed at Miami Airport, Alex and Michael got off the plane and Alex was able to get a taxi for both of them. And Alex and Michael stayed in a fancy hotel room that over looked the ocean. Michael then set up his spy watch to contact Alex and also be a field coach to him as well "So where are we going first?" Michael asked "well for your starters, your going to stay here and see if there any strange activity going on in Miami and for me I'm going to explore the city and see If we can get some information about the Sandinistas and then once we have information then we can para-shoot into Nicaragua" Alex said "Oh okay that sounds good man" Michael said and then after getting ready, Alex then got on a 1980's style suit and tie and he walked out of the hotel room and he went down the elevator and he started heading to a lot of different parts of Miami. This included going to like the Hispanic zones of the city as well and as well as the rich people zones as well and looking for any person that was available. As Alex was getting really hungry, he then walked into a Mexican food restaurant and then ordered himself a chicken burrito. And then he saw a Hispanic teenager walk into the restaurant and he was wearing a normal Nicaraguan bracelet that just had the normal Nicaraguan flag on it. The boy was also with his parents as well and he was speaking Spanish to them. Alex then lowered his sunglasses and then the boy sat down somewhere. And Alex while memorizing a little bit of Spanish back in high school with all the books that he read in the past, Alex then titled his head up and he began to speak "Hey amigo, ven aquí." Alex said with perfect pronouncing of the words and with an accent as well. The teenager then started coming to Alex. Also Alex knew a little bite of Spanish because of also being around Sabrina Fiorina and Morella's Fortuneteller spells made Alex's brain smarter and more intelligent and it was another reason why Alex was able to read a lot of books as well "¿Sabe Señor?" he said in Spanish "no you do not man. But I saw a Nicaraguan bracelet on your arm. And I was wondering if you knew anything what was going in Nicaragua and why the Sandinistas are getting powerful?" Alex asked, "Look man, I do not want to talk about those evil monsters, they killed all my family and I can't tell you" he said, "You can with me. I'm Alex Aussmen; I'm a private investigator. I don't work for the government. And I know what the Sandinistas are like as well" Alex said, "How old are you?" Alex asked, "I'm 17 years old" he said, "Oh that's wonderful. I remember when I was your age; I actually took on the Sandinistas back in the 70's and I really understand how evil they are" Alex said "Can I get you drink?" Alex asked "Sure I will have a doctor pepper" he said

And then as Alex was eating with the teenager from Nicaragua. "So I have a question for you Alex, How were you able to speak Spanish so well?" he asked, "It's all because of memory kid, I was raised by really smart people and I had really good role models as well" Alex said "Oh wow that's really incredible" he said "By the way, what's your name?" Alex asked, "My name is Pablo. My parents and I both came here to start a new life here in America and there is so much freedom here" Pablo said "Do you ever think you will ever become an American citizen when you turn 18?" Alex asked "Yes I want to really badly" Pablo said "Well that's good kid" Alex said "but I really need your help as well. Have you seen any strange people here?" Alex asked and then Pablo kept on drinking and he started thinking about it for a couple of seconds and then finally he came up with an answer "Well...I did see someone name Mr. Tyler Smells who is a assistant to a US senator from Florida and I herd on the news that he really supports anybody that wants to impeach the current U.S. President especially with los contras as well" Pablo said as he was mixing his

English and his Spanish words but Alex was able to understand him really well. "Oh okay I see what your saying, There is someone who is secretly supporting the Sandinistas and giving them money and at the same time is attacking President Reagan on the Contra affair…Where is this person now?" Alex asked "Yo no sé Señor…But I do know that he goes to the capital building and then goes to a United Nations building as well" Pablo said both in Spanish and English "And I also saw some strange people with him as well" Pablo said "…Your a very smart kid. How would you like to be a secret agent apprentice of mine?" Alex asked, "Are you sure?" Pablo said, "yes I am very sure" Alex said

And then after Alex was done eating lunch and as Pablo was done drinking his soda, Alex then started heading to the beach that was in Miami, Florida. And then as Alex was at the beach, he then was sitting around tropical like bar and then Alex was able to order a tropical drink. And then while Alex was sitting down in the bar, Alex was then watching a lot of beautiful and really stunning and really gorgeous women all around him. Alex kept on turning his head left and right and checking out the girls. But there was one girl that really stood out and she came out of the ocean and she was wearing a red bikini bathing suit and she also had green eyes, her hair was a little bite of a mix between blonde and brown hair, she looked very athletic and overall, she had the face of a princess. She then started walking to the same bar table that Alex was in and then she ordered herself a margarita drink and then she started drinking it. And then Alex then put on his sunglasses and the girl then turned back at Alex and the girl really loved Alex's sense of style and she got really happy "I really love your suit that you are wearing" she said "Oh thank you" Alex said "So do you come here very often?" Alex asked her "Yeah sometimes, just when I want to get away from school. Cause I know School can really hard" She said, "Where do you go to school at?" Alex asked, "I go the University of Miami" she said "Oh wow so your hurricane then. Well I went to the University of Washington and I'm a Husky" Alex said "Oh okay" she said, "I'm Ashley Owelmen and you are?" Ashley said, "Names Aussmen…Alex Aussmen" Alex said, "it's a pleasure to meet you Mr. Aussmen. So what brings you to Miami?" Ashley said, "Well other then looking at beautiful and stunning girls at the beach. I'm actually here on a businesses trip. And I also do really risky businesses as well" Alex said "What sort of businesses. Please tell me!!!" Ashley said, "Well right now I'm going after terrorist groups that are from Central America" Alex said "What kind of groups?" Ashley asked "I'm thinking about going after the Sandinistas down in Nicaragua" Alex said "Oh wow that sounds really crazy and also really hard as well" Ashley said "But I know from experience however, I am very skilled with using a gun. So I really believe that I can help you" Ashley said "So when do we start?" Ashley asked and then all of a sudden Alex then put one of his hands into his pockets and then he was able to give Ashley his phone number through a business card "Thank you Alex. Yes I will defiantly call you" Ashley said though Ashley was very beautiful and very stunning, Alex really made sure to stay focus on what was in front of him and also remembering what Pablo said to him and then after being at the beach for quite some time and also going swimming himself, Alex then started heading back to his hotel room to meet up with Michael "Hey man how was your little exploring around Miami?" Michael asked "Yeah it was really good my man. I was able to find some more information about what might be really going on." Alex said, "What do you mean Alex?" Michael asked, "Well for starters a new ally that might be helping us said there is a senator that is attacking president Reagan. But also at the same he is funding the Sandinistas with government aid as well" Alex said "That really does not sound good" Michael said "No it does not Michael" Alex said "And I can only imagine that he is also working with Victoria Borodina as well" Alex said "But the new allies/agents that might be working with us are a girl name Ashley Owelmen who is a University of Miami student and also a teenager from Nicaragua name Pablo who knows the facts about our first operation" Alex said "That sounds really great Alex. Where do we start?" Michael said, "First, we just have to wait Intel they get here my man" Alex said "Oh okay" Michael said

And then later that night, Pablo and Ashley then started heading to Alex and Michael's hotel room in Miami. And then as they got there, Ashley then knocked on the door and then Alex was able to answer the door "Come in you guys" Alex said and they both came into the hotel room and they both sat down on Alex's bed "Alright well since we are all here, The reason I called you guys here is because we are going after the Sandinistas in Nicaragua and they have the power to become the most evil party in all of the world. And they are now led by a Ukraine mastermind name Victoria Borodina who also funds them from Ukraine as well. And both of you have really bright minds and both of you guys will bring something to the table as well" Alex said "My friend Michael will also be helping us once we start our first mission" Alex said "any questions?" Alex asked and then Pablo raised his hand "Yes Aussmen, I believe I know where Smells is heading to and he is heading to the Miami City Council building. And I know he is transferring the money there" Pablo said "Thank you Pablo" Alex said, "So how do you think we are going to get into the building?" Ashley said, "Oh I think I have my ways Ashley" Alex said "So is what I said clear?" Alex asked and then both Pablo and Ashley said yes and then all of a sudden, Alex, Pablo, and Ashley then started getting black jumpsuits and then they headed out of the hotel room and they got into one of Alex's new car and then as they were in the car, Pablo then got out a map and he was able to tell Alex the directions on how to get to the city council building and Alex listened to him and from there they got to the building.

As they got to the city council building in Miami, Alex was able to park the car in a parking lot. And then as Alex parked the car, Alex then saw a strange person with a suit and eyeglasses go into building and he was able to un-look the door and get into the building. And then Alex, Pablo, and Ashley were able to get out of the car and they started going to the back of the building. Alex then got out a hook shot gun and then Alex shot the gun on to the roof and then Alex zooming up to the roof and then Pablo and Ashley then climbed up the rope and they started fallowing Alex. Alex then found an air vent and Alex broke the air vent door and Alex started climbing down the vent and he started crawling Intel he found another door and he was able to break the door using a laser pointer pen, Alex broke the door and then Alex got out of the air vent and Ashley and Pablo joined him as well. They both landed on the ground and they then got through an office room. Alex then pulled out a gun and Alex using his brain, started fallowing the conversations of both Smells and another person as well. And they kept on walking and then Alex saw both Smells and Cruz Manuel talking to each other inside another office room. "We appreciate your kind generosity of giving us around 3 million dollars. I always knew average Americans were always so dumb and really stupid" Cruz said "Don't worry we will make sure that your operations really go really well" Smells said and then Cruz then walked over to the computer and then he started typing on the old apple computer and transferring a lot of the money into a "unknown" account but in reality, it was really a forging bank account that was held by the Sandinistas "This account will really work in terms of keeping the Sandinistas in power for 90 years. And we owe it all to you" Cruz said

And then as Cruz said that, Alex got really angry and he was really steaming and really mad. And then all of a sudden broke the door down as the door was shut and then Cruz and Smells turned back and they saw Alex in complete shock "La Raza, La Raza, La Raza, La Raza!!!!!! El Gringo!!!!!!!" Cruz yelled and then all of a sudden a lot of Sandinista thugs showed up out of nowhere. And then Alex took out his gun and then he dodged the bullets firing at him and then Alex hid behind a wall and then he started shooting around 60 bullets at the Sandinista thugs. And then as Alex shot the thugs, more thugs then started coming towards him and they started throwing a lot of punches and kicks at Alex and Alex was able to dodge the attacks. And then all of a sudden, they took Mexican swords and they tried to stab Alex in the stomach and also tried to stab him in the arm. Alex then got punched in the face by another Sandinista thug and then another tackled him really badly and punched Alex in the face and caused Alex to get a bloody noise "No nos detendrá de tomar el dinero que es nuestro maldito Gringo!!!!!" One of them yelled at Alex "You know what FUCK YOU!!!!!! AND FUCK YOUR PARTY!!!!!!!" Alex yelled and then Alex kicked 2 of the Sandinsta thugs in the face and grabbed one of the Mexican swords and stabbed two of them in the head really badly and then Pablo joined in the fight and kicked another in the stomach and took out a gun and shot the Sandinista solider in the head and then Ashley then grabbed another gun and she then pointed the gun at both Smells and Cruz "Oh my dear, you really believe helping this stupid gringo from Seattle is going to help your country. This problem is a lot more bigger then you" Cruz said and then Ashley really didn't say a word and she held the gun really firm and she was really getting fire at Cruz "You will not get away with this Manuel!!!!" Alex yelled "Oh I think I already have because of my really smart brain I was able to go on your manzana computer and I was able to transfer all the money to my party.

Which means for you, the Sandinistas will be even more powerful then the whole United States of America under Victoria Borodina's orders!!!!!" Cruz said "Yeah the fuck that is going to happen Mr. Gold teeth and Sandinista suit wearing piece of shit!!!!" Alex yelled with complete fire and anger built in him and then Cruz laughed and chuckled "I grantee you will regret saying that to me señor Aussmen" Cruz said and then all of a sudden as Cruz went really close to Alex, Alex then all of a sudden head-butted Cruz really hard and then Alex wanted to beat the living stuffing out of him and more Sandinista thugs came and they were holding Alex back "And now it is time to say good bye Mr. Aussmen" Cruz said and then as Cruz said, Pablo then saw a gun that was on the ground and quietly, Pablo then started loading up the gun with some bullets that he had and all of a sudden, he then shot a gun bullet at Cruz's arm and then he loaded up another bullet and then he shoot Smells in the arm and forced him to the ground "You will fucking regret that you stupid boy!!!!" Cruz said and then Pablo then flipped off Cruz and then gave him his middle finger. And all of a sudden there was Sandinista thugs that showed up and they picked up Cruz and they put him inside of a Sandinista helicopter and then the helicopter left Miami. Smells then was on the ground and then Ashley punched him in the face and then she also pointed gun at Smells "You are going to tell us everything!!!!!" Ashley said and then Alex walked towards Smells "People like you are the reason why I never vote democrat!!!! Good job Ashley, we have a lot of bones to pick with you" Alex said

Pablo, Alex, and Ashley were able to escape out of the City Council building and they took Smells back to Alex's hotel room. As they got back to Alex's hotel room, they then placed Smells on a chair and then Pablo took out a gun and he pointed the gun at his head "So I'm going to ask a lot of times!!!!, How much money did you give the Sandinistas?!..." Alex asked, "I can't tell you" Smells said "why not?!...Is it because you will run out of liberal donors and then you won't be able take down president Reagan is that why?!..." Alex yelled and then Alex bitched slapped Smells really hard "And also I know that most of that money is going to be used to attack the president of false stories that relate to the contra affair as well" Alex said ".....Man I really don't know who the hell you are?!...But I really hate pro America people like you that are very toxic and deplorable!!!!!" Smells said and then all of a sudden Alex punched Smells in the face and shoved him against the wall "That was for using the word toxic" Alex said "I will ask you again, where is the money?!..." Alex said "I don't know" Smells said "You are a traitor to your own country" Alex said and then Alex grabbed by his wrist and then all of a sudden Alex hung Smells over the balcony "I'm going to give you one last final chance!!!" Alex said "Where is it!!!!?" Alex yelled again "it's in Nicaragua!!!" he said then all of a sudden, Alex then dropped Smells off the ledge and then Smells started falling to the ground and he started yelling and screaming to his death and he landed on a car and Smells was dead

But even though Smells was dead, Alex had the information that he really needed. And he knew that Alex, Michael, and now Pablo and Ashley they knew that this evil plan was really big and really huge and Alex knew that he had to go down to Nicaragua and find Victoria Borodina and also find and defeat the Sandinistas as well. Unfortunately however, since Alex was banned from going to Nicaragua back in the 1976 but also secretly going there again in that same year, Alex knew that he had keep himself at a very low profile and they need a vehicle where they can drive down to Nicaragua through the Mexican boarder without being seen or caught by the Sandinistas. And from there on, they started driving down south.

Chapter 3 Secretly Entering Nicaragua and finding the technology building in Managua

As they were driving south and went through the Mexican boarder, Alex, Pablo and Ashley were inside of the RV and it was colored in black from the inside so that way nobody knew who was driving the RV. During this drive, they went through a lot of countries and ate a lot of the food that was in those countries. And they also stayed in the RV as well. But then around the 3rd day, they all were getting close to the Nicaraguan boarder and that's when trouble really started to hit. As Alex was driving they saw a lot of Sandinista groups with riffle guns in their hands. "So what's the plan Alex?" Pablo said, "Sadly I really do not know my man. But I will come up with something" Alex said and then Alex turned his head back and he didn't see a lot of cars behind them. And then as one of the guards was coming towards them Alex then was able to get an idea in his head. Moments later, the guard came to the window of the driver's seat "¡¿Qué diablos?!" the guard said in Spanish and then he kept on looking around and then all of a sudden he was able to open the car. And all of a sudden, Alex tapped the guard on the shoulder holding a little American flag and then Alex grunted his teeth and punched the Sandinista guard in the face and kicked him in the balls. Alex then took out his pistol gun and shot the Sandinista guard in the forehead and killed him. Pablo and Ashley were able to come out of hiding and Alex grabbed the guard's key and they entered into checkpoint box that controls the gate and Alex was able to use the key to open the gate. The gate was able to open and then Alex, Pablo, and Ashley were able to go back into the RV and then they just kept on driving south.

As they entered into the country, Alex noticed right away that Nicaragua looked very different from the last time that he was there back in 1976. While Alex was driving the whole capital of Managua looked like a complete hellhole and there were houses that were not built properly, a lot of garbage on the street, and all around Alex there was a lot of poor people as well in the streets. But sadly most of all, there was a lot of Sandinista and communist propaganda in the country. And overall the whole country looked like a complete mess and Alex even noticed a lot of American fast food chains as well. And then there were even people that were also waiting in line for food and clothes as well. Alex kept on driving and he knew at some point, they had to stop somewhere, lucky however Alex saw a hotel from far away that really looked like the rich part of town and Alex started driving up there. As they were able to find some parking, Alex didn't know what he should do next because he didn't know if the country still banned him from ever coming to Nicaragua ever again especially around the 1st time he went there. "Ashley do you think you can check us in?" Alex asked "yeah sure Alex" Ashley said

And then moments later, Ashley then walked up to the counter and she started getting a hotel room and they easily give her a key. Alex and Pablo then fallowed her to their hotel rooms. Michael also was with them and he also got a separate room as well. Alex then lay on his bed and he started looking at the window of the palm trees outside and then also of the swimming pool. The swimming pool really made Alex think of teenager years back when he was living with Morella and swimming in her pool back in Edmonds, Washington as well and then also back when he was jumping on the trampoline in Morella's backyard as well. And then right around 1AM or so, Alex then got out of his hotel room and he started looking around the hotel room and he went inside of a bar and there was like nobody in there and it was closed but the staff didn't really care to lock it up. Alex went in there and he sat on a chair and he drank some whisky that on the table. As Alex was drinking, he then saw a businesses office that had an old IBM computer inside of it. Alex then stopped drinking and as he got to the door, he then used his spy watch to unlock the door. Alex then went into the room and he noticed right away that the computer was not working very well. Alex even was able to turn on the computer and he noticed right away there were a lot of viruses on it that would be easily fixable with American interference. As Alex was on the computer he noticed a lot of dark things on the computer. And then all of a sudden, there was a strange door that opened up and it was from behind the computer and Alex went inside the room. And then all of a sudden, Alex then started sliding down a really huge slide and then Alex fell off of the slide and he landed flat on his face. And then from out of nowhere, Alex then started hearing a lot of liquid machines that were making computer with corrupted Silicon crystals and Alex was on the ground and he hid from the guards and there was a lot of scientist that were creating them. And inside of the factory there was also old IBM computers that were getting melted like crazy and being turned into futuristic computer that were using a lot of technology that American computers were really not using. But then all of a sudden Alex then crawled and he hid behind a lot of boxes and all of a sudden, Cruz came into the room with a lot of other Sandinista thugs "Perfecto, esta computadora realmente Detroy todas las cuentas bancarias en Estados Unidos y también destruirá SILCON Valley" Cruz said "También estoy muy seguro de que estos ordenadores también nos harán muy ricos y que será capaz de bajar por el oeste, así." Crus said again and then all of a sudden, a women in a dark green dress with black hair and with some gray hair as well and wearing a communist bracelet with the USSR flag on it walked into the room "I am very proud of your progress Cruz. And from there I know that we will be able to kill the contras and get Reagan out of office on false clams and nobody will be able to stop us" Victoria said but as Alex was hiding he didn't that Victoria was there because he didn't see a lot of Victoria's characteristics. And he also knew that something was defiantly different from before.

"Oh yeah I agree Ms. Borodina that this time we will be able to use Nicaragua and blow up both the United States and then also blow up Nicaragua and draining everything out of both countries especially the money" Cruz said "And the best part will be that nobody knows about the damage that my funds are doing by supporting your operation and your socialist party as well" Borodina said "perfect" Cruz said and then all of a sudden, Borodina and Cruz left the room and Alex took out a gun and he shot the Sandinista guards with a silenced pistol gun and shot them in the head. Alex then came out of hiding and he started looking at the Sandinista computers and Alex started taking pictures of them. As Alex was done taking pictures of them. Alex then was able to sneak out of the room the way he got in. Alex then was able to get out of the bar and he started heading back to his hotel room. As Alex got back to his room, he then started looking at a map of Nicaragua and then Alex saw a phone book and he saw a random business called "Joyería del agua" and Alex noticed on the picture that it didn't look bad and broken down at all and the company was around gulf of Mexico. As Alex kept on walking, he then started walking on the beach and he started walking towards the businesses. As Alex walked in, he saw a lot of jewelry everywhere especially in many different colors and shapes. Alex then started walking around the store and as he did so, he started having flash backs of when he walked into Morella's store for the first time in 1976 in Edmonds, Washington. As Alex kept on walking around, he then saw an older Hispanic looking gentlemen. "¿Puedo ayudarle en algo, señor?" Alex turned his head and he Alex simply responded with "No gracias sólo estoy mirando alrededor." Alex said and then as Alex kept on looking around he noticed a lot of pictures on the wall and he saw that Morella before moving to Edmonds was in this store. Alex started looking at the picture more and more closely. And then he also noticed a picture of Paul Millet also in the photo as well. And then as Alex was looking at the picture, the same owner went up to Alex "¿Conoces a ese hombre en la foto?" he asked "De hecho, sí. ¿sabes cuando vino aquí?" Alex said "Sí. Él vino en 1967 y él y la muchacha con la muchacha negra estaban en una misión juntos y estaban detrás de muchos matones de Somoza." The owner said "Y también durante ese tiempo cuando muchos matones de Somoza los estaban atacando, luego me preguntaron si podían quedarse en mi tienda y yo le dije que sí también." The owner said "¿Sabes lo que buscaban?" Alex asked "Nadie turly lo sabe. Pero puedo decir que te pareces a los persom de Francia que vinieron aquí." The owner said

Moments later, the owner and Alex went to his kitchen and Alex had some fish tacos that had beans and rich and cheese on them. And also Alex had the meal with a Mexican Pepsi "¿tuviste suficiente para comer jovencito?" he asked "Sí,

Señor. Entonces, ¿qué pasa con toda la joyería que tienes en tu casa? ¿y cuánto tiempo lo has estado guardando?" Alex asked "Oh, la joyería. He tenido esta joyería desde la década de 1950. Y lo he escondido de los Sandinstas y los Somozas por mucho tiempo. Se dice en la leyenda que pueden alimentar a muchas computadoras." The owner said "¿Crees que la joyería nunca ha sido probada dentro de un ser humano?" Alex asked "No creo. Pero he visto otra joyería que colocó dentro de un niño hace años." The owner said and then as Alex herd that statement, Alex then started to be in shock and he started puzzles together in his head. And Alex then started to realize that the boy the business owner was talking about was Cruz. And then as Alex was done eating, the business owner then took out some old footage of both Paul and Morella in 1967 and in the footage they were shooting guns at Somoza thugs and Nicaraguan soldiers. And then the footage then went blank and then went back on and Alex saw Paul's face on the screen "Hello my name is agent Paul Millet and I'm a French intelligence agent from France and my partner Emily Romney have discovered the Somozas and the Sandinistas are starting to create very smart soldiers using liquid jewelry and liquid silicon. There is no doubt that the Soviet Union is funding the Sandinistas and making them powerful every minute and every second right now. Also we have found out that the Borodina family has been helping the Soviet Union and the Sandinistas down here. We also have footage of them creating a very smart human." Paul said and then all of a sudden in the footage, the footage cuts to a younger Cruz and he strapped on to a medical chair and he is trying to get free. And also a lot of Sandinista soldiers are giving him liquid silicon and liquid and they are grabbing his mouth to make sure it stays open and Cruz is grunting and screaming like crazy. And then as Cruz drinks the liquid jewelry and the liquid silicon, Cruz then starts getting really powerful and he keeps on screaming and yelling. And then also some parts of his eye start to break down to the point where you see nothing but a sliver circle with infected eye coloring. As the screaming in the footage stopped, Cruz then broke out of the table and he started killing people and killing a lot of Somoza and Sandinista soldiers. "Yeah so right now in this footage you see a young boy being turned into a cyber like human and it's believed that his brain has become much more smarter then other human. And right now who ever is seeing this footage, I hope you send this to President Johnson or to the UN because I repeat Nicaragua in the future will become a country full of terrorism and we must do something about this!!!!" Paul said in the video and then all of a sudden, the footage then started to break down and Paul and Morella started fighting more Sandinista thugs and then a young Cruz started fighting Paul and Morella at the same time and throwing a lot of objects at them in the process.

The footage was completely cut off and Alex really couldn't believe what he just saw as he knew in his mind that years later he would meet those two people but in different points in time. And also Alex thought in his head why Morella never mentioned anything about working with Paul back in the 1960's. And also thought why Morella mentioned her own secret mission in

Nicaragua. "El hombre que realmente me sentí tan mal por ellos que les estaban atacando por realmente sólo hacer la obra del Señor." The business owner said "Lo sé." Alex said but then the business owner then went to safe and he brought over to Alex a jewelry that was blue and purple and had the Nicaraguan flag on it "He guardado esto durante muchos años Intel un americano vino. Y no dejes que esta joyería caiga en manos de los Sandinstas o de los rusos." The business owner said "No se preocupe, realmente me aseguraré de que no lo haga." Alex said and then all of a sudden, Alex then started running from the business and he started running on the beach. But as Alex was running on the beach and he saw a strange looking building. Alex then saw a surfboard and he grabbed a flashlight and Alex changed out of his clothes and he put on a wet suit and he started heading towards the water. As Alex was on the water, he was able to get closer and closer and he saw that it was a fancy looking building. But also as Alex was getting closer, he did notice a lot of Sandinista boats that were guarding the building. Alex then dived into the water and he started swimming under water to avoid the guards. The soldiers then saw Alex and all of a sudden, Alex climbed on to the boat and right away, Alex then punched the soldiers in the face and kicked them in the stomach and Alex started fighting the Sandinista soldiers and Alex punched one of them in the face and then one of the Sandinista soldiers tackled Alex and Alex was able to get up right away and Alex grabbed one of the sniper guns and Alex shoot two of them in the eyes and killed them. Alex then threw the Sandinista soldiers in the water and then the mako sharks in the water started eating them and there was a lot of blood in the water. Alex took hold of the boats and he started driving the boat towards the building and the island.

As Alex was getting closer and closer to the building, he was able to get in through the back of the building and kill a bunch of guards and Alex opened the door. As Alex got into the building, Alex then started looking around and hiding from guards at the same time. As Alex kept on walking he did notice a lot of flags from Central America and South America and then Alex saw Cuba's flag in the building as well. And Alex ducked and he peeked his head to see some sort of visual on what was going in the room. And as he did so, he saw some people in suit jackets that had the pins of the flags of where they came from, one of them was Nicaragua and then the other one was Venezuela and then the other one was Cuba "Creo que hasta ahora en una cuestión de tiempo, vamos a tener toda la joyería y luego utilizarlo para construir un arma enorme que destruirá los Estados Unidos y también poner a Estados Unidos en el E.O., así." One of them said "sí sé cuando hemos terminado aquí. Apuesto a que Ortega y Chávez y Castro nos darán mucho dinero por nuestros esfuerzos también." The man in the suit jacket said "Y también espero que la chica de Ucrania finalmente destruya América y entonces ese país será nuestro." The one from Cuba said and then all of a sudden, Borodina showed up again "Hola a todos, espero que todos ustedes tengan la pouds de la joyería que les pedí. Para matar a los contras." Victoria said "Sí, señorita Borodina. Lo tenemos aquí mismo." One of them said and then all of a sudden one of the men in the suits got out a bag full jewelry and liquid silicon and showed it to Victoria "Buen trabajo. Estoy seguro de que sus líderes estarán orgullosos de usted. Y pronto el Sandinstas gobernará el mundo y destruirá a los Estados Unidos de América. Y entonces no habrá nada que el estúpido Alex Aussmen pueda hacer al respecto." Victoria said "Oh, sí, estoy de acuerdo. Él no sabe nada y estoy seguro de que Ortega enviará mucho al ejército para ir tras ese estúpido americano." And then all four of them in the room started to laugh. And then all of a sudden, Victoria turned on the TV in the room and all of a sudden it was Ortega, Hugo Chavez and Fidel Castro on the TV screen "Buenas tardes señorita Borodina. Me complace mucho que haya podido ayudar a la Unión Soviética. Y sabemos que no importa lo que suceda con el muro de Berlín, nuestros gobiernos van a ir tras los Estados Unidos de América y destruir todo lo que aman tanto." Castro said "Es mi placer Castro, pronto mis hombres y Organzation darán mi dinero al Sandinstas y a Venzula y a la Unión Soviética y de allí, todos gobernaremos el mundo y destruiremos la civilización occidental tal como la conocemos." Victoria said "Pero entonces, ¿qué vamos a hacer con los contras que intentan derrocar a Nicaraguia y a los Sandinstas?" Chavez said "Es fácil me aseguraré de enviar a mis matones después de ellos y capturarlos y matarlos." Victoria said "Victoria perfecta. Excelente estoy seguro de que Ortega será muy pleasued y América en cuestión de días será destruida por las computadoras de joyería y courpted." Castro said

And then all of a sudden, the computer screens turned off and they all started leaving the room "Asegúrate de que nadie venga y se rompa en la caja fuerte." Victoria said and then as Victoria left the room, Alex then saw an air vent and he was able to use his gun to break open the air vent and Alex then was able to climb into the vent and he started crawling to the other room. As Alex was able to get to the other room, Alex then from behind grabbed one of the guys in the suits and slammed him against the wall and then the other men in suit jackets took out guns and they pointed their guns at Alex "La Raza, La Raza, La Raza!!!!!!!" They yelled "Mata al Gringo!!!!" They also yelled again.

Alex then started fighting the men in the suits and Alex punched one of them in the face and then kicked another one in the head and forced him against the wall. Alex then grabbed a liquor bottle and slammed the bottle at one of the men and the men screamed and yelled in pain. Then one of them grabbed Alex from behind and slammed him to the table "Te vamos a llevar a Cuba y te han tourdo por Castro!!!!!!!!!!!!" The man said and then Alex grunted in rage "Fuck you!!!!" Alex yelled and then Alex elbow punched the man in the stomach and threw an upper cut punch and then another men had a machete in his hand and he tried to cut and stab Alex. Alex was able to dodge the machete attacks and Alex did another kick attack towards the man with the Venezuela pin on his suit jacket. And Alex was able to knock the knife out of his hand, Alex was able to grab the knife and he stabbed the man with the Venezuela pin on his suit and stabbed him in the neck and killed him. Then the other man grabbed Alex and punched Alex in the face 4 times and Alex started coughing out a lot

of blood. Alex then was able to duck and dodge the 5th punch and head butt the man punching him. Alex then grabbed the man's head and whacked him with his knee and Alex punched the man in the face 5 times. The last and final thug grabbed a Mexican sword and tried to stab and cut Alex really bad. Alex was able to the dodge the attacks and Alex kicked him in the face and then kicked him again in the stomach. Alex then was able to find a magnum gun and Alex loaded up the gun and he was able to shoot the last thug in the head 15 times. And the man wearing the pin that had the Sandinista flag on it was dead. As he was laying down on the ground dead, Alex then walked up to him and he started looking either a key to the safe or a combination code to the safe. Lucky though however, Alex was able to find the key and he then ran to the safe and he used the key to open up main safe. As Alex was able to open the safe, he then found a lot of blue prints of the weapons that Chavez, Castro, and Ortega were going to build to destroy the Contras. Alex then kept on looking at the documents he saw transaction papers of Borodina giving money and funding the Sandinistas since 1976 "holy mother of god!!!" Alex said to himself. And then Alex kept on looking through the papers and he saw that there was a underground base that was in the country of Venezuela and the base itself was a computer factory that making a lot of IBM computers that had super advanced technology and the computers would ultimately brain wash a lot of people and also had bombs with jewelry that would destroy a lot of public places in the United States of America. And then Alex was able to grab the papers but then all of a sudden, a lot of Sandinista soldiers came into the room "La Raza, La Raza, La Raza, La Raza!!!!!!" The Sandinista soldiers yelled and then Alex did a summersault and Alex took out a magnum gum and a lot of Sandinista soldiers started firing a lot of bullets at Alex out of their riffle guns. Alex was able to take cover and he loaded around 20 bullets a round and Alex would turn around and shoot the Sandinista soldiers in the head and also shoot them in the stomach and in the chest as well
Alex was able to shoot and kill around 30 Sandinista soldiers and he started running out of the building. And one of the Sandinista soldiers was able to hit the alarm. Alex then started running downstairs and Alex was able to steel a riffle gun and Alex kept on shooting at the soldiers and killing them. "Conseguir que el americano se escapa. No dejes que se vaya del edificio!!!!!" One of the Sandinista soldiers said and then Alex kept running away and Alex was able to jump on a table and Alex turned around and he was able to shoot around 100 bullets at the Sandinista soldiers and kill around 300 Sandinista soldiers coming at him. More of them started coming at Alex and shooting at Alex and Alex was able to kick some of them in the face that were coming at him. Alex then kept on running and turning back and shooting at more Sandinista soldiers that were coming at him and as Alex kept on going, he then was able to get outside and he was able to find a motor boat and Alex got on the motorboat and a lot of Sandinista soldiers started chasing him around the gulf of Mexico. And as Alex was driving, Alex would turn back and he fired more bullets out of a A33 riffle gun and shoot around 50 bullets and killing more Sandinista soldiers in the process. "Se acabó el Señor Aussmen. Dé

vuelta al barco!!!!!" One of the Sandinista soldiers yelled, "Fuck you!!!!" Alex yelled and then Alex was able to grab a grenade and throw 6 grenades at the boats that were chasing him and Alex was able to blow up 6 boats that were coming at him from behind.

And then Alex was able to get back to shore and he was able to park the boat around the dock. And then all of a sudden more Sandinista soldiers and government police showed up and they started shooting at Alex. Alex then ran back to the boat and he was able to find some pistol gun and he was able to load new bullets into the gun. And Alex hid behind the wall and then he would turn his body towards the soldiers and police shooting at him and Alex was able to fire around 40 bullets at them and kill them. And then Alex kept on running and he started running back to his hotel room. But Alex did a summersault and more Sandinista soldiers started going after Alex and kept on shooting at him and Alex was able to strike back them and shot more bullets at them but sadly also destroying a lot of property in the process. And then all of a sudden the Sandinistas started firing a lot of rocket launchers at Alex and Alex was able to the dodge explosions and the rockets that were firing at Alex. Alex then hid behind more walls and he kept on firing more bullets at the Sandinistas and killing 50 of them "No dejes que escape con los planos!!!" one of the Sandinista soldiers yelled and then Alex loaded up his gun again and with rapid fire trigging in Alex's little finger, Alex then started to firing 100 bullets at more Sandinistas that were coming at him and shot them in very different places including the head, shoulders, and sometimes in the neck. But then as Alex running out of bullets to load, Alex then started running and he was able to hide inside of a underground base and from there, the Sandinistas then retreated and started heading back to their headquarters.

Alex then was able to get out of the base and he was able climb through the latter. And Alex after a really huge night of fighting and also sneaking into an island base, started heading back to his hotel room. And as Alex did this, he really started think a lot about what the businesses owner said. And then he started thinking about Morella and Paul and the old footage of both of them from the 1960's was very visible inside of Alex's Brain. Alex was able to get inside his hotel room and he then went to sleep and in Alex's mind, he knew that he had to go find the contras very soon and help them in anyway that he could.

Chapter 4 Finding the Contras and Breaking into the Main Sandinista base

Alex then woke up the next day and he was able to take a shower and get dressed. And then right away on the phone, Alex then got a phone call and it was from Michael "Hey Michael" Alex said "Hey Alex, what's the statues in Nicaragua so far?" Michael asked "Yeah so far I was able to break into an island base and I was able to steel the blue prints and Borodina is helping the

Sandinistas and the socialists in Cuba and also helping Chavez and Castro as well" Alex said "oh my god that's awful. Do Pablo and Ashley know anything about this?" Michael asked, "No they don't Michael. But I'm going to tell them very soon" Alex said "Alright good. What about finding the Lewis?" Michael asked "no sign of them yet. But I believe I am getting very close to finding them" Alex said "well I just herd word the contras in San Ramon up in the hills and you should be able to find them. And I believe I also herd word that they are going to break into a Sandinista computer headquarter building. Good luck Alex" Michael said "Thanks Michael" Alex said and then Alex was able to hang up the phone and then Alex then started calling both Ashley and Pablo and they didn't pick up the phone, but Alex then started to leave a message "Hey guys, I'm about to help the contras and we are going to break into computer base. I don't know anymore then that. But I will keep you guys updated" Alex said and then Alex hung up the phone and then Alex headed out the door.

Alex then started heading north part of Nicaragua and during his drive, Alex through a lot of poor villages and poor people and he knew that in his heart and these socialist people really had to be stopped. Alex then kept on driving and then he saw some Nicaraguan people with a lot of weapons and he was able to meet them in the woods. And then one of them turned around and they saw Alex "Hello Mr. Aussmen" one of them said to him "I am Rivera Sanchez from Spain and a junior operative of the United States government" Rivera said "The names Aussmen…Alex Aussmen" Alex said "It's a pleasure to meet you Mr. Aussmen. In a matter of minutes our people were able to steel a bus and we are heading to see release American hostages from the Sandinista head quarters. And one of them is being torched with jewelry and liquid silicon as well" Rivera said and then all of a sudden, the bus was able to come and Alex and contras were able to get on the bus and they started heading to Managua. And as Alex was able to get on the bus he saw a lot of Nicaraguan people with guns and other weapons as well. The bus ride itself took around 3 hours but then around 6PM or so they were able to get to the main Sandinista headquarters building in the capital. "Ready to save the world Alex?" Rivera said "Not only am I ready to save the world, I want to kill the monster that is helping these shit-heads!!!" Alex said

And moments later, inside of the building, Victoria Borodina was walking in the hall way and a lot of Sandinista soldiers were bowing down to her like she was an empress or like the freaking queen of England. And then she walked into the main room where she had another office inside of the Sandinista building and there was a lot of Americans that were getting torched by liquid jewelry and they were shoving their faces on to a computer screen. And the screen itself was showing a lot of socialist propaganda and the Sandinistas were shoving their heads into the computer and destroying their eyesight and destroying their brains as well. And then there was also a lot of screaming and yelling as the Americans were getting tortured as well. "Soon I will be able to create a lot of very smart and intellectual beings that will be able to destroy a lot of people and destroy first world nations. And then I will be able to create a new world order!!!!!! And then I will have these new computers controlling everybody and making them believe the Sandinistas and Soviet Union's ideology and then we will also remove President Reagan from office as well....MUAHAHAHAHAHAHAHAHAHAHAHAHAHAHAHAHAHAHAHAHAHAHA HAHAAHAHAHAHAHA BRAHAHAHAHAHAHAHAHAHAHAHAHAHAHAHAHAHAHAHAHAHAHAHAHAH AHAHAHAHAHAHAHAHAHAHAHAHAHAHAHAHAHAHAHAHAHAHAHAHAHAHAH AHAHAHA!!!!!!!!!!!!!!!" Borodina laughed as more Americans were getting torched by the Sandinistas and also more corrupted IBM computers and liquid jewelry was being created.

And then moments later, Alex and the contras were able to sneak into the Sandinista building and then they were able to kill some soldiers. And as they were entering the building, Alex then started having flashbacks of 1976 and flashing back to Amber Wade's death and then also fighting Kramer Quinne as well. "Alright well Alex. All you have to do is find the power switch and destroy the Sandinistas assets. This will stop all the operations of creating the silicon and the jewelry and also stop the computers being made as well" Sanchez said "and then also there is another base that in Venezuela as well that are doing the same things as well" Sanchez added. And then during that time, Pablo and Ashley were able to catch up to Alex and there wearing American flag jumpsuits and they were able to beat up some Sandinista soldiers and also shoot them in the head and kill around 8 of them using a silenced PP7 gun. "That must be the entrance to get in, we have to help Alex as much as we could" Pablo said

And then Alex was able to get into the main hall and around the main room of the building, and Alex everywhere he turned was Sandinista artwork and propaganda everywhere including pictures of Castro killing President Reagan and burning an American flag and also a painting of Ortega pressing a button and firing nuclear weapons at the United States of America and bombing America, England, and also other first world countries as well. And as Alex was seeing all of this, Alex just started steaming and it really burned him really bad and Alex had a very angry and very pissed off look on his face and inside of his mind, he really wanted kill Ortega, Chavez and also kill Castro as well. And then as Alex kept on sneaking around, one of the Sandinista soldiers saw him and they quickly got out their guns and they were about to shoot at Alex "La Raza, La Raza, La Raza, La Raza, La Raza!!!!!!!!" The Sandinistas yelled and then Alex grunted his teeth and anger and Alex got really angry and mad and Alex right away took out an A33 riffle and he started firing 900 bullets at the Sandinistas and killing a lot of them in the building. And then all of a sudden, more Sandinista soldiers saw Alex and they hit the alarm and the alarm in the building started going crazy "DIE MOTHERFUCKERS DIE!!!!!!!!" Alex yelled in anger and Alex kept on firing a lot more bullets at more Sandinistas and killing more of them "Consigue el!!!! Americano" The Sandinistas yelled and Alex kept firing and firing more bullets at more Sandinista soldiers coming at him "ALL OF YOU COMMUNIST AND SOCALIST PEOPLE CAN ALL GO TO HELL!!!!!!!" Alex yelled and Alex kept on shooting and there was a lot of explosions and the building itself was catching on fire. More Sandinista soldiers and police from the Nicaraguan government got into the building and they also started shooting at Alex. But with every cell in Alex's autistic body and in his finger, Alex was just bleeding red, white, blue and bleeding the American flag inside of him "GO BACK TO CUBA YOU CHILDREN AND MOTHER KILLING SON OF A BITCHES!!!!!!" Alex yelled "Esta es su última ADVERTENCIA, señor Aussmen. Y deja de disparar y entrega tu arma." The Sandinistas yelled over a blow horn "DIE, DIE, DIE, DIE, DIE!!!!!!!!...FOR AMERICA!!!!!!" Alex yelled as he was yelling like a manic and like a crazy person and Alex kept on firing a lot of gun bullets at more Sandinista soldiers. And then more of contras helped Alex in fighting the Sandinistas and Nicaraguan government. "Alex, we got to this, go save the hostages!!!" Ashley said and then Alex started running up the stairs and Alex fired more bullets at more Sandinista soldiers and killing them as he was running.

Alex then got to the main floor and he saw 30 American hostages in jail cells and Alex started freeing all of them. Alex then out a walke-talkie and he started talking in it "Michael, we need some big American planes to get the hostages out of here" Alex said "Alright perfect. I will do that" Michael said and then all of a sudden a lot of huge cargo plans started flying to Nicaragua and firing a lot of bullets at Sandinista air planes chasing them and was able to destroy 5 planes that were chasing them.

Then Alex kept on running and then as his mind was going at a face pace, Alex then set a mine bomb on the main door and Alex shot at the bomb and was able to blow up the door and huge explosion happened. And all of a sudden, in the other room Borodina forced against the wall and so where Chavez, Ortega, and Castro "¡ ¿Qué coño está pasando?!" Castro yelled and then Alex walked into the room and Alex and more Sandinista soldiers kept coming at him and Alex jumped on a desk and Alex kicked one of them in the face and fired more bullets at more soldiers that were coming at him. Alex then jumped in the air and whacked more of them in the face and shot another bullet at another explosive and causing another explosion. And then as Castro tried to tackle Alex and then without really thinking, Alex right away turned back and he just flat out punched Fidel Castro right in the face and kicked him in the balls and then Chavez forced him against the wall "Te voy a enseñar cómo matamos americanos como en Venezuela" Chavez said and then he grabbed Alex by the neck and then Alex head butted him really bad and Alex did a boxing pose and Alex dodged all of Chavez's punches and punched Hugo Chavez in the face 7 times and kicked him in the stomach and Chavez punched Alex in the face and slammed his head against the wall and Alex started grunting really bad "Es una lástima que los americanos sean tan débiles!!!" Chavez said and then Alex right away saw a machete on the table and grabbed it and swung the machete knife at gave Chavez a cut around his eye and then Alex kicked him in the face and stabbed him in the arm and he started screaming and yelling and blood started coming out of his arm.

And then Ortega tried to attack Alex but Alex turned back and did karate kick and kicked Ortega in the face and then he fell flat on his back and he got back up again and Alex grabbed the same machete knife and gave Ortega a cut and caused more screaming and yelling and Alex grunted his teeth and stabbed Ortega in the arm And Alex had a very angry and no remorse stair on his face. And then grabbed Ortega by the head and slammed him to the wall and pointed his riffle at his head "It's time finish you off once and for all and then Alex pushed him in the ledge and he started falling to his death and he landed on sharp rocks and was knocked out. And then Chavez and Castro were also knocked out on the floor with blood coming out of their arms.

Alex then walked over to the Americans and was able to untie them "There is a cargo plane that will take you back to the states" Alex said and then the hostages were able to escape. But then as they did so, all of a sudden out of the shadows, an evil red and black shadow was walking towards Alex "I have to admit Alex, you were able to destroy this building in no time" Borodina said "but you are going to loose the war against me and it doesn't matter what you do, I will always be around to haunt you!!!" Borodina said, "I am not afraid of you Borodina!!!!" Alex said, "I knew you would say something like that Alex. But I believe it's really too late to save the rest of the American hostages that are in Venezuela as we speak. And I will really enjoy once they kill you and I will be watching from my castle in Ukraine as well!!!!" Borodina said, "You will never get away with this Borodina!!!! And I will tell everybody about your crimes as well" Alex said And then all of a sudden, Borodina took out a rocket launcher and she pointed the weapon at Alex and she was about to fire at him "Good bye Mr. Aussmen!!!!!!" Borodina yelled and then Alex did a summersault and he grabbed a magnum gun and shot Victoria's room and Victoria screamed in pain but she was also able to fire the rocket launcher and cause a really huge explosion and Alex was able to survive the explosion and Alex was grabbing on to a rope and more Sandinista army and police started running towards the building and firing at more American agents and also firing at the contras as well. The contras were able to fire back with a lot of weapons from the United States and cause a lot chaos and explosions and blowing up a lot of Sandinista army tanks in the process as well. "Muerte a América!!!!" The Sandinistas yelled and more contras and Americans including Ashley started firing their guns at the Sandinistas and killing them. And then whole thing was caught around the Nicaraguan media and then to CNN as well.

Alex then let go and he was able to land on the ground and then as more of the fighting was going on, Alex then saw a jet, and then Alex started running towards the jet that was at the Nicaragua airport and more Sandinistas were chasing and going after Alex and firing bullets at him as well. Alex was able to get into the jet and then as he was turning on the jet, he saw some machine guns and he started firing the machine gun at more Sandinista army tanks and more Sandinista cars coming at him. And Alex was able to cause a lot of explosions and fires all around the airports and army tanks and other cars were catching on fire. And then Alex started flying the plane and the plane started to go in motion and started going really fast and more Sandinistas kept chasing after Alex. But then with all his force and might, Alex pulled the main lever inside of the jet and all of a sudden, the jet took off in the air and Borodina and other Sandinista soldiers saw the jet up in the air "God almighty!!!" Borodina said, "Alex just does not know when to take a fucking hint!!!" Borodina said and then Ashley and Pablo caught up to the Sandinistas and started firing around 900 bullets at the Sandinistas and killed around 500 of them and then were able to knock out 700 of them and arrest them in chains and Ashley pointed a gun at some of them "By the authority of the United States of America all of you are placed under arrest and taken to Washington DC to be killed" Ashley said And then Ashley and Pablo started rounding up a lot Sandinista soldiers and policemen and putting them on a cargo plane to Washington DC to be executed would be in chains and hand-cuffs.

Ashley then saw Alex's plane as Alex heading to Venezuela to stop Borodina once and for all and also stop Cruz as well. "Good luck Alex" Ashley said

Chapter 5 Borodina's 2nd base in Venezuela

As Alex was flying the jet, he kept on flying more and more south. Intel he was able to see the Venezuela flag from a distance. And then that is when Alex started to land the airplane around one of their military bases. And once Alex got there, the country of Venezuela looked like a normal country but there were still signs of poverty in the country. Alex got off the airplane and Alex knew that he had to go really fast because he knew that 700 something Sandinistas were on his tail and were also after Alex as well. Alex then was able to run through the villages and he knew that the main computer base was located somewhere. And then Alex saw a motorcycle and he was able to steel a motorcycle and he started heading to Caracas. As Alex was on the motorcycle he saw a lot of Venezuela's history and culture but also he saw the buildings of the corporations that they had there and then he saw the stores there as well. But Alex did notice right away that everything in there was so expense that not even an average American couldn't buy it. And then also there was an apple computer that Venezuela flag colors on it as well. And during that time it was starting to reach around 7PM and then without thinking, Alex then went into the very expensive store and he started looking around. And all though the prices were concerning to Alex, he knew that he had to stay focused. And then as Alex kept on walking he then opened another door and he saw another store and another grocery store that was short on supplies and other food. And then Alex saw lever that was by the check stand and he also noticed a lot of pictures of the wall of a little girl with blonde hair with her father. And Alex knew that he was not in friendly waters and not in a very good environment. All of a sudden, an elevator showed up out of nowhere and Alex went on the elevator and the elevator started taking him down. As the elevator kept on going down, Alex saw more apple and IBM computers and then also rooms of CPUs everywhere that had people speaking Spanish and saying a lot of socialist and communist propaganda. And then as elevator stopped, Alex then looked around and he saw workers with wearing uniforms of Sandinista colors and also the colors of the Venezuela flag as well. And then as Alex kept on walking, he then all of a sudden turned back and he saw Cruz wearing a general outfit "hello Alex!!!!" Cruz said and then all of a sudden Cruz punched him in the face and Alex was hand-cuffed and Venezuelan soldiers started taking Alex to a very fancy room in the base and then all of a sudden, sitting in a blue fancy office chair was Victoria Borodina and then as Alex opened his eyes, he saw that he was in a very fancy room that had the colors of the Venezuela flag but also the Venezuela flag and also the Sandinista flag as well and Alex saw a lot of fancy elements in the room and all of a sudden, Victoria got out from her chair and she grabbed a pistol gun "Alex, what an unpleasant surprise that you were able to make it to the very corrupted and the very scary and evil country of Venezuela" Borodina said "You will never get away with this Borodina!!!!" Alex said and then all of a sudden, Borodina snapped her fingers and all of a sudden a lot of Sandinista soldiers and Venezuelan soldiers showed up. And not only that but also Ashley and Pablo also were tied up and guns pointed at their heads and Ashley started grunting "It really sounds like that tables have now turned Mr. Aussmen. In a matter of minutes my computers that I built will brainwash a lot of Americans and thinking that socialism and communism are good. And then from there, the computers will blow up the United States of America and then, I will then use Cruz to take over both Nicaragua and Venezuela and over throw all the countries in central and south America. And then create our own version of the Soviet Union in both continents" Borodina said "And then last but not least, we will also frame president Reagan get him out of office and then kill the vice president and then put our candidate in the democratic party that will embrace all the stuff I just talked about only to continue making America a very weak and clueless country" Borodina said and then Alex had a very angry and pissed off look on his face "Yeah like the hell all that stuff is going to work Victoria!!!" Alex said "Oh that's what you think, and once all that stuff is done, I will then be Ukraine and then make my gateway to Cuba. And as you!!!!!!...You have melted and annoyed me and feared with my evil plans for the last time Mr. Aussmen!!!!!!!" Victoria said in complete anger "And it's time that I killed you once and for all!!!!" Victoria said and then all of a sudden Victoria then grabbed a Venezuelan sword and pointed the sword at Alex's neck and then as Victoria did this, Alex did notice the same blue jewelry that the businesses owner was talking about and he saw it. And then Alex started to flash back to the old

1960's footage of both Morella and Paul. "And I will enjoy killing you and leaving to die in Venezuela!!!!" Borodina said and then all of a sudden, Alex right way head butted Borodina in the stomach and then stepped on her foot. And then Alex jumped up in the air and he was able to get himself unchained and break through and then Pablo then started fighting some of the soldiers and Ashley grabbed one of the soldiers and punched one of them in the face and she also started fighting some of them as well.

Alex then kept on fighting a lot of Venezuelan soldiers and the Sandinista thugs inside of the room. Alex then was able to grab a gun and he started shooting around 600 bullets at them and killing them. And then Ashley did a lot of jumps and backflips and she loaded up her gun a couple of different times and she kept on shooting at them. Pablo then kept on fighting some of the thugs and then Pablo was able to grab the blue diamond that was on the wall and he was able to throw it to Alex "Alex, I believe that this diamond will destroy the computers don't let them be processed. Go!!!" Pablo said and then Alex started running and chasing after Borodina and Victoria started running and Victoria kept on turning back and she started shooting an A33 riffle at Alex and Alex was able to dodge the bullets and also shoot back at her. Alex then kept on chasing Borodina and then Alex was able to get to a really huge computer room and then a lot of red, blue, and yellow colors started flashing inside of the room, and then all of a sudden Victoria grabbed a sword and gave Alex a really huge cut on his arm and Victoria punched Alex in the face and slammed his head on to a computer. And then Alex grabbed Borodina's arm and slammed her head on to another computer screen and caused one of the screen to break and Alex started to burn parts of Borodina's face and Borodina's face really bad. And then Borodina punched Alex from behind and then Alex grabbed a staff as Borodina was getting ready to strike at Alex, Alex then grunted really hard and whacked Borodina in the face and was able to knock her out and a lot of jewelry was able to get into her face and also a lot of flames were starting to burn parts of the left side of face around her chin. And then all of a sudden a trap door appeared and Borodina fell through the trap door. And even though Borodina was knocked out very badly, Alex knew it wasn't going to be the last he saw of her.

And then all of a sudden, Cruz then showed up and he slammed Alex against the wall and Cruz started throwing a lot of punches and kicks at Alex then Cruz punched Alex in the face 6 times. And then Cruz throw Alex against a couple of keyboards that powered the corrupt computers. And then Cruz attacked Alex again but Alex was able to dodge the punch and another kick and grabbed Cruz by the leg and slammed him to the ground and Alex punched Cruz in the face and then Cruz kicked Alex in the face and Alex ended up on the ground and Cruz used his metal arm to crush and punch Alex on the ground. And then Alex got up and he grabbed on to a sword to protect himself and then Cruz grabbed Alex's wrist really hard and slammed him against the wall again. "Le debo una muerte muy dolorosa, señor Aussmen." Cruz said and then Alex dodged another attack and then Alex grabbed the staff again and whacked Cruz in the head 6 times with the staff. And then Alex saw the blue jewelry diamond on the ground and Alex started racing to get it but then Cruz was able to catch up to him and grab him by the leg and then Cruz grabbed Alex's leg and threw Alex up in the air smashed him against a glass window. Alex felt the glass of the window cracking and then Cruz took out a Venezuelan sword and started walking towards Alex "You can't win Alex!!!! There is nothing you can do about it. I will now rule over the country of Nicaragua and Venezuela!!!!" Cruz yelled and then saw a knife and then Alex grabbed the knife and he threw the knife and cut Cruz in the face and then Alex started to running towards the blue jewelry and Alex used the point tip of the blue ruby and Alex all of a sudden with all the force that he had, then just stabbed Cruz right in the fore-head and then all of a sudden Cruz's brain started getting really weak and his brain cells started dying and parts of his body also started dying as well. And then Cruz started screaming and yelling in the process. And then Cruz's skin started turning blue and his eye colors just started black and then Alex grabbed the Venezuelan sword and stabbed Cruz in the head and Cruz feel to the ground and a lot of blood started coming out. And then all of a sudden, Cruz's forehead exploded and Alex saw that Cruz's brain a lot of artificial chemicals and grey and blue liquids inside. And then also Alex saw a piece of metal in the brain that was really making Cruz really smart as well.

And then without wasting anytime, Alex then started running to the computers and with staff in his hand he then started destroying all the computers and the blue jewelry started destroying the corrupted computers and there were a lot of explosions and flames. And then as the computers exploded, then more them underground that were getting shipped, also started to explode and a really huge explosion in Caracas and a lot of people saw the explosion happening. And then Alex was able to grab the main keycard and also grab Cruz's credit card and Borodina's credit card and he started running back to the main part of the room. And then Alex, Pablo and Ashley started shooting at a lot of bad guys and they started running and more explosions started happening and the base was catching on fire like crazy. And then more of the computers inside of the base and all over the country of Venezuela and Nicaragua started to explode into flames and destroying a lot of Sandinista buildings in the country.

Alex, Pablo, and Ashley were able to escape from the base and then more explosions started happening and a lot. And then they were able to grab a car and Alex was driving the car and all of a sudden a lot of Venezuela soldiers and police started chasing them and shooting at them. "We have to get out of here Alex" Ashley said "Don't worry we will" Alex said and Alex started to hear more the police sirens coming after him. "¡ abran fuego!!!" they yelled and then Pablo got out a gun and he started shooting at them and killing them. Ashley then poked her out and she started firing a lot of rockets at the Venezuelan soldiers and blowing up their cars and some of the cars went up in the air and landed on the top of the car and crashed into a building and caused another huge explosion with fire and flames everywhere. Alex then kept on driving really fast on the road and going around 700 miles per hour and they were able to get to the airport. They then got out of the car and more soldiers showed up and started shooting at them. Alex then got out a riffle gun and started shooting 900 bullets at the soldiers and killing them and Pablo also started firing a gun as well. They then started running to the airplane and Ashley started powering up the plane and Pablo was also inside of the plane as well. Alex then stopped firing his gun and he started running to the plane. And with the plane being really bumpy, Alex grabbed on the jet stairs with all of his might and he started climbing into the plane and more soldiers kept on firing. Alex, Pablo, and Ashley were able to escape and they flew up in the air and they then started heading northeast. "So where to Alex?" Ashley asked "we have to get to Washington DC and get there fast" Alex said "And then once we get there we have to find a way to testify and tell the government about the Sandinistas and about Victoria Borodina as well" Alex said and then Alex got on the microphone and he then pressed the button and he then started talking "Michael we are heading to Washington DC. Met us around Capitol Hill and I will give you more information on what to do next" Alex said, "Alright sounds good Alex" Michael said and from there Alex, Pablo, and Ashley started heading to Washington DC and Alex finally in front of the country can explain what the true intentions of Sandinistas and Borodina truly are.

Chapter 6 Testifying in Washington DC and The Sandinistas strike back in the Nation's capitol

And then as Alex, Pablo, and Ashley were able to get to Washington DC. Alex was able to land on the jet in an airport in Washington DC., they then got off the plane and it was around 7PM which was very late and they knew that they had look for a hotel and also buy some new clothes as well. As they got to their hotel room and checked in, Alex then was looking at the window and he still felt a little bit of emptiness. And it's mainly because he was able to save the people that were trapped inside of the Sandinista building in Nicaragua but he wasn't able to find the Lewis in Nicaragua at all. And Alex really thought at this point that they could be dead and that Sandinistas might have killed them. And then during that night, Ashley came into Alex's room to have a conversation with him "So are nervous at all for being inside the capitol building?" Ashley asked, "Sadly I am very nervous. Because I know everything about them and who their inner connections are as well" Alex said "Well I think you are going to do just fine Alex. And we will be there with you" Ashley said and then during that night, Ashley then gave Alex a kiss on the check and then she headed to bed.

Alex then also went to bed as well and as Alex was sleeping, he then started having dreams and flash-backs of all the missions that he went on that were Nicaragua related and he knew that the Sandinistas were very powerful and how many bad guys that they have created to stop Alex. And Alex also had a dream that the Sandinistas were able to destroy the United States of America and take over the world with Borodina leading the charge and that there was nothing Alex can do to stop it.

Alex was able to get up the next morning and as he did so, he then saw the sun rise on our nation's capital. And then sun itself was shinning on the Lincoln memorial and other memorial sites as well. Alex then got up and he put on a 1980's suit and tie and also for good luck, Alex also brought aviator sunglasses to wear. As Alex was getting closer to being ready and getting ready to head out the door, Alex also prepared a briefcase of every single detail and lots of documents to prove how evil the Sandinistas truly are. Alex then got ready and he got out of his hotel room wearing a 1980's suit wearing his aviator sunglasses and Alex was able to take a taxi to capitol hill in Washington DC and the taxi started taking him to the building. And during the ride, Alex saw a lot of the key elements of Washington DC and he was looking at the window through out the whole car ride. Alex was able to get out of the car and he was able to pay the driver. And without turning back, Alex then started walking into the capitol building and he went through all the customs and the X-Ray machines just fine and from there, he just kept on going. As Alex kept on walking, he also saw his name on a very fancy schedule sheet of paper inside of a gold frame. Alex then sat down and he started waiting Intel it was time for him to go in. And as Alex was waiting, he then saw a lot of senators walking and it appeared that Alex was going to be part a committee meeting as well. Then as the time got closer and closer, the doors then opened and Alex got into the room and he sat down on one of the chairs. Alex set his briefcase on the table and he put the microphone very close to him. And then Alex saw a lot of the senators walking in and they sat down and then was some other people that sat down in their seats to watch the meeting as well.

The door then started to close and the meeting was about to begin "Alright we here and ready to begin our new meeting that is related to the Iran contra scandal. And we are trying to look for as much information about possible" one of the senators said "Alright plaintiff will stand up and raise their right hand and repeat these words and start with your name as well" the main senator said "State your name" one of them said "Alexander Aussmen" Alex said "repeat after me" one of them said "Do you swear to tell the truth and nothing but the truth" one of them asked "Yes" Alex said "Alright good" the main senator said "Alright now please be seated" they said and then Alex sat down "Now Mr. Aussmen I understand that were in Nicaragua in Central America during the contra scandal. Is that correct sir? Yes or no" the senator said "Yes" Alex said "And what was your purpose for being in Nicaragua Mr. Aussmen" the senator asked "Well senator the reason I was down there is because the Sandinistas are a very powerful socialist party in Nicaragua and they are just as evil as the Nazis were in World War II and also they are working with the communist in Russia as well. But they also want to take over the world and destroy the United States of America as well" Alex said "Do you know who else is funding them?" another senator asked "Yes I know who is helping and funding them as well. They are being funded by Fidel Castro and Hugo Chavez and by an evil communist name Victoria Borodina who is in Ukraine right now as we speak" Alex said "I even have papers to testify" Alex said and then right away, Alex was able to open his briefcase and as he did so, Pablo and Ashley were able to get into the room and sit behind other crowds of people. And then other senators were able to see all of Alex's documents that he prepared for quite some time of every record and stat of how evil the Sandinistas truly are "wow these are a lot of documents Mr. Aussmen. What do you do for a living sir?" the senator asked "I am a private investigator and I have been a private secret agent since 1976" Alex said "Oh wow that's very long sir. So you have been going after mad people and criminals since you were 16 years old. You must have had good training by good people" the senator said "yes sir" Alex said "Did you know when you were working with the contras that they had weapons from Iraq yes or no?" the senator asked "No sadly I did not know that senator" Alex said "But I also believe in the future however that we must take down dictators and provide peace through out the world as well. Because I know the lot of countries do not have the same freedoms like we do. And eventually those same dictators are going to try to destroy the United States of America" Alex said and then as Alex was on TV, there some Sandinistas that saw Alex on TV, and they then started going on fighter planes and they started heading to Washington DC and around 66 airplanes were in the air and started heading Northeast.

"Is they're anything else that you want to add Mr. Aussmen?" the senator asked "No I have no further comment" Alex said, "oh okay. Well I believe that conclude this meeting I believe and hopefully someday we will go after the Sandinistas as well" the senator said and then Alex started walking out of the room and Pablo and Ashley were able to catch up to Alex "Alex you did a really great job" Pablo said "oh thanks man. Yeah I tried the best that I could" Alex said "Well I believe you did a great job" Ashley said and then as they were able to get out of the capitol hill building, they then started walking down the stairs "So where to?" Ashley asked, "sadly I really don't know. I know that I am pretty hungry so we can go somewhere for lunch" Alex said but then all of a sudden, Alex herd a lot of airplanes that were in the air they were all black and red airplanes that were coming towards him "Oh no we have to get out of here right now!!!!!! Come on!!!!" Alex said and then all of a sudden Alex, Pablo, and Ashley then started running to avoid the guns firing bullets at them and some of the Sandinista jets landed around Washington DC and around 33 jets landed on the ground and destroyed a lot property as well.

Alex and Ashley and Pablo hid around the Lincoln memorial and then more Sandinista surrounded the Lincoln memorial and one of them pointed a gun at Alex's head "No se mueva, señor Aussmen. Sabemos lo que dijiste de nosotros. Y te vamos a llevar a Nicaragua para ser arrestado!!!" one of the Sandinista soldiers said and then Alex turned back and he raised his hands but then all of a sudden Alex then punched the Sandinista solider in the face and kicked him in the stomach and Alex was able to grab his riffle gun and then Alex started shooting the gun at a lot of Sandinista soldiers coming towards him. And then Ashley and Pablo started fighting other Sandinista soldiers and they were able to grab their guns and they also started shooting at Sandinista soldiers coming at them. And then some of the Sandinista soldiers started shooting at them non stop and more of them started coming out of the airplane and they started firing rocket launchers and grenade launchers at Alex, Ashley, and Pablo. They all kept on running and they kept on shooting a lot of bullets at the Sandinistas. And Alex was able to blow up 5 more airplanes that were coming and he was able to kill around 200 Sandinista soldiers in the air. And the airplanes then started falling through the sky and a lot of airplanes were exploding in the sky. And around 7 Sandinista jet airplanes exploded.

Alex kept on fighting a lot of Sandinista soldiers that were coming at him. And Alex was able to fire around 600 bullets and he also kept on reloading the bullets and he kept on firing and firing "Necesitamos copia de respaldo ahora mismo" One of the Sandinista soldiers said And then more of them just kept on coming after Alex and then Alex, Ashley, and Pablo were able to find shelter and they kept on running Intel they got to the main street of the capital and more Sandinista airplanes started landing everywhere and Sandinista army tanks started chasing after them. But then after running, Alex saw a couple of grenades and mine bombs and then Alex started throwing the bombs at the Sandinista army tanks and Alex was able to cause 9 different explosions. Alex then was able to find more rockets to reload his rocket launcher gun and he kept on firing more rockets at Sandinista army tanks and blowing 19 more of them causing more explosions and fires around Washington DC.

Alex and Ashley were able to duck around a broken car and Alex kept on using his rocket launcher to fire and strike back at the Sandinistas and he was able to kill around 90 of them. And then as they did so the chaos around them really stopped and it appeared for a moment that Alex was able to kill all the Sandinistas. But then all of a sudden a fighter jet with a Ukraine flag on it was able to land on the ground. And then as it landed on the ground, Borodina got out of jet and she was wearing a Sandinista general uniform on. But only this time however she had blue jewelry scares on her face and with parts of her face burned up as well "Well hello Alex. You truly believe all your guns and weapons are going to stop me and my new huge group of allies that I have." Borodina said and then all of a sudden huge number of Sandinista and Venezuelan soldiers showed up with riffles in their hands "You are out numbered Alex, The whole world knows who you are. And will want to kill you including myself" Borodina said and then all of a sudden, Borodina then took out another remote that had a Sandinista and Venezuela flag on it "I also was able to create new computers in the states while you were in capitol hill and soon a lot of jewelry is going to be create a lot of super smart humans to destroy Mr. Aussmen and in a matter minutes I will have the information of every American in the states as well with my new Sandinista and Venezuelan powered computers. And there will be nothing you can do about it" Borodina said "Your wrong Borodina, there is always something I can do about it" Alex said and then Borodina was looking at him, Alex started flashbacking to the codes that Millet and Morella had in the footage and then Alex saw another remote in Borodina's pocket and then as Borodina was about to attack Alex, Alex then was able to get out a gun as a prop and he hit Borodina in the face with the gun and right away remote fell out of her pocket and Alex was able to grab the remote and Alex got out his gun and he shoot Borodina in right eye and Borodina started screaming and yelling and a lot of blood started coming out of her eye. Alex then closed his eyes and he took a leap of faith and he started trying to remember the codes that Cruz was typing on the old IBM computers back in 1976 and in the old 1960's footage. Alex then was able to type the codes on the remote and the remote that Nicaraguan flag was able to destroy the red silicon jewelry inside of the courted computers built by the Sandinistas and the computers were able to shut down and they started breaking down and the screen fell off of them in different places around the capitol and around the United States as well. And then out of the computers was a red ruby that had jewelry and poison inside of it.

But then as Alex was able to stop Borodina's plane once and for all, then Borodina was able to get up and she had a riffle gun in her hand "You might have stopped my plan. But the bad guys will always win Mr. Aussmen!!!!....." Borodina said and then all of a sudden, Borodina fired a bullet at Alex then all of a sudden, the bullet knocked out Alex and he saw and shot in the arm really bad. "Alex!!!!" Ashley said and then Ashley took out a gun and she kept on shooting at Borodina and she started to escape using a Sandinista jet and more the Sandinistas started to escape from Washington DC. And then the local police show up and they started firing at the Sandinistas and also federal Unites States troops showed up and they also started firing at the Sandinistas and they were able to kill 66 of them and capture around 88 Sandinista soldiers. But Alex was not able to see all of that stuff and Alex was put on a medical table and he was taken to the hospital "It's okay, it's going to be okay Alex..." Ashley said and then Alex kept on closing his eyes and from there his vision was pitch black.

During all that time Alex was knocked out, he really felt like in that moment he was going to die. And then in his dream Alex got a glimpse of the future in 30 years from now and he saw that the country was very different but also in the worst ways possible. He saw a lot of the smart phones people were using and a lot of futuristic cars. But then he also noticed a lot of people that were brain-washed by the government and have become very left and having bull-crap ideas and worst of all, the dream turned into a nightmare and that everybody started going after Alex and they kept saying "Capitalism is evil!!!! Get him!!!!!" they yelled and then Alex started running and he Seattle burning up in flames and the rest of the country getting destroyed as well. And Alex really wanted the dream to be over because it really was like his personal hell and he really hooped this was a future that would never happen and while he was knocked out, he kept on shaking his body around.

The doctors then took Alex to Washington DC and they were able to get the bullet out of his arm while he was asleep. And then they also put him on medicine while he was sleeping. Ashley and Pablo were also watching Alex from a far in the hospital. And then moments later, the doctors decided to send Alex back to Seattle, Washington for future treatment. And then Alex was carried on medical airplane that was sending him to a hospital clinic in downtown Seattle. And during that time, Alex kept on having a lot of good and bad dreams while he was sleeping and while he was knocked out and they were all dreams that were about the future and also about Ashley and also about Michael as well and hoping that he was alright as well. But overall, Alex really didn't know what was truly happening and all he could do now was sleep and rest Intel he was able to get back to reality again.

Chapter 7 Waking up in the hospital and Back in Seattle again, and finding the Lewis's again

After a couple of days in the hospital, Alex then was able to wake up around 5 weeks later. As Alex woke up in the hospital, he then looked at the window and he was so happy to be home in Seattle again and he was really happy to see the Seattle skyline again. But as Alex opened his eyes, he saw a beautiful and very stunning female nurse that was walking towards him. "Well good morning Mr. Aussmen" she said "Are you feeling okay?" she asked, "Yeah what happened?" Alex asked "parts of your circle was able to get you here and 5 weeks ago, you were in Washington DC and I believe you were fighting a lot of Sandinista soldiers in our nation's capital. Your hero" She said "Was I able to stop them?" Alex asked, "that part I don't know but I do believe you have some people that are going to pick you up" she said "Do you want me to get you anything to drink?" she asked "Um just a glass of orange juice" Alex said and then she walked away and Alex started checking her out head to toe. But then as he did so, all of a sudden an older woman in her late 40's showed and also with a man in his 50's also came into the room as well and it was Emmy and Matthew "Hello Alex" Matthew said "Matthew, Emmy, thank god you guys are alive!!!" Alex said, "Are you okay Alex?" Emmy said, "I'm okay. I just feel very light and sadly very weak but overall I'm okay" Alex said "Oh okay good" Matthew said "I thought you guys were trapped in Nicaragua and I thought I was never going to see you guys again" Alex said "We were able to get rescued by some American troops. And I believe one of your friends saved us while you were dealing with Borodina" Emmy said "Well I am just glad you guys are okay" Alex said and then the same female nurse walked back into the room "Alright Mr. Aussmen. The doctor checked all of your boxes and I will get your clothes and you will be free to go" The nurse said "Thank you so much my dear" Alex said "You need me to give you a lift somewhere Alex?" Matthew asked "sure why not" Alex said

And then later that day, Alex was released from the hospital and he was able to get on his suit he was wearing 5 weeks ago. Alex then started walking to Emmy and Matthew's car and then they started driving Alex back to his apartment. They then stopped the car and then Matthew and Emmy looked up "So is this where you live?" Matthew asked, "Yeah this is my apartment that I live in" Alex said "Wow its very beautiful Alex" Emmy said "oh thank you guys" Alex said "Well if you ever need anything Alex, you are always welcome to call us" Matthew said "Alright okay" Alex said and then Matthew and Emmy drove off and Alex started walking into the building and going inside the elevator. As Alex got to his apartment, he then was very lucky to be alive and he sat down on his couch and he started playing Nintendo on his big screen TV and also started drinking a bud light and eating junk food as well. But then around nighttime however, Alex then looked at the Seattle skyline again from his window and then he also noticed a reflection in the window and it was Ashley and Alex turned back. "Man I am so glad to see you" Alex said "oh well I was here guarding your place. And also waiting for you to come into bed with me..." Ashley said. And then all of a sudden, Ashley took off her rob and she was butt naked in front of Alex and then Alex started making out with Ashley and he started touching her naked body more and more. "Oh Alex" Ashley said and then Alex right away turned off the lights in his apartment room and he started making out with Ashley on the couch. And overall, Alex was really weak and didn't have the same stamina, he was just glad to be alive and glad that there was a beautiful girl waiting for him in his apartment. And also Alex was very lucky that he was able to live in a great country like the US and destroy parts of Borodina's evil plan and hopefully be able to finally stop her once and for all.

Sadie Mackenzie Holbrook
001

001:
Sadie Mackenzie Holbrook & The Moving Nights

Prologue 1 the tale of the girl who loved to travel and wanted adventure, Minnesota 1971

In the early 1970's, it was a really cold day and a lot of snow was falling down on the ground. And it was a normal January day in 1971, But then there was a rich couple who were well dressed, the man had on a nice 1970's suit and tie, the wife had diamonds on the rings she was wearing, And then also the couple had 2 beautiful little girls. The oldest one had very golden hair and she had blue eyes, the other one had brown hair and had green eyes. And every time this couple went anywhere such as the mall or any fun places, the oldest girl in the family would love going places with her parents. And this girl was very curious about the world around her, and this girl really had big dreams for herself as well. She didn't really know what she wanted to do yet, but the little girl kept an open mind. The couple went back home and they stayed in a really nice house in a suburb in Minnesota. And the girls had a very wonderful childhood, the dad worked as a normal minimum wage job working at a Wendy's, he didn't really make much at his job, but however that being said, he would stop into his bank branch on the way home from work and meet with his banker and his banker would go over with him which companies to invest in. And with the paycheck he had, he would use his paycheck to find companies that didn't have a lot of value to their name and buy somewhere 600,000 stocks with that company. The girls would grow up and they right away be sent to college with money that their parents gave them. Both girls went to the University of Minnesota around the same time Alex went to University of Washington in 1980. Accept this girl was a little bite older then Alex. And she also worked for her parents before going to college as well.

But then as the girls got there, some of the roommates that they had were sadly not very good common sense people. And some of the roommates would always problems with the older girl going to gas stations and getting snacks and getting beer. And they even said at one point it was not very lady like. The girls also went to normal and really crazy college parties and there was people being silly and dancing to 1980's music and people wearing a lot of 1980's clothes and having crazy 1980's fashions. And also people were drinking some drinks, some people were watching TV, playing pool or playing darts. And then other crazy people were playing beer pong as well. The girl was then at the party and she was drinking a coke and eating a hot dog. But then as they were, there was also another gentlemen at the party and he looked very little but also very athletic at the same time and he was drinking a beer. And the girl saw him and started flirting with him. "Hey sweetie, this is a great party" she said "Oh yeah it's a really wonderful and a really wild party" he said "Oh yeah I agree" she said "I'm Spencer by the way" Spencer said "I'm Sadie" Sadie said "So what brings you to this wild little place?" Spencer asked "Well my sister and I found out that there was going to be party here and we came" Sadie said "Oh that's awesome" Spencer said "So what do you do when your not going to school?" Spencer asked "Well I actually work at Penny Mora's here in the city" Sadie said, "Oh that's a great store, I hear they are just like Nordstrom's in Seattle, I hear on the news that place is getting really good" Spencer said "Oh yeah I have herd that too" Sadie said "So what are you studying Spencer?" Sadie asked "So far…. nothing…At least not yet anyway" Spencer said "Well for me I do like to travel, and I do want to be a traveling personality and share my adventures to the world" Sadie said "Well that's really ballsy baby girl" Spencer said "I know…" Sadie said and then Sadie smiled at Spencer. And then during that night, they both got to know each other very well and right away the two had a lot in common, and they both wanted to travel and see the world. And then in the same night, Spencer and Sadie were making out in Spencer's dorm around the University of Minnesota campus. And all of a sudden in the coming months, Sadie and Spencer flunked out of school and the three people started working very different jobs. Sadie worked at the same job and she also told her boss about the plan and her boss was all in as well. Sadie's sister April would also be part of this adventure of hers in making a TV program where they talked about traveling and going places as well. And Sadie using the knowledge from her mom and dad, started investing in the stock market as the economy is getting really good. And Sadie bought a lot of stocks from small companies and in one year alone, she got around $900,000 in shares and Spencer would invest even more then Sadie would around 900$ and then getting 9,000,000$ in shares.

And from there, they just really wanted to move somewhere else. And both Sadie and Spencer decided to move to Seattle, Washington. And they moved into a really fancy house that was in the Seattle area that had a swimming pool and a hot tub, a gym, and also a huge basement where there was a big TV room and video game room as well. That, and also a bar where there was a lot of alcohol as well. And from 1980 to 1989 and started recording on their adventures on an old video camera from the 1980's. And they went to a lot of places all over the world such as in Europe and went to a lot of countries such as Italy, England, France, New Zealand, and also go to Mexico, Brazil, and then to Ireland and then to Australia. And then she also traveled around the United States of America as well. And then there would be times where also explored Canada and all the territories in that country as well. But whenever Sadie, Spencer, and April went anywhere, they always were really smart; they also made sure not to spend a lot of money as well. And then also make sure they were around safe people as well. And by the late 80's her popularity and her fame really grew a lot. And when Sadie, April, and Spencer returned to the states, she then was called on the phone to go on a radio show in San Diego. And when she was on the radio, she was really happy, really bubbly, and she just really loved to laugh as well. And not only that, but she also answered her questions correctly as well.

But then also on that same day Sadie was on the radio, Alex was coming back from working at Seattle agencies going over reports and then attending gun practice. And as Alex was driving home in downtown Seattle and heading to his apartment, he then was listening to Sadie on the radio and explaining her adventures and how she has able to travel the world on a budget. Alex right way from listening to her on the radio, loved her voice and thought in his little brain "Ah yeah she is a very beautiful and a very gorgeous and a very stunning and a very sexy baby girl" Alex said and thought as he was driving home, and then as Alex came home from Seattle Agencies, he then took a shower and he was only wearing a T-shirt and boxer underwear and not wearing any pants as well. And then all of a sudden, Alex started making an ice coffee and then he also put whipped cream on the coffee and then Alex was able to make something to eat as well. And then Alex turned on TV and he started slipping through the channels. And sometimes Alex really does not take the little tiny local channels seriously and he mostly focuses on the sports channels and also the higher channels as well. But as Alex was flipping through, he then saw Sadie's show on TV and it was on channel 5 and the show was called "Living Adventures with Sadie" and Sadie spoke and it was mostly set up like a normal talk show but with traveling and the show always started out with a bing and then some music would play and then the crowd would start clapping and making a lot of noise "Hi everyone this is Sadie on Living adventures and I do this program everyday Wednesday. And my goodness it is really great to be back. And today I got to go to Germany, and we will have clips of that real soon. And we will have a guest on the show very soon as well" Sadie said and then as Alex kept on watching, he was also really amazed at how beautiful and gorgeous, and very stunning and very happy and she just loved to laugh a lot. And she also wore a lot of really beautiful and really gorgeous 1980's style dresses on her show. And then Alex was really amazed at how beautiful and athletic her body was. And then Alex kept on thinking "Ah wow she is super pretty and very beautiful and damn she is fine" Alex thought in his head and from there, Alex was hooked on Sadie's TV show about traveling and talking about her adventures and also having special guests on the show as well. And every time Alex didn't have any missions from 1984 to 1988 Alex always watched Sadie doing her TV shows. And whenever Alex heard the bell noise on TV, he really knew something was about to go down and Alex always had popcorn with cheese zits under the piles of popcorn and also some goldfish and cheese related snacks under the popcorn. And then he would drink a lot of junk drinks such as soda, beer, a milkshakes, icey's, and the list goes on and on of junk drinks and junk food.

And then there would even be times when Michael and Tony would come over to watch Sadie's show on TV. And as they were watching the show, they were watching an episode on her program were she went to Russia. And this episode was a lot of more serious because she was interviewing someone who was an Indian-American who was a young ambassador to Russia. And his name Salem Suyog Jadon. And the man was really muscular and he had dark skin and he also had black hair as well. But he spoke really well with an American accent. And Salem was talking about Russia and how the berlin wall could fall at any point after Reagan's speech in Berlin. And then there was also a much important detail in that interview as well where Salem said he was going to do a rally in Portland, Oregon to rally behind President Regan and also rally behind America as well against the Communist. "Alright yes defiantly well this was Living Adventures With Sadie. And I will see you guys next time" Sadie said and then the episode ended.

And back the studio around in downtown Seattle, Salem was leaving the building and he was heading to his house that was around the University of Washington neighborhood. But then as he went to sleep that night, there was a lot of evil Sandinistas from Nicaragua that were spying on him. And not only that, but they also had contact with more Sandinista groups that were in the United States including in Portland, Oregon as well. And the next day, Salem got up and he took a shower and he got into his car and he started driving to Portland, Oregon and it was around a 2-hour drive. But as he got to the city, he then stayed in a really fancy hotel. And once he was checked in, around that same point, once Alex saw Salem on TV, he knew that Salem in some way was going to be in grave danger because Alex knew from being in Portland back in 1976 when he was 16, he knew there a lot of anti-America people that refuged to that part of the country just like did with San Francisco and anything that supports an anti-America agenda, those evil people would go there. The next day, Alex went to Seattle agencies and he reported to Rivers saying that there might be an attack in Portland and wanted Rivers grant him approval to go on a mission there. And Rivers ended up saying yes. Alex also told him about Sadie's new show as well. And from there, Alex was on his way to Portland and Alex actually took the train to get there. And as Alex was on the train, he really thought about what he was going to run into. And he also knew he had to find Jadon before any bad people did.

Prologue 2 The Sandinistas and Borodina's attack at the pro America rally in Portland

As Alex got to Portland, He then got off the train and he took a bus that was heading to downtown Portland. As Alex was on the bus, he did notice a sign that said, "Support for the Berlin wall coming down" and then Alex also checked into a hotel as well. "Can I help you?" the hotel lady asked "yes the names Aussmen…Alex Aussmen…I would love to check into a hotel here" Alex said "Alright okay, we will get your room very soon" she said and then the lady was able to get Alex a hotel key and she was able to hand it to him "Here is your key sir" she said "thank you so much sweetie" Alex said and then Alex went to the elevator and he pressed on the 7th floor and the elevator started going up. Alex got off the elevator and he started heading to his hotel room. Alex set his bags on his bed and Alex started changing out of his suit and tie and started putting on normal 1980's style clothes. Alex was able to get out of his hotel room and he started heading more towards a park area that was is around a couple of department stores. Alex then kept on walking and he saw Salem go into a bar that was inside of Nordstrom. Alex went into the Nordstrom and he saw Salem getting a beer and also drinking shots before speaking. Alex then walked up to that same bar counter and he didn't really get any beer he just got water and was eating some pistachio nuts. And then while he was there, Alex then saw more alcoholic drinks and he started mentally writing notes in his head and writing down and memorizing every alcohol brand that there is. And then Salem turned to Alex and then turned away from him and then Alex turned to him "Today is a great night for a speaking rally" Alex said "oh yeah defiantly we need to get the Berlin wall to come down" Salem said "wait, my man, you watched my interview with Sadie" Salem asked "Yeah I did. I'm Alex Aussmen, private investigator. And I believe you maybe in danger" Alex said "What do you mean dude?" Salem said, "I'm saying that a lot of anti-America people live here in Portland and they always support a lot of anti-America causes and they come here" Alex said "But doesn't that happen in Seattle as well?" Salem asked "it does but we have a lot of business people in Seattle and Seattle has a lot going for it" Alex said "let me at least come with you to the rally" Alex said "Alright okay be my guess man" Salem said and then as Salem was done drinking his beer. Alex and Salem started walking to the rally and at the rally; Alex saw a lot of people wearing T-shirts in supporting George H.W. Bush and people had a lot of American flag T-shirts. And people were going crazy and wissleling and making a lot more crazy sounds as well. And then Salem started walking up to the podium "Good evening everyone, it is my pleasure to be here. And really soon we are going to create peace in Russia and the Berlin wall will come down. And we don't want socialism or communism getting into our country. And we don't want to be like everyone else, we want to be the United States of America. And when Reagan is out, we must support a candidate that will continue the path of patriotism and the free market and also the rule of law as well. And we must end socialism and communism once and for all" Salem said and a lot of the people there roaring and clapping and chanting "USA, USA, USA, USA, USA!!!!!!!!!" and but then all of a sudden as Alex was listening to the speech, he saw a lot of Hispanics that were wearing black and red suit and ties and sun glasses. And then he also saw some evil people in blue and yellow tuxedos. And then all of a sudden an evil huge mob of evil Ukraine and Sandinista thugs showed up and created a riot and a huge fight broke out and also gunfire broke out as well. And everyone was going crazy.

And then a lot of Sandinistas and Ukraine thugs started attacking and shooting at people. All of a sudden, Alex took out a PP7 gun and he started firing 30 bullets at them "LA RAZA!!!!!, LA RAZA!!!!!, LA RAZA!!!!!!!, LA RAZA!!!!!!! MATA EL GRINGO!!!!!!!" They yelled in Spanish and then Alex grunted his teeth in anger and was very pissed off and he started firing 300 bullets at 60 Sandinista thugs coming at him with riffle guns. Alex then took cover and he hid behind objects and he kept on shooting and then one of the Sandinista thugs tried to tackle Alex, but Alex was able to dodge the tackle and he punched the thug in the face and then dodged another attack and kicked another Sandinista in the balls, and then another one tried to stab Alex with a machete knife, Alex then dodged the machete attacks and Alex punched the Sandinista thug in the face and grabbed him and slammed him into a car.

And then Alex started running and he grabbed Salem "come on we have to get out of here" Alex said "who are these fucking people?!..." Salem said, "They are the communist down in Nicaragua, they are the Sandinistas, and they are just as evil as the communist in Russia" Alex said and then Alex and Salem hid behind a car and Alex took out another gun and he loaded up his gun and started shooting 90 bullets at them and Alex was able to kill 40 Sandinistas thugs and shoot them in the head and also shoot them in the neck. And then Salem saw a lot of Sandinista thugs were coming close at them and shooting A33 riffles at Alex, Alex kept on shooting at them. And then Alex and Salem started running and they started running and Alex saw a early 1980's car and Alex was able to break into the car and Salem was riding shot-gun. "Hold on" Alex said and then the Ukraine thugs started coming at them as well "Ne dozvoljajte amerykans'komu pity!!!!!!!" The Ukraine thugs yelled and then Alex put the pedal to the medal and he started driving the car really fast. Alex drove the car really fast all over Downtown Portland

and Alex kept on taking four different turns. And then Alex was going around 500 miles per hour and then more Sandinistas and Ukraine thugs kept on chasing after Alex as Alex was going really fast. "LA RAZA!!!!!!!, LA RAZA, LA RAZA, LA RAZA!!!!!!!!" the Sandinistas kept on yelling at Alex "Vamos a llevarnos de vuelta a Nicaraguia por todos los crímenes que cometieron a nuestro país, el Senior Aussmen!!!!!" they yelled "Yeah fuck all of you!!!!!!" Alex yelled and then Alex was able to find a bomb in his pocket and then Alex threw the bomb at the other cars that were chasing Alex and then the car exploded into flames and caught on fire and then more thugs started firing more bullets at Alex. Alex then kept on taking sharp turns and then as he was driving, Alex then loaded up PP7 gun and Alex kept on firing bullets at the Sandinistas. And then as Alex was going really fast and going around 900 miles per hour, a lot of Sandinistas that were black and red helicopters started chasing after Alex and firing a lot of advanced missiles and causing a lot of explosions and more buildings and cars were catching on fire and Alex kept on driving with a lot of energy in his little right pinky. And then a lot of motorcycles with USSR flags started chasing Alex and they started rocket launchers at Alex, and then Alex dodging all of the rockets firing at him. Alex then took out his gun and Alex fired 50 bullets and reloading and shooting at the tires and shooting at their arms and causing them to crash in the process and more explosions happening. Alex kept on driving really fast and he ended up around the bridge by the Columbia River and by the Washington state boarder. And then Alex was driving and then he parked the car and drifted car really fast and then put the car on park. Alex then turned back to Salem "stay here man" Alex said and then Alex took out another pistol gun and he reloaded the gun with more bullets.

Alex then heard the motorcycles and more helicopters coming towards him. And then Alex took out his DD4 gun and Alex started shooting at the Ukraine thugs coming at him and shooting around 90 bullets at them. Alex then took out bombs and he was able to throw around 5 different grenades at a lot of Sandinista thugs that were coming at him at a rapid pace. And then Alex kept on running and he saw one of the ropes. Alex jumped on to one of the ropes and Alex started climbing up the top of the rope and Alex was able to get to the top and the Sandinistas helicopters kept on shooting at Alex. Alex was able to dodge the bullets and Alex saw a rocket launcher and Alex picked up the rocket launcher and Alex with careful aim and holding on to the launcher very tight. And as the Sandinistas were coming after Alex in very intense fashion and at a really fast race, Alex then shot around 3 rockets at the Sandinista helicopters and Alex was able to blow up 5 different Sandinista helicopters as well "El día de mayo vamos a bajar. Nos han golpeado!!!!" The Sandinistas inside of the helicopters yelled and then there was a huge explosion and the helicopter landed in the Columbia River and killed the Sandinistas inside of the helicopter. And then Alex climbed off of the bridge and he was able to get back on the ground and Alex saw a lot of motorcycles that had a lot of Ukraine and USSR flags coming at Alex. "MY tebe teper pan AUSSMEN!!!!!!!!!!" They yelled and then Alex grunted his teeth and Alex started firing 10 different rockets at the Ukraine thugs and causing a lot of explosions and their motorcycles caught on fire. And then the thugs flew off of the motorcycles off the bridge and into the water. And then more thugs started coming at Alex and shooting at them, Alex was able to dodge the attacks and then the thugs turned back and Alex reloaded the rocket launcher and fired another rocket back at the Ukraine thug and blew them up in flames and smoke. And then another van full of Sandinistas thugs waving the Sandinista flag "Te tenemos ahora Señor Aussmen!!!!!" they yelled and then they started throwing a lot of bombs at Alex and then Alex started running away from the vans and Alex and they started firing a lot of bullets at Alex. Alex then jumped on another rope that was on the bridge and Alex took out another gun and reloaded the gun and Alex started shooting at the tires and then Alex grunted his teeth and Alex shot at one of the Sandinista thugs in the van and killing two of them as well. And then the Sandinista thugs came out of the car and they started shooting at Alex. Alex was able to do a summersault and dodge the bullets coming at him and he was able to take out another gun and reload the gun and Alex started shooting around 300 bullets at the Sandinista thugs and shooting them in the head and in the neck and also in the chest as well. And then the van was rolling on the bridge and drifting and then all of a sudden, the Sandinista thug van started going in the air and turning in circles. And then it landed on the ground and it crashed on the ground and then Alex started running to the van with the rocket launcher in his hands. "Who sent you?!...." Alex yelled in a very angry voice "We will get you and take you back one of these days gringo!!!!" the Sandinista thugs said "Yeah like fuck that is going to happen" Alex yelled in anger and then all of a sudden out of the shadows more Sandinista and Ukraine thugs showed up as Victoria Borodina showed up again "Making fire piles Zero, Zero One?!...." Victoria said and she is wearing a red and black jumpsuit with Blue and yellow boots and also one part of her hair was blue and blonde, and the other half was died red and black "One of these days, I will capture you Alex and torture you in Nicaragua and run away as much you want little boy, but I will always be better" Victoria said "I'm not running Victoria, I am protecting an innocent person from being killed by one of your thugs!!!!" Alex said "very well then little boy!!!!" Victoria said and then Victoria took out a remote and she pressed a button on it and then all of a sudden, a lot of metal arms started growing out of her watches that she was wearing and the metal claws tried to grab Alex, Alex then grunted his teeth and he was able to throw 6 different punches at the arms. And then Alex was able to use a flame thrower gadget to burn the metal arms that Victoria Borodina had, then she took out a king staff and she tried to whack Alex in the face and she threw around 14 different staff attacks and Alex was able to dodge all 14 of them. And then Alex kicked Borodina in the stomach and then Borodina recovered from the attack and she whacked Alex in the face and then she grabbed a very hot glove to try to burn Alex's face "This is going to cause a really huge sting to your face Little boy!!!!!!!..." Victoria said as she was grabbing Alex by the neck and then Alex kicked her in the face with both of his legs and then Alex saw the rocket launcher and he picked up the rocket launcher and Alex all of a sudden, fired a rocket out of the rocket launcher and he shot Victoria Borodina in the stomach and then she started yelling and there was a huge explosion in flames and then Alex ran to the ledge of the river and saw parts of the fire go into river "Welcome to hell Borodina!!!!!" Alex yelled and then all of a sudden, Alex turned back and he saw Borodina's little Rottweiler dog growling and making a lot of evil and nasty and very mean dog barks at Alex. And then from there even though the dog didn't attack or bite Alex, he did notice something was not right and he knew that this time in fighting Victoria Borodina that he knew he was going to need more help and if Alex learned anything from the past, it's that Victoria Borodina is a lot like the evil and creepy and nasty monster that children are afraid of and is like the monster under the bed that can crawl up and snatch you and kidnap you and torture you and overall kill you as well.

Alex was able to leave Portland and he was able to take Salem back to his hotel room in Portland. But as this was happening, all of a sudden, there was communist submarine that was able to find Borodina and Borodina looked very beat up from fighting Alex, and all of a sudden the doctors inside the submarine started operating on Victoria and all of a sudden, they put her through plastic surgery and her skin started getting wrinkled, she started growing a lot of zits on her face, her hair started turning gray and white behind all of the hair dye that she put into it. And then also Victoria's teeth were getting yellow and ugly and also starting to turn black as well and started gaining wrinkles around her eyes some of her face as well. And then as the operation was completed, Borodina stood up and her hands were all wrinkled and old and her finger nails were dirty and smelly and had a lot of dirt and bacteria in them "Mirror!!!!!" Borodina yelled and then one of the Ukraine soldiers gave her the mirror and then Borodina broke the mirror and she broke the glass on the mirror "Ms. Borodina, I'm really sorry that you look very ugly, we tired to do the best that we could…" the solider said and then all of a sudden very aggressively she grabbed the solider by the neck and start chocking him very badly and her nails were stabbing him and a lot of blood was coming out his neck and Victoria was able to kill him and she threw him to the floor. "YOU FUCKING FOOL, YOU RUINED MY BEAUTY AND YOU RUINED MY STUNNING LOOKS!!!!!!" Borodina said in a very creepy and very witch like voice "BUT SOON I WILL TAKE OVER THE WORLD AND SOON I WILL BECOME EVEN MORE RICH AND NOT ONLY WILL I USE THE MONEY TO BECOME BEAUITFUL AGAIN, I WILL USE TO FUND THE SANDINSTAS AND THE SOVIET UNION AND MY PLAN WILL BE VERY SIMPLE!!!!!!!!…I WILL FIND A RICH PERSON IN AMERICA AND KILL THAT PERSON, STEEL THEIR MONEY AND THEIR FORTUNE JUST LIKE I DID EMILY ROMNEY AND SABRINA FIORINA AND THEN JUST LIKE I DID WITH AGNET PAUL MILLAT AS WELL!!!!!!!!!…AND THIS TIME I WILL SUCCED AND I WILL KILL ALEX AUSSMEN ZERO, ZERO ONE ONCE AND FOR ALL!!!!!!!!!" Victoria said and then Victoria looked a magazine and she then saw Sadie on the magazine "oh that will be perfect to kidnap a TV host on a talk show and ruin her and destroy her life and steel all of her fortune and kill her boyfriend…and I will get that pretty girl and use her DNA as well. And as for Alex Aussmen, I will get you this time little boy!!!!!!!!…AND NOTHING CAN TRULY STOP ME NOW!!!!!!!!!!…..EHEHEHEHEHEHEHEHEHEHEHEHEHEHEHEHEHEHEHE

HEHEHEHEHEHEHEHEHEHEHEHEHEHEHEHEHEHEHEHEHEHEHEHE
HEHE……MUAHAHAHAHAHAHAHAHAHAHAHAHAHAHAHAHAHAHA
HAHAHAHAHAHAHAHAHAHAHAHAHAHAHAHAHAHAHAHAHAHAHA
BRAHAAHAHAHAHAHAHAHAHAHAHAHAHAHAHAHAHAHAHAHAHAH
AHAHAHAAHAHAHAHAHAHAHAHAHAHAHAHAHAHAHAHAHAHAHAH
AHAHAHAHAHAHAHAHAHAHAHAHAHAHAHAHAHAHAHAHAHAHAHA
HAHAHAHAHAHAHAHAHAHA…EHEHEHEHEHEHEHEHEHEHEHEHEHE
HEHE
AHAHAHAHAAHAHAHAHAHAHAHAHAHAHAHAHAHAHAHAHAHAHHAHA
MUAHAHAHAHAHAHAHAHAHAHAHAHAHAHAHAHAHAHAHAHAHAHAH
AHAHAHAHAHAHAHAHA!!!!!!!!!!!!!!!!!!!!!" Victoria laughed and then as
Victoria was laughing, parts of herself was reveled and there was
thunder and lighting outside and Victoria kept on looking at the picture
of Sadie in the magazine and the whole room was turning dark and
there was more thunder and lighting as well.

Chapter 1 A Big surprise in Ballard, Seattle, Washington 1989

As the sun was rising in downtown Seattle, there is a special place in the
heart of Seattle and it's a neighborhood or a borough, as some people
from the east coast would call it. And the name of this neighborhood
was Ballard, the neighborhood is really known for a lot of fishermen
boats and a lot of fishermen going up to Alaska and getting a lot of fish
and crap and also some shrimp as well. But it's really important to know
that Alex was able to get released out of the hospital in downtown
Seattle after the attacks that he in Washington DC. Alex was released
from the hospital and there were two people that picked up Alex and
those people were Tony and Michael. And as Alex was released from the
hospital, Michael and Tony took Alex to get some lunch and they took
him out for fish and chips and they took him to a restaurant called
Anthony's. And from there, Alex was eating fine once again and he was
also drinking his soda just like he would drink any other drink. "How do
you feel Alex?" Michael asked him "Sadly I feel very light-headed and my
brain feels like complete dog-shit" Alex said "Yeah I'm sorry to hear
about that home boy, I mean I have been watching the news, and yeah
hommie those Sandinistas in that country are just very awful people"
Tony said "Did you find anything else about them?" Alex said "well…not
really it's just another mission of me attacking them and blowing up
parts of their country and them yelling at me and saying a lot of racist

things at me" Alex said "oh dear yikes I'm sorry Alex" Michael said "Hey you don't have to be sorry buddy" Alex said and then all of a sudden, the food came and Alex, Michael, and Tony started eating the food and munching all of it like big husky dogs eating a bone. And then they also drank 4 big shots and gulps of soda and felt very hyper and very silly as well.

They then were able to take Alex home back to his pen house apartment in downtown Seattle. As Alex got home, he then started all the things that were mentioned in the prologue especially with him starting to watch Sadie and her boyfriend and her sister on TV, and then also the events of him going to Portland, Oregon. And then also before that, Alex was going to Seattle agencies but he just didn't have missions assigned to him and he there for gun practice, working out at the facility weather it was him swimming in the pool, working out and doing cardio workouts or also lifting weights as well. Alex also had a sheet of paper recording every single set and every workout stat. And everyday Alex ended up burring around 1,000 calories a day. And then as he was done working out, he would also be studying other agent reports coming in and also writing stuff down and taking notes on the blue prints handed to him. And then also Alex would go to meetings and listen to other operative officials talk about missions that were coming up even though he was not assigned to go on those missions. And then also one day as Alex was swimming, he then saw Jenny in a very beautiful and a very gorgeous and very stunning and a very sexy 1980's bikini bathing suit and she had a very beautiful and a very gorgeous smile on her face. "Hey Alex, I didn't know you were coming here for a swim?" Jenny said and then as Alex saw her and as he was getting done swimming his 100th lap in the pool, Alex then got out of the pool and since Alex was not seeing anyone, Alex just started walking up to Jenny and started making out with Jenny by the pool and Alex gave her a really smooch on the lips and also Alex started touching her. "You doing anything later today?" Alex asked "no…I'm not…I'm all yours" Jenny said, "oh I love the sound of that baby girl" Alex said and then after Alex was done swimming, Alex and Jenny took showers and they got dressed and they were wearing really cool looking 1980's clothes. And then Alex softly put his arms around jenny and Jenny had a really big smile on her face "So where were you. I haven't seen you in a while" Jenny said "I was on in a mission in Nicaragua and also in Washington DC as well" Alex said "oh that sounds really exciting, I really wish I can come with you on all those missions Alex, Rivers just has me doing office work all the time and I have never really been anywhere" Jenny said "you were on my last local mission that was in Bellevue" Alex said "Oh that's right I forgot" Jenny said "So where are we going tonight?" Jenny said, "I actually really didn't know, we can go to a fancy restaurant in Seattle, and then come back to my apartment, does that sound like a great idea?" Alex asked "Oh that is a fantastic idea Alex" Jenny said and then Alex raised his left hand and a taxi car showed up and Alex and Jenny got into the car. "Where to?" the driver asked "Any fancy place in Seattle" Alex said, "yes sir" the driver said

The taxi driver started taking Alex and Jenny to a fancy restaurant in downtown Seattle. And the driver dropped them off and they got out of the car and started heading into the restaurant. Alex and Jenny were able to get seated and they sat upstairs and had a view of the Seattle skyline from their table. "Wow this is really wonderful Alex, this is the first time you have actually took me on a date" Jenny said "Well I am really glad you were free Jenny" Alex said "I just really can't believe I'm 29 years old, it just felt like yesterday I just became a secret agent all those years ago" Alex said "How did you become a secret agent?" Jenny asked Alex then paused for a little bit and then he was able to take a deep breath "it's kind of complicated" Alex said, "What do you mean Alex?" Jenny asked "well I am saying that how I became a secret agent was not a very normal way, you see Jenny, there are parts of my life that are very dark and very scary and also my life was never easy because my parents never thought I was going to be anything in life and basically treated me like I was nothing. And...I also ran away from them as well and I raised by a fortune teller as well" Alex said "That sounds really cool" Jenny said "it may be cool to you but I have done things and seen things that I am not proud of" Alex said "you can tell me Alex, were adults" Jenny said "okay well Jenny...I have just always a lot of people come after me and even a lot of evil and messed up people come after me" Alex said "Like what Alex?" Jenny said "I don't know like I know when I was 16 I had to go to creepy medical building in downtown Seattle with my guardian name Emmy Lewis and I had to get tested for disability. At least that is what was suppose to happen but instead I got hunted and I had run through an obstacle course and run through the building and swim in very cold water butt naked, it was not good" Alex said "Oh you poor baby" Jenny said "oh dear I'm sorry Alex" Jenny said "Are you okay personally Alex?" Jenny asked him "Yeah it's fine, I'm over it and it was many years ago. But my point is that I have a dark past and my life is very edgy and not very clean as well" Alex said "it's okay Alex, I understand, we all have dark things in our past" Jenny said and then Jenny put her right hand on Alex's hand and she started touching Alex and then from there, Alex started feeling a lot more relaxed and they eating the food that they ordered and then Alex was able to pay for Jenny and himself and pay the bill. And then from there, they started heading to his apartment.

And then as they got back to Alex's apartment, Jenny and Alex started making out and kissing each other on the lips and went into Alex's bedroom and started taking each other's clothes off. And then Alex landed on his bed and then Jenny kept making out with Alex on the bed and they started laughing "oh my" Jenny said and they passionately making love with each other. "Wahoooooooooo!!!!" Jenny said as Alex was making out with her and kissing her on the lips. And then they started making out and having sex for the remainder of the night. And then next day morning, Alex saw the sun rising up at around 7:30AM and as Alex was getting up, Jenny was sleeping on Alex's chest and she was kissing Alex's chest and then Jenny kissed Alex on the lips and then both of them were kissing each other. Alex then got up and he put a towel to cover up and Alex looked at the sun and he also looked at the Seattle skyline. And then Alex started heading to his bathroom and he turned on the water and the water started coming down on him. And then as Alex was in the shower, Jenny went into the shower with Alex and they started kissing and making out in the shower. For the rest of the morning, and then after they took a shower, Alex and Jenny started heading to breakfast and Alex paid breakfast and he made sure to tip the waiter that served both of them. "Anyway thank you so much for breakfast Alex" Jenny said "Your welcome Jenny" Alex said "Well I am really sad that I have to leave you but I think Rivers is sending me on another mission where I have to go to Europe and go on my first overseas mission" Jenny said "that sounds fantastic Jenny" Alex said and then Jenny got up from the chair and she walked over to Alex and she was able to give Alex a kiss on the check and she started walking to the door in her beautiful high heels and Alex just smiled as he was eyeing her, but trying to be clam and cool, Alex knew that at some point, he was going to be assigned a new mission from Rivers.

Alex then left the restaurant and since he really didn't have anything else on his calendar, he then started looking around downtown Seattle and he started going to a lot of stores. And as Alex was in downtown Seattle, a communist Russian in the city started fallowing Alex as he was in the stores, and as Alex was walking into a book store, Alex started looking at another different novels at the store, but then as Alex was reading, the same communist Russian thug and an anti-America guy with a T-shirt of him mocking president Reagan fallowed Alex as well. And little did Alex know, he was about to be in mortal danger. And then as Alex kept on reading, both of these guys came at Alex and notice his style of suit he was wearing "HEY FUCK REAGAN!!!!!!! FUCK YOU WHITE BOY!!!!!!!" the anti-America guy yelled at Alex and then the ugly looking young man got really upset and he started screaming and yelling and he also had a big sharp pocket knife and he threw 19 different knife attacks at Alex. Alex then right away jumped in the air and he landed on the ground and Alex started dodging the attacks that the anti-America guy was throwing at him. And then Alex dodged more attacks and then Alex kicked him in the face and then the guy tried to stab him in the chest and Alex got really aggressive and slammed anti-America guy against the wall and Alex grabbed his shoulder and Alex slammed his head against 5 glass windows and Alex grabbed a hard edge book slammed him from behind 7 times in the head. And then the ugly anti-America turned back and he threw more punches and more kicks at Alex and then he also bull-rushed at Alex and caused Alex to land on the ground "I'M GOING TO MAKE SURE YOU CONSERTIVES DIE IN A BURNING FIRE!!!!!!!" he yelled in complete anger and then Alex got up and then Alex dodged another attack and Alex punched him in the face and threw another kick at the attacker. And then the communist Russia wanted to kill Alex he took out a Russian sword and tried to stab and cut Alex and threw around 30 different attacks at Alex. Alex was able to dodge the attacks and then the communist Russian punched Alex in the face and Alex had a bloody lip and then both of the aggressive men tried to tackle Alex and then grabbed the Russian's wrist really hard and slammed him against the wall. And then he tried to attack Alex with Russian sword and then Alex punched the gun in the face was able to kill him. And then Alex was fighting the anti-America guy and he threw more punches and kicks at Alex. Alex kept on dodging the attacks and then did an upper cut punch at the guy and Alex grabbed the guy and slammed him against the wall and then took out an electricity gun and Alex electrocuted the anti-America guy really bad and he started screaming and yelling in pain and Alex was able to kill the guy. And then Alex noticed at the anti-America guy that he had a microchip and a lot of liquid soy milk coming out his cuts and Alex knew right away that something was not right. And Alex started running out of the bookstore as a lot of people in the store were shocked at just what happened. Alex then started running upstairs in the mall and he noticed some anti-America thieves wearing black outfits and wearing a lot of communist propaganda T-shirts on them. Alex saw them and he started running and he ran out of the building. Alex ran out of the mall and started running towards one of the west lake buildings and then Alex turned back and all of a sudden, a lot of motorcycles and black cars started chasing Alex, Alex then saw a Lamborghini Countach car Alex sadly had steel the car and Alex got into the car and Alex was able to steel the car, and Alex was able to get the car out of it's parking spot. And Alex turned back and he got really shocked and saw a lot of communist cars about to come at Alex and then right away Alex put his foot on the gas pedal and Alex started going fast on the road in downtown Seattle. Alex then started driving the car really fast through the streets and Alex speed through up 5 red lights. As Alex got around Pike place market, Alex then took a sharp turn and Alex kept on going really fast and more people started saying a lot of crazy things as Alex was speeding, more of the Anti-America in black cars and black motorcycles kept on chasing him "We are going to kill you Reagan lover!!!!!!" they yelled as they were driving their vehicles and going after Alex. And then they took out grenade launchers and started firing at Alex and causing a lot of explosions in the process. Alex then kept on going really fast and Alex parked the car and Alex looked his coat pocket and he was able to find a DD4 gun and Alex found the gun and Alex reloaded the gun and Alex pointed and aimed carefully and Alex started to fire 19 bullets at lot of anti-America people that were going to ram into him. And Alex was able to blow up their tires really badly and cause a really huge explosion and Alex reloaded his gun again and Alex pointed the gun at another motorcycle coming at him and Alex shot at that particular motorcycle and was able to cause another explosion.

Alex then pulled the stick shift lever on the car and Alex was able to back up the care really fast while turning his head back. And then Alex was able to put the car back on drive from reverse and Alex kept on going fast on the road and a lot more anti-America people kept on chasing after him. Alex kept on driving and Alex started heading towards Lower Queen Ann and around Seattle Center, Alex put the pedal to the medal and Alex's car started going off a lot of hills and slamming on the ground and kept on going. More anti-America kept on shooting at Alex and Alex started drifting the car left and right and Alex would throw a lot of bombs from behind at the bad guys. As Alex kept on driving, he sadly was out of bullets in DD4 gun and Alex knew he really needed to use a weapon and fast. Finally, Alex while he was driving remembered that his watch could fire lasers even from far distances. Alex was able to take off his watch and Alex aimed his spy watch as more anti-America were on his tail, as they took out more guns and more weaponry, Alex pressed the sliver button and Alex started firing 12 lasers at the thugs chasing him, Alex while he was driving was able to blow up a lot of black cars and motorcycles that were chasing after him and Alex kept on going really fast on the road, he noticed that he was in Ballard and was on the Ballard bridge and Alex kept on going really fast and then Alex was able to take sharp right turn and more of the thugs kept on chasing him. Alex then turned the car around and then Alex started going really fast and then the car started heading towards a ledge that was towards the water. As Alex flew off the ledge in the car, Alex jumped out of the car and Alex was falling in the air and Alex fell into the water in Ballard. Alex was able to swim back to the surface and he started swimming to the ledge and he was able to climb up the docks and he around where the boats, Alex then hid behind a wall and he was soaking wet and he smelled really bad, and more anti-America people showed up and they had guns and riffles in their hands. Alex then noticed some of them walking towards him and Alex hid behind a crate and Alex was able to grab him from behind and punch him in the face knock him out and Alex was able to steel his riffle gun and then a lot of anti- American thugs in anti-America cars showed up and then they took out a lot of riffle guns and they started shooting at Alex. And then Alex hid behind a wall and Alex loaded his gun and he started shooting around 44 bullets at the thugs and Alex was able to kill around 8 different thugs and then the thugs that were alive, kept on shooting bullets at Alex and Alex kept on running and more explosions kept having and some of the Ballard port dock started catching on fire. And then all of a sudden, one of the anti-America people took out a rocket launcher and blasted a lot of rockets at Alex. And Alex did a lot of summersaults and did a lot of backflips and front flips and landed on his feet and Alex took out his spy watch and firing at a lot more anti-America people and caused more explosions and the Ballard port building started catching on fire. And Alex kept on running and Alex took out the riffle gun and he started shooting 99 bullets and also kept on reloading as well. And then another anti-America person tried to punch Alex in the face, but Alex dodged the punch and kicked the thug in the balls and punched him in the face and threw in the harbor.

And then at the same time, Alex was in Ballard, Sadie and Spencer was in their car and they saw the fire and were shocked "Spencer what's going on over there?" Sadie asked, "I don't know" Spencer said but then they just kept on driving.

Alex meanwhile, kept on running and he kept on shooting at more thugs that were coming at him like crazy. Along with one of the port buildings that caught on fire. As Alex kept on running, Alex then started running on the street and he started running to Ballard. Alex was also able to find a pathway that led to the admiral house by the dock and Alex sneaked on to the property and was able to loose the anti- America thugs that were chasing him. And then Alex went into the house and he was able to see the view of downtown Seattle and also the buildings and the space needle as well. And then Alex went back into the house and he started looking around the house and none of the staff of the place haven't come back yet. And then Alex turned on the TV and he was able to see a commercial that Sadie and Spencer did and found out that a local meet up with them was in Ballard. But Alex didn't think very much of it. And also around the same time, Alex was around the Admiral house, Sadie and Spencer then drove around the Ballard port dock fire. And also since Spencer had military and former police experience he saw the sight and got out of his car. "What happen over here?" He asked "A lot of pro USSR and pro communist people attacked a normal guy in a suit and tie" the police officer said "oh dear that's terrible" Spencer said "is he alright at least?" Spencer asked "We have no idea where he might have gone" the officer said

And then after that social conversation, Spencer then went back into his car and him and Sadie started driving to Ballard. And at this point, it's very important to know that Sadie and Spencer own a nightclub and bar called the ruby league. Now you may say why it's called that but the real reason is because the city of Ballard in Seattle is home to a lot of strange and crazy people. As Alex was still at the admiral house, Alex then lie down on the bed and then fell asleep and then one of the staff saw him and they grabbed Alex and they took to a van and put him inside the trunk. And the van itself just so happens to be going to the Ruby league. And then as Alex was asleep, the two staff members then picked up Alex from both his feet and his head and then they went inside and they threw Alex on a coach while he was sleeping. And at first the club and bar was a very quiet and not a lot of people and Alex was able to sleep peacefully. But then around 4PM or so, Alex started hearing some noise and he slowly started to realize he was in a very strange place, and Alex looked around he saw people in the bar drinking, pool tables, and people playing a lot of interesting looking games, people playing arcade games and watching TV games. Alex got off the couch and Alex looked around and there were posters of Sadie everywhere and then Alex kept on walking and Alex then saw a person wearing A Sadie shirt that looked like he was a fan of her work. And Alex reluctantly sat by him and then same gentlemen as he was drinking his beer then turned to Alex "Are you here to Sadie as well?" he asked "I don't think so, I don't even know how the hell I got here, I have been sleeping for 3 hours or so" Alex said and then little did Alex know, he was sitting on a trap door and then all of a sudden, the trap door opened and then Alex fell through the trap door and the chair he was sitting on dumbed Alex on to a moving slide and Alex started going really fast on the slide and Alex had a concerned look on his face as he was sliding faster "Hello welcome to the Ruby league, you have been chosen to be in my special nightclub, and you stepped on the VIP chair and have been chosen to me in person. And you have entered into the girl made house. Wahooooooo" Sadie's voice said, as she was super excited to meet Alex. And then Alex kept sliding down the slide and saw a lot of clips of Sadie talking to many of her guests on her talk show and seeing a lot of people dancing in lights. "What in the hell am I watching?" Alex thought inside of his head.

And then all of a sudden, Alex fell off the slide and he landed on to a sofa and felt the force very rapidly and then Sadie started doing a girly laugh.

"Welcome" Sadie said and then Sadie laughed again "Welcome to my crazy night club Alex Aussmen" Sadie said and then the lights turned on Sadie showed up as she walked out of another moving object and Sadie showed up in a very beautiful and very gorgeous and very stunning 1980's dress that was purple and she was wearing pink high heels and wearing 1980s sunglasses "I have herd so much about you Mr. Aussmen" Sadie said "Like what kind of things?" Alex asked "Well a lot of good things. Such as from reading my viewer chart that you watch my show and have been doing so since the early 80's. And you also like very beautiful women as well" Sadie said "Oh okay that's actually very accurate" Alex said "And I have read your reports that you are like the best secret agent in the Seattle area as well" Sadie said "And you are finally here in my sight and it's a huge pleasure to meet you as well" Sadie said and then all of a sudden, Sadie got very very close to Alex and she put both of her hands on Alex's face like she was going to kiss him on the lips and Sadie right away was fascinated with Alex's good looks and how handsome he was. "Well I really love your energy and how free spirited you are. But I think I might already have a girl I like" Alex said "Hmmmm oh what's the matter Alex..." Sadie said and then all of a sudden Sadie started bending down and showing her cleavage to Alex to get more of his attention and then all of a sudden, Spencer came in the room, "I don't your funny tricks won't work Sadie, I'll see what I can do" Spencer said and then Spencer was wearing a white suit and tie with 1980's sunglasses and Sadie walked back to Spencer "Good evening Mr. Aussmen, I'm Spencer, and Yeah my girlfriend Sadie loves to hit on guys all the time just to really get into your head" Spencer said "Yeah I can really see that" Alex said "Anyway reason we choice you on the trap door spotlight chair is because we may not be staying in Seattle for very long and planning to move our headquarters back to Minnesota and won't be on the Seattle channels anymore, and since things are getting full, we would be honored if you came with us and be our bodyguard in Minnesota?" Spencer asked as Alex herd the sentence and the question, he then had a lot of thoughts going through his head and the question sounded very crazy as well "Look it was very nice to meet you and Sadie but I'm already employed by Seattle Agencies and I can't leave that agency I'm sorry" Alex said "Oh come on Alex, if you work for us, you will get paid double at what your working currently, also Sadie and I saw video tape of you taking out the Sandinistas in Nicaragua as well and also back in 1976 as well, And if you come with us, I will show a lot of different women as well, and then you will also see more of the world as well" Spencer "But I can't just leave however my current job, also I am not made out of money and…" Alex said but then Alex was interrupted as Spencer pulled out a check for 400 million dollars, "Is that 400 million dollars?" Alex asked, "It is Mr. Aussmen this would be money that would double everything, not just that but I can set you up with a lot of stocks as well and have multiple sources of income other then being a secret agent" Spencer said "also you don't need to move anywhere, you can still live in Seattle, but just be with us for a while. What's it going to be Alex?" Spencer said Alex then started thinking about it for a couple of minutes and then he was able to come up with a choice "Alright, I will go and be you guys new bodyguard" Alex said and then Sadie got really excited and she started hugging Alex "Thank you, thank you, thank you, you will not regret this one bet" Sadie said "Oh your going to have so much fun Alex" Sadie said

And then during that same night, Alex started drinking a lot of beer with Sadie and Spencer and eating food with them as well. And as they kept on talking, Alex really enjoyed their company as well and love their personalities and Sadie and Spencer got to know more about Alex as well. And then as Alex was laughing and having fun with Spencer and Sadie, there was a robotic dog with robot eyes that started spying on Alex and the transmission was going to a submarine in the ocean around where Forks, Washington is. And then Victoria Borodina started looking the TV of Alex laughing with Sadie and Spencer "Go to Minnesota Alex, but even if you go to Minnesota, your evil granny Victoria is going haunt your thoughts and I will send more communist soldiers into the USA and go and capture you and kidnap my little prince Alex and my evil plan will be so harmful that you won't be able to stop me. And prepare to bomb the United States and the USA will be no more....MUAHAHAHAHAHAHAHAHAHAHAHAHAHAHAHAHAHAHAHAHAHA HAHAHAHAHA HEHEHEHEHEHEHEHEHEHEHEHEHEHEHEHEHEHEHEHEHEHEHEHEHEHE HEHEHEHEHEHEHEHEHEHEHEHEHEHEHEHEHEHEHEHEHEHEHEHEHEHE HEHEHEHEHEHEHEHEHEHEHEHEHEHEHEHEEHEHEHEHEHEHEHEHEHEHE HE" Victoria laughed as her laugh was sounding more and more like an evil witch and even though Alex was excited to go on a new adventure of sorts, he knew that there was a lot of evil waiting for him.

Chapter 2, Meeting Sadie and Spencer's bodyguard in Minnesota

Alex kept on hanging out with Spencer and Sadie under the nightclub and they all had really wonderful conversations as well that night. And then around 11PM or so, Alex then was able to call a taxi and the taxi was able to take him back to his apartment in downtown Seattle and then as he got there, Alex started packing a lot of clothes in his huge bag including a lot of suits and other clothes and bathing suits as well. And then Alex took a shower and then he shaved some of his left over facial hair that was on his face and then he took off his clothes and then he went to sleep and then he was able to set an alarm to wake up around 4AM. And as Alex was sleeping, he really didn't know what to expect when being Sadie and Spencer's bodyguards but he knew doing this was a trip of a lifetime that was somewhat a break from his usual secret agent missions that he did in the past. And then he was also thinking about Jenny as well and while he was sleeping, he started developing a lot of sexual feelings for her and he often would get erections that would last for 9 hours as well. As Alex's alarm started to ring and go off like crazy, Alex then got up and he was able to take a shower, get dressed and he was able to put on a 1980's suit and tie and also put a par of 1980's sunglasses on his head as well. Alex was able to go out the door with his bag and his other important items as well. Alex then was able to call a taxi through a pay phone and in 30 minutes or so, the taxi arrived and Alex went into the cab and the cab started driving to Sea-Tac airport. And Alex knew that this one of his top secret missions that he was going on and also he didn't have enough time to tell Michael and Tony that he was leaving and going to be out of town and knew that this was going to be a long trip.

The car was able to get to Sea-Tac airport and the car was able to drop off Alex around the gate, "Glad you can make it Alex" Sadie said and then as Alex got out of the car, Sadie was so happy, that she ran up to Alex was able to give him a really hug that lasted for 20 minutes or so and Sadie just loved touching Alex especially his backside and touching hit buttocks as well. And then all of a sudden, Sadie released him "So are you ready to go to the mid-west?" she asked "Oh I am ready, also another thing to point out is that I have been to mid-west back I believe in 1985 or so when I went on a mission in Chicago and stopping a crazy highway from being built" Alex said "Oh okay, sounds like you know where your things are, that's great" Sadie said "And also that's really amazing Alex" Sadie also said "Oh thank you" Alex said "Well we better get going otherwise we are going to miss our flight" Spencer said "Oh yeah I agree man" Alex said and then Alex, Spencer, and Sadie started heading to the ticket counter and they were able to get their tickets and then from there, they also went through customs well and Alex was able to use a special gadget so that the metal detectors wouldn't get triggered. As they all got to the terminal and got to their gate number and just sat down in the chairs. As Alex was sitting down, he then went to go get a Wendy's cheeseburger and fries and lemonade and also get himself a frosty as well and then as he came back to his seats Spencer turned his head and saw Alex eating "yo man that's a lot of food, do you always use a lot?" Spencer asked "Oh yeah I always do my man, mainly because I'm always on the move and walking and running and always have energy and never get tired" Alex said "you must have a very hard time sleeping I assume" Spencer said "Not really, I always drink milk before I go to bed or a milkshake" Alex said "How many calories do you end up burning?" Spencer asked "Somewhere around 5,000 maybe" Alex said "Oh that's really amazing Alex" Sadie said "Yeah your like the terminator my man" Spencer said And then after one hour later, Alex, Sadie, And Spencer then herd the announcement in the airport and that their plane to Minnesota was about to take off and boarding was about to begin. And so they all started getting up on their feet and they started heading in line. And then as they got in line, they then sat around the middle part of the plane and Alex got to sit in the aisle seat. And from there, the airplane started taking off from Seattle, Washington to St. Paul, Minnesota and on the plane, Alex was sleeping on the plane and Alex was dreaming a lot about Jenny and having crazy dreams where Alex was making out with her on the beach and they were in very sexy swimsuits as well. And then as Alex was sleeping, Sadie and Spencer were able to get their food on the airplane and then Alex would get up around certain times during the plane ride and also drink like a coke or a ginger ale as well.

And then after a couple hours, the airplane landed and landed in the airport, and then everybody in the plane then I started getting off the airplane. And then Alex, Spencer, Sadie got off the airplane, Alex was really looking around with his eyes because he staring at the elements in the airport. Especially at the culture elements. And then they all started heading to baggage clam and went to get their suitcases and then they started heading to a rent a car on one of the buses. And then as they got to the rent a car place, they then got to the place, the three of them got in lane and then they all started waiting. "So what kind of car do you guys want?" Alex asked "you know that's a really good question Alex, I think we really need a car that is really good when it comes to travel" Sadie said "Like a RV or motorhome or a trailer?" Alex asked, "Yeah something like but a little small" Sadie said "Sounds good. If you actually want to know a story, My best friend Michael and I actually drove in one when were heading to Dallas, Texas on a mission" Alex said "That must have been really fun, and Texas is a very beautiful state" Sadie said "It is" Alex said "What kind of mission was it?" Sadie asked "Well it was a mission where we with a French painter and he was selling art at an art convention" Alex said "oh wow" Sadie said "Oh yeah" Alex said and then as the line kept on moving, the three of them were able to get the front of the line. "Can I help you people?" the rent a car person asked "Yeah we really need a traveling car?" Sadie asked "Alright I think we have the car for you sweetie" the rent a car person said and then all of a sudden, they then went outside and they saw a van that looked like a hippie van but it was more modern looking as well "This car is a good mix between car and a motor-home" the rent a car person said "Oh sweet that's really wonderful, we will take it" Sadie said "And also the car rent is around 300$" the person pointed out "Alright that's pretty cheap" Spencer said and then as they got the car, Spencer and Sadie started packing their things in the car, and then so did Alex as well. And then as they all got into the car, Alex went to the back seat and he started looking around and he right away started getting flash backs to 1978. "So who is driving?" Alex asked "why don't you drive and give it a go" Spencer said and then Spencer threw the keys to Alex and Alex was able to catch the keys. And then Alex climbed into the driver's seat and he put the keys into the main car hole and then Alex then started turning on the car and right away, Alex started driving the car and Alex started to drive on a highway and he was driving on the highway and heading to downtown St. Paul and Alex saw a lot of the different buildings and then Alex saw the mall of America and Alex started driving there "I would imagine you guys need some champing gear cause of your traveling stuff right?" Alex asked "Yeah defiantly for sure Alex" Sadie said "And then also some cameras as well" Spencer said

"Sounds good" Alex said and then Alex started driving to mall of America.

And then as they got there, Sadie and Spencer started going into stores and they started getting a lot of different 1980's camping gear, and then Alex was with them and he also looked around and looking at the different clothes that were there. And then Sadie would come out of the dressing room "Alex how does this look on me?" Sadie asked "I love it Sadie, it looks very beautiful and very stunning on you" Alex said "oh thank you" and then in another store, Spencer was looking at different cameras that were both video and normal cameras as well. And Spencer was able to buy them with new sweat what so ever. And then as everyone was done shopping, they then started heading to the car and Alex got into the driver's seat "So where are we going next?" Alex asked "We are going to my house that is in one of the suburb neighborhoods" Sadie said "Sweet" Alex said and then all of a sudden, Sadie was able to hand Alex was directions and Alex started driving and fallowing the directions to get to Sadie's house. And then as Alex kept on driving, he then turned his head to the left and he saw a normal looking 2-story house that had a normal backyard and the style of the house looked very castle like and then Alex stood in his tracks and he just starred at the house in amazement "So this is your home?" Alex asked "Oh yeah this is where Spencer and I live and also April lives here as well" Sadie said, "That's really cool" Alex said "you have to see more things, it does a lot of other cool stuff, especially underground" Sadie said And then Alex was able to park the car, and then they all got unloaded the car with all the things that Sadie and Spencer bought and they started heading into the castle house.

As they all got into the house, Inside of the house was really fancy and there was a lot of paintings and art everywhere, a TV room, and then a really fancy looking kitchen and then also there was bedrooms around the other side of the room as well. "Man guys, this house is amazing and really incredible" Alex said "Oh thank you Alex, this is a house that is been in my family for a lot of generations and it was built by my ancestors that came from England and also from France as well" Sadie said "Oh that's really amazing" Alex said "What about your parents?" Alex asked, "Well my mom and dad were also really wealthy and you know he didn't really have a big time job, but he just always invested in the stock market a lot, and then that's what April and I and Spencer did as well" Sadie said "That's actually really smart, That's something I really need to do, cause I know that I can't be a secret agent forever" Alex said "Well how much do you make Alex?" Spencer asked "Well so far around 400,000$ a year but it use to be a lot less when I was a teenager" Alex said, "I see" Spencer said "But yeah if you stick with us Alex, we will teach you how to make a lot of money" Spencer said "Thanks Spencer" Alex said "But you also have to see underground part of the house as well" Sadie said And then Alex, Sadie, And Spencer then started walking downstairs and then Sadie pressed a button and then parts of the wall started to open up and they all went into the elevator and then all of a sudden, the elevator started going down. And then as the elevator stopped, they all got out of the elevator and Alex was really amazed and around the basement and underground parts, there was a swimming pool, hot-tub, a lot of arcade games, and then also some darts. And then also a basketball court and other forms of entertainment. And then there was also a gym down there as well. "Oh wow this is amazing" Alex said "Yeah this were we all come down and play and chill down here as well" Sadie said "And then we also even fire pit as well to cock marshmallows" Spencer said "This place is like my apartment on steroids" Alex said "So Alex buddy, what do you want to do first?" Spencer asked "I don't know, I'm going to try out the game room" Alex said and then all of a sudden, Alex then started trying out the game room and then after a couple of hours, Alex and Spencer then played each other in one on one basketball. And then after doing that, Alex, Sadie, and Spencer had some food as well and they were all having Hot dogs with cheddar cheese on them along with relish and onions and they also had popcorn with butter on them as well "Well I must say you guys, thank you so much for letting me come with you guys, and your house is incredible" Alex said "oh thank you Alex" Sadie said "So what is planned for tomorrow? if you don't mind me asking." Alex asked, "Well, we are going to do another show in downtown Minnesota. You don't really have much to do, you just are bodyguard and you wear a suit and make sure nothing happens to Spencer and I. And then we also get ready to travel again" Sadie said "Sounds really good, I can't wait" Alex said

And then during that night, Alex then went to sleep and as Alex was sleeping, he heard a lot of noises and also the snow that was falling down on the ground. And then the next morning, Alex then woke up and he then took a shower and then he also got dressed into normal 1980's style clothing and then before Sadie and Spencer got up, Alex then started looking around the house. And Alex even looked at the window and he saw the snow falling down and then all of a sudden, Alex herd one of the doors in the house open and it was Spencer and Sadie walking towards him "Morning Alex" Sadie said "Morning Sadie" Alex said "How did you sleep?" Spencer asked him "I slept really well. What about you?" Alex asked "really good, yeah in this house, you will always get a nights rest" Spencer said "That's awesome my man" Alex said "Well I better make us some breakfast and we have a big show to do" Spencer said and then during that morning, Alex, Sadie, and Spencer all started eating breakfast and then after breakfast, everyone started getting dressed and then Alex got on a suit and tie and he was able to brush his teeth. And then Alex got into Sadie's car and he was able to drive Sadie and Spencer to downtown Minnesota and started driving to their studio. And as Alex kept on driving, he was really amazed at how big everything was, and then Alex drove into the parking garage and he was able to park the car. And then as Alex was able to park the car, Sadie, Alex, and Spencer started heading to the elevator and the elevator started going up and they were going to the 60th floor. And then as they got to the floor, Alex then saw a lot of directions and posters of Sadie and Spencer and Alex fallowed them to their dressing room and then Sadie stopped and turned around "Alright what you do is just check for tickets and that's all you do." Sadie said, "Alright sweet, shouldn't be that hard I don't think" Alex said "good luck and be careful Alex" Sadie said and then all of a sudden, Alex then started walking out of the stage and he was guarding the main stage and checking for tickets from the people coming in. And for the most part, Alex was able to do this really well, and also just incase there was a bad person that was coming in, he also had a pistol gun in his suit pocket. But then as Alex ticketing people, there all of a sudden, was another beautiful and a very gorgeous and very stunning girl with blonde hair and she also eyes that were a mix between green and blue eyes, and she walking in there with her mom as well, Alex wasn't really paying attention anybody that was coming and was just mainly doing the job he was tasked to do. And then the same girl with those same features, just smiled at him and just said "Thank you"

And then as the show was going to start and everybody start getting in their seats and as the lights got shut off, there was a lot of lights that were flashing and then the song "Papa don't preach by Madonna" and then Spencer did the announcing work "Live from Minnesota in front of a live studio audience it is the Living With Adventures with Sadie. And now without further a do, here is Sadie Holbrock" Spencer said on the microphone and then all of a sudden, a lot of the crowd started clapping and really going crazy and also screaming with excitement as well. And then all of a sudden, the curtain opened and Sadie was in a very beautiful pink 1980's style dress as well. "Thank you, thank you, thank you everyone, my name is Sadie Holbrock and I do this show every week, and if your someone that really loves to travel and see the world, well this show is for you" Sadie said with a smile on her face.

And then as Alex was behind the door, little did Alex knew there was a lot of evil looking people that had scares and ugly finger nails that were starting to come towards Alex while he was guarding, then one of the guards ended up punching Alex in the face and Alex ended up being knocked out, and then Alex fell to the ground, and then the thugs grabbed Alex and they put him inside a bag and they started taking to the top parts of the building and around a basement. And then after a couple of hours into the show and around some of the breaks in between, Sadie noticed that Alex was gone and she really started getting concerned for him. "Oh my god Spencer Alex is gone" Sadie said, "Do you know where he might be?" She asked "Sadly I don't know. And yeah I noticed that he is gone as well. And I think some shady looking people kidnapped him and they didn't look very nice either" Spencer said "I'm going to go look for him Sadie" Spencer said and then Spencer then went out of the studio and he had a gun in his coat and he started looking around the building for Alex.

And then all of a sudden in the abandon room of the skyscraper in Minnesota, the bag was lifted from Alex's head and Alex had duck tape on his mouth and his hands were tied up and in duck tape as well. And then Alex started hearing a very evil, very creepy, and a very evil witch laugh coming towards "HEHEHEHEHEHEHEHEHE HEHEHEHEHEHEHEHEHEHE!!!!!!!! Good evening Mr. Aussmen!!!!!!! And hello, hello, hello my handsome little boy!!!!!!" the witch voice said and then all of a sudden, it turned out the evil Victoria Borodina and Alex for the first time saw her new look. And Alex started grunting in anger and he was trying to get free "I have right where I want you Alex, and you nowhere to run and even though you are in Minnesota, I was always going to be around to make your life a living hell. And also I am a lot more uglier and more witch like because I have had more plastic surgery done on me and now I look like an evil witch from all the scary stories, and if you really thought my Social justice Warrior and colored hair was scary, I think my new look will give you a lot of nightmares Alex" Victoria said "And then I also have these yellow zits on me as well Mr. Aussmen!!!!!!" Victoria also added and then she did another soft and evil witch laugh. And then Alex kept on grunting and trying to get free "Do you even know why I am in Minnesota to begin with Mr. Aussmen?" Victoria asked "It's mostly because your friend Sadie Holbrock's ancestors stole a lot of money and gold and treasure from my ancestors and I tend to kill her and her sister and her boyfriend to have it back and this time you will not stand in my way little boy" Victoria said "Put him outside to freeze to death" Victoria said to her thugs "With pleasure boss" one of her thugs said and then all of a sudden, Victoria's thugs grabbed Alex and they started going upstairs and they took the elevator to the top of the skyscraper building. And then the thugs started tying up Alex and they even ripped the duck tape off of his mouth and Alex was in a lot of pain.

And after Sadie's show was all done, then all of a sudden, there was a lot of shooting that happened and a lot of people were screaming and people were really scarred. And then all of a sudden, Sadie also got really scarred and then all of a sudden, Victoria and her thugs showed up into the room "Good Evening Ms. Holbrock" Victoria said "Who are you?..." Sadie said in a very scarred voice "Oh I'm someone that really knows your family history really well and I do believe you have money that belongs to me" Victoria said "And if you don't give it me, I will kill or kidnap someone in this room or someone that did go to your show" Victoria said in a very evil witch like voice and then all of a sudden, Victoria and her thugs started getting really close to Sadie and Sadie started getting really scared and all of a sudden, they grabbed Sadie and they tied her up somewhere on the stage. And some of her thugs tried to get one of the 1980's computers that was around the backstage on the studio and they started hacking into her bank account and they were able to put all of Sadie's money into a keycard.

Meanwhile at the same time, Spencer found Alex as he was tied up and he un-tied him on the roof and the snow was coming down on him like crazy. Spencer then had some hot water in his bottle and dumped some hot water on Alex to warm him up. Alex's body got trigged and warmed up and Alex was able to get back on his feet. "Are you okay Alex?" Spencer said "Yeah I think so buddy, we have to stop Borodina and her thugs cause I know she is up to something. Come on!!!!!" Alex said and then all of a sudden, Alex and spencer started running down the stairs and going at a rapid pace. And then as they got to the main floor, they saw a lot more thugs and they had deadly hand guns in their hand, and then all of a sudden, they started shooting around 77 bullets at Alex and Spencer, Alex and Spencer were able to avoid the bullets and were able to take cover. Alex then reloaded his Walter gun and Alex pointed his gun and grabbed his gun with two hands and Alex started firing 99 bullets and Alex was able to shoot around 9 thugs coming at him and was able to shoot them in the head and kill them. And then all of a sudden, more thugs started coming at them and they had A33 riffles in their hand and they started shooting around 900 bullets at Alex and Spencer and they able to take cover. "I got these guys, go save Sadie, go Alex!!!!" Spencer said and then all of a sudden with all the speed in his strange and weird body, Alex then started running to the show room for dear life, and then as more thugs were shooting at Alex, Alex then dived on the floor and then Alex was sliding on the floor and then as Alex was sliding on the floor, Alex then kicked one of the thugs in the legs and then Alex was able to use both of his legs and grab and slam to the ground head first. And then a lot of thugs that didn't have any weapons started coming towards him and they started throwing a lot of punches and kicks at Alex. And then Alex was able to dodge the attacks and throw some punches and kicks back at 4 different thugs that were coming at him.

And then Alex was able to punch one of the thugs in the face and also grab another one by the arm and slam against the wall. And then Alex was able to kick another in the face and then kick another one in the stomach and knock that one out as well. And then Alex kept on fighting more thugs and then Alex was able to punch 3 more of them in the face and then Alex grabbed a fire department axe and stabbed 4 more of them in the stomach and kill them. And then after killing the thugs, Alex then kept on running and Alex breaked the door open and Victoria was on stage and more thugs were pointing their riffle guns at Alex and Victoria had the keycard in her left hand and showed it to Alex "Looking for this!!!...." Victoria said and then Victoria was pointing a gun at Sadie "you are very too late Mr. Aussmen, I have already gotten most of Sadie's money and in a couple of minutes I will use her money to build more weapons from my castle in Ukraine and then I will rule the world and destroy everyone that stands in my way" Victoria said "You will never get away with this Borodina!!!!!!!" Alex said "Oh I think I have already have little boy!!!!, and now the time has come for me to escape in my helicopter" Victoria said in her evil witch voice "it ain't going to happen you ugly Ukraine bitch!!!!!" Alex said in anger in his voice and then without Alex knowing, Sadie was able to get herself free and then all of a sudden, Sadie was able to kick Victoria in the face and punch her in the face and knock the keycard out of her hand. "Alex grab the card!!!!" Sadie said and then Alex started running and all of Borodina's thugs started shooting a lot of bullets at Alex and then Alex reloaded his gun and then Alex started shooting at the thugs and Alex was able to fire around 15 bullets and Alex was able to kill around 5 thugs that were shooting at him and then Alex reloaded his gun and more thugs were shooting at him and then Alex started shooting 20 more bullets out of his gun and then Alex started running and he jumped on stage and Alex kept on shooting at the thugs coming at him and Alex was able to kill 40 thugs that were coming at him and shoot them in the head and then also shoot them in one of the eyes. And then Alex finally was able to get to Sadie and un-tie her "Thank you Alex" Sadie said "Your welcome Sadie" Alex said "Go find Spencer and find a safe place and get out of here" Alex said "Alright okay" Sadie said "Alex be careful they have a lot of guns and a lot of Ukraine thugs as well that hate America" Sadie said "Don't worry I'm going to be okay. Trust me" Alex said and then Sadie started running out of the skyscraper and she went into one of the elevator with Spencer "Where's Alex?" Spencer asked, "He is going after the thugs" Spencer said "Man that guy has a lot of fight in him" Spencer said

And then as Alex was in the room, one of Borodina's thugs threw a bomb at Alex and there was a huge explosion and all of a sudden, the building started catching on fire and then Alex did a summer-sault and then all of a sudden Alex saw the same girl with blonde hair that said thank you and the girl was looking at Alex and the girl was looking for her mom who was trapped in the building. And then all of a sudden Borodina grabbed the girl with blonde hair and she started getting really scarred and Borodina grabbed her by the wrist and then she took out a pistol gun and pointed the gun at her "Somebody help me, someone help me!!!!" she cried "Shut up you stupid American girl!!!!!" Borodina yelled and then Borodina threaten her with a taser. And then Alex was able to catch up with Borodina and Alex had a Walter gun in his right hand "If you fallow me the girl dies!!!!!!" Borodina yelled and then the girl started screaming as she was really scarred and then Alex saw a window and then Alex broke one of the windows and Alex jumped out the window and then Alex started sky diving and falling and then Alex pressed a button his spy watch and then all of a sudden, Alex had wings come out of his fancy shoes and then Alex started gliding in the air and then Alex saw Borodina in a blue and yellow limo. And then on the ground, Borodina forced the girl with blonde hair to get into the limo and then the car started driving really fast. And then moments later, Alex then landed on the ground and Alex started looking around and then he saw a motorcycle and Alex was able to steel the motorcycle and then Alex started up the motorcycle and then Alex all of a sudden, started going really fast and he started going around 200 miles per hour on the bike.

And then as the limo started going really fast on the road in snowy Minnesota, Alex then started going really fast on the motorcycle and he was speeding through a lot of cars and speeding a lot of red lights as well. And Alex was wearing special sunglasses that were protecting his eyes from the snow. And then Borodina turned and saw Alex chasing her "Aussmen, Only Aussmen, Kill him!!!!!" Borodina said and then all of a sudden, her driver started pressing a lot of buttons and throwing a lot of weaponry at Alex. And then Alex was able to put on the pedal to medal and go really fast on the motorcycle and then Alex pulled out a ZMG gun and then all of a sudden, Alex started firing around 200 bullets at Borodina's limo and shooting at her window. And then Alex was able to dodge a lot of cars that were coming at him and then Alex was able to go off a lot of ramps and Alex was doing a lot of front and backflips while he was on the motorcycle while he was up in the air and then Alex was able to land on the ground and keep on going really fast. And then Borodina inside of her limo, she then pressed a lot of buttons and she fired a lot of machine gun and rockets and missiles at Alex and then Alex was able to dodge the missiles and rockets that were coming at him and then the rockets and missiles caused a lot of explosion in downtown Minnesota and some buildings started catching on fire. And then as the chase was going on, Alex saw Borodina's limo that was going towards a warehouse that had a landing roof on top of the building. And then Borodina was able to park her limo and then she got out of the limo and grabbed the girl "Get out!!!!!" She yelled and then she pointed a gun at her head "Otrymaty vertolit hotovyj!!!!" Borodina said in Ukraine and then all of her thugs started getting ready to get the helicopter ready to go. But then all of a sudden, Alex was able to get into the building and then more thugs saw him and they started shooting a lot of bullets at Alex and then Alex took out his gun and then he started firing more bullets back at Borodina's thugs and also taking cover as well. Alex then reloaded his gun and then he kept on shooting more bullets at the thugs and shooting them in the head and also in other areas as well. And then Alex kept on running he then saw Borodina taking the girl into the helicopter "let her go Borodina!!!!!" Alex said as he was pointing and aiming his gun at her "you loose again Alex!!!!" Borodina said and then all of a sudden, Borodina threw a bomb and Alex was able to dodge the bomb and all of a sudden, there was a huge explosion and the warehouse started catching on fire. And then Alex started looking around and he saw a snowboard object that was in the warehouse and Alex stepped on to the snowboard and it actually turned out to be flying board and then Alex pressed on the button and board started zooming up in the air and then Alex took his gun and he saw Borodina's helicopter and her helicopter started heading towards the mall of America stadium and then helicopter turned back and the helicopter started firing a lot of missiles and rockets at Alex. And then Alex was able to control the flying board really well and he was able to dodge all of the missiles and rockets coming at him. And then Alex was able to reload his gun and then Alex kept on shooting at the helicopter as he was in the sky and then Alex was able to do a lot more damage to the helicopter and cause some explosions as well. And then Borodina's face got really burned up really bad and then all of sudden, the girl with blonde hair then feel to the ground and she started screaming as she was falling in the sky and then all of a sudden, Alex then started diving down really fast and then with all of his might, Alex was able to catch her in his strong arms and then Alex turned his back and he saw Borodina's helicopter flying in the dark and snowy skies of Minnesota

"We will meet again Mr. Aussmen" Borodina yelled as the helicopter was flying away

And then as Alex was going back to the ground on the flying board, the girl with blonde hair then snowy looked up at Alex's face and with her beautiful and sparking blue eyes that she had "Oh you rescued me. Oh you're my hero, who are you by the way?" She asked "The names Aussmen...Alex Aussmen" Alex said to her "Aussmen that is a really strange and a very un-usual last name. But anyway, thank you so much for saving me, Sadly we do need to find my mom, and I think she was in the building that evil witch lady attacked" She said "Yeah I can imagine" Alex said

"Anyway what is your name?" Alex asked her "Oh I'm Rebecca by the way" Rebecca said "Rebecca who?" Alex asked again "Rebecca Olga" Rebecca said "That's also a very strange last name as well" Alex said "Anyway I will get you back on the ground and then hopefully we will find your mom as well" Alex said "So do you know Sadie Holbrock yourself?" Rebecca asked, "Yeah I do, both her and Spencer are good people" Alex said "So are you originally from Minnesota or are you from somewhere else?" Rebecca asked, "I'm from Seattle, Washington" Alex said, "Oh wow that's really cool and really amazing, I hear that's a really amazing state to live in" Rebecca said "Oh yeah it is" Alex said

And then once Alex and Rebecca landed on the ground, Alex and Rebecca started running to a pay phone and Alex was able to call a cab from the pay phone and then the taxi was able to find them. And then as they got into the cab, they then started driving back to downtown Minnesota and started driving back to Sadie's building. And then Alex was able to pay the driver and then moments later, Spencer was able to find Rebecca's mom in the building and it turned out she was trapped in one of the rooms once Rebecca was taken by Borodina "Mom are you okay?" Rebecca said and then Rebecca started running to her mom and hugging her "Oh yeah I'm fine Rebecca, I'm just glad you are okay. Anyway thank you guys for saving my daughter. I really appreciate it a lot" Rebecca's mom said, "Oh no problem you have to give it Alex, it was him that did everything" Spencer said, "Do you have the keycard Alex?" Spencer asked, "I actually have it" Rebecca said and then all of a sudden, Rebecca handed the keycard that had a lot of Sadie's money inside of the keycard and she handed to Spencer, "I was able to jack it on that witch lady's helicopter before Alex saved me" Rebecca said "alright good girl, I will try to see if I can get this back to Sadie" Spencer said

Sadie was able to catch up to Spencer and Alex and Spencer was able to hand Sadie the key card and then Rebecca and her mom went back home and Alex headed back to Sadie's house and she was able to put the keycard into the computer and get every single dime back into bank account "Oh thank god" Sadie said "Oh wow today was just so scary and horrifying as well" Sadie also added "Yeah tell me about it, Alex who were all those people?" Spencer asked him "....Sadly those are people that are after me, their leader is Victoria Borodina who is from Ukraine and she has wanted to kill for almost 12 years ever since I was teenager, and she has her evil witch claws into every terrorist organization that is out there as well" Alex said "Sounds like she knows a crazy amount of information about you" Sadie said "Oh you have no idea" Alex said "And then not only that, but she works very closely with the Sandinistas in Nicaragua and also the soviet union as well which is also really bad" Alex said "oh my god, that reminds me of someone I interviewed on my show" Sadie said "you mean Salem?" Alex said, "How did you know?" Sadie asked "Well I remember watching one of your shows and episode where you had him on and I actually saved him when he was in Portland, Oregon and Borodina and her goons were trying to kill him" Alex said "Oh my god that is terrible" Sadie said "Yeah it just goes to show that there are a lot of bad and messed up and very evil people in this world baby girl" Alex said "So what do you think we need to do Alex?" Spencer asked, "Well for the most part, I actually really don't know Spencer. But I know Borodina did try to kidnap Rebecca and I was able to save her, and I believe I'm going to try to know her a lot more I believe" Alex said "Well sounds like a really good idea Alex. Do you want Spencer and I to come with you?" Sadie asked "Yeah sure why not" Alex said and then later that day at Sadie's castle like house, Sadie then started going through her phone book and she started looking for Rebecca's first name and her last name and then finally around 4PM, Sadie was able to find Rebecca's information and also her occupation as well. And apparently Rebecca was a freelance model and she would also be in front of people in art classes. And then the next day, Alex then took a shower and then he found a way to get a bus fare card and he went to downtown Minnesota because Spencer was able to drive him. And then as Alex got to the bus office that was there, he was able to fill in his information really well and was able to get a bus pass. And then as he got out of the office, he then took a bus to the community college that was around downtown. And Alex got off the bus and then he started looking around the campus, and then Alex saw an ad that was on a bulletin board that said, "art models needed" and then Alex looked at the piece of paper really closely and then Alex started heading to the classroom and as a lot of the students were leaving the room, the main art professor looked at Alex and he had a puzzled look on his face "can I help young man?" he asked "Sure you can sir, I saw that you needed some art models for some of your classes I believe, I was wondering if that was still open?" Alex asked and then the professor looked at him for maybe 20 seconds "Yeah it's still open, have you modeled before?" he asked " Yes I have actually back in 1976 when I was teenager and then there was also other times where I had to be naked a lot as well" Alex said "yeah you're a really handsome guy. And I can tell the girls love you and you seem very boyish as well" the professor said "How much are willing to be paid?" the professor asked him "I'm willing to work minimum wage" Alex said "Alright...perfect" he said and then all of a sudden the professor gave some Alex some papers and it was some- what like a release forum and Alex gave every sort information that he knew that was in his head. And then as Alex was filling out the paper work, he then gave the paper work back to the professor "perfect" he said "Also robes are in my office and your welcome to grab one and once you strip everything off" he said "Alright sounds good sir" Alex said and then Alex walked to the back room and then Alex started taking his clothes and his underwear intel he was butt naked and then he put one of the robes to cover his naked body, and all of a sudden very slowly he then pecked his head and all of a sudden, he saw Rebecca in the class room and Rebecca had a normal look on her face. And then Alex had a smile on his face and Alex was really excited and then as the clock strikes the start time of the class, Alex then went to the middle room and he had a huge smile on his face as he saw a lot of beautiful girls wearing a lot of 1980's clothing and then the girls smiled at him back and some even chuckled did a soft laugh and then the professor gave a lecture before the class started "Now everyone we are going to draw a naked male body, it's not a test and do your best" he said and then all of a sudden, without hesitation Alex then took off his robe and Alex was butt naked and he started doing a lot of model poses and Alex then started doing a lot of poses that he did when he was modeling in New York City when he was with Dr. Jasmine Thompson that one time. But this time was completely different because he wanted to get Rebecca's attention and get to know her. As Rebecca was drawing Alex's naked body she was softly shocked as she saw how huge Alex's pennis really was but then she then smiled and then she slowly gave Alex eye contact and she started looking at Alex with a dreamy look on her face. And then Alex kept on posing and Alex felt his pennis getting bigger and bigger the more he posed. 3 hours later, as students left the room, the professor gave his own submission of the class and as the students left, Alex then put his robe back on and the professor turned to him "Well bravo young man, I can tell you really enjoyed yourself up there and a couple of my students that were girls loved your body as well" he said "oh yeah it was nothing sir" Alex said and then all of a sudden, the professor went to his desk and he started writing a Alex for 40$. Now to put this in perspective, 40$ is not a lot of money, but Alex had some very special plans for this normal check of 40$ and Alex put the money in his wallet and he started heading to nearest bus stop that was around him.

As Alex was waiting for the bus, then 20 different college girls that were in the same art class started coming up to him and they really wanted to know more about Alex as well "we really loved your body…" one of them said and then one of them really were just laughing and chuckling "so what's your name?" one of them said again "I'm Alex…Alex Aussmen" Alex said" Alex said "well it's a pleasure to meet you Alex, and we really loved your model poses as well. And we are actually having a party at an apartment, and I was wondering if you wanted to come with us?" they asked "Um…sure why the hell not" Alex said and then Alex went with the girls and he rode with one girl that had brown hair, she had blue finger nails, and she wore a lot of 1980's make up on her as well. And also she was a white girl but Alex was just amazed how beautiful she was as she was driving and also her other gestures she would make as well. And then as the car kept on going, they then parked in the parking lot and Alex started walking with the girl with blonde hair "Oh your going to like where we are taking you Alex baby boy" she said and then they went up to the elevator and then they were around 20th floor of the building and then they got off the elevator and they started walking into the building and all of a sudden, as they walked into the room and there was around 60 beautiful girls that were in 1980's bikini underwear and wearing Victoria Secrets and other ladies underwear brands as well. And then inside of the party, they were playing Papa don't preach by Madonna and there was a lot of alcohol at this party and a lot of girls being wild and really crazy. And then Alex just smiled and he said to himself "Wow" Alex said and then all of a sudden, Alex during that party drank around 4 beers and got really wasted and then 5 girls took Alex to a huge bedroom and one of them placed him on the bed "awwwwwwe such a handsome baby boy he is, I think it's time to take his clothes off" one of them said "ah okay ladies" Alex said and then all of a sudden they started tickling Alex and they were laughing and then started stripping Alex and Alex was laughing and then the girls started off their clothes, the first one that was butt naked was an African American girl, the 2nd one was a Hispanic American girl, the 3rd and 4th ones were white girls, and then the last one was a Hawaiian looking girl that had tan skin and her breaths and her bottom were really big. And the girls kept on making out for at least 5 hours. And Alex ended up sleeping with all five the girls and then as night time came around, Alex was really tired and all five of the naked girls in bed with him were softly touching him everywhere and saying "Oh Alex hold me" one of them said and then one of them even kissed Alex on the lips and went on top of Alex as well. And then all of a sudden, Alex saw the faces of the girls and then they started laughing but then all of a sudden, as Alex was making out with girls, then Alex herd a door open and Alex took a quick peak and then Alex's eyes lit up and then some of girls that were butt naked in the room all of a sudden saw a riffle gun pointed at them and then they started shooting 900 bullets at the girls and the girls were screaming in fear and crying and tears were coming out of their eyes. And then all of a sudden, the thugs and all of a sudden Victoria Borodina went into the room and saw Alex with girls he was sleeping "I got you now little boy!!!!" she said with a witch like voice "Get down!!!!!!" Alex yelled but it was too late, Victoria and her thugs sadly shoot the girls that Alex slept and all of a sudden there was a blood in the bed and then Alex was really sad as he saw the girls dead in his bed "Oh my god!!!!" Alex said and a tear fell through one his eyes and then with tears in his eyes Alex kissed all of five of them in the back and their bottoms as well and also their neck and Alex kept on breathing really hard as tears were coming out of his eyes.

And then Alex then tried to run but then one of the thugs grabbed Alex from behind and Victoria took out a whip and Alex started grunting and trying to get free "Don't be sad Alex...this room was my personal pen house and I knew I was going to trick all those college girls to be here and then kill them once I found out you were here as well" Victoria said "you fucking monster!!!!!" Alex yelled and then all of sudden Victoria hit Alex with a whip and hit him right around his private areas and Alex felt the sting very badly "You know Alex even though your 29 years old, I will always be smarter then you and I will always be a social cancer to you as well" Borodina in a very evil witch voice and then all of a sudden without Alex knowing, Spencer and Sadie were able to track Alex down from her castle house and they slowly start getting to the pen house and then as they got there and Victoria were about to whip Alex really bad, then Sadie grunted her teeth and then she fired 6 bullets at Borodina and shoot her in the arm and in back of her skull and Borodina screamed like a witch and then some of her hair fell out and then Alex got free and then Alex then punched 4 of her thugs in the face and then kicked more of them in the stomach as well. And then Victoria tried to whip Alex more but then Alex grabbed Victoria's face and pushed and electrocuted her face badly and then Victoria screamed and then Alex while he was naked started running away with Sadie and Spencer "GET THEM!!!!" Victoria screamed and then as they kept on running and Sadie and Spencer started firing bullets at Borodina and her thugs "yo man what happen to your clothes bro?" Spencer asked "it's a very long story" Alex said and then they kept on running and more of Victoria's thugs kept on shooting at Alex, Sadie, and Spencer and then as they got to the first floor, Sadie and Spencer brought their big car and Alex hid in the back so no other people would see Alex's nudity "I can imagine the art model thing went really well for you I believe" Sadie said "oh yeah it went really well" Alex said "Good" Sadie said "And then I also saw Rebecca as well and she really loved my modeling as well" Alex said "Oh that's awesome and really wonderful Alex" Sadie said and then all of a sudden, Spencer started driving and then Sadie started firing a lot of guns and gadgets at Victoria's thug cars that were chasing them. "And we also may take Rebecca with us because I believe they may have our information and Rebecca's information as well" Spencer said "Alright okay, we may need to meet her at a certain place here in St. Paul" Alex said "oh yeah for sure man" Spencer said Spencer then kept on driving and Sadie was able to throw around 19 mine bombs at the cars and was able to blow up them in flames and they kept on moving from there. Luckily however Sadie had Rebecca's information as well and it looked like she lived in an apartment complex place in the city. And then as they got there, they then parked the car and Alex, Sadie, and Spencer ran to Rebecca's door and Sadie knocked on the door 30 times and Alex could tell Sadie had a lot of energy in her body as well because he could tell that there was a lot of allergen in her legs and Alex saw her privates moving like crazy which in Alex's mind started turning him on but Alex stayed focused and said to himself "Sadie is Spencer's girl. Focus Alex" his mind said to him and then all of a sudden, Rebecca opened the door and Rebecca saw Alex naked "Alex you're here in my apartment, what are you doing here?" she asked "Rebecca, I don't think your safe here, sadly a lot of girls from your college were killed by an old enemy of mine from the past and her thugs and her coming here and we have to leave Minnesota right now" Alex said Rebecca looked at Alex at first with a confused look but then Rebecca also was distracted by Alex's naked body and him covering his pennis in the cold water and then Rebecca smiled and said "oh okay I will go pack, I would love to come with you" Rebecca said in a very cheerful voice and then all of a sudden, Rebecca then started packing a lot of clothes and underwear and shoes and other things as well. And then as she was done packing, Rebecca and Alex then went back into Sadie and Spencer's big car and they started driving "Don't worry Alex we are going to get you some clothes to wear" Spencer said "or we could just put him in a bag and sneak him on to the barrage clam Intel we get out of the states" Sadie said in a joking matter "Oh my god" Alex thought and then Sadie started laughing and giggling in a very girly way. But then as they got there, Spencer being a police officer in the past, was able to speculate Alex's pants size and shirt and shoe size and he was able to buy Alex some normal 1980's style of clothing. And then as he was done paying for it, Alex then started putting on the clothes and in the end, Alex was wearing blue jeans, normal American tennis shoes, a normal green T shirt and a gray winter coat as well. Alex sadly didn't have any ID with him or his money because of what happened at the pen house with a lot of the college girls, but without telling Alex, Spencer was able to create a new bank account for Alex put around 800,000$ in there as well, and it was from a special world wide bank that would be used in almost every country in the world. And Spencer did all this with his computer and college knowledge as well.

And then moments later, Alex, Rebecca, Sadie and Spencer then after creating Alex's bank account, they then started to the St. Paul airport and they checked in through customs really well. And then after that, they then they got to their first gate and then they all started "So where are we going Sadie?" Rebecca asked "I don't know I think we might be going to Greece I believe mainly just because of the beaches" Sadie said with a very beautiful smile on her face "Oh I really love the sound of that baby girl" Spencer said and then Spencer and Sadie kissed each other on the lips and then as Alex was with them, Rebecca then smiled at Alex "Oh I can't wait to go to Greece with you Alex" Rebecca said "I will really enjoy being on the beach with you" Rebecca said "Yeah me too" Alex said And then as boarding began, they all sat in the middle part of the airplane and through the plane ride, Alex would drink around 6 ginger ales and then he fell asleep in the chair he was sitting on the plane. Rebecca was also sitting with him and she laid her head on Alex's right shoulder and then Rebecca started doing a lot of feminine moans. But the plane ride itself was not all fun and games and Alex thinking about Rebecca romantically, sometimes he had dreams in his head about Victoria Borodina and really hoped that she wouldn't find a way to kidnap Alex and also Sadie as well.

Chapter 3 the trip to Greece

As the airplane landed in Greece, Alex then woke up and so did other people on the plane including Sadie and Spencer. And everybody on the airplane was able to get off just fine. And then everybody including Alex went through customs and immigration very well and Alex was able to show the main person his passport and the customs person was able to stamp Alex's passport and see his papers that he filled out on the plane as well. They then went to baggage clam and right now Alex kept turning his head left and right and staring a lot of people that were speaking Greek and just observing their culture and certain mannerisms as well. And then as everybody got their bags, Sadie was able to call a taxi and they then started going to a hotel that was very normal looking. And then as they checked in, they all started exploring the country and going everywhere. Alex was wearing normal 1980's American clothing and having 1980's sunglasses on his head and Rebecca was also wearing short shorts and sandals as well. Around this point as they were traveling, Alex also noticed a very tan looking person with black hair also in Greece and he was a normal suit and tie and it looked like he was heading to a meeting somewhere.

Later that night, Alex was having a drink in the hotel lobby and Sadie and Spencer were talking about the country and Greece was really beautiful and Rebecca was drinking a martini drink as well and then all of a sudden, the same person that Alex walked by turned out to be Salem Jadon and he was meeting with the ambassador of Greece as well and Salem approached Alex very quietly and he tapped Alex on the shoulder and then Alex turned around "Hey Alex" Salem said "Salem hey buddy, what's up? How are you doing? What are you doing in Greece?" Alex asked "well the reason I'm here is because I'm here for another meeting with the Greece Ambassador and so far I think you're the only American on this trip that I have ran into" Salem said "Oh and I can also see your with some friends" Salem said "Yeah this Sadie and Spencer and Rebecca" Alex said then Sadie and Spencer introduced themselves to Salem and then Salem started drinking a Greek alcoholic drink and joining Alex as he was with Sadie, Spencer and Rebecca "So how have you been Alex?" Salem asked, "Good I think. Unfortunately in Minnesota I sadly ran into Borodina again and she sadly killed a lot of college girls as well" Alex said "dude that's terrible Alex. I'm sorry buddy" Salem said "Anyway that's one of the reasons I came to you is because I think Borodina's people might be in Greece and I think they may try to steel money from Greece government and something really fishy is going on" Salem said "Oh shit!!!! Well I will keep my eyes open Salem" Alex said and then during that night, Alex was then in his hotel room and he started looking at the window at the islands that were in Greece and he really wanted to check them out for himself. And then Alex climbed back into bed and he put his arms around Rebecca and started kissing her on the back and on the shoulders as well.

As the trip around Greece kept on going, Alex and everyone else really started exploring the country and going through many different places and saw all of the big time tourist destinations and Sadie was able to take pictures on her camera and then the coming days they then went to more places and explored more the country and Alex was really enjoyed a lot of Greek food as well. And then finally after traveling and exploring, Alex and Rebecca and Sadie then saw a nude beach and they all started taking off their clothes and they all laid in the sun butt naked and they then started putting sunscreen all over their bodies as well and sun tan oil as well. And then Rebecca and Alex started making out on a towel and smooching each other on the lips and then moments later then they ran and jumped in the ocean. But as they did so, there were a couple of strange looking people that didn't look like they were Greece that fallowed them. Alex and Rebecca swam underwater and they saw more of the ocean and the fishes and since both of them were both butt naked, they felt completely invisible to fish and other big sea-life in the ocean. And then as they were in the water, Alex and Rebecca started making out underwater and they started rising back to the surface and then both of them started breathing heavily and Rebecca did a very girly gasp. And then as Alex was going close to her, Alex then felt something strange as his body was really getting cold and Alex started feeling his body begin to shut down very drastically "Alex are you alright. Baby talk to me!!! Alex!!!!, Alex!!!!" Rebecca said and then all of a sudden, Alex passed out in the water, and then Alex started drowning in the water and Rebecca dived under a water and then all of a sudden, her body started to shut down as well and then all of a sudden, the same people swam towards and it turned out unfortunately while Alex and Rebecca were under-water, the thugs were able to lightly stab them with a ruby jewel that had sleeping slime like liquid and it cause them to pass out or get killed in the process as well.

And then the thugs were able to grab Alex and Rebecca and they started taking them on a boat and the boat started taking them to Athens. And then later that day, Sadie and Spencer also noticed that both Alex and Rebecca were missing and right away they started looking for them all over the country. And then they even checked out of their hotel and started looking for them.

And then moments later, Alex and Rebecca slowly started to wake up and Alex noticed that both of them were inside of a freezing water and then Alex started hearing big time laughter and Alex knew right away if was Victoria Borodina and she was laughing like an evil witch "Good evening Mr. Aussmen" Victoria said "Borodina!!!!" Alex said in anger "when will you ever learn that I have people everywhere even in a country Greece. And also I know that I am getting closer to not only killing you but also steeling Sadie Holbrook's money and destroying the western world as well" Victoria said "Well kidnapping me and taking away my clothes is not going to change anything" Alex said "Oh yes you are correct little boy. Once I make a new European union, then it's off to Israel to try to do the same thing and blow up every country has any American influence and destroy them in everyway possible" Victoria said "And you see Alex, the communist will win the cold war and as for you, you will end up being a homeless person with no money what so ever" Victoria said "You know that's a complete fucking lie" Alex said with anger in his voice then Victoria then walked over to Alex touched his face and Alex could feel the cold and freezing glove that Borodina had and Alex started to shiver "Good-Bye Mr. Aussmen" Victoria said and then Victoria then left and her guards fallowed her and then Victoria went into an elevator and the elevator went up.

"Alex how in the world are we going to get out of here?" Rebecca asked and Rebecca was starting to get really scarred and then Alex then started freezing and thinking and then all of a sudden, Alex used all his strength and he was able break through some of the steel and then he climbed out of the water and he ran to the switch that was freezing the water and turned it off and then Rebecca climbed out "Oh Alex" Rebecca said and then all of a sudden, Alex noticed that this was not a normal building and it looked like the same building he saw when he was younger and it looked like the same medical building and then all of a sudden Alex herd Victoria's voice again "Good luck trying to escape Alex. I set the timer to 60 minutes and it's same obstacle course building that you had to go to when you were little. Only this time, you are timed very badly. Not enough time to escape" Victoria said and then Victoria did a very evil witch laugh and then all of a sudden, Rebecca and Alex started running and they then ran to a door and Alex open the door and he saw a lot of climbing elements and Alex and Rebecca started climbing really hard and they had to jump over different things and a lot of dangerous weapons were being thrown at them like crazy and they then ran more and more and then they found another door and as they were running there was trap doors that would appear and Alex would grab on the metal bars that were above his head and Alex would hold on for dear life and then as they got to the next part, it was even more dangerous and it was a path that also had traps but under them was a huge swimming full of great white sharks and Alex and Rebecca kept on going but then Rebecca felt the force of one of the flying objects hitting her and Alex grabbed on to her hand really tightly and Rebecca started crying and Alex was able to pull her in and Alex then hugged Rebecca really tightly in his arms and Alex felt Rebecca's naked body pressing towards him and Alex and Rebecca were able to get out of the building and they saw the ocean and they jumped off the building and building exploded into flames and they jumped into the water and Alex sadly got knocked out and Alex then began to sink really badly and more bad guys showed up and grabbed Rebecca and started taking her away and they were able to kidnap her.

And then 3 hours later, Alex was in the hospital in Athens and one of the doctors that was able to speak English recognized Alex from his face and was able to contact Sadie and Spencer right away and they raced to the hospital and saw Alex "Alex are you alright?" Sadie asked and then Alex started moaning and then he saw Sadie's face and her blonde hair and her beautiful and gorgeous and stunning blue eyes "Where am I?" Alex asked "Your in Athens, one of the doctors called us and told Spencer and I that you were here" Sadie said "And Rebecca?" Alex asked "she sadly got kidnapped Alex" Spencer said, "Fuck!!!!" Alex said and then Alex started breathing very heavily "It's okay we are going to get her back man" Spencer said "It's okay, I may know where she is" Alex said "and I think you guys may need to go back to states right away" Alex said and then right away as Alex said that, more thugs came and a lot of chaos happened and all of a sudden, Borodina's thugs were able to break into the hospital and poison Sadie and Spencer really badly and were able to knock them out and kidnap them and also take them away, Alex then right away got out of the hospital bed and he was able to steel some normal doctor clothes and he started chasing the thugs and they had guns in their hands and they started shooting at Alex.

Alex then felt a grenade come towards him and a huge explosion happened and Alex saw Borodina's helicopter up in the air and Alex knew he must go to Ukraine and must defeat Victoria Borodina once and for all.

Chapter 4 Never Try to Kill a Ukraine Woman

As the explosions happened, Alex then started running and he found a car and he started heading towards the main airport in Greece. And even though Alex had no ID with him, he was able to memorize his ID and passport number with flying colors and also know his bank number as well. Alex then got through the customs really well. But then another strange thing happened where Alex fell through a trap door inside of the airport and Alex fell on a sofa under the airport in a strange and secret room and it Salem "I think I can help you defeat Borodina Alex. And your going to need my help getting into Ukraine" Salem said "Thank you. I really appreciate it a lot" Alex said "No problem Alex" Salem said and then all of a sudden, Salem was able to hand Alex one of his clothes and he was wearing normal 1980's clothes again and a door started to open a fighter airplane with blue and green and yellow was on the airplane and Alex climbed into the plane "There is a couple of things of thing you have to do before going to Borodina's castle in Ukraine. I will guide you through everything" Salem said "Sounds great thanks" Alex said and then as Alex climbed into the plane he then felt the power of the airplane "Alright Alex, now what you have to do is that Borodina is going steel a lot of money from all the countries that on the United States side and she will steel it using a satiate and you have to fire at all of them" Salem said "oh okay" Alex said

And then all of a sudden, Alex took off from Greece and Alex started flying all over the world and started heading east and Alex started seeing a lot of Borodina's satellites that had Ukraine colors on them and as Alex was getting closer, there all of a sudden was a lot of communist fighter planes that were firing and chasing Alex. And then Alex started firing a lot of missiles and gun bullets as well. And then would do a huge roll over on the plane and then Alex was able to fire at the communist airplanes and then all of a sudden a lot of Sandinista communist fighter planes also started showing up and firing at Alex and Alex then was able to fire around 99 missiles at the Sandinista airplanes and 900 fighter planes were firing at Alex non stop. Alex then kept on going and he fired more missiles and he was able to blow up satellites that were created by Victoria Borodina and destroy around 30 of them around different parts of the world. And then Alex kept on flying in the fighter plane and more Sandinista and communist jets kept on firing at him. And then kept firing a lot of missiles and rockets at the airplanes and then all of a sudden, Alex flew over the country of Ukraine and all of a sudden in the dark clouds and over the thunder and lighting, Alex saw Borodina's Ukraine castle that gray and black and had some communist colors and also some colors of the Ukraine flag all over it. "Alright Salem, I'm going in and I'm going to blow up the communist castle" Alex said "Alright be-careful Alex. And very soon I'm going to call the United States army and air-force to help you and we are going to take Borodina down buddy" Salem said "sounds great" Alex said

And then all of a sudden was able to find a landing spot in Ukraine and he saw more thunder and lighting all over the castle and Alex right away started running as fast as he could. And as Alex was going towards the castle himself he then ran into a couple of Ukraine guardsmen guarding Borodina's castle and the pointed their guns at Alex "Vin vy tut ne nalezhyte!!!!!!! Zupynyty!!!!!" and then all of a sudden with a lot of rage built up, Alex then pulled out a kitchen knife from his pocket and stabbed the guardsmen in the neck and blood started coming out and then more guardsmen showed up "Vbyvaty amerykans'kykh!!!!" and then Alex took out a handgun and he was able to shoot 50 bullets at different times and shot the guardsmen in the heads and then Alex was able to get into the castle and he blew up one of the main door and sneaked in. And then all of a sudden, Alex saw Borodina in a very queen like outfit with one side of her queen with the Sandinista colors and then the other side was communist USSR colors as well "Very soon. Once I still all of Ms. Holbrock's money I will be the new queen of the world and I will blow up every leader's home and kill of them, and I will create the Borodina Empire and nobody will be able to stop me. Not even the stupid Americans" Borodina said in a very evil feminine voice and then all of a sudden as she kept on walking she saw a Queen Crown with blue, red, black colors with diamonds and rubies and gold jewelry on it. And Borodina grabbed the crown and put it on her head and in her room she also had computers that showed much money that she had. But worst of all in the room, Sadly Rebecca and Sadie were in huge containers of water and both of the girls were butt naked and Borodina had a remote in her hand that controlled the tempter and then also different advanced wires that were going to suck up a lot of information they had from the brain. "Oh Sadie, I knew this day would come where my own people would get revenge on your people for becoming good friends with all of the royal family and taking everything from the Ukraine and if you can't tell I also despised your mother and father as well in the shadows" Borodina said in a very evil witch like voice and then Borodina walked over to Rebecca and Rebecca sadly had very sad puppy dog like eyes and she banged on the tank a couple of times "I have seen this type of look before. And this is what little boy Alex looked like before I told him the truth about me back in 1976. And now only with you I will kill you and steel your money and I will use your DNA to make me young again and make myself beautiful again….MUAHAHAHAHAHAHAHAHAHAHAHAHAHAHAHAHAHAHAHAHA HAHAHAHA" Borodina laughed and then all of a sudden Alex had a very angry look on his face and then he broke through the doors and he pointed his gun at Borodina "It's all over Borodina. Your under arrest!!!!!!" Alex said "Ahhhhhh Mr. Aussmen!!!! I am very glad you are here. It's pitty that I didn't kidnap you once again and put in the water with Ms. Olga and Ms. Holbrook as well. And then as for Spencer, he is also here as well" Borodina said all of a sudden Borodina pressed a button on her remote and all of a sudden Spencer was then tied up in ropes and he was about to be lowered to grinder and Spencer was scarred out of his mind and screaming "With Spencer I'm going to drop him into a grinder where not only will his balls and penis get destroyed but his whole body will get destroyed as well little boy" Borodina said "And then you won't be able to save either of them because I will be the queen of the world and start a new dynasty and a new empire and destroy the west once and for all" Borodina said and then all of a sudden Borodina grabbed a giant queen staff "And this time unlike the past, he will not inter-fear with my plans this time Mr. Aussmen!!!!!" Borodina said "and also you will now for once pay the price of being a hero of the west Mr. Aussmen!!!!!!...."Borodina said in a very witch like voice and then all of a sudden Borodina grabbed her staff and pointed the staff and killed one of her own guardsmen and then Borodina smiled like the evil queen from snow white and hey ugly yellow teeth were showing and she yelled "GOOD BYE MR. AUSSMEN!!!!!!!!.....AND IT'S TIME THAT YOU DIE AND GO TO HELL!!!!!!" Borodina yelled and then all of a sudden Borodina then started firing a lot of missiles and exploding liquid and causing explosions all over her castle and then Alex got forced against the wall and then more of Borodina's decorations started falling on Alex and Alex felt the pain very badly. And then Borodina started screaming in angry and she started screaming and yelling more and more like a witch and throwing more staff attacks at Alex and then Borodina hit Alex in the head and hit him in the stomach and stabbed Alex in the chest and Alex yelled in pain and blood started coming out and Alex got the knife out of his chest and then Alex kicked Borodina in the face and he grabbed a knight sword and Alex threw a lot of sword attacks and then Alex gave Borodina a cut on her arm and then Borodina then grabbed 30 grenades and threw 30 of them at Alex causing a lot of explosions and her castle started to catch on fire and Alex then got forced to the ground and Borodina yelled again and tried to stab Alex in the head with her queen staff and she kept on yelling and screaming very violently and then all of a sudden found a wine bottle and hit Borodina in the face and nose broke off of her face and blood started coming out and then Borodina grabbed Alex by the neck and started chocking him and stabbing in the neck with her dirty and her long witch like finger nails and then Alex was able to swing his body and all of a sudden was able to kick Borodina in the face and forced her to the ground and then all of a sudden Borodina got even more angry and grabbed her queen staff and then Alex was able to see a metal fireplace fork and Alex grabbed the item and then whacked Borodina with two hands and hitting her like a golf ball and then all of a sudden there was 99 United States Helicopters and army tanks and air force and military and then all of a sudden an army solider showed up and he spoke inside of a blow horn "THIS IS THE UNITED STATES ARMY AND THE AIR FORCE, WE KNOW THAT YOU ARE A COMMUNIST AND WORKING FOR THE RUSSIANS AND FOR THE SANDINSTAS IN NICARAGUA!!!!!! AND IF YOU DO NOT COME OUT, WE WILL FIRE AT YOUR CASTLE BLOW UP THE CASTLE AS WELL!!!!!!!!" the solider said

But it just didn't really mater as Borodina kept on attacking Alex with her staff and Alex just getting more and more hurt during the fight as well. And then Alex had around 6 different cuts around his body and then Borodina did more attacks at Alex and then all of a sudden Alex was able to dodge one of her attacks and then grabbed the staff and kicked Borodina in the face and then Alex grabbed another wine bottle whacked Borodina in the face and then Alex punched Borodina in the face with no remorse and then Borodina tried to stab Alex with a sword and then Alex kicked Borodina in the face and knocked her to the ground "WHY YOU LITTLE FOOL!!!!!" Borodina said in anger and then all of a sudden Alex saw a bucket of chemicals and then Alex poured the pocket of chemicals and all of a sudden all of Borodina's long hair started coming off of her and her skin started getting older and older and Borodina started screaming and then Borodina grabbed her queen crown tried to stab Alex with her crown and her queen staff and then all of a sudden Alex grunted his teeth and anger tackled Borodina to the ground and Alex with all his might and his strength started chocking her and Borodina started screaming pain and then Alex then grabbed the knight sword and then stabbed her in the forehead and then more of her skin and her blood started dying as then all of a sudden Borodina's body and her head started turning into a skull and into a skeleton's body and Victoria Borodina was dead.

And then all of a sudden Alex started running to the tank and he was able to disable everything on the keyboards and then water was dumped on the ground "Oh Alex" Rebecca said and then Alex also hugged Sadie as well "I'm glad you guys are alright" Alex said and then all of a sudden Alex then pressed another button and was able to save Spencer "thanks buddy, I really thought I was going to be dead meat" Spencer said "Your welcome Spencer" Alex said and then all three of them were able to find their clothes and all of a sudden they started running out Borodina's castle and there were a lot of explosions. And then all of a sudden as they got out of the castle, Alex then turned back and he saw Borodina's Ukraine castle on fire and started falling to the ground and then there was another explosion that happened as well.

And then all of a sudden, during that same night, Alex, Sadie, Rebecca, and Spencer were then taken to the United States embassy in Ukraine and Salem started handling everyone's paper work as well. "Alright guys, I was able to do your paper work and the good news is that you guys can go back to the states. And the army and everything else about Victoria Borodina will be investigated" Salem said "Thanks Salem" Alex said and then after that visit, they all then started heading to the airport and heading back to the United States and going through customs and immigration through New York City and through Newark, New Jersey and then as they were in the airport, Alex then was finally happy to have real American food and he got himself a Wendy's triple cheeseburger and a Dr. Pepper and some fries and then after he was done eating, he then used a napkin and whipped his face clean and then he went into the bathroom and used water to clean his face as well. And then after he was done doing that, he then went back to his seat and sat down "hopefully Borodina didn't do too much damage to you Sadie" Alex said "oh are you kidding Alex, my money is completely saved and in fact, I know have 99 trillion dollars in my bank account because of all the stocks my dad invested as well." Sadie with a huge smile on her face "So are you still going to keep doing this secret agent stuff Alex. Cause I think it maybe time for you to settle down, you just been on the run from life for a long time" Sadie said "I don't know" Alex said "come on Alex, you can start investing in stocks and making a lot of money, and you can live in a house like a normal person" Sadie said "I'm never going to be a normal person, my life is very fucked up and it will always be fucked up" Alex said "Plus I mean I can be around to help you Alex and be a good influence as well. I can imagine you have lacked that for a long time" Sadie said

And then later that day, Alex then headed back to Seattle, Washington and Sadie and Spencer headed back to Minnesota. And Alex was just tired and just really burned out from everything and all the missions he did and how he was almost 30 years old. And thought about what Sadie said to him and really he had nothing to loose, he just killed Borodina and with the cold war on the brink of being over, Alex then made the choice in his head that he will maybe not retire but just start settling down with someone.

As the plane landed in Seattle, Alex was able to grab a taxi back to his pen house apartment in Seattle, and when he got home, Alex then started looking his bank account and right away he went to stock market place in Seattle and they talked about which companies had a lot in shares and Alex started investing 9,000$ in buying shares around the millions and he started growing his money a lot more. And right away, Alex then started looking for some houses and he then was able to find a mansion in Kent, WA and around that point Alex had around 9,000,000 million dollars built up in stocks and he moved into his new mansion that had both a basketball court and also a tennis court and also a hot tub and a swimming pool that was both an indoor and outdoor pool. And then as he moved into his new house, he then quit working at Seattle Agencies and Alex professionally retired as a secret agent. And then Alex was able to give Jenny a phone call and Jenny was able to drive to Alex's new mansion in Kent and they both had a really wonderful time and even went skinny dipping in Alex's new pool and then watched movies wearing ropes and made out on Alex's couch "Oh I am really glad that you invited me to come Alex" Jenny said "Yeah me too. Anyway the reason I wanted to invite you to my house is because I really love you Jenny and I wanted to ask you...Will you marry me?" Alex asked and then Jenny just really smiled and she then said yes to Alex and then days later Alex and Jenny got married and their weeding was at Alex's new mansion in Kent, WA and a lot of people that Alex knew came to his weeding and their honey moon was in Brazil and then also Alex and Jenny both traveled the world and then they went to beaches and then to other parts of the world as well. And then during the trip they then were able to catch up with Sadie and Spencer in Italy and also travel with them as well to other places as well.

And then as Alex and Jenny's honeymoon was over, Alex then days later got a letter from Sadie saying that she moved back to Seattle and she lives in a new house that is very castle like. And then as they got the letter, Alex and Jenny then went to Sadie and Spencer's new castle like house in Kirkland and it was a very causal party with Alex drinking a beer and having steak and salad with ranch and mashed potatoes as well. And during the visit Alex took look around the house, Alex started having flash backs to Morella's house in Edmonds and that the house itself was very similar to Morella's house accept however it was more castle like then golden mansion, Alex also saw more English culture and paintings all over the house and Alex just sat down on a sofa and he saw a Dr. Pepper drink and he felt more relaxed then ever before in his life. And then all of a sudden, Jenny was able to find Alex and then Alex and Jenny started making out on the sofa and they started laughing and kissing each other on the lips "Oh Alex" Jenny said

www.ingramcontent.com/pod-product-compliance
Lightning Source LLC
Chambersburg PA
CBHW081326090726
47907CB00010B/2392